Flower and Tree

Flower and Tree

a novel by Sharon Rose

DANCING MOON PRESS
NEWPORT, OREGON

Flower and Tree

Publisher's Note: This book is a work of fiction. The characters, incidents, and dialogue are drawn from the author's imagination and are not to be construed as real. Any resemblance to actual events or persons, living or dead, is entirely coincidental.

Paperback ISBN: 978-1-937493-90-5
EBook ISBN: 978-1-937493-96-7
Library of Congress Control Number: 2016935994

Rose, Sharon
Flower and Tree
1. Fantasy-fiction; 2. Young adult fantasy; 3. Magic; 4. King Arthur myths; 5. Welsh folklore; 6. Celtic ideology; 7. Magical twins
I. TITLE

Book editing, design & production: *Carla Perry, Dancing Moon Press*
Cover design & production: *Sarah Gayle*
Manufactured in the United States of America

DANCING MOON PRESS
P.O. Box 832, Newport, OR 97365
541-574-7708
www.dancingmoonpress.com
info@dancingmoonpress.com

FIRST EDITION

Acknowledgements

I thank all of those who helped me in the creation of this book, no matter how small a part you played. Without you, this story would not be what it is.

Contents

Chapter 1

SHE'S FLYING, SOARING OVER THE TREETOPS. The sky darkens, thunder rolls, lightning flashes, rain pounds her back. She's falling, falling....

"Ella!"

Rosella sat up. "What is it?" she asks.

"It's time to get up. It's moving day!" Her mother, Hannah, said.

She sighed. "Yes, mother."

Her mother turned to leave, then stopped. "Oh, and Ella, do comb your hair."

"Yes, mother," replied Rosella when the woman left to wake younger brother and sister, John and Mary.

Rosella sighed again. She often felt like a raven among cardinals because her mother, father, sister, and younger brother all had red hair and brown eyes. She and her twin brother, Rowan, had black hair and blue eyes.

Rosella pointed her finger at the wall. "Opinaum."

She smiled when the wall melted away to reveal an elegant wooden door. Rosella and Rowan, both had magical powers, and not only did those powers become stronger every day, they were the only ones that knew about them. She pulled open the door, revealing a cavernous room, its walls lined with shelves full of thick books and strange knick-knacks. The only divisions between the shelves were silver arches hung with rich curtains. These led to other rooms within Rosella's "hideout."

Rosella walked over to one of the bookcases and stroked its ebony-and-pearl surface. Then she ran her finger along the bindings of the thick books on one shelf, looking for a certain volume.

"Ah, here it is, *Dream Interpretation,* by Annaea Sorco."

She removed the book from the shelf, sat down in a chair, and opened it to the table of contents. Soon she found the correct page and read what her dream supposedly meant, according to the book. Rosella put the book away and went to one of the arches, pulling aside its sea-green curtain to reveal a dressing room. When she was done there, she had on a deep blue, button-up shirt, black trousers, and tall black leather boots. Her ears were adorned with small gold earrings. Then she went into a room that branched off from the first, and from a fountain filled a silver pitcher with water, which she then poured into a large shell. Rosella brushed her straight black hair using a silver-and-pearl brush until it felt like silk, then went to a cabinet and got out a deep-blue silk ribbon.

She sat in front of a silver-framed mirror and braided her long hair, then tied it off with the ribbon. Afterwards, Rosella went back to the main door.

"Opinaum."

The door opened again and Rosella went out. She met her sister, Mary, in the hall.

"Hello, Mary."

"Hello, Ella."

Rosella held back a scowl. She did not like that nickname very much.

Then Mary saw Rosella's braid. "Can you do my hair like that to match my dress? Please?"

Rosella smiled at the younger girl. "Of course."

"Thanks, Ella!"

Rosella took Mary's long, straight red hair in her delicate, long-fingered hands, and braided it tightly before tying it off with an ivy-green ribbon that Mary had with her. The ribbon matched Mary's short play dress. Then Rosella and Mary went downstairs for breakfast.

They saw John and Rowan on the stairs, and Rosella grinned when she saw Rowan's hair. The hair of her twin was longer than most males', reaching two inches past his shoulders. But it was different today. It was pulled back into a ponytail and held with a deep green ribbon. Normally he tied his braid with leather.

Rowan was dressed similarly to Rosella, except his shirt was emerald, and he had no earrings. John, however, was dressed in a lime-green short-sleeved shirt and light blue jeans with orange trainers.

Just then, their father, Brian, called up the stairs for them to come down for breakfast.

After breakfast, their dad said, "We're leaving for the new house in an hour. Go pack what you need for now, the rest will come in a few days."

"Okay!" John and Mary said at the same time as Rowan and Rosella said, "Yes, Father."

At that, the two elder children cleared away their dishes as the two younger ones ran upstairs. Once the dishes were clean, the two elder children followed their siblings. Rosella went straight to the door of her alcove.

"Opinaum."

The "door" slid open, then closed. The raven-haired girl walked through one of the many silver arches that lined the walls. This particular one had an emerald curtain. The room was small and empty except for a backpack. Rosella picked it up and strode out, the arch disappearing as she left the room. Then she went through another arch, this one hung with a pearly-white curtain. Her keen blue eyes surveyed the room.

"Elkanaea," she said.

Everything in the room became tiny and fit into the backpack. Rosella then went from room to room, doing the same in each one. As soon as Rosella left a room, it disappeared, so soon only the main room was left.

"Elkanaea."

Then the room was empty. Rosella turned towards the door.

"Opinaum."

Rosella left the room. The door disappeared. Rosella, carrying her backpack, went into the hall, nearly running into Mary, whose eyes went big when she saw Rosella's backpack. It was so deep a blue that it was nearly black, and had green borders the same shade. Embroidered on the front was a large, deep-blood red rose edged in gold and silver, with golden zipper pulls on its many pockets. Mary glanced at her own backpack, which was bright pink with a design of ivy-green plants and purple, turquoise, and-magenta flowers. Mary walked off.

Then Rowan walked up. "Hello Ro."

Rosella looked at him. "Hello, Ro."

Rowan's backpack was similar to Rosella's, except that the base colours were red with blue borders, and instead of a red, gold, and silver rose, he had a green, gold, and silver tree.

The two elder twins began their descent of the stairs and ran into John. The younger brother's backpack was lime-green, had a brown border, and for some reason, there were bright yellow star stickers scattered across the front.

Rosella raised one eyebrow at Rowan, and he replied with the same expression. *What is with our siblings' backpacks?* their silent message seemed to say. The raven-haired twins shrugged simultaneously and then continued on their way to the living room.

When they arrived, the rest of the family was already there, so as a group they went outside and piled into the van. Rosella and Rowan moved into the back, pulled out their MP3 players and began to listen to music, drowning out the sound of Mary and John arguing about who got to sit behind the driver's seat this time. The blue-eyed twins leaned their heads back and closed their eyes, letting the music wash over them. Soon they were asleep, though it was closer to a doze. For them, the drive passed quickly, and they awoke as the van pulled into the driveway of their new house.

The house had three stories and a basement. Well, technically two stories, an attic, and a basement. Behind the house was a small yard. John asked if they could put a trampoline and a waterslide back there.

The raven twins scoffed silently. Of course, John would ask for something like that, and their parents would probably give it to him, as they would give Mary anything she asked for as well. After the younger siblings got out of the van, the elder ones followed. They walked to the back of the van, opened the boot, and began hauling luggage into the house. They placed each item in the entryway. After a while, Brian joined them, taking the heavy bags that the two could not carry.

Soon the van was empty and the luggage delivered to each person's room. Hannah and Brian, and the younger twins, were on the second floor. John and Mary had their own rooms across the hall from each other. Hannah and Brian's room was near the stairs leading to the living room on the first floor.

Behind a closet door near Brian's study was a staircase leading to the attic where Rosella and Rowan's rooms were to be. Once John and Mary's bags were in their proper places, the raven twins carried their backpacks and single suitcases up that staircase, entering the attic through a trapdoor. Daylight came in through two large, round windows that lit up the bare wood floor.

The attic contained two small rooms that seemed to have been created after the house was bought. Rowan looked at Rosella and raised an eyebrow. She mirrored his expression with a shrug.

"I'll take the left?"

He shrugged as well. "Why not?"

With that settled, they carried their bags to their new rooms. The rooms were sparse, just like their old bedrooms, each with a simple twin bed, chest of drawers, a few shelves, and a mirror. The mirror was full-length, as opposed to their previous mirrors, from which they could see only to their hips. That gave the twins an idea.

What if, instead of making the entrance to their magic chambers a hidden door in the wall, they stepped through the mirrors instead? With that thought in mind, the twins set down their bags and returned to the first floor.

When they reached the entryway, they found the rest of the family standing there. Rowan glanced at his twin as Brian caught sight of them.

"What took you so long?"

They did not answer, as they knew he did not truly expect a reply.

They just shrugged. The red-haired man shook his head, then directed them all back to the van. They were headed out to visit the school the children would be attending the following Monday. Rowan held the door for Rosella, then merely left it open for John and Mary who were once again bickering about who would sit behind the driver's seat.

The raven twins began to listen to their music, just as they had on the drive to their new home. However, instead of going to sleep, they paid close attention to the route Brian took to the school. Leave the driveway, drive two blocks, right turn, drive three blocks then take a left. Drive five blocks, take another left. Go four blocks and there it was, on the right. The school was a long, squat, red-bricked building with deep burgundy trim around the windows and doors. A reddish sign at the entrance to the parking lot read "*RUMEN PRIMARY*" in blocky white letters.

A man was standing on the top of the low, wide stairs leading to the glass double doors. He was tall, lanky, and dignified, with short light-brown hair slicked back, a pair of silver-rimmed glasses perched on his nose, and an immaculate reddish-grey suit. His expression was stern and he carried himself imperiously. As he descended the steps, his sharp grey-brown eyes surveyed them with faint curiosity.

"I am William Torell. I am the principal of this school."

When the man spoke, it became clear to Rowan that he did not like this man. A glance to Rosella showed that she agreed. This 'Principal Torell' was most definitely not someone they could trust. Rowan had the feeling that most of the teachers would be that way as well.

Greetings were exchanged, then Hannah and Brian took Principal Torell aside and spoke to him in low tones. Whatever it was that they said caused him to look at Rowan and Rosella attentively. He stared at the blue-eyed twins the entire time he chatted with their parents. Thus began the tour of Rumen Primary School.

The first room they entered was the lunchroom, with its long metal tables and benches, and a rusty tile floor. Next were a succession of classrooms, all following the same pattern and faintly red colour scheme. Finally, they entered the gym, which opened into an outdoor ball court and set of jungle gyms. Once the tour was concluded, the

Tiger family piled back into their van and returned to their new house.

Rowan and Rosella went up to their rooms to unpack. Not that they had much to unpack. However, it would take a while for them to set up their alcoves behind their bedroom mirrors.

Rosella placed her backpack on the floor in front of her mirror, then stepped back, making sure to cast a strong concealment ward over her room. If she hadn't cast one, or if she hadn't cast a strong enough one, well then the redheaded Tigers would definitely find out about her powers. That would not be good at all.

The raven-haired girl raised her hands and they began to glow with a bright blue light. Soon the light turned to beams that struck the mirror, and slowly pierced and warped the reflections. For perhaps an hour, Rosella stood there, magic emitting from her palms, eyes closed, forming the only retreat she had—behind and through her mirror. Eventually, the light faded and she lowered her hands. The mirror looked no different, at least at that moment, and the backpack appeared to be empty.

"Opinaum."

The mirror's surface rippled and turned transparent, showing the cavernous chamber exactly as it had been at their old house.

Rosella picked up the backpack and stepped through the glass. It flowed like silver water around her. After she passed through, the mirror showed no sign that anyone had touched it at all. All seemed ordinary in the to-be-unused attic bedroom of Rosella Tiger.

On the other side of the attic, Rowan's room showed the same image. Bare walls, plain bed, small chest of drawers, and a full-length mirror just a few metres away from the foot of the bed.

Chapter 2

MONDAY CAME ALL TOO SOON for the raven-haired Tiger twins. The two twelve-year-olds had been spending most of their time in their Alcoves, either by themselves or with each other, and they liked it that way. But now, they had to deal with people who had known each other all their lives—children and teenagers—not to mention Principal Torell. Neither of the blue-eyed twins was anxious to be around *him*.

From a room in the alcoves, the twins took simple, plain backpacks—blue for Rosella and green for Rowan. They dressed in black boot-cut jeans, plain loose long-sleeved T-shirts, and short black boots. Both had braided their hair. Rowan's was tightly coiled and bobby-pinned to the back of his head, to be less obvious. Rosella wore no jewellery except a pair of dark grey stud earrings and a silver-and-blue-moonstone ring that she never took off—the ring was hidden from those who did not have magic. Rowan had one just like it, except his was green. So far, only the twins were able to see them. Perhaps that would change at this new school, but most likely not.

Either way, children and teens are ruthless when it comes to bullying those they do not like or think "odd"—at least in the twins' experience. Therefore, they were apprehensive about the first day of classes. The thought of a new library, though, was indeed intriguing. They wondered what kind of books it would have, and how large a collection. They hoped the librarian would like them well enough to let them spent their lunch breaks reading. If he or she didn't let them, well then, that might become a problem. If that was the case, they could bring their own books to read.

The drive to the school was quiet. Apparently, John and Mary were apprehensive about starting the new school as well. The red-haired twins never had to deal with bullies before, so Rosella and Rowan wondered what they were worried about. With simultaneous mental shrugs, the raven-haired twins turned to watch the roadside foliage and houses pass by.

They arrived at the same time as the bus. After cheerful goodbyes—in the case of John and Mary, and stern goodbyes—in the case of Rowan and Rosella, they joined the throng of students entering the school. The two sets of twins split up after passing through the door, each pair going to their respective classrooms.

Rowan and Rosella found their class and they made their way to the seats farthest from the teacher's desk, and the rest of the students. They were in no mood to deal with anyone today. Class began.

* * *

The blue-eyed twins made it until lunch without having to deal directly with their fellow classmates. However, after they sat down at a table to eat, a burly boy with spiked platinum-blond hair bumped into Rosella. The boy's ice-blue eyes leered at her.

"I'm sorry, are you okay?" he said with mocking concern.

When she did not answer, the boy continued, "You know, I don't think I've seen you before...you must be new."

Rosella raised an eyebrow. "What an astute observation."

The boy appeared confused, then he shrugged it off and said, "I'm Ed Carson. Who are you?"

"Rosella...." she began.

Rowan said, "...and Rowan...."

"...Tiger." They finished in stereo, attempting to get the boy, Ed Carson, probably short for Edward, to leave them alone. They just wanted to eat their lunch in peace and go find the library. But the boy didn't give up.

"You have strange names."

"We are aware."

Then Carson noticed Rowan's bun. "Does he have long hair? He has long hair!" He turned to the group that had gathered behind him and pointed at Rowan. "He has long hair!"

Rowan's eyes narrowed. "You have said that already."

Carson sneered at him. "You're weird!" The boy tilted his head and whispered loudly to one of the boys next to him. "I think he likes guys."

Rowan's eyebrow went up. *Hmm.* He glanced at Rosella. She shrugged. He cocked his head. "Does hair length somehow determine whether or not someone likes their own gender, Rosella?"

His twin pursed her lips. "I do not believe so, Rowan."

With that, they stood and left, taking their empty trays with them and ignoring the Carson boy's glare boring into their backs.

Once they were out of the lunchroom, the black-haired twins leaned against the wall of the (thankfully) empty hallway. One would think that having to deal with nearly twelve years of peer ridicule and scorn would make it less impactful, but that was never the case.

They sighed as one, then Rosella spoke. "I suppose we should locate the library."

Without looking at her, Rowan replied, "Indeed we shall."

They walked in lockstep down the hall. After a few moments, Rowan said, "I wonder why Principal Torell did not include the library in the tour...."

His voice trailed off, and Rosella gave a noncommittal hum, then they fell back into companionable silence. Their quiet footfalls were the only sound in the hall since the rest of the student body was still in the lunchroom.

After about fifteen minutes, the two finally found the double doors that led to the library. With a joyous, yet nervous glance at each other, they gently pushed open the light wooden doors.

The library had two levels joined by a spiral staircase made of the same dark wood as the furniture, cream-coloured walls and ceiling, and a lightly patterned carpet in the exact burgundy tones as the upholstery and curtains on the large windows.

"Can I help you?"

The twins turned. At the desk sat a woman, undoubtedly the

librarian. Her near-black red hair was piled high in a knot on top of her head, and her sharp green eyes peered at them calmly. There was a hint of inquisitiveness lurking in their depths.

Rowan shook his head. "We just wanted to look around."

Rosella tilted her head at the woman. "Beg pardon, but what's your name? We are Rosella and Rowan Tiger."

The librarian cocked an eyebrow. "I am Mrs. Natser."

The twins nodded and spoke in unison. "It was nice to meet you, Mrs. Natser."

With that, they headed towards the rows upon rows of shelves.

..*

Jenny Natser watched the two raven-haired kids wander throughout the library. They showed obvious curiosity. There was something familiar about them, something that didn't match with their last name. There was a chance the Tigers had black hair, but she had a feeling that that was not the case. Just to be sure, she clicked on her computer and looked up their registrations. There. 'Tiger, Rosella,' 'Tiger, Rowan.'

Oh, interesting, there were more...a John and Mary Tiger, three years younger...both with *red* hair. That was odd.

Jenny scrolled down the registration pages until she found Parents/Legal Guardians. Brian and Hannah Tiger, both redheads. Her brows furrowed and she opened another page, typing into the search bar the names of the parents, looking for something that would indicate a black-haired gene was close enough to make the two in the library actually related to the Tigers.

"Hmm...."

According to her Internet search, it appeared the Tigers had a history of being predominately red-haired, and the Duncans, Hannah Tiger's relatives, were mostly blonds and gingers, yet the two children wandering her library, supposedly Tigers, had hair the shade of a raven's wing.

Now that she thought about it, Jenny realized that not only did the two have a different hair colour than the rest of their family, their eyes and facial features were dissimilar too. Rosella and Rowan had blue eyes, whereas the Tigers and Duncans had mostly brown or dark-grey eyes. Another thing to put on the list. Their facial features, in fact, were not very different from each other. Jenny did not exactly see as much as feel a faint blurring of the twins' faces that she recognised as a glamour charm. This was getting curiouser and curiouser.

The librarian pondered. It was obvious that Rosella and Rowan were adopted, and somehow they did not know it. How they could not know was beyond Jenny, but perhaps they did not care. Either way, it was not her place to tell them, for she sensed the time was not right and they would need to find out on their own. However, there was still that faint sense of familiarity she had to contend with.

* * *

Rosella headed towards the fiction section, searching for a particular book, one she couldn't believe she hadn't bought yet: *The Phantom of the Opera* by Gaston Leroux. It was a favourite book for both her and Rowan, along with a few sci-fi fantasy novels. She wandered the sci-fi section for a bit, then headed upstairs to look for the mythology.

After reviewing the library's material on Greek and Norse myths, Rosella returned downstairs. Rowan was waiting for her at the counter, holding a copy of *Macbeth*.

Rosella's eyes lit up. "Trade when you're done?"

Her brother looked at her and grinned. "Of course."

They checked out their books and, after putting them in their backpacks, walked back to the lunchroom just in time to follow the throng of their grade-mates to the next class.

As they walked home that afternoon, the raven twins reflected on their day. Meeting the teachers was not as bad as it could have been, but it was obvious that Principal Torell had told all the staff, except perhaps librarian Natser, whatever it was that Hannah had said to him the day he gave the Tigers the tour of the school. The teachers seemed suspicious of the twins, always watching them out of the corners of their eyes.

Then there was the Carson boy. The twins had rapidly recognised him as the school bully. His treatment of them, and his treatment of others that they witnessed throughout the day, left no room for doubt.

Other than that, the day had gone pretty well.

When the duo arrived home, they went up to their rooms to begin their homework. They had just started however, when they were called down to make supper for the rest of the family. That they did, and afterwards, the twins returned to their rooms to finish their assignments.

* * *

The next day was similar to the first, although Rosella and Rowan walked to school. They again sat in the back of all of their classes, ate lunch quickly, and spent the rest of their break in the library—attempting to avoid Carson and staying out of the way as much as possible.

For the next few weeks, life fell into a familiar routine. The twins rose early, made breakfast, went to school, came home, did homework, and made supper. They cleaned the house on weekends. Life was...good enough. Then, one day, a fortnight before their birthday, one of the things they dreaded most happened.

Chapter 3

THE DATE WAS OCTOBER 17, exactly a fortnight until their birthday, and on a hunch, Rosella and Rowan decided to transfer some of their clothes and most of their precious items into hidden compartments in their unused bedrooms. Neither of them knew why, they merely sensed that it was a wise thing to do.

It was a good thing, too, because the previous day Hannah Tiger had entered the twins' attic rooms and found them unused. When the duo returned home that afternoon, the woman secretly followed them up the stairs and witnessed Rosella entering her mirror-sanctuary. She told Brian.

When the twins arrived home from school, the adult Tigers met them at the door, arms crossed in a stern countenance.

"John, Mary, go to your rooms and do not come out until we call you, no matter what you hear."

"But Mom...."

"Now." Hannah's tone brooked no argument, and the younger twins obeyed without further protestation. The raven twins were confused when the adults grasped their wrists and drug them to their rooms, or rather, to where their rooms had been. The dividing wall had been knocked out. The duo's eyes widened in shock as they looked upon what had previously been their rooms. The mirrors had been smashed, destroying the only ways into their sanctuaries, which meant the sanctuaries were destroyed as well. They now had nowhere to hide, to escape.

They turned to the adults, not bothering to hide their feelings of despair. Then, as one, they bowed their heads, accepting what they knew would come. Brian picked up a piece of mirror frame and ordered them to place their backpacks on the floor. The raven twins faced the wall and closed their eyes. Whack! The piece of frame impacted with Rosella's back and she cried out in pain. Rowan's turn was next and he, too, made the same cry of pain.

Soon, the sound of wood hitting flesh filled the attic and the twins' grunts of pain soon turned to crying. Both sounds continued long into the night. The twins fell asleep that night on their stomachs on the floor because their backs, from their shoulders to their calves, were covered in welts and dark-purple bruises.

The next day, when Rowan awoke, he attempted to roll over but stopped and let out a gasp. His back *hurt*. He managed to stand. Looking around he again saw the walls were missing and the floor littered by broken mirror glass. *Oh, that's why.*

The blue-eyed boy gently woke Rosella, and then painfully dressed for school. At least, being non-magical, the adult Tigers did not find the hidden compartments in the chests of drawers, so a good deal of their clothes and their most precious possessions were safe, at least for now.

During lunch period, they did not even enter the lunchroom. Instead, they went straight to the library and decided to hide in the back until break was over. They were in no shape to deal with people.

The two must have fallen asleep, because they were awakened by librarian Natser telling them that lunch break was over. With a nod of thanks, the twins headed to their next class in silent lockstep.

* * *

Jenny watched the twins she had come to think of as *her* children leave the library. There was an odd stiffness to their movements. After a moment, she realized what that the stiffness could mean. She phoned her husband.

He picked up instantly. "Hello?"

"Rupert, this is Jenny."

His voice seemed to smile. "Jenny!" Then a frown. "Why are you calling during work? What is wrong?"

"I need you to look up everything you can find about the Tiger family."

She could almost see him raising one eyebrow when he asked, "Any particular reason?"

"There is a set of twins in the sixth grade that have that name but not the appearance, and today they came in walking stiff, as if from pain."

Her worry must have been apparent in her voice, for her husband said, "I'll see what I can do."

"That's all I ask. Goodbye, Rupert."

"Goodbye, Jenny."

With a click, the phone connection ended and Jenny leaned back in her chair, covering her face with her hands.

* * *

That evening, the blue-eyed twins found that they had been moved to the basement, with only a curtain dividing the area into two private spaces. No mirrors at all. A list of chores had been placed on both cots, which had replaced their beds. The chores had to be completed by suppertime, which the duo would make, as usual. With a simultaneous sigh, they began their duties.

Thus began a new routine. Every day, they would rise early, complete the tasks on their chore-lists, walk to school, go to their morning classes, spend lunch break in the library, go to their afternoon classes, walk back to the house, complete their chores, do homework, go to bed, repeat the next day. Days they were able to do everything on their lists were good ones, but sometimes there was just too much to get done before supper. Those were horrid days. For each task not completed, the twins received five strikes *each*, with the piece of mirror frame Brian Tiger used the first time. He kept it as a reminder that they could find out anything, no matter how secretive the twins were being.

Then, Rowan and Rosella's birthday came: October 31. Luckily, it was not on the weekend, which meant they would be away from the house most of the day. Somehow, librarian Natser knew what day it was, other than Hallowe'en, and she wished them a happy birthday. Though it was doubtful that this day would be happy for them, the two thanked her anyway, appreciating the thought.

That day, at lunch, the Carson boy made his appearance.

"Hello, freaks."

They ignored him.

"What are you going to be this evening?" He sneered. "Demons? Witches?"

The twins raised their eyebrows at him. "We will not be dressing up, because we are not going out, and if we were, why would we tell you?"

The platinum-blond boy scowled and the twins paid him no more mind, though he stood there for a good while.

The day seemed to crawl, and the twins were glad for it. They were not excited about returning to...the house because it was "home" no longer. They doubted it had ever truly been so.

When the school day ended and it was time for them to return to the house, the duo would have liked to take as long as possible, but that would only delay the inevitable and likely make it worse. They did their best to remain undetected—at least until they managed to address their homework. Luckily, they succeeded, and were able to complete a few of their afterschool chores before the adult Tigers came home from work.

Rosella had just finished setting out supper for the four redheads, and Rowan was putting away the cooking dishes when Brian and Hannah returned. Brian ordered them to the basement, and it was with a silent sigh of relief that they went. Perhaps nothing bad would happen that night.

The blue-eyed magicals' hopes seemed to be enough, and nothing horrid or painful happened that night.

* * *

The months passed, and soon the four children's first semester at Rumen Primary ended and report cards were due. The blue-eyed twins did not expect the trouble that occurred when cards arrived.

They returned from school to find the school envelopes waiting in the mailbox. After staring at the unopened letters for a few moments, the duo placed them on the dining table. Somehow, they managed to finish their chores early and were working on their homework when the adults returned.

The first sign that something was not right was when Hannah's voice cut through the stillness, calling for the raven twins to get up there this instant. They complied silently, dreading what they would see. It appeared that they had gotten excellent marks, better than those of the red-haired twins. Ah. So, that's the problem.

Meekly, the raven twins walked the steps towards the attic and waited. A minute later, Mr. Tiger appeared through the trapdoor, carrying the piece of mirror frame. The small room resounded with cries of pain, and bits of blood speckled the floor after a few hours of continuous hitting of the backs and legs of the blue-eyed twins.

Rosella woke slowly. The pain in her back caused her to wince as she sat up. Rowan woke soon afterward. Rosella cast a time charm to see how late they were. Luck was on their side, for it was not even midnight. Silently, the raven twins slipped down to their basement rooms to get some more sleep before school.

When morning came, it was clear-skied and sunny, as if the weather wished to mock the duo's wounded backs and downcast minds. It appeared that in the minds of the adult Tigers, being intelligent was a crime if one had magic. At least getting better grades than the 'normal children' was a crime. They would either have to purposefully drop their grades, or learn to forge signatures. The latter seemed much more appealing as the two did not wish to appear anything less than intelligent. Intelligence was not something it would be wise to hide. They had hidden enough already.

At school, they managed to conceal the stiffness of their backs and the pain inflicted the night before. They skipped lunch again, once more choosing to spend their time in the back of the library reading Shakespeare and Poe until the bell rung. They did not see the look the librarian cast at them as they left for their next class.

Throughout the day, it was apparent that the twin's grades and their good behaviour during the past semester had made an impact on the teachers. Well, most of them. While most of the teachers viewed the magical duo positively, there were still a few who held onto Principal Torell's initial assessment of their character, no matter how incorrect it proved to be. They were not the kinds of kids to fake poor grades out of spite. They were mature adults, after all.

Either way, the fact that they now were no longer looked down upon as much by most of the teachers cemented the twins' decision to learn to forge signatures on their report cards. That way, they would not be lying to their teachers, and they would perhaps escape the pain of "being better" than the younger Tiger twins. Never mind that they would be hiding yet another thing from the adults they lived with. Once they could do it well enough, they would not be found out. And if they were caught...well, they would just have to take that risk, because they would never get bad grades on purpose.

That afternoon, school was let out early for a reason the twins never discovered. They decided to explore the town. Perhaps they could find a church to attend. Luck was with the duo that day because they came upon a small church just a few blocks away from Rumen, and within walking distance of the house. They went there that Sunday, and all the Sundays after that until they transferred to secondary school. How they managed to do so, without being caught, they had no idea.

Over the next few months, Rosella and Rowan spent their lunch breaks in the library, researching and practicing forging signatures, starting with those Mr. and Mrs. Tiger. Their magic unconsciously assisted in that learning and soon they could imitate just about anyone's handwriting and signature, with some studying of the original, of course.

The year flew by, with only a few altercations and soon it was once again report-card time. Thanks to the magicals' new skill, the receiving of said cards passed without incident and the summer holidays began.

Whenever they could, the raven twins spent their time in the town library. Mrs. Natser, and a man who seemed to be her husband because he had the same last name and they did not look blood-related, worked at the public library when school was not in session. While the twins were in the library, they hid in the back recesses of the stacks, reading mostly Shakespeare, Sci-Fi/Fantasy, and Gothic Fiction. And listening to music.

And then, on Friday the 13th of August, the magical twins had enough money—from savings and from doing odd jobs for the librarians—to buy a few certain items they had wished for ever since inspiration struck. That morning, instead of departing straight to the library after finishing their morning chores, Rosella and Rowan went to the local craft store and purchased a large deep-blue leather-bound journal. When they arrived at the library, they disappeared into their usual spot.

From his backpack, Rowan pulled a sheaf of notebook paper tied with string and covered with writing from two different hands. He also pulled out a black ink pen etched with silver feathers. He held the pen and papers out to Rosella, but she pushed them back at him and handed him the leather journal. "You have swifter and better penmanship and you know it, brother-mine."

"Very well. What shall you do while I transcribe?"

She tilted her head for a moment then replied. "I saw a book a few days ago that I feel we may be interested in. I shall read that. If it is good, I shall recommend it. If it is bad, I will read *Dracula* again."

He nodded, and Rosella disappeared behind the stacks, searching for the book. The blue-eyed boy uncapped the pen, opened the journal to the second page and began to write, losing track of time as he transcribed. After what seemed mere seconds as well as an eternity, his ears registered the near-inaudible sound of Rosella's footsteps returning. He glanced up as she sat beside him and opened her book. He caught sight of the title: *Les Misérables,* by Victor Hugo, Volume 1. Hmm. He shrugged slightly and returned to his writing.

A few hours passed. Rowan completed three pages of the notebook and was on the second side of the fourth. Rosella was a quarter of the way through her book. Mrs. Natser's voice came over the loudspeaker.

"The library will be closing in five minutes."

With near-mechanical steadiness, Rowan packed the writing things into his backpack. Rosella went to the front desk to check out her book. They met up at the library's front door with two minutes to go and departed for the house where they resided.

As on every day, the raven pair managed to arrive at the house before Mr. and Mrs. Tiger returned from work and picking up the younger twins. After stashing their backpacks under their cots, the duo began their chores. However, since they were cleaning every day, there was not much *to* clean. Once they had washed and put away the supper dishes, Rosella and Rowan were able to escape down to the basement and read, or in Rowan's case, to work on the manuscript.

* * *

After five weeks, what was written of the manuscript was transferred, and Rosella had finished her book. She handed it to Rowan and said, "Read this. There are a few slow parts, but it is an excellent story."

He did not even blink. He set down the book and continued writing. She rolled her eyes and stared at him until he looked up again.

"What?"

"Nothing," she smirked.

"Okay," he said, returned to his writing.

* * *

Soon school began again. The Carson boy had formed a "gang" made up of four other boys in their class. Carson was the leader. Taylor's tan hair fell in dreadlocks around his pointy face. Jameson had sneering dark eyes. Harper's mousy-blond hair was shorn close. And Roberts had spiked black hair and light green eyes. Now that Carson had a gang, he was not shy about irritating the Ro twins. They had sworn to never use their powers at school for fear of being found out, but Carson sensed something was different about them.

Chapter 4

IT WAS DURING THE THIRD WEEK OF SCHOOL that Carson's gang caused problems for the magical twins. Somehow, Principal Torell had gotten wind of the fact that they had been spending all their time in the library when not actually attending a class, and he decreed that they were permitted there only to retrieve a book for a class. He did this on the grounds that they needed to socialize more. The twins accepted the order because they knew they could not do anything about it. They simply ate in the farthest corner of the lunchroom. Luckily, Carson and his gang were not observant enough to notice Rosella and Rowan's routine change until Monday of the fifth week.

The duo was just about to begin to eat when a shadow fell across their table. As one, the magicals looked up. It was Carson and his gang.

"Hello, freaks."

They did not answer, merely gazed at him. He scowled at their lack of response and the two gang members closest to him attempted to appear more intimidating.

After a moment, the twins glanced at each other out of the corner of their eyes and replied in tandem, "Hello, Edward Carson."

He glared harder at the mention of his full name, and after another short staring contest, left since the twins were no longer paying attention to him, having gone back to eating their lunch.

The next day, Carson tried another tactic. He insulted them until he became bored with their lack of response, and left again.

Then, one day near the end of winter break, when Rosella and Rowan were walking home from the town library just before sunset, they decided to take a shortcut through an alley. Unfortunately, it was less of an alley, more of a really long alcove ending in a brick wall. They turned around and headed back the way they came. However they were soon surrounded by a group of larger teenagers, one of whom bore a significant resemblance to the Carson boy. Most likely an older brother.

"Aw, look at the little children out all alone in the dark...."

The twins each raised an eyebrow. Seriously? He didn't look much older than they were, at least not enough to call them "little children." Wait... in the dark? Sure enough, the sun had set and the alley was lit only by the harsh glow of streetlamps. Now the ten older teens appeared a good deal more menacing, and the twins backed up until they were against the brick wall again. The gang closed in on them. It seemed the only way to escape was to fight or negotiate, and the gang did not look like they would be up for the latter.

Instinctively, the twins spoke in tandem. "What do you want from us?"

The leader did not even blink; he merely leered. "Just some fun." He directed his next sentence to the gang members closest to the twins: a spiked-haired young woman and a shaved-headed young man. "Grab them."

As the two older teens lunged, the twins thrust out their hands in defence. Their eyes flashed, and the older teens flew backwards, knocking against the walls of the alley. They slumped, and did not move. The twins hoped they weren't dead.

The older Carson boy scowled and jerked his head in their direction. Nearly all of the gang pounced. He sent another one off in the direction of the street.

Rosella and Rowan moved to stand back-to-back. They raised their hands, palm out in defence. Their eyes glowed softly as they threw the gang members back one-by-one. Their brief luck did not hold, however. As soon the gang members realised that the twins could throw only one person at a time, four of them attacked at once, two per twin, and Rosella and Rowan were restrained.

Though the twins were good using the magic they knew, they had never seen a need to learn combat, nor how to get out of someone's grip, so they could not escape. Although the gang members held them securely, they continue to struggle and the glow in their eyes never dimmed. But no matter how hard the duo fought, the grip of those who restrained them did not weaken.

After a few minutes, the gang member the elder Carson boy had sent off returned, with Principal Torell in tow. The brown-haired man's eyes were hard as he observed the twins' glowing eyes and the unconscious gang members slumped against the alley walls.

He approached the elder Carson boy. "I assume those two did this, Paul?"

Paul Carson nodded. "It appears they have magic, sir."

Principal Torell spun on his heel and walked away. "Bring them."

Paul nodded at the two goons that held the twins, and the five of them set off after the middle-aged man.

Eventually the group arrived at what appeared to be Principal Torell's house—a squat, grey-panelled building with cream-coloured trim and a cream-coloured front door. He unlocked the door and inside they all went, following him through the house and down the stairs to the darkened basement.

Principal Torell flipped the light-switch revealing what was a perfectly ordinary basement, except for what was hanging on rows of hooks on the opposite wall. Even Paul Carson seemed surprised at the dozens of chains, shackle-like bracelets, and chokers lining the wall. Although it seemed odd that a middle-aged man had so much untypical jewellery, Rosella and Rowan could feel a deadness humming in the air that explained exactly what those bands on the wall were—magic suppressors. Their eyes went wide and they began to struggle once more.

However, just as before, the magicals' struggles were in vain and they were manhandled to the other side of the room. Principal Torell ran his finger along a row of shackle bracelets before selecting a pair of narrow, silvery chains with no visible clasp.

The twins fought even more against their captors as the sharp-eyed man approached, binder-chains jingling in his hands. He went to

Rowan after handing one to Paul Carson, who walked to Rosella. The twins whimpered as the bracelets clinked closed over their left wrists. The connection to the power that had been with them for all their lives, the power that sheltered them and kept them from harm, was blocked. With that, they blacked out.

* * *

Rowan came to first, slowly. Rosella woke a few moments later. They were in their basement, on the floor. No light was coming from the windows near the ceiling—it must still be night. Something was different. The colours weren't as bright and shapes not as clear or sharp. Something was missing. A comforting feeling was gone. The pathways to their magic were blocked.

They looked at each other, wondering how long they had been unconscious and when they got back home since nothing, as far as they could tell, had been taken from them. Although they no longer had their power, they still could sense that someone had gone through their things and removed certain "odd" objects. If that someone was not Principal Torell, then it was most definitely Paul Carson. After crawling to the loose bricks of a wall, the twins sighed in relief at the sight of their book—safe in its spot with their rings, which they had stopped wearing a few weeks earlier when Ed Carson had ramped up his bullying.

After sitting on the floor and staring blankly for a few minutes, the raven-haired twins clambered into their beds and fell asleep. They dreamed of rivers and rushing air and waves and cold.

When morning dawned, Rosella sat up hesitantly, then closed her eyes as once again she felt the lack of magic within. Life would be very different without that comforting blanket-shield around her, ready to act whenever she directed her thought. One thing was for certain—they had no protection against Ed Carson anymore. Unless...no, they did not have the money to start training in martial arts, at least not formally. However, the library was sure to have books on it.

Suddenly, the fourteen-year old realized something very important.

Now that they could not access their magic, they could no longer put glamours over the bruises they would undoubtedly receive for not being there to make dinner the night before. Oh dear.

With a faint groan, Rowan sat up. Their eyes met, and even without the telepathic bond their powers had given them, he knew by her expression exactly what she had been thinking, and the conclusions she had arrived at. His brow knit in worry and matched her own. What were they to do?

It seemed the only safe option was to continue with life as they had before the blocking, and so they did. Once winter break was over, their grades dropped a bit, what with the lack of the slightly enhanced learning that their powers had given them. But they managed.

* * *

The next few months passed without incident. Rosella and Rowan still attended church, but they did so now with a hungry fervour, searching for the warmth that the blanket of their power had provided, albeit on a smaller scale than the church did. Whenever they were not at school or doing chores at the house, the azure-eyed duo were sequestered in a corner alcove of the church entryway, reading and writing, or just sitting in silence. They took to carrying their Bibles wherever they went. And once they saved enough money, they planned to go to the local jewellery store in search of a certain something—a pair of plain, matching cross necklaces. Then they planned to give the rest of their meagre monies to the church, for it to do what it wished.

It was a grey, drippy day when the two fourteen-year-olds opened the door to the jewellery shop. A small bell attached to the top of the glass and metal panel jingled. The shopkeeper, a tall, balding man, looked up briefly from the watch he was fixing, then turned his attention back to his work. The twins scanned the shelves and glass cabinets before identifying one in the farthest left corner of the shop.

In that cabinet, all alone on a dusty faded cushion, a pair of plain silver crosses lay, each on a nondescript black leather cord. Rowan and Rosella were drawn by the pure simplicity of the pendants. The shopkeeper noticed them looking and approached.

"You like those?"

"Yes, and we would like to buy them."

"You would? I have never had a customer even look at these. Usually they want something gaudy or elaborate."

"How much are they?" Rosella's eyes were quizzical, her voice firm.

The keen-eyed man pondered. "Usually I would say... thirty pounds, but since you are the only people interested since I made them five years ago, I'll make it fifteen."

The twins glanced at each other then back at the shopkeeper. They nodded. "Fair enough. Yes, we will buy them."

The shopkeeper took the necklaces from the case and rang up the sale. The twins paid him and put the necklaces on as they walked out the door, causing the little bell to ring again.

* * *

The next day was Sunday. The duo walked into church the same as they always had, right on time. The only difference was the silver crosses around their necks. Only one person noticed. That person also caught sight of the chain-link magic-binders locked around their left wrists. The person's eyes narrowed in thought as she studied the twins more closely: Raven-black hair, bright blue eyes dulled with the hardships of a life unusually cruel, light skin, slightly blurred features...wait, what? Slightly blurred features—someone had these kids under a glamour-charm, and by the looks of those chains, it was not the twins who had cast it. Someone else wished these twins to be kept hidden.

The woman's winter-blue eyes narrowed further as she noted the age of the twins. They appeared to be around fourteen...the same age her brother's children would be...and that made her think of her brother and his wife, who believed their twins were dead. The woman firmly believed her niece and nephew were still very much alive.

She ran one caramel-coloured hand through her long ink-black hair absently. How to tell if the two here in church were the two she was thinking of. Had their magics not been blocked, she could read their auras to see if they held similarities to those of her brother and his wife. Actually...perhaps....

The woman contemplated a loophole. If she sent a tendril of power to unblock the duo's magic, just for a second, she could read their auras. Yes, she would do that.

Out went the tendril and for perhaps a millisecond, winter-blue eyes glowed as the woman observed the two teens' auras, completely unnoticed by the twins. Her eyes widened slightly as she recognised a familiar tinge of bluish-silver. The shade was faintly different, but that could be due to the glamours and magic-binders. If so, then it was the same tinge of blue-silver that graced the auras of every member of the Balaur family, whether from the bloodline or married into it. This woman was a Balaur, as was her brother, sister-in-law, sister, parents, and so on and so forth. Therefore, if she was correct, these twins were her brother's children, for there were no other Balaur children of that age. In fact, as far as she knew, there were no other Balaur children at all since neither she, nor her sister, married and their father was an only child.

And yet, how could she be sure? Glamours could be created to disguise auras, though that was extremely difficult. Only a full-fledged Mage could properly cast one. She did not know who glamoured these two teens, so she could not know how powerful he or she was.

Perhaps the best course of action was to merely walk up to the children and introduce herself.

***

After the church service, when Rosella and Rowan were just about to leave, they were approached by a tall woman with caramel-coloured skin. The woman had winter-blue eyes in a fair, angular face framed by hip-length curtains of thick inky-black hair. She was studying them keenly. Then she held out a hand. "Hello, I recently arrived here. I'm Araunya Balaur."

They shook her hand.

"Rosella..."

"...and Rowan."

They gave no last name and the woman did not even blink. In fact, she seemed to be expecting something of that sort.

"Well, Rosella and Rowan, it was a pleasure to meet you." With that, she walked away, and the twins glanced at each other and shrugged. They left the church and headed home since the library was closed on Sundays. They did not notice the woman was following them.

* * *

Araunya tailed the twins discretely because she did not know how sharp their senses would be without their powers. After about nine minutes, they approached what appeared to be a three-story brick house with a small front yard and white picket fence. In the driveway were a white van and a red hot-rod.

The twins entered the house, and with a blink, Araunya became invisible and followed them, slipping through the door just before it closed.

The house where the twins lived showed no sign of resident adolescents, which did not surprise Araunya considering the lack of family name given in their introduction, and the pain and loneliness threaded through their auras. Most people did not realise that auras were not only representations of an identity, they were also a map of that person's experiences, and so they had the tendency to shift as a person aged.

The pictures on the walls and on the side tables showed no hint of the raven locks or blue eyes possessed by the twins. Instead, the photos were of brown-eyed, redheaded children. There were also photos of a man and woman, and two children, one male, one female, clearly also twins, and obviously offspring of the man and woman. What was the name of the host family?

Discreetly, so the raven twins would not notice, the caramel-skinned woman picked up a photograph showing the redheaded family at a lake and looked at the back. "Fun Day at The Lake for The

Tiger Family!" it read in loopy, flowery script. She set the photograph down. The Tiger family. So, that's who held her niece and nephew and the reason for so much pain in their auras. Silently, Araunya growled and clenched her hands into fists. Those...people had better be glad she would never seriously harm another person unless directly antagonised.

Cause a bit of mischief, sure, but she feared anything she did would be pinned on the twins, and therefore she would be indirectly responsible for even more pain inflicted on them. Therefore, she would not act now—now being the key word. They would get their due eventually, if she had anything to say about it.

Araunya followed the raven twins into the basement and her anger at the adult Tigers grew. The room was almost completely bare—the only furnishings were two cots, a cheap card table, and two folding chairs. There was not even a carpet on the cement floor, just a small rug alongside each of the cots.

Rosella and Rowan went to a wall and removed a few loose bricks, revealing a dark blue journal and a pair of silver rings—one set with a deep green stone, the other with one of deep blue. The rings caught Araunya's interest. They were obviously made with magic and fashioned in a manner that allowed only those with magic to see them. Luckily, the binders the twins wore around their wrists could not take away magic, only block a person's access to it.

The twins each picked up a ring—Rowan the green one and Rosella the blue. They held them, just staring, for a moment. Then, as one, their hands closed over the bands of silver and gemstone and then they placed them back in the hole. Rowan opened the journal to the last page where there was writing. Araunya saw small and narrow, elegant writing in a pitch-black ink. She wondered who had written the words, but then Rowan picked up a black ink pen and began to write. The pen was etched along the sides with spiralling silver feathers. Rosella mumbled into Rowan's ear every once in awhile. While Araunya could easily have taken a step forward to hear what was being said, she refrained out of respect for what was left of the twins' privacy.

She looked around the basement once more, then nodded grimly.

She had found her brother's children and now knew where they were housed. Now she needed to find out if the twins' foster parents had legally adopted them, or if they had just been left on the doorstep. If the latter, that was the fault of whoever had kidnapped the children, not the host family. However, if the Tigers had chosen not to legally adopt the twins, then that was another black mark on their record in her opinion—though not much of one since a parent should care for any child in their keeping, legally required or not.

With a final nod, Araunya Balaur teleported home.

Chapter 5

NEVA LOOKED UP WHEN SHE SENSED HER SISTER APPEAR. "How goes the search, Araunya? Or have you finally accepted that you are wasting your time?"

The black-haired woman could feel the older woman's glare even as she added another touch to her drawing. It was a charcoal sketch of tiger lilies in a field of daisies. She liked drawing plant life.

Eventually Araunya spoke. "I have not been wasting my time, Neva. I found them. I have found them!"

When hearing the winter-blue eyed woman shout, Khulai, their younger brother, approached the door with curiosity. His braids cascaded over his shoulder. "What did you find, Ara?"

"I found the twins."

The man's gunmetal-blue eyes widened. "What?" he asked in a low baritone voice.

"I. Found. Durriken and Charani's. Long. Lost. Twin. Children." Araunya's tone was final, and though she joked occasionally, she never did about something like this. And she did not lie.

Khulai entered and shut the door behind him. "Where? Do they need medical aid?" Always the doctor, their brother asked first about their health. Not that that was a bad thing. Neva just found it amusing.

Araunya shook her head. "Not at the moment, but from what I saw of their home life, and what I read in their auras, glamours are concealing their appearance and magic-suppressors are on their wrists. They will need medical assistance soon."

Khulai's eyes darkened. "Magic suppressors?" The caramel-skinned man's tone was dangerously calm. His mind cast back to the last time he had to deal with something of that sort.

He had just turned twenty-five and been captured, though he couldn't remember by who anymore. Whoever it was had wyrms under their power. The slippery, long-bodied, wingless, hornless, dragon-like creatures supposedly existed only in legend. Yet there they were. And, whoever it was had many magic suppressors, one of which was attached to him. Until that band of shining metal clicked shut, Khulai had been confident he would escape. But immediately afterward, he felt his sharpness of sight, clarity, and the comforting power of his magic fade. At that moment, all hope failed him.

He had let loose ear splitting screams of loss and rage, and then gone limp in the chains that held him stretched spread-eagle against a wall. His head drooped to his chest. The person—he remembered now that it was a man, deathly pale, dark-haired, with a face that would have been considered handsome before it was marred by his evil nature—seemed to revel in his screams. The man's black eyes shone with malicious joy.

Then the tortures began. He could not defend himself. White-hot pokers and knives, whips tipped with glass, spiked clubs—though his face was left untouched. With each scream of pain Khulai emitted, the man had smiled more. He could do nothing to save himself.

Eventually Araunya, Durriken, and Neva arrived to rescue him, and he killed the man with a stake to the heart, then decapitation. But the memories still haunted him. He often woke screaming from dreams of the daggers and whips digging into his skin, muscle, and bone.

Khulai rolled his shoulders. All of the physical wounds had healed, leaving his body covered in silver-white scars. But every time he heard the word "magic-suppressor," he could not suppress a shudder.

His handsome face contorted into a dark scowl. "We need to get those children out of there as soon as possible."

Araunya nodded. "You are right, brother-mine, but we must be patient. They may free themselves from the suppressors' bonds." She fixed him with a hard stare, daring him to challenge her when she had the authority, and he had believed, just as the others did, that the twins were long dead.

He nodded, still scowling. "I will defer on this matter, but that does not mean I have to like it."

"Very well."

Neva, who had been sitting quietly since Khulai entered, spoke. "'Are you sure it is them, Araunya? Are you sure you're not mistaken?"

The older woman turned her hard gaze upon her younger sister. "I read their auras, Neva. I am not mistaken."

"Okay...." Neva's tone indicated she would not believe that until she had proof, which would be soon enough—the winter-eyed woman would bring the twins to Ynys Golauglas, the Island of Blue Light, where Clan Balaur resided, and where their Gorhendad, their Great-Grandfather, Barsali Oaksword, reigned in the Lodge on the west coast of the isle.

Araunya was just about to teleport to her room to plan, when Neva stopped her. "Just so you know, Ara, Charani, and Durriken have had another child, a son."

She stopped short. "What? Since when?"

"Since three years ago. His name is Jardani, and he has Charani's sapphire eyes."

"The twins had midnight-blue eyes, similar to Durriken's, but brighter." Araunya had no idea why she said that....

"What colour were the eyes of the twins you saw?"

"Just plain blue, but I know they were glamoured. I saw the feature-blur."

"Ah."

Shaking her head at her sister's disbelief, the lithe and shapely woman disappeared to her room to plan and plot.

* * *

Rosella and Rowan awoke to the sound of rain. By the time they arrived at school it was pouring, and they were soaked. Mechanically, they put their backpacks in their lockers and went to their first class. Classes on a whole went perfectly fine, but at lunch a familiar annoyance made himself known.

Just as they finished eating, Carson and his gang approached. The usual insults were heard and cast off, but then he said something new. His voice and face took on a false friendliness and sincerity.

"I heard something interesting the other day that I think you may be interested in, freaks, especially since you don't know about it yet."

"Oh? And what might that be, Edward Carson?" the twins said.

He smiled in mean glee. "For all your good grades, you can't figure something like this out. No wonder your parents didn't want you, freaks."

The twins' eyes went cold, and had their magic not been bound, their hands would have been sparking. As it was, there was a faint smell of ozone in the air and the temperature dropped slightly.

Carson did not notice. He opened his mouth again. The twins stood suddenly and walked off. They placed their trays on top of the rubbish bin with the others, then made their way to the library.

Once the raven twins had passed through the double doors, they walked to the adult fiction section where they curled up in a corner, their backs to the wall and their faces on their knees.

* * *

Jenny, the librarian, watched. Her eyes fell on the chain-link bands around their wrists, and their fingers where their silver rings used to be. The green-eyed woman thought back to something she had not tried to reach for a very long time. She felt the apple-pie-scented warm blanket of her magic wrap around her.

Every person's magic has a different scent to it, just as each person's aura has a different combination of colours. It is not a physical scent, but that is the only way it's been described. Rupert's magic smelled like freshly baked peach cobbler.

In any case, Jenny shivered slightly as her magic encompassed her, sharpening her senses and filling her with power for the first time in five years. She searched the library for the twins with her re-awakened senses and wondered why she had put her magic aside in the first place. Then she remembered and her shoulders drooped slightly.

The dark red-haired woman squared her shoulders then realised she did not have to hide anymore. She made up her mind to never put away her magic again. She decided that when she found the twins, she would attempt to contact her family again. Perhaps she and Rupert could move back to Ynys Golauglas. Rupert had liked it there with her family, and she had been sad to leave.

She quickly located the twins and brushed aside the thought that she could have found them just as quickly without magic. Nodding once, after giving them a discreet scan for wounds, Jenny returned to her desk. It was time to see if she could contact one of her cousins.

All of a sudden, she had an idea and pulled a knotted string-and-bead bracelet from her purse. She tied it on her wrist, closed her eyes, and thought hard about one cousin. She asked the cousin to call her and provide her mobile number.

A few moments later, Jenny's cell phone rang, filling the library's silence with the sound of fast-paced cello music.

"Hello? Jenny Natser speaking."

"Hello, Zujenia. How have you been doing these past five years?" Araunya's voice was deep for a woman, and she had a thick Welsh accent. She also sounded somewhat sarcastic.

"It worked!" said Jenny.

Her second cousin chuckled. "No need to sound so surprised, Zu." She paused for a moment. "So, why do you wish to speak with me? Does it have something to do with Cojiñí and Scoruș?" Then she clarified, "The raven-haired twins at Rumen."

"How...?"

"I happened to be in the area and ran into them at church. Followed them home and surveyed their residence once I read their auras."

"Then you know they need out as soon as possible."

"You are indeed correct, cousin-mine."

"What should we do?"

Araunya was silent for a moment. Then she asked, "Do you still have that bracelet on?"

"Yes."

"Give me a minute and I'll be right there."

When the woman hung up, Jenny put down the phone.

A moment later, the tall woman appeared at her side. She became invisible when the class bell rang.

And as the class bell rang, the twins looked at each other, stood, and left the library. They did not know the gaze of librarian Natser and an invisible woman followed them until they exited the library doors.

For the rest of the day, the twins operated on autopilot. They did not even know why the platinum-haired boy's jab had hurt them so much, they just knew that it did. They felt like complete idiots for not realizing they were not related, at least not very closely, to the Tiger or Duncan lines—unless black hair and blue eyes were recessive traits in their long-ago history. The twins were educated enough about genetics to know that black hair is a dominant trait, not a recessive one.

That afternoon, Jenny took Araunya home for a dinner they shared with Rupert. Afterwards, they spoke about the raven-haired duo.

When Rupert had heard all that had been going on, he ran a hand through his short, dark brown hair and said, a bit testily, "And why did you not tell me any of this before, Jen?"

Jenny shrugged. "Honestly, I have no inkling of an idea, Ru."

Araunya piped up. "She probably didn't tell you because she didn't want to worry you or rile you into doing something that would get you in trouble, no matter how well-intentioned it was. You are in the habit of acting impulsively, which was the case for a year and a half after you two wedded."

The stormy-eyed man conceded to the logic of that statement and Araunya changed the subject. "You now know the twins are bound by magic-suppressors. And you noticed that this afternoon, Zu?"

Jenny nodded, and the winter-eyed woman continued. "Well, I have reason to believe they will attempt to break the bonds tomorrow."

The married couple frowned. The conversation turned to what they would do if that happened.

* * *

When the twins arrived at home, they went down to the basement and lay on their cots. As they stared at the ceiling, an idea struck. They still thought the same, even without their telepathic bond.

When Carson had insulted them and they became angry, they both felt their magic again, even through the suppressors' blockage. Their idea was, perhaps if they became angry enough, and used their rings, then the suppressors would break and they would be free once more.

They decided to wear the rings, which they had made themselves at age eight, because the rings had been crafted to enhance and amplify magical power. They originally made the rings to help them create their secret alcoves behind the bedrooms, but the raven twins figured the silver-and-gem jewellery could break the suppressors' power, too.

With that pleasant thought in mind, the blue-eyed, raven-haired, blurry-featured (not that they knew that) twins went to sleep, their dreams full of what they would do when they were free. They would pray to God in thanks that their scheme had worked, that was certain.

The next day dawned mostly clear, but with a hint of oncoming storm. It was as if the weather was mirroring the mood and plans of the twins. They were prepared in case they would have to make a break for it. In their backpacks were an extra change of clothes, the silver feather-etched black ink pen, the blue leather-covered manuscript journal, and a fairly good supply of non-perishable foodstuffs.

Rosella and Rowan went through their first classes as if in a dream. Time was their enemy that day and it seemed to crawl slower than a sleep-sliming slug with a rock on its back.

Finally, after what felt like a trillion years, the lunch bell rang and they joined the throng of students making their way to the lunchroom. They grabbed food and ate their lunches quickly so they would have time to digest it before the "showdown," as they had begun to call it.

So far, everything was going to plan. But soon the Carson boy and his gang came over to them.

"Hello, freaks."

The twins would recount later that they never really registered the exact words Carson said, and could not even recall the gist, except that it was all very insulting and succeeded in making the twins very angry.

This time, faint sparks emanated from their hands, and the smell of ozone became prominent as the temperature dropped. Their rings began to glow. But it seemed as if the Carson boy did not feel the cold, and must have a plugged up nose because he did not notice the changes in the atmosphere and kept up his tirade.

Eventually, the twins reached their breaking point, and Carson took a step back. The temperature around the raven-haired duo dropped further, and a wind manifested inside the room. Outside, the storm finally broke and rain poured down in torrents. Lightning struck the ground outside the building. Lighting struck the floor inside.

As the indoor wind increased in speed, the teens' bracelets began to shake, then they shattered with a high-pitched clatter of glass breaking. Rosella and Rowan's eyes closed as they felt the warm, comforting blanket of their magics wrap tightly around them once more, and their bodies began to glow as they rose a few metres off the floor.

Just then, the lunchroom doors swung open, banging the walls on both sides. Two figures appeared, both women. One was familiar to the students of Rumen Primary School—librarian Jenny. The other had black hair pulled up and back, away from an angular, fair face. She had keen winter-blue eyes that glinted sharply. One caramel-skinned hand grasped a long, black wood staff tipped with a garnet set in steel. Araunya Balaur. Her long grey coat whipped around her long black-clad legs due to the wind the twins had created.

The red stone on the staff began to glow, as did Araunya's eyes as she pointed the staff at the floating duo. She muttered something and a bolt of white light hit them, sending them to the floor in a heap. The woman winced slightly, then rushed to them. She held onto the arm of both children and teleported away in a faint puff of air, leaving Zujenia to take care of the students huddled against the walls.

Chapter 6

KHULAI SENSED ARAUNYA TELEPORT IN, and after identifying her location in the West Wing, he teleported to join her. As soon as he saw the unconscious twins, he took charge, and the older woman deferred to his expertise in all matters of healing.

"We need to put them in separate rooms, but near each other...the ones in the centre of the wall on the top floor. I have a feeling that when they awake they will enjoy the height."

Araunya nodded, and the lithe man continued, "I will fetch another doctor skilled in the art of healing intense magical exhaustion while you put them there, if you would please, sister-mine."

She nodded once again, and Khulai disappeared with a faint puff of air. With a sigh, the slender woman hefted the two fourteen-year-olds onto her shoulders and carted them to the requested rooms, as she would rather not teleport again without her passengers being conscious. Especially since she did not know how being in the mid-space would affect their magical and mental states. She had teleported them to the Lodge because that was the only way to get there, as it was not on any maps, and ships were turned away by the wards.

Khulai reappeared as soon as she had laid Scoruș down on the bed that was to be his. He brought a brown-haired, brown-eyed young assistant named Tara Nighthand with him.

"Right then, Tara. You know how to kick-start the healing process for intense magical exhaustion. I want you to do so on the girl in the next room. Do not come back until you are done. I will be doing the same to this boy."

With a nod of understanding, the short young woman left the room to do as she was told. Khulai knelt beside the boy and laid his hand on his forehead, then closed his own eyes. He reopened them immediately and called for Tara to come back at once. She appeared in the doorway, confused.

"Tara, your patient and mine forcefully broke a powerful set of glamour charms, which have not been completely undone. They were not able to unravel them. I suggest you start by setting your patient's appearance to what it should be."

Tara nodded again.

"You may go back to continue your work now, Tara, and remember, this is your test."

After Tara left the room, Araunya asked, "Okay, why is she so quiet, and what do you mean, her test?"

"This is her last practical test on becoming the leader of the IMIH ward. As to why she's quiet, I have absolutely no idea."

"Remind me what IMIH stands for...."

"Intensive Magical Incident Healing."

"Ah."

"Now I need you to be quiet so I can focus, sister-mine."

Araunya nodded, then sat on the floor beside her younger brother to watch him work.

Placing his hand on Scoruș' forehead once again, Khulai Silvertouch focussed his magic on finding the glamour woven into his nephew's form. He found it quickly, and with a slight—but well-practiced—flick of thought, the net of magic unravelled and faded away.

Opening his gunmetal-blue eyes, he watched as the boy's features morphed and defined themselves, and his skin darkened to the light caramel tone characteristic of the Balaur Clan. The man cast an appraising glance over the face of his nephew, taking stock of which elements came from which relative. The angularity of prominent cheekbones was common in the Chief's line. The straight nose and almond-shaped eyes were similar to those of Charani, his and Cojiñí's mother. The cleft chin came from their grandmother Jaelle, Durriken, Araunya, Khulai, and Neva's mother. And the tall forehead and widow's peak were reminiscent of relatives far back, but Khulai could not recall their names. Perhaps it was from Charani's side of the family, but he could not be sure.

Khulai tossed one of his braids behind his back and focussed again, flexing his fingers ever so slightly. His eyes closed as he delved back into Scoruş' magic, making his way to the boy's core, a ball of light in the general area of his heart. The ball's colour, also reflected in the boy's aura, was bright emerald green.

Khulai's magic was purple. Araunya's was red. Neva's was pale greenish-yellow. Durriken's was silver. Charani's was also purple, but closer to violet.

The colour of Scoruş' core was not relevant at that moment due to his depleted state. It was barely even glowing—more like a ball of intangible green smudge. The caramel-skinned man frowned. This was bad. What else had the children done?

Khulai opened his eyes and turned to Araunya, taking his hand off the boy's forehead. "When you found them today, what exactly were they doing?"

She thought for a moment. "Floating in the air, eyes closed, unconsciously simulating a strong wind throughout the room." Her gaze turned quizzical. "I knew that was bad, but why?"

Khulai rested an elbow on the bed. "It's bad because they were using magic when their cores were at dangerous depletion levels from breaking the suppressor-bonds and the glamours. I picked up something else in my scan—they may have broken a memory block, which means I need to assimilate their blocked memories."

"Are you going to tell Tara?"

He shook his head. "If she finds it, she knows how to take care of it. This is her last test, after all."

"Ah."

With that settled, the tall man turned back to the boy, laid his hand on the boy's forehead again, found his magical core once more, and began repairing the torn channels and feeding in some of his own magical energy.

The effort exhausted him. A quick glance at the clock indicated he had been focussed on the boy for more than two hours. Araunya was still sitting there, watching him.

Khulai shifted his other hand, bumping it into something. He looked down and saw that Araunya had brought him a glass of water. He drank the water in three gulps.

"Thank you, Ara."

"I thought you would need it."

He turned back to Scoruș. "I've done all I can for now. I've mended the channels he tore by using too much power too quickly, after not using it at all for a while, and I've given him enough magic from my core to replenish it. I've also gone in and assimilated the blocked memories into where they should be. The memories were his earliest ones. Why anyone would block memories of someone's infancy, I have no idea."

"Do you think Tara also found the memory block?"

"Undoubtedly she did, and assimilated them just as I have done." He tilted his head. "In fact, I believe she should be coming back...now."

Indeed, as he said the last word, the brown-haired young woman, just a few years younger than Khulai, entered the room.

"I have done what I could...." She trailed off, uncharacteristically. The bell-voiced young woman had always been concise and to the point, really a spitfire. But Araunya noticed that now she was quiet and...meek. She was avoiding Khulai's eyes, as if it was a game. Khulai seemed oblivious.

"That is all I ask, Tara. Now, show me your patient. If you did this correctly, then I will file the necessary paperwork; you will be elevated to Head of the IMIH ward; and your apprenticeship under me will be fully completed. If you did not complete the task correctly... well, I believe that you did." With a kind smile, Khulai followed the short, young woman out the door. Araunya went too, out of curiosity.

When they entered the room, it was clear that at least the glamours had been removed because the girl's skin had darkened and her features were almost a perfect copy of Scoruș' face. The differences were fuller lips and a faintly softer, more feminine jaw line and eyes.

Khulai knelt down beside the bed, laid his right hand on Cojiñí's forehead, just as he had done with Scoruș, and closed his eyes. A few moments later, his gunmetal-blue orbs opened and he stood up, held out his right hand, and he smiled at Tara.

"Tara Nighthand," he began, "Ignoring the paperwork and formal ceremony, you are now Head of the IMIH ward and have fully completed your apprenticeship. Welcome, my friend."

Tara's smile could have lit a continent as she vigorously shook the black-haired man's hand, letting go just before it would be considered improper, but longer than necessary. Araunya watched with amusement, but quickly made her face expressionless as Tara turned to her.

"Okay, I know this will sound horrible, but I have to thank you for providing the opportunity for this test."

The winter-eyed older woman chuckled, and nodded. "I do suppose the best thing for me to say is, you're welcome, so, you are welcome, Doctor Nighthand."

Khulai clapped his hands together, causing the two women to look at him. "Since now we must just wait for the twin's recovery, complete the paperwork, and arrange a ceremony—and the latter two can be put off a few hours—how about we go out for drinks and a meal, on me. And Tara can choose where we go."

Araunya and Tara turned to each other. "Alamina's?" said Araunya.

Tara nodded. "Alamina's."

Khulai sighed slightly, as if in relief.

* * *

Alamina's was a small café and bakery off to one side of the Lodge on Main Street. When the trio entered through the glass door, they were greeted with the sound of soft classical music and the smell of freshly baked pastries, breads, and hot soup. It was not an overly busy day, so there was only a short line approaching the counter. The menu hung from the ceiling.

Araunya ordered a dark chocolate mousse cup and a baguette-ham-cheese sandwich. The mousse cup had a strawberry on top. Khulai and

Tara both ordered a blueberry croissant and a bowl of the soup of the day. All three got water.

While they ate, they talked about everything and nothing, Araunya carefully steered their conversation away from anything embarrassing—though it was her job as eldest sister to embarrass her younger siblings. But today, she only made Tara laugh. Tara was a good woman, and as far as Araunya could see, she would be a fair match for Khulai—if only he would notice the brown-eyed woman was fonder of him than is typical in a teacher-apprentice relationship.

When they were done, Khulai paid for their meals, as he had said he would, and they all went their separate ways. Khulai returned to his office to file the paperwork and arrange a formal ceremony. Tara headed to her parents' home to tell them the good news. And Araunya went back to the Lodge's West Wing to wait for the twins to awaken.

* * *

Many, many kilometres away, in an elaborate mansion in the mountains, a voluptuous, slender young woman looked up, a lock of her long, pale-golden hair falling across her beautiful face. Her perfectly arched eyebrows were creased, and her ocean-aqua eyes were puzzled and worried. She stood up gracefully, elegantly extracting herself from behind her carved mahogany desk, and glided over the white marble floor to the spiral staircase in one corner. The spiked heels of her tall, white leather boots clicked on the gleaming stone. As she walked, her low-collared, deep wine-burgundy dress stretched tight across her shapely, fishnet-covered thighs.

She walked up the stairs and stepped onto the smooth, grey, stone floor of an octagonal room very different from the one she just left. The first room had many large windows with a view of the mountains; this room only had only one window, shuttered. The first room was elegantly decorated and elaborately furnished, but this second one was Spartan, though the furniture was well made.

Lining the walls were shelves and cupboards, most of them full of bottles and boxes and jars of powders, liquids, stones, and things of that sort. In the centre of the room was a fire pit over which hung a large cauldron on a three-legged stand. Beside the pit was a metal rack holding assorted instruments used for stirring and stabbing hanging from hooks. There was a sturdy table and chair, and a box containing paper and parchment, and assorted pens and inks.

The beautiful woman pulled from a cupboard: a wide, shallow bronze bowl, a large vial of oddly glinting burnt-orange powder, and a large jar of thick, oily liquid. She set all three items on the table. Into the bowl, she poured the liquid until the shallow dish was full. Onto the mirrored surface that the liquid in the bowl created, the fair-skinned woman sprinkled some of the powder, then pursed her full, red-painted lips and blew on it softly.

The powder dispersed over the top of the liquid and dissolved, turning the liquid a colour darker than dried poppies. She spoke a few urgent words in her rich, musical, bell-like soft voice.

The liquid began to swirl rapidly, and the woman watched with sharp oceanic eyes. After a few moments, the liquid settled and became transparent, but it did not show the bottom of the bowl. Rather, she saw a pair of figures lying flat. The rise and fall of their chests as they breathed proved they were living.

As the figures became more defined, it was evident they were one male and one female, no older than fifteen, caramel-skinned, raven-haired, with similar facial features. One could even say that had they been of the same gender, they would be identical.

The woman made a gesture with one flawless hand, and nimbuses of coloured light surrounded the figures—one emerald green, one electric blue. The nimbuses were threaded with various colours, including the dark lapis-sapphire of Clan Balaur. The woman's lips pulled back into a snarl, revealing even, pearly-white teeth.

Suddenly, she slapped the table, nearly upsetting the shallow bowl filled to the brim with liquid. Ripples coursed through the surface, disrupting the image and causing it to disappear. Sighing elegantly, the woman poured the liquid from the bowl into the cauldron, and put the bowl, jar, and vial away. She lit a fire with a click of her fingers. When the liquid was completely burned, she descended back to her office.

With her heels clicking on the white marble, the statuesque woman glided to the huge, elaborately carved double doors that led to the hall. She closed the doors behind her, entered a hallway, and went into the third room on the left.

This was an office as well, with the same white marble floor and similar mahogany furniture, although the room had a clean, masculine feel. A man sat at the desk. He was exquisitely, alluringly handsome—an equal to the exquisitely and alluringly beautiful woman. Their facial features were similar. They were twins. The man looked up when he heard the woman's footsteps.

"Anwyn? What is wrong?" His voice was just as handsome as his face, a perfect voice to either sing love songs or shout battle orders. Hers was the feminine mirror of his.

"You did not sense it, Aneirin?"

"I sensed something, but I had not yet gotten up to check." As he said the last word, he gestured at his still-seated, well-muscled form.

Anwyn rolled her eyes. She and Aneirin were only nineteen years old, though their age was not obvious in their manner or speech.

"I assume you know what it was then, sister-mine?"

She nodded, and sat down suddenly on the edge of her brother's desk. "You remember the twins... *she* told us about them when she explained our heritage. The twins she glamoured and memory-blocked?"

The ravishingly handsome man thought for a moment, his oceanic eyes focussed on the wall behind the ravishingly beautiful woman. He nodded. His chin-length pale gold hair caught the light just so. "Yes, I do remember. What of them?"

"*Her* bonds and charms have been broken."

His eyes opened wide. "Oh!"

"Yes, oh!"

"We have to find them...soon."

"Yes, we must, but I think we can hold off a little longer."

"Very well."

Chapter 7

ARAUNYA RAVENHEART STRODE PURPOSELY through the halls of Glamdring Secondary school. Although it appeared as if she knew where she was headed, she really had absolutely no idea how to get to the principal's office. For some reason it was on the fourth floor—the top floor—and the directions given to her by the secretary were confusing, especially since she had forgotten them. She ended up wandering, completely lost, yet moving in a purposeful manner.

Eventually, she poked her head into a classroom and asked for directions. The teacher, Ms. Bond, gave much clearer instructions than the secretary had, and Araunya soon reached her destination.

The door to the principal's office was unassuming, with a single frosted-glass window. Beneath the window was a brass plate inscribed "Principal A. E. Jones."

Aidan Jones had been a friend of Araunya's for five years, though they'd had minimal face-to-face contact during that time because she'd still been travelling all over the globe looking for Cojiñí and Scoruş. She thought back to the first time they met.

She was fighting a pack of wyrms, creatures thought to be mythical until she saw them the night the twins were stolen. Wyrms are similar to dragons, but they do not have horns or wings. Their long, sinuous, yellowish bodies, and short, jagged teeth that drip with venom, were also clues they were most definitely not dragons.

Either way, she was fighting a pack of five nasty beasts when a man suddenly walked around the corner. Sensing the easier prey, the

wyrm pack turned to face him, leaving themselves completely open to her. A well-thrown dagger took out the one closest to the man, and sharp bolts of magic and strikes with her staff took care of the others.

Once all the wyrms had been slain, she focussed on the man. He was about the same height as she was, perhaps two inches taller, and slender, with a mop of curly dark-auburn hair, sharp cheekbones, and pale green eyes with a faint glint of gold. He was clad in a long coat, so dark brown that it was nearly black, a gold button-up shirt, black trousers, and black shoes.

His lips were pressed tightly together. His striking eyes were narrowed and calculating. He seemed stuck in thought, so Araunya waved a hand in front of his face. He blinked, grabbed her hand, and studied. She did not sense a threat, so she let him examine her hand and wrist. It was as if he was trying to figure out where the bolts of magic had come from.

After a moment, the man let go of her hand and started looking around. He finally registered the wyrm bodies on the ground, the fact that the hand he had just been studying was attached to a woman, and that the woman had a large stick tipped with metal.

He blinked, and opened his mouth to speak, then closed it again. After another moment, he said, "Aidan Jones, Professor at Glamdring Secondary School—most of the time. Private Investigator during summers, and whenever an interesting case comes up."

He stuck out his gloved hand, and Araunya shook it. "Araunya Balaur, full-time Mage, part-time whatever I want to be."

Mr. Jones was not fazed. "You just saved my life. Thank you for that. Would you like to use my shower since you are covered in blood, and join me for a cup of tea? My flatmate won't mind."

It was Araunya's turn to be surprised. "Okay... sure. I don't see any reason why not."

Mr. Jones smiled. "Follow me. My flat's not far."

The black-haired woman did as requested, and thus began their unusual friendship that the two of them shared since that day.

The caramel-skinned woman returned to the present and knocked four times on the door. She heard a muffled crash, as if a stack of papers fell off a desk. Then there was a moment of silence, as if the person was contemplating the mess, then sounds of rushed movement and the rustle of paper. Araunya was patient. Eventually, a voice came from the other side of the door.

"You can come in, if you want. It's not locked."

Why would the door to a principal's office be locked in the first place? She turned the knob and opened the door. Inside, it was not exactly what one would expect of a school administrator, but then the man was not what one would expect for a principal, either.

The office was small, with one window, a desk, a filing cabinet, and a few bookcases—one full of books, the other empty except for a few trinkets. The man was tall and lanky, and his mop of curly hair was mussed from his running his hands through it so many times, an action he was doing at that exact moment. It seemed as though he was looking for something as he bent under the desk.

Araunya's eye caught on a file just to the left of her feet, and she picked it up. "Is this what you're looking for, Principal Jones?"

There was a thump as Aidan smacked the back of his head on the bottom of the desk. "What?"

His eyes came into view. "Araunya?"

"Yes?"

He stood rapidly. "It's nice to see you again. How long has it been...two years or so?"

"About." She held up the file. "Is this what you were looking for?"

His unusual eyes lit up. "Yes! Thank you."

Araunya handed him the file and he set it on a pile of other files on his desk. He arranged the pile just so, then gestured for her to sit down. As she sat, he did too.

"So, what did you come here for?"

"Well...I see you received a promotion. When was that?"

He smiled. "Last year, just before school started."

"Ah."

"But that's not what you are here for, is it, my friend?"

Araunya leaned forwards, her winter-blue eyes twinkling. "I am in need of a flat to rent. Do you know of one?"

Mr. Jones leaned forwards as well, deep in thought. "I don't know, but James might."

Araunya nodded as the two leaned back. She recalled the first time she met James Allen, Aidan's flatmate, and best friend.

It was just after Mr. Jones' offer of tea and the use of his shower to clean off the wyrm blood. They had just reached his flat, and Mr. Jones unlocked the door to find it blocked by a broad-shouldered, short, sandy-haired, older man, his grey sharpshooter's eyes screaming in frustration.

He jabbed his finger in to Mr. Jones' chest with every word. "Where. Have. You. Been? I come home, and find your note stating where you are and when you expect to be home, that was fine. But then you didn't come home on time! I turn on the news and it says there was an attack where you said you would be! You had me worried sick!"

Mr. Jones reacted as if he was used to that behaviour. He pushed past his accuser, bringing Araunya with him and closing the door behind them.

He gestured at Araunya. "James, this is Miss Araunya Balaur. She saved my life a few minutes ago. Miss Balaur, this is my flatmate and best friend, James Allen."

Mr. Allen looked at Araunya and his expression changed completely. "Please, call me James. Thank you for saving this idiot's life. I suppose he hasn't thanked you yet...."

She interrupted him. "Actually, he has."

James smiled. "Well that's good. It appears he does have manners."

Mr. Jones cut in. "If you haven't missed it, James, Miss Balaur is covered in blood and is in need of a shower."

James paused, then hurriedly began speaking again. "Right, sorry, Miss Balaur." He pointed at a short hallway. "The bathroom is that way, second door on the left. Umm... here, I'll get a dressing gown for you to wear, if you would like."

The caramel-skinned woman smiled. "Thank you, and please feel free to call me Araunya."

"No problem, Araunya."

She turned to Mr. Jones. "I will see you in a few minutes, Mr. Jones."

"Aidan, please; Mr. Jones is my brother," he scoffed.

"Very well."

Araunya emerged from the bathroom, clean and wrapped in Aidan's dressing gown, which reached her ankles. They had tea and chatted. Then Aidan starting talking about wyrms.

Araunya brought her mind back to the present and focussed on what Aidan was saying...something about wyrms.

"What? Could you say that again, please?" she said.

He started over. "I heard from one of my contacts in the homeless network that something similar to wyrms was seen in an alley by the north train station."

That was extremely worrying information. Even though she had obviously fought wyrms before, they were supposed to be extinct now. Having them just show up here was very suspicious.

All of a sudden, an alarm she had set in her mind started ringing. She needed to get back to the Lodge. Tara's Journeyman and Ward Head ceremonies would start in an hour and a half. She was required to attend, and to look pretty.

She stood. "I have to go, Aidan. There are two ceremonies I must attend and I have to look prettier than this." She gestured at her black jeans and knee-high boots, long-sleeved red t-shirt, trademark long grey coat, and hair pulled back in a severe bun.

Aidan looked her up and down, then muttered something like, "You always look pretty."

Araunya raised an eyebrow, then discarded the notion as wishful thinking. He saw her as a friend, nothing more. Nothing less.

With a final farewell, the black-haired woman returned to the Lodge to get ready.

An hour later, Araunya's hair was done up in braids, she had applied a little makeup, put on a necklace and earrings to go with her silver-and-garnet ring, and donned a simple blood-red gown with a high neckline and long flowing sleeves, as well as a floor-length, detachable, loose skirt. Underneath the skirt, she wore trousers and a pair of her nicer-looking boots, just in case something bad happened, and because she was not comfortable in hose and heels. Her staff, luckily, was something she was allowed to bring, since she was a high-ranking Mage and the eldest daughter of the eldest grandson of the Chief.

Araunya ran a hand over the long, black, rune-carved wood with a steel tip at one end, and a gem-and-iron-tip on the other. She let her fingers trace the markings she made when she created this beautiful weapon. Every Balaur, at fifteen years of age, made a weapon of their own. She set the stone in her shaft back then. That act preceded choosing—or being given—a surname. Araunya chose to carve her Mage-staff, which is what she held now.

She inspected a slight scuff in the steel tip. She'd had this wood shaft twenty years. She twirled the staff around her body a few times to check the range of movement for her dress. Araunya pondered about turning thirty-seven in two weeks, and the fact that she'd never had a romantic partner. She didn't have the time, but mostly, she hadn't been interested. Yes, she'd had a few crushes, but those were based on fantasies, so they didn't count.

Setting her staff's steel-tipped end on the floor, Araunya conjured up a large full-length mirror and checked her appearance. It would most definitely not do for a person of her rank to go to a function of this manner looking anything less than meticulously arranged and formally dressed, even though she would rather wear full battle dress.

Out the door she went, closing it carefully behind her, and then down the stairs and along the corridors to the courtyard in the centre of the four wings of the Lodge, each of which was its own self-sufficient house. The courtyard was where the formal and official ceremonies of Clan Balaur took place. Unless it was storming, in which case they used the East Wing Ballroom.

She arrived just in time to join the group, just before the ceremony began. Luckily, she did not have any official act or speech to make, though she wouldn't have minded joining the police force once this whole thing was over. Perhaps, she could eventually become Prefect....

Ah. The ceremony was beginning. The winter-eyed woman discreetly made her go to where the rest of the Mages stood. Usually, they preferred to mingle with the rest of the guests, but because this was an *official* function, they were not permitted to do so. Slipping in between two people she had not seen for a very long time, Araunya turned her gaze to the High Chair where her Gorhendad Barsali was sitting. His shoulder-length, white hair was loose, and the braid in his short beard wagged as he spoke to someone just out of sight, though she could see the shape of a Mage-staff.

Then, a fair-skinned, black-haired woman with sky-blue eyes, clad in a purple gown and holding a toddler and a Mage-staff blocked her view. It was Charani Duskflame, named Violet Williams before she wedded Araunya's elder brother Durriken and became a part of Clan Balaur. In her arms was her son, Jardani.

"Araunya! How are you?"

"Well enough." The caramel-skinned woman could barely restrain herself from adding, 'Oh, I found those twins of yours who have been missing for thirteen years—you know, the ones you assumed were dead and spent barely a year searching for...,' but she managed to get out, "And how are you?"

"Good, but tired. Taking care of this one," Charani hefted the three-year-old wrapped around her waist.

Araunya shrugged. "Never had a kid; wouldn't know. However, I can sympathise, I think."

She glanced at the toddler's aura since she could often tell by the nimbus of coloured light how a child would turn out. Huh? *That was interesting,* she thought. "I can tell you one thing, Charani, this boy will be most definitely a handful when he's older, more so than a usual fifteen-year-old boy."

The fair-skinned woman made a hmmm sound.

Suddenly, something popped into Araunya's mind. She needed to look at the auras of the twins to see what they might become when grown, now that the charms and blocks had been removed.

A trumpet sounded, turning everyone's attention to the dais on which the High Chair rested, and to the slightly smaller, beautifully carved chairs where Chief Barsali Oaksword and his wife Dorenia Stareye sat. Above them both, pinned to the wall, was a banner displaying the coat of arms of Clan Balaur: a silver Celtic dragon with blue eyes, displayed on a field of inky-black. And above the banner, sewn in silvery thread, were the words *Pur O Ysbryd, Pure of Spirit,* in flowing script.

Barsali and Dorenia sat regally in their silver-edged black ceremonial Mage robes, embroidered on the breast with the Balaur coat of arms in fine stitching. Araunya's father and grandfather, Kennick Bloodmace and Danior Ironfist, stood next to the Chief's wife, and at their side stood Araunya's brother (Charani's husband), Durriken Stormeye, with his red-wood Mage-staff in his hand and wearing his dark grey formal robe and boots.

Standing in front of them were Khulai and Tara, both in formal robes, ready to participate in the ceremony being held in their honour.

Barsali lifted his staff. "My friends, you are gathered here today to witness two things. One: the raising of this young woman from an apprentice to a journeyman. Two: the bestowing upon her the title and position of the Head of the Intensive Magical Incident Healing Ward, a mantle not held since my eldest son, Camlo Lightfoot, died." Although Barsali was one of the eldest people on the island, his voice and stature had not diminished.

Barsali slammed the end of his grey-wood staff on the stone floor of the courtyard, which caused a loud boom that could have been created only by magic. As the boom's echo subsided, Khulai and Tara bowed to Barsali, Dorenia, Kennick, Danior, and Durriken, before turning to face each other. Khulai raised the ceremonial sword that was used only on special occasions such as this. He spoke, and his powerful baritone voice resonated throughout the courtyard.

"Do you, Tara Nighthand, believe yourself ready for this next step in your life? Are you ready to leave the sheltered extension of childhood apprenticeship and take the last step to full adulthood?"

The brown-eyed young woman nodded. "I do, and I am."

With that, Tara knelt at Khulai's feet. She pulled a braided cord of entwined hair out from her pocket. It was the symbol of their relationship as master and apprentice.

As Araunya watched this happen, she mused on the similarities between this ceremony and the inter-woven cord made from the hair of a couple being wed. Then she cast the thought to the back of her mind. She really was becoming a bit of a meddler.

The winter-eyed woman turned her mind back to the proceedings as Tara stretched the cord in her hands, drawing it taut. Khulai's silver-bladed sword flashed, and the cord separated, sliced cleanly through the centre. Tara let both halves fall to the floor as she bowed her head.

Khulai sheathed the sword and placed his hand on the top of Tara's head. She shivered for just a second, but Araunya saw it.

Khulai and Tara both closed their eyes. Khulai's voice was softer as he said, "Tara Nighthand, I hereby release you from being under my teachings."

There was a flash of magic-light, and Tara stood, somewhat shaky. But it was not over yet. There was still another ceremony to conduct.

Barsali slammed the end of his staff on the ground again and Khulai unbuckled the sword from his belt. He handed it to one of the armourers who had been standing there just for that purpose.

A medical official handed Khulai a medal-like badge. Khulai held it in the air before Tara. "Do you know what this is, Journeyman Tara Nighthand?"

She did not answer, as was customary, and he continued. "This is a Ward Head badge. It once belonged to Camlo Lightfoot and now it belongs to you. Take care of it, and do not lose it, for if you do, it shall be handed to your successor."

With deft and gentle fingers, he pinned the badge to Tara's robe, just above the breast. Stepping back slightly, he held out his hand, and she shook it.

"Welcome, Ward Head Tara Nighthand."

Her grin could have lit a small city with its brightness.

* * *

Aneirin sauntered silently through the alleys and backstreets of the city, which was a great distance from the mountains where he and his twin lived in their mansion. Behind him trailed three or four wyrms. Three or four because one kept running off. But one wyrm more or less was not much of a problem since there were plenty of wyrms in those mountains and they were easy enough to control using power and concentration.

He didn't mind if the stray wyrm killed and ate a few people out late at night. It was hunting time, though he was not intending to kill his prey, not yet anyway. No, he would let the wyrms do it themselves. You see, he and his sister had a certain game they liked to play and they needed more players.

* * *

Aidan Jones lounged in the chair behind his desk in the principal's office. Today was slow. He had already caught up on his paperwork tasks and could not think of anything that required his immediate attention, but he had to stay put in case he was required to mete out discipline to a wayward student.

So, what was a principal with nothing to do, to do? His eyes scanned the bookcases. He could read...but he didn't want to read. He softly sang from a favourite musical, then thought, hey, he could read *Phantom of the Opera* again. But nah, not right now. Ho, hum.

The curly-haired man stood suddenly and performed a slight twirl, shouting, "BORED!" as loud as he could. "BORED, BORED, BORED!"

Having gotten that out of his system, the lanky man sat down on the floor with a thump. Now what? Hummm...hum-de-dum-dum. He flopped backwards and lay stretched out on the floor.

He sat up suddenly. Hey! He had a computer. He could research something! He flopped down again. He didn't know what he wanted to research. His eye was drawn to a book because it didn't look familiar. Hmm.

Aidan rolled on to his stomach, stood up and walked over to the book to get a closer look. Perhaps he had bought it, then placed it on the shelf and forgotten to read it. The book was a greyish-green hardback with the title, *The Silmarillion* by JRR Tolkien, in swirly gold lettering. The image of a sun within a rhombus was also in gold ink. The book looked interesting. He would read it, he decided.

* * *

The ceremonies were over and the party had begun. Araunya did not like parties, so she excused herself as soon as she could. She changed her clothes, put her face and hair back to rights, and headed up to the roof of the West Wing to watch the stars and moon come out. Of course, as soon as she reached the top, she remembered she had to look at the twins' auras, so she climbed back down.

Standing in the room where Cojiñí lay sleeping, the battle-experienced woman closed her eyes and opened her aura-sight, letting the changed vision wash over her and alter her perception. Everyone had some form of aura, and all magicals can sense them and see their colours, but only a few could read them as well as Araunya. She could tell the person's past, and sometimes his or her future. True, auras can be disguised, but it took a Mage of high calibre to have enough power to do so. This exercise was to see if the twins' auras had changed. It would also reveal how powerful the person was who stole them.

Letting out a slow breath, Araunya opened her eyes and stepped back in surprise. Part of the glamour spell, or something, was restricting the twins' magic levels.

Encasing Cojiñí from head to foot was a star's worth of deep, bright, electric-blue light, threaded with a network of eerie emerald-green and shining silver threads. There were also multi-coloured threads of experiences and possible destinies. This girl was most definitely a Mage, perhaps even an Archmage, like Gorhendad Barsali's younger brother who died at the hands of a woman known to the Balaurs by the name of the Wyrm Queen, a woman who had not been seen or heard of since.

Araunya stared a few more moments before leaving the room and hurrying to the next one where Scoruș lay. Her aura-sight was still on.

The boy was surrounded by near-identical nimbus to his sisters', except the blue and green colours were switched, and a few of the experience and destiny threads had a different tone.

The thirty-six year-old-woman stumbled and staggered as she exited the room into the hallway. She was stunned by what she had seen. Those twins were powerful, exceedingly powerful, but they did not know it. They were completely untrained. Which was very dangerous.

Perhaps, yes, that may work, Araunya mused to herself for a moment, then re-entered Cojiñí's room. She opened the glass door and stepped onto the balcony. She closed the door and climbed to the roof. The stars were beautiful that night.

* * *

Tara Nighthand sat on her bed, contemplating her existence. Or something like that. Actually wasn't that deep. She was attempting to decipher her feelings centred in the direction of a certain Master Healer named Khulai Silvertouch. She knew he had gained his surname due to his excellent talent for healing, but some part of her always giggled like a blushing schoolgirl whenever she thought of his name.

Whatever it was that she felt for him was driving her insane. She was confused and didn't know how to decipher her feelings. She respected him, and she was pretty sure nothing could change that. But during the past few years, something else stirred in her mind whenever she thought of her former teacher. It didn't help that he was only five years older than she was, and that he was, indeed, handsome. She had heard other young women talking about him the same way, so she was not alone in that assessment.

She flopped on her bed and stared at the ceiling. She had painted a canopy of branches and leaves on it two weeks ago, but now she imagined a canopy of embroidered cloth, brocade or velvet, in blue or deep purple, for surely his canopy would be his favourite colour. She imagined herself in a snow-white gown, trimmed with pale flowers, and a bouquet of white roses and forget-me-nots. And, for Khulai, a coal-black suit with a rose and forget-me-nots in the buttonhole.

Tara pulled herself out of her musings using a smack to the forehead. Khulai Silvertouch certainly didn't feel the same about her, even though she loved him. Sure, she'd had boyfriends before, and thought she'd loved them, but she had never, ever had wedding-imaginings before. So, that counted for something.

The light-tan-skinned woman snatched the Ward Head badge from her nightstand and turned it over in her hand. The bronze pendant on its short white ribbon glinted dully in the light of her table lamp. It was a strange feeling, having the responsibility and privilege finally given to her after ten years of hard, dedicated after-school apprenticeship work. She was proud in herself for having completed her goal and knew what this position required of her. But there was still that feeling of—what do I do now?

Sighing, just because she felt like it, the brown-eyed woman turned on her room light with a flick of thought and got up to stand before the mirror next to her closet. Her thoughts returned to the man who had presented the badge to her. *Why would he even give a thought to me, aside from the fact that I'm a fellow Ward Head and his former apprentice?* she mused, her eyes raking up and down her reflection.

She was pretty, but plain in her opinion, nothing like Emanaia Greenflower with her hip-length wavy dusk-red locks, dazzling sea-glass eyes, and striking figure. Tara was average height, though a bit taller, with brown hair, brown eyes, and a slightly snubbed nose. She was slim and lithe, but not voluptuous or foxy. Training with Femi Redstave and Ferka Arrowfoot had left her well muscled and swift, however.

Ferka was a difficult taskmaster, and ironically, appeared as if a strong wind would blow him away. His frail appearance assisted him in winning nearly all the races and it was quite fun to watch him run—his pale hair streaming in the breeze and contrasting well with his tan skin. Femi, however, looked just as hard as she was. Broad-shouldered and tall, she was built like a man and she kept her ink-black hair drawn back in a clubbed braid, away from her strong face.

Both of Tara's instructors had keen dark-grey eyes that were always watchful for students' mistakes. But even with their opposing appearances and personalities, they had been wed for nearly seventeen years and loved almost every minute of it.

Tara decided that whomever she ended up marrying, she wanted to have a relationship with her husband like Femi Redstave and Ferka Arrowfoot. She sighed again, then set the badge back on her nightstand and flopped down on her bed once more. Eventually, she fell asleep.

Chapter 8

ROSELLA WOKE SLOWLY, her brain registering the information her senses gave her one-by-one. First, was the sensation of touch. She was lying on her back. She must have been unconscious and arranged this way because she normally slept on her stomach. She was in a bed—soft, yet firm, with silk sheets, and the covers drawn up under her chin. The cover on the duvet was soft, somewhat fuzzy. The pillow was firm, but soft enough to conform to her head and keep it straight—an odd feeling. She felt a faint breeze, so a window somewhere was open.

The next sense was sound. Someone was in the room. Or at least something that was playing a low-toned instrument like a flute. Then smell and taste returned: a faint scent of roses, a foul taste in her mouth. Sight came next.

Her lids stuck together at first, then Rosella's eyes fluttered open. She saw deep-blue cloth, embroidered or printed with a brocade of dark silvery grey. The bed had a canopy with two sets of curtains—one sheer blue, the other the same heavy fabric as the top. Only the sheer curtain was closed so she could see the room beyond the bed.

The walls were pale grey, as was ceiling. The floor was a warm red wood. Off to the right was a sliding glass door leading to a balcony. Double sets of black curtains, sheer and solid, hung open by the door, which was also open. The breeze was coming through the door.

To the left of the bed were dark wood doors; their colour contrasted well with the pale walls. One door had a small frosted-glass window, showing that the room beyond had white walls. Perhaps it was a bathroom. A dressing screen, tall chest of drawers, small vanity, and a fairly large wardrobe were all made of the same wood as the doors and doorframes. To the left was a full bookcase, corner desk with shelves, a rolling chair, and a very comfy-looking, oversized armchair with a pale grey fuzzy blanket that contrasted classily with the black leather.

On a whole, the room was tastefully decorated in black, touches of green and brown, and shades of blue and grey.

Rosella focussed on the armchair again and was surprised to see a familiar black-haired, caramel-skinned woman, playing an elegant, slender, carved wooden recorder. How she had not noticed Miss Balaur before, she had no idea and it made her suspicious. She sat up, slowly, making no noise, and stared at the woman.

Miss Balaur stopped playing and looked at her. "I'm glad to see you're awake, Cojiñí."

Rosella's face scrunched in bafflement. "Cojiñí?"

"Yes, that is your birth name, the one your parents, my brother and his wife, gave you. Your brother's name is Scoruș." She snorted at the look Rosella gave her. "Search your memory, Cojiñí. You know I'm telling the truth."

Rosella cast her thoughts back, and her memory proved just as reliable as it had been before the binders. In her memory was a fuzzy image of a fair-skinned woman and caramel-skinned man, both with black hair and blue eyes, though his were darker and deeper. They were both leaning over her. The woman's mouth formed a word and though slightly distorted, she heard the exact name Miss Balaur had just uttered. She heard, ***'Hello, Cojiñí, my dear little rose.'***

She brought her thoughts back to the present and stared at Araunya. Her aunt smiled and tossed her something. She caught it without looking. It was a small mirror, the reflective side face down.

The raven-haired girl turned the mirror over and almost dropped it in shock. Her face had changed. Her skin was darker, her forehead wider, and her hairline came to a widow's peak. Her eyes were almond-shaped and darker. The colour reminded her of a cloudless sky after dark. Her nose was straight and turned down at the end. Her lips were the same, but her jaw was stronger and a bit more angular. Her chin had a faint cleft and seemed more pointed than before.

Cojiñí let the mirror fall from her hand and stared off into the distance. She refocused her gaze when the woman spoke.

"There is something else you should be aware of, Cojiñí."

"What is that, Aunt Araunya?" the girl asked, trying out the name on her tongue. It was not too bad, though it would take getting used to.

"You may not have noticed, but your magical core was bound until you used magic to break the suppressors. Now it is what it is supposed to be—two or three times more than it had been before the suppressors were put on you."

The surprises would not end! Cojiñí did not react, though she continued to stare at Araunya, who chuckled. Cojiñí came back to herself, most of the way. "How do you know this?"

The winter-eyed woman gave her a knowing smile. "I can see auras, if I let myself. And auras reflect both experiences and possible destinies—and a person's magical core. The former is represented by threads of colour of a certain...texture, and the latter is represented by the size and colour of a person's aura."

She paused, and Cojiñí waited patiently. "Both your and Scoruş' auras are what is known as a star's-worth, one of the largest—and if I'm remembering correctly—contains *the* largest amount of magic. Even the smallest amount more could completely fry the mind and body. That is how my great-grandfather, the Chief of Clan Balaur's younger brother died, saving someone from a magical parasite by drawing the magic of the parasite into himself. He destroyed the parasite, but he destroyed himself when doing so."

She sighed. "He was the first and last Archmage in at least a century, until you and your brother came out of the womb."

Cojiñí's eyes were stuck wide open and her mouth would not be closing anytime soon.

Araunya continued, "The last recorded Archmages before him—I say Archmages because there were four of them—were the highest number of Archmages to appear in one country at one time. You may know one's name through popular legends. Two are less well known, and almost never portrayed with magic, though they are often assigned the morals—or lack thereof—of the other. The fourth rarely appears in the legends, and her morals, too, are often confused. Can you guess who I'm referring to?"

Cojiñí took a wild guess. "Could one of them be Merlin, maybe?"

"Myrddin, yes, you are correct. That is the first. How about one of the others?"

"Umm...Morgana?"

"Morgaine, good, two more. Another appears in the tale of King Arthur's death...."

"Mordred?"

"Correct. The last is Morgause."

Cojiñí frowned. "They were real?"

Araunya nodded. "Yes, they were very real."

The midnight-eyed girl pondered a moment. "When I said Merlin and Morgana, you corrected me on the pronunciation. May I ask why? And when you corrected me on Merlin, it didn't sound very different."

The woman shrugged. "It didn't sound very different because it isn't, not in pronunciation. More in spelling. Merlin is M-E-R-L-I-N, Myrddin is M-Y-R-D-D-I-N. One is English, the other is Welsh. He was Welsh, but he is remembered as English. That is how it is."

She popped a few of her knuckles, and continued. "It is essentially the same with Morgana/Morgaine. One is simply another name for her. According to the Mage-Archmage records, however, her name is entered as Morgaine. That's all."

"Oh. That's a much simpler explanation than I was expecting."

"It is what it is."

"I suppose it is that."

They looked at each other, then burst out laughing. Once their giggles subsided, Araunya stood and tucked her flute-recorder away—in the...air? "Scoruș should be waking soon, if he is not already awake. So, I am off to explain to him as I did to you, and then I have work to do. Please do not leave this room, though you may go onto the balcony. When you get hungry, ring this bell." She set a small silver bell that appeared from nowhere on the desk. "A staff member will bring you food."

With that, she was out the door and Cojiñí thought she heard it the lock turn.

Cojiñí leaned back on the bed and stared up at the canopy. A few moments later, she sat up, tossed the covers aside, slid her legs over the edge of the bed, stood, and walked over to the bookcase. Her first few steps were a bit wobbly because she stood up too fast. She felt dizzy, but it did not take long for her to reach her destination.

She found a familiar title and curled up in the armchair, the throw blanket wrapped around her. She started reading *Frankenstein* by Mary Shelley for the third time.

* * *

Neva Whitefeather, youngest child of Danior Ironfist and Jaelle Fanghand, and sister to Durriken, Araunya, and Khulai, stared at the picture before her. She had been doodling, not really paying attention to what she was drawing. On her paper was a rowan tree and a rose bush entwined, coming from the same root.

She sighed and put down her pen, then ran her hands over her face, unknowingly smearing it with ink and charcoal. The cornflower-blue-eyed woman stood, drawing her soft lime-green dressing gown around her slender form. Everything would be changing now that the twins had returned, or at least Araunya said they had. She had not seen them yet, so she didn't know what to believe, not that Araunya had a habit of lying. Yet Neva could never be sure. This all may be a cruel joke, she thought, though deep in her heart, Neva knew the truth.

The young woman suddenly slammed her hand on the table, nearly knocking over her inkwell. If Araunya planned to reveal the twins now, Neva would put her foot down. Araunya may be the second eldest in the family, but she still listened—sometimes—and Neva would make certain that the older woman listened now.

Revealing the twins would cause disruption. Jardani was only three. He needed time with his parents before his "wayward" elder siblings returned. And perhaps the twins needed more time out in the world before coming back to Ynys Golauglas permanently. Unless they ended up with a mission or adventure.

With a decisive nod, Neva Whitefeather stripped off her dressing gown, revealing brown jeans and a long-sleeved green t-shirt. She headed towards the door. She had a sister to talk with.

* * *

After speaking with Neva, Araunya admitted that the younger woman had a good point. She didn't like the deception. Khulai, standing at her side, agreed. So it was decided. The twins would stay in the Lodge's mostly unused West Wing until Araunya found a flat for her to rent for the three of them.

The twins would still attend the last few weeks of the school year at Rumen Primary, and then continue their education until they graduated into university training at Glamdring Secondary. Araunya selected Glamdring because Principal Aidan Jones was at least tolerant of those with magic, something that could not be said for the principal of Rumen—based on her meeting with him the day before. Principal William Torell had attempted to "discreetly" get one of those magic-suppressors on her. Let's just say that it did not end the best for him. The official story, provided by the secretary—who did not distain magic—was that he went on an extended holiday to America. Which was not too different from what really happened. He *was* in America, just not exactly on holiday, and most likely, he would never be returning. However, Araunya had had nothing to do with the planning or spreading of that tale.

In any case, Rumen Primary had begun searching for a new principal, one who would not be as bad as William Torell.

Araunya knew the twins might not be happy with the delay in meeting their birth parents, but they were capable of being patient. She knew that much about them. She would need to tell them the whole story, and introduce them to Khulai at least. Neva had not seemed enthused about the situation, but perhaps she would show up.

After that, Araunya would talk to James Allen about flats to rent. That would mean finding Aidan Jones' office again since she did not know if he and James were still flatmates, or if they had moved due to Aidan's promotion and larger paycheque.

* * *

Scoruş waited for Araunya to come get him. He was sitting on his bed, leaning his head against the wall near the hole he and Cojiñí discovered and used to communicate when they did not want to speak telepathically through their twin-link. Eventually the winter-eyed woman appeared, and he stood.

"Follow me," said Araunya. "I don't want you to get lost. The West Wing is large and labyrinthine. All of the Wings are."

Scoruş hurried after her. Neither noticed that the door closed itself behind them, and a faint noise, as if some disembodied person were making an 'hmmm' sound as it floated down the corridor.

* * *

The central chamber that joined the four wings of the mansion was held up by four huge pillars, but was open to the weather and sky. A ghostly figure of indeterminate gender and age hovered near the top. It opened Its eyes and smiled. Its children were home, if only for a time. Perhaps It should give each of them a portion of It to carry with them, like an...artificial intelligence...so that they would always have It near them in case they needed It, or It needed them. Yes, It would do that. The question was how. It had done this before, with Its' two other children.

Ah, It had more time—they were not going out to die again. It had been allowed by the White God to seize what was left of them—the elder children who did not go up to Paradise and get tossed into the timestreams. And that was a good thing. They had more to do. And, apparently, the White God agreed. They had more to accomplish in this new time, especially because Morgause and Mordred, who they had fought against, were back as well. In much the same way.

* * *

Araunya led Scoruş to the library by the quickest route not requiring use of secret passages. They did not stop to admire the huge oak double doors, magnificent as they were, but simply opened one and went through. She felt the boy's surprise at the size of the room that contained all the books of the West Wing. The ceiling was at least fifteen metres high, with shelving that lined all the walls. The shelves were full of books and a few artifacts. With pride, Araunya said the West Wing library was the best library in the Lodge. Of course, the other three wings had rooms that held special collections, but Araunya liked the library best. The fact that in the deep centre of the library was a space for high-intensity magic and combat training had nothing to do with that. No, not at all.

In any case, it was truly a massive room. But they were not there to admire the architecture. Araunya's gaze focussed on a small table upon where a bright-shining lamp was set. Sitting at the table were Cojiñí and Khulai sitting in amiable silence.

As she and Scoruş joined them, Araunya asked, "Have you two spoken to each other since I introduced you?"

"Yes," they said at the same time, which made Scoruş smile.

Man and girl looked at each other, and Khulai motioned for Cojiñí to continue.

"Yes, we've talked. Uncle Khulai might teach me how to play the pipe organ."

The tall man spoke. "And I think she may have a fair aptitude for healing."

Araunya nodded. "That's good." She turned to the twins, now seated next to each other. "And if either of you wish to learn how to play the shepherd's flute, I will be glad to teach you once summer comes."

Cojiñí was interested, but Scoruş said, "I've always wanted to play the violin...."

The winter-eyed woman and gunmetal-blue-eyed man looked at each other. "I think Neva can play violin...." Khulai said.

Araunya shrugged, then composed her face into a stern expression. "Either way, we are getting off track."

"We weren't on track to begin with, sister-mine."

She glared at Khulai and continued, directing her words at the twins. "As much as I would rather otherwise, unfortunately you cannot 're-meet' your parents for a while."

The twins frowned and nodded, clearly disappointed, but resigned to the decision.

"The plan I've made is that we—meaning you two and I—will stay here until I rent a flat, at which point we will move there. You will finish out this year at Rumen, which should not be as bad as it was because the school is looking for a new principal. During breaks and the summer, Khulai and I will teach you magic, combat, healing, and whatever else is needed. Scoruş, I may be able to convince Neva to teach you violin. If not...well, we can always hire someone."

The twins nodded in understanding.

"Any questions, comments, concerns?"

"Not that we can think of."

"That's good."

That settled, they all returned to where they had all been before meeting in the library. Well, not really. Khulai returned to his hospital. Cojiñí and Scoruş returned to their rooms, but then decided to explore the West Wing, which they had permission to do as long as they did not go through the white double doors on each floor. Araunya left to speak with Aidan Jones about James' help with finding a flat.

* * *

The entity in the chamber at the top of the pillars in the centre of the courtyard watched as Its' reborn children explored Its West Wing, poking in the cracks and crevices with the curiosity that children—and a few adults—displayed. The children were awed by the size of Its library, and intrigued by the labyrinth of secret passages twisting through Its West Wing walls, joining many of the rooms together. It tightly locked the doors leading to the outside. Even though It wanted Its children to explore the rest of It, It understood the need for caution.

It was amused at the twins' antics using props in the theatre-cinema room, and smiled at their amazement of the West Wing's pool room and the various types of pools contained there. It watched contentedly as the twins roamed during the small timeframe they had for exploration.

Eventually, however, they had to go to sleep and It subsided into a watchful rest. It had slept long enough. Now that Its children were back, It did not need to sleep anymore.

* * *

Araunya arrived at Aidan's office by way of teleportation, now that she knew where it was located, and startled him so much that he dropped the book he had been reading.

"Hello, Aidan."

"Hi."

"How are you doing this fine day?"

"Perfectly fine until you surprised me like that."

Araunya chuckled, Aidan chuckled, and soon they were full-out laughing. Once they caught their breaths, the curly-haired man asked, "So, what did you come all the way out here for, my friend?"

Araunya sat on the edge of his desk, deliberately sitting on a stack of papers. "My purpose is to discover first where James lives, and to ask him about flats for rent."

Aidan looked quizzical. "We live in the exact same place as before, Araunya, except I pay all the rent and James bakes for me every once and a while."

She spread her hands in a gesture of helplessness. "Well I didn't know if you had moved because of your promotion or something."

He shrugged. "Fair enough."

"Anyhow...."

"Yes, go." The green-gold-eyed man made a shooing motion with both hands, and the caramel-skinned woman disappeared.

Araunya reappeared in the living area of James and Aidan's flat. It hadn't changed since she had been there the last time—before Aidan's promotion—which said much, and nothing, about the two men who lived there.

James was lying on the sofa, watching a swords-and-sorcery show on the telly in which a young man who was supposed to be a young Myrddin was talking to a large golden-toned dragon.

"Greetings, James Allen."

James jumped slightly, sat up, paused the show, and turned to face the woman. "Oh. Hello, Araunya. How are you doing?"

"I am well. I am in search of a flat to rent. Aidan said you knew of a place?"

He nodded. "Yes, I do. Actually, it's in this building."

"Oh? Which one?"

"Number 332C."

"The one across the hallway from you and Aidan? Does it have room for me and two teenagers of different genders?"

He thought for a moment. "I don't know. You'll have to look at it to find out."

"Who do I contact, and when would be the best time to do so?"

James stood and stretched, then shook out his arms and legs. When he had returned to a normal stance, he replied, "You can talk to Ms. Holden in 332A. She's the landlady, and you might be able to talk to her right now. Come on, I'll introduce you."

He led Araunya out the door and down the stairs to flat 332A.

Ms. Holden turned out to be a friendly, motherly, older woman with short, dark-brown hair and merry—yet strangely piercing—light-brown eyes. She was perfectly happy to show Araunya flat number 332C.

She smiled like a beacon when the younger woman decided the flat would work for her. Not for the income, she explained, because she was not short on money, but for the extra company—another woman to talk to. The brown-eyed woman was also eager to meet the twins. She said she had thought about having kids once, but then her husband did.... Araunya missed the last part of the sentence, but she did not pry, as it was not her business.

And so Araunya received the paperwork and filled it out on the spot even though Ms. Holden said she could return it the next day. Araunya was given the key, and permission to make as many copies of the key as needed. James said the older woman had given him the same permission, though she hadn't extended that permission to Aidan. Then he asked if he could give a copy of the 332B key to Araunya and the twins. That permission was granted, though Ms. Holden's eyes did an odd twinkle at that exchange. James looked straight at her and Ms. Holden deflated. But then he nodded once, and the older woman smiled.

As they walked back to flat number 332B, Araunya asked, "What was that about?"

The sandy-haired man shrugged. "Just something I picked up a while ago. That's all."

"You didn't answer my question, James."

"I don't intend to, Araunya. Not yet, anyway."

"May I ask why?"

"You'll learn soon enough, without me telling you. Well, I think it may be time to say goodbye. See you later, Araunya." With that, he entered the flat he and Aidan shared and shut the door, giving her a last smile and wave.

Araunya frowned. That was more cryptic than she expected from James. Those were perfectly normal speech patterns for Aidan, but coming from James, they were...unexpected. Well, each person has many facets, and she didn't know much about James' history. Even Aidan didn't know much about James' history. He learned a few facts about him the day they met by deducing his life based on a few glances, but that is not the same as knowing his history. Not at all.

Shaking off the thought, Araunya teleported back to the Lodge to inform the twins they had a flat. However, she decided to keep the information to herself for one more day, since the flat needed furnishings—something not too difficult to take care of.

* * *

Two days later, the twins met Araunya in the library once more. This time, they each had a small messenger bag that had been left at the foot of their beds.

"Ready?"

They nodded.

"Good. Grab hold of my arms, and whatever you do, don't let go of me or your bags."

They did as requested. All of a sudden, they were somewhere else.

It was somehow dark, and yet at the same time bright as day. Everywhere they could look was crisscrossed with faintly glowing purple threads leading in different directions. A glance in front of them made it clear that they were travelling along one of those threads by way of a tendril of red-coloured magic coming from Araunya's chest, pulling them along.

The tendril moved, and though there was no sensation of changing direction, they could tell they were travelling a different way. After an indeterminable amount of time, the tendril disappeared and a short corridor materialised around them.

Directly in front was a small window. Behind them was a narrow staircase. To their right and their left were identical doors with brass numbers just above the knocker. One read 332B. The plate below the knocker indicated it was the flat of *A. E. Jones and J. E. Allen*. The other door indicated it was flat number 332C, rented to *A. R. Balaur, C. Balaur, and S. Balaur.*

Araunya took out a key ring and unlocked to door to flat 332C. "Welcome to our new home for the next four years, kids." She pushed open the door.

They entered a short hallway with walls painted a pleasant pale blue and patterned with a white brocade design. The wood floor was a rich red colour, and the ceiling was white. On one wall was a wooden coat and hat rack on which Araunya hung her long grey jacket. A few metres further, facing right, was a large living area with a telly, sofa, and two armchairs, two bookcases, and two window seats. To the left was a door, presumably leading to the bathroom, and directly ahead was a kitchen-dining area, fully equipped with all the kitchen necessities and a table that sat five.

To one side of the kitchen was a recessed staircase with a single landing that led up to a second level with the same square footage as the first. Behind and under the staircase was a storage space. As soon as the twins saw it, they transformed it in their minds as a perfect study/reading/writing room. It even had a power outlet into which a power strip could be plugged, which meant they would have access to at least a floor lamp and two computers. There was just enough room in the storage space to stand upright, and just enough floor space to fit the lamp, a small bookcase, and a pair of beanbag chairs, which left barely enough room to step around the objects. Right now, the room could be locked only from the outside, but that was easy enough to change, especially with magic.

On the second level were three small bedrooms, another bathroom, and an office for Araunya. All the bedrooms were simple and identical, leaving plenty of room for personalization. They each had a twin bed, wardrobe, chest of drawers, nightstand, and a small window with a curtain rod. The flat was decidedly different from the house they had just left, but it was better than the twins' basement or attic rooms of the Tigers' house.

The twins claimed the adjoining bedrooms, leaving Araunya the third. As soon as they set their bags on their beds, however, they approached the woman, curiosity shining in their eyes and a question on their lips.

"What was that thing you took us through to get from there to here?"

Araunya's first instinct was to reply with something snarky, such as "the door," but she knew that would not help and probably make them glare at her.

"This may not be a long explanation, and yet it may. Shall we sit?"

The twins curled up on the sofa like large, attentive cats, and Araunya floated one of the armchairs so that it faced them.

"We teleported."

They opened their mouths, but Araunya held up a hand to stay their questions and comments. "This is done by travelling through the mid-space, the Void. It is similar to a half-way parallel dimension that overlays every universe, like uncountable layers of tightly woven, sheer blankets. Each thread leads to a different place. Each place has its own...signature...for a lack of a better word. Once I teach to you how to teleport, you will be able to 'save' or 'bookmark' the signatures of important places, such as this flat and the Lodge. And your secondary school, whatever that school may be. I'm hoping that school will at least be tolerant of you using your magic on the premises."

The winter-eyed woman took a breath, let it out, then continued. "Teleportation works by attaching a tendril of magic to a thread and sending it to find a certain signature."

She held up her hand again seeing that the twins were about to interrupt. "You are aware of things that are bigger on the inside, and rooms that are entered through doors in walls that lead nowhere, yes?"

At their nods, she elaborated. "Those work by creating a pocket in the mid-space and forming the room within that pocket. Items can be stored in the mid-space as well, but only if you can identify them. Otherwise, they will be lost there, as vanished things are. Never, ever, ever detach yourself from a thread while in the mid-space. Those who have done so have never been seen or heard from again and we can only assume they have perished. Do you understand this?"

"Yes, we understand, Aunt Araunya."

"Good. It is possible to have a chamber in a mid-space pocket and enter using something as small as the tip of your smallest finger. That does not matter, for you can use the threads to travel to it, and you will remain unreachable—as well as anyone you bring with you. The space will be a fortified hideout or lair. You two have enough power that you might even be able to make a small pocket dimension all by itself, with more than just a room contained within the mid-space pocket."

The twins looked a bit lost, but soon their faces caught up with their brains, and their confusion melted into understanding.

"Did I give you too much information?"

They shook their heads. "We understand, and no, that was all very interesting, and just enough information."

She nodded once, smiling. "That's good."

They stood, and Araunya put her chair back in its place. "I saw you both paying special attention to the closet under the stairs. Do you have anything in particular in mind for it?"

"Yes we do." And they explained what they had been planning since the moment they saw the room.

The next day, Araunya drove the twins to school, using the car she had rented the day before. She was planning to buy one, because four years was an unreasonably long time to rent just about anything other than a flat, a house, or an office.

The day went well for the raven-haired duo, at least after the impromptu interrogation from the school nurse when they delivered the medical report that Khulai had made up to explain the reason for their sudden absence.

The first class was science, followed by history and math. Those teachers, Mr. Bond, Mrs. Barnett, and Mr. Ingram, treated the twins the same as they always had, though perhaps they were a bit more polite than when William Torell was principal. On the whole, however, the teachers were just as indifferent to the twins as they were to the rest of the class.

English class, however, went a bit differently. Halfway through, the teacher, Mrs. Alexander, was called out into the hall and the person that sat behind Cojiñí tapped her on the shoulder.

"Hey."

She turned around. "Hi."

It was a boy from a sports team. His green eyes were bright and keen, and his floppy dark blond hair had a stripe of bright purple in the bangs that kept falling over his eyes. He was tan, and the hand she shook politely was strong and warm with life.

"My name is Gareth Archer," he said in response to her calculating glance. "I always sit behind Rosella Tiger during English and History. Do you know what happened to her?" Gareth then shook his head. "Sorry, you just got here, you wouldn't know...."

She interrupted him, a slight smirk on her lips. "Actually, Mr. Archer, I do know what happened to Rosella Tiger because I entered this school under that name when I arrived here with my brother, then known as Rowan, a few years ago."

"Call me Gareth, please," he said automatically, then his mind caught up with what she said. "Wait, you're Rosella Tiger? But you look nothing like her, except that your hair is exactly the same as hers...." He trailed off, realising that he was rambling, and blushed.

"Something was fixed while I was away, and that is all I will say." She chuckled at her rhyme. "For now."

Gareth accepted that. "I didn't have the nerve to talk to you before, but would you perhaps be interested in being friends?"

"On one condition. Do you like sci-fi, fantasy, classic gothic lit, and Shakespeare?"

"I like sci-fi and some fantasy, and I might be able to like the others."

"Then sure."

* * *

That evening, after Araunya drove the twins home in her new car, she imparted a tidbit of information—they would be having tea with their neighbours, the residents of flat number 332B, in half an hour. The landlady, who lived in 332A, would be there, too.

They accepted the information with grace, and seemed eager to meet new people. Although they had been burned by life—and most of the people around them—they were still extroverts at heart.

Half an hour passed and they crossed the hall. The door was answered by a sandy-haired man with grey, sharpshooter eyes, who was a bit shorter than Araunya. He smiled brightly at the sight of the twins.

"Hello. I'm James Allen, but please, call me James. I'm a friend of your aunt's. What are your names? Araunya hasn't told me yet."

They were glad of the opportunity to creep someone out.

"Cojiñí...."

"...and Scoruș...."

"...Balaur." They finished together, and James smiled wider.

"I like you two already, and I think my flatmate will as well." He paused briefly. "If he stares at you at first, don't be bothered. It's what he does to try and figure people out. It actually works fairly well, if I may say so as someone who had been a subject of his...gaze."

They nodded, and promised to not be offended.

The man led them into the kitchen/dining area. The layout of flat

332B was similar to the layout of number 332C, though, of course, the furniture was different. The dining table here sat seven.

James' flatmate was a tall man with a mop of curly, dark-auburn hair, cutting-sharp cheekbones, and strange piercing green-gold eyes. His name was Aidan Jones.

"Call me Aidan. Mr. Jones is my brother."

The landlady, Ms. Holden, was a grandmotherly woman with short, dark hair and cheerful, keen brown eyes. She was very glad to have them in her building, she said, because it would be nice to hear young feet walking around, and young voices ringing through the halls. They did not have the heart to tell her that they were not the type, at least now, to make their voices ring.

* * *

During the following weeks, the twins and their neighbours became friends, and the tea dates became a regular thing. For some reason, Ms. Holden kept looking at Aidan and Araunya strangely, but the twins mostly ignored it until they saw the glances the two gave each other when the other person wasn't looking. And when they thought no one else was looking.

The twins brought up the subject to James, who merely made a shushing motion and asked them to keep it to themselves. It became a game then, to see how long it would take the two—whose first names started with the letter 'A' to acknowledge the looks they were giving each other.

And then, a week after that, something somewhat interesting happened.

Chapter 9

AT THE TEA-DATE THAT AFTERNOON, for which James had asked them to arrive fifteen minutes early, the twins discovered that the grey-eyed man had made a big pumpkin pie loaded with whipped cream and drizzled with caramel sauce instead of the usual scones or biscuits. When asked the reason, the sandy-haired man shrugged and smiled.

"I thought it would be an interesting experiment. I haven't made pie in a while."

They accepted that explanation. Then he put party hats on them, which confused them. He winked, and directed them to hide behind the furniture. He turned off the lights and hid behind the sofa near the light switch. The twins began to understand.

When Aidan walked into the flat, James jumped from his hiding spot, flipped on the lights, and the twins joined him shouting, "HAPPY BIRTHDAY, AIDAN!"

Aidan blinked in surprise, thoroughly startled and a bit stupefied, then he smiled the biggest grin the twins had ever seen. He embraced James, though they quickly broke away from each other. James spun the taller man around and put a cloth over his eyes.

After spinning the sea-eyed man in a circle a few times, James pinched Aidan's nose so he couldn't smell the pie, and led him into the kitchen and sat him down. James jerked his head at the twins indicating they should get the pie and place it on the table. Which they did. At that point, James removed his fingers from Aidan's nose and the cloth from his eyes.

Aidan's eyes widened at the sight of the decadent caramel-and-whipped-cream-covered dessert.

"How did you know?"

The older man shrugged. "I asked Hadrian."

James then went to the kitchen to fetch plates and forks.

Aidan seemed to deflate. "Oh. Okay." Then he shook his head and the grin was back.

Scoruș asked, "Who is Hadrian?"

"My meddling older brother. You wouldn't like him at all. He has a low tolerance of magic, no matter if the wielder is Christian or not. Actually, he's not Christian himself. I've tried to convince him to come to church with me, but he always refuses."

"Ah."

James returned with plates and utensils, and the mood instantly brightened again. The pie was absolutely delicious, and everyone had two pieces.

After eating, they went to the living room and the topic of school came up.

"I'm planning to send the representative in two days," said Aidan. The four others looked at him. "I think I have someone picked out to send, but I'm not completely sure since there are a few who would be good." He paused. "Could you help me choose?"

"Of course." Araunya was the one who spoke, and Aidan glanced at her.

"Thank you, Araunya."

She shrugged one shoulder. "Aidan, we've known each other long enough that you can call me Ara."

He smiled. "In that case, you have my permission to call me Ed." His smile widened at her confusion.

"Ed?"

"My middle name is Edgar, and aside from 'Dan,' which I don't think suites me, the only name I could think of was Ed."

"Edgar..." Cojiñí said, hesitantly, "after Edgar Allen Poe?"

He nodded. "Yes, actually."

The twins smiled. He had gained another good mark in their book.

"Time to pick out a representative," the dark-auburn-haired man said. He fetched his briefcase from where he had set it by the door and pulled out five files. He spread them out on the coffee table.

James was surprised to see that one of the files had his name on it. Actually, more than surprised, because he had started teaching at Glamdring only the year before.

He read the names on the other files: Ms. Abigail Bishop, Aidan's replacement as the Literature and Linguistics professor, a post that had been expanded to two—English & Literature, and Linguistics. Linguistics was now an elective. The remaining files were labelled: M. César Bertrand, the French and Art professor; Mr. Albert Lee, the German professor; and Ms. Alice Cole, the secretary. The final file was for him, Mr. James Allen, the History Professor.

After an hour of debate, it was decided that Ms. Cole would be sent, as she did not have anything to teach, and it would be easy enough for Aidan to handle any paperwork that day, since there wasn't overly much, and anyways, it wasn't as if he had an awful lot to do.

Two days later, just after the twins and Gareth finished eating lunch, they were approached by a woman in a dark grey pantsuit. Her curly, light-auburn hair was pulled back in a severe bun. On the pocket of her blazer was a coat of arms showing a silver diagonal sword surrounded by four white, four-pointed stars. It was the coat of arms of Glamdring Secondary School, a school that most of the students were hoping to be selected to attend.

The woman's sharp brown eyes rapidly surveyed the crowd of students before they landed on the black-haired, caramel-skinned twins she was to pay special attention to, and their companion, a blond boy with a purple stripe in his floppy bangs. She recognised the boy from a file Principal Jones had given to her.

She walked through the throng to where the three special students were—all the way in the back corner, away from everyone else. On her way there, she gave a cordial nod to the representative from Galben, another secondary school—less prestigious than Glamdring.

"Hello. I am Ms. Cole, secretary of Glamdring Secondary School.

You are...?"

Alice was glad to see the happy look in the twins' eyes, especially with what her friend Jenny said about their home life before Jenny's second cousin found them.

The girl spoke first, her midnight-sky eyes shining with intelligence. "Cojiñí Balaur."

The black-haired boy whose eyes shone with the same spark as the girl said, "Scoruş Balaur, Cojiñí's twin brother."

Last, the green-eyed blond boy with the purple stripe said, "Gareth Archer, no relation to these two." His voice had a tone of friendly ribbing.

Alice nodded, then handed a packet of papers to each "You have been selected to attend Glamdring Secondary School. Should you accept, all you have to do is take this packet and turn it in to Glamdring's office no later than two weeks before term starts."

Alice smiled at them, put a check by their names on her list, and then left to find the rest of the students she needed to contact. She paused a moment. It appeared that the youngest Carson of this generation would not be joining the student body of Glamdring. Just like his brother, who also had not been extended an invitation.

There weren't many students on her list from Rumen this year. Most of the invitations were for students attending the primary school on the other side of the city—Temple Primary.

* * *

Scoruş looked through the folder that Ms. Cole had handed him. His sister and Gareth did the same. The folder's cover was same charcoal grey that her suit had been, and the sword and stars that decorated her pocket graced the front of the folder and the upper right corner of all of the papers within.

The first page merely had the words *Glamdring Secondary School* in calligraphy above the coat of arms. The second page listed the current staff and professors. The staff was: Aidan Jones—Principal, Alice Cole—Secretary, Rupert Natser—Librarian, and Jaina Bayley—Nurse.

The list of professors read: English and Literature—Abigail Bishop; Physical Education—Aaron Abbot; Science—Adriana Baldwin; Math—Gregory Walters; History—James Allen; French—César Bertrand; German—Albert Lee; Art—César Bertrand; Music, Dance, and Drama—Erik Chaput and Cathrine Baudin; Linguistics—Abigail Bishop.

The blue-eyed boy smiled at the two familiar names, and turned the page. This page indicated which courses were mandatory, and which were electives. Two years of either French or German was mandatory, as was one year of Phys-Ed. Three years were mandatory for Math. Everything else except Linguistics and Art was mandatory for all four years.

A glance at Cojiñí told him they were thinking the exact same thing, and from out of their pockets, they each produced a small ink pen. Araunya had given the pens to them the day before, though she had not said why. They were pretty sure now that it was so they could fill out the form in the folder indicating their choice of electives and foreign language.

Gareth looked at his new friends as if he saw something odd in their behaviour, but shrugged it off. They did seem to be a bit spontaneous at times. The green-eyed boy looked at his own folder, thumbing through it a few times before setting it aside to study in-depth later. That's when he would decide the electives he would take. He could not make up his mind as quickly as the twins did.

The blond young man took his lunch tray and set it on top of the used trays, returned to the table, and settled back in his chair. He tried to not focus on how Cojiñí's hair caught the light just so. But he failed, although not miserably. Luckily, she did not notice he had been staring at her hair and therefore felt not awkwardness.

A few minutes later, the twins left to take care of their trays, and Gareth had the opportunity to redirect his focus elsewhere, which he did. He focussed his attention on a very interesting loose piece of floor tile.

* * *

Later that day, when the twins arrived back at their flat, they went to the study to read. After the twins headed up the stairs, Araunya snuck over to number 332B where James was making tea. After a short whispered conversation, she returned to 332C. She felt like taking a shower before their daily, neighbourly tea-dates.

After her shower, the winter-blue-eyed woman put on her favourite red shirt and well-worn blue jeans. Leaving her hair down—which she usually never did, and not bothering to put on shoes, she padded across the hall to talk to James again and to ask if he needed help.

As it turned out, he did not, so she crossed the hall once again to check on the twins. They were still reading and Araunya chanced a peek at their books—Scoruş was reading *Les Misérables* by Victor Hugo, and Cojiñí had Bram Stoker's *Dracula*. Both were curled up in their window seats with a plush throw blanket wrapped around them.

After a few moments, Araunya spoke up.

"It's time to go over."

They looked up, marked their places, and set down their books. They tossed aside their blankets and walked over to her. They stepped out the door as the clock struck 3:45.

* * *

All the lights were out when Cojiñí, Scoruş, and Araunya entered flat number 332B, and the caramel-skinned young woman had a sneaking suspicion that James and Aidan were hiding behind the furniture. Why? The reason was completely unknown. Her brother probably didn't know either.

The door closed behind them and suddenly the lights went on. James and Aidan were not hiding behind furniture, but they were blocking the view to the kitchen and dining room. Cojiñí peered at them. What on earth was going on?

Then they stepped aside, revealing a cake, frosted in dark grey, the Glamdring Secondary School coat of arms on the top.

Cojiñí opened her mouth, and then closed it with a snap. Right. Of course. They had been accepted to Glamdring, and they accepted the school's offer. So, James made a cake. A very large cake. Cojiñí hoped it was either a red velvet or dark chocolate cake, and most definitely NOT lemon, strawberry, or anything with coconut.

The cake was chocolate, and very delicious—as was everything James baked. It was also very rich. Each of them had a large piece, but half the cake still remained. Aidan divided it and the twins and Araunya took some back to their flat.

Later that night, Cojiñí lay in bed, watching the moonlight make patterns on the ceiling through the lacy curtains she had hung a few days before. Eventually she fell asleep, and dreamed.

She saw a man who looked an awful lot like Scoruş, but older, with a neatly trimmed beard. His hair was loose except for a braid behind his ears that kept it away from his face. She saw herself, but she was older as well. Her hair was wavy. They both wore medieval/Renaissance clothes: she was clad in a flowing blue split-skirted gown, and he in a forest-green knee-length tunic. Both of their ensembles had wing sleeves and high collars. Beneath her split skirt and his tunic, they both wore black trousers and tall, laced boots.

Hanging from the wide belts at their waists were bastard swords, silver-hilted and sheathed in black leather worked in Celtic designs by their own hands. In their hands were tall, smooth, pale-wood staffs carved with runes on both ends. On the end directed at the darkening sky was set a dangerously glinting stone of midnight blue shot through with an eerie green and silver. On the end resting on the ground, at least an inch was encased in silvery steel.

They stood on a ridge, an army at their backs, and at their side stood another man, fair of face, tall and broad-chested, with shoulder-length golden-red locks, a well-trimmed beard, and eyes the same clear, warm blue as the sunny midsummer sky. Upon that golden head rested a golden crown, and from his maille-clad shoulders streamed a cape the same colour of fresh blood, emblazoned with a rampant golden dragon. King Arthur Pendragon.

Cojiñí started nearly awakening when she realized the implications. If this man was King Arthur, then who were she and Scoruş? Myrddin, or Merlin, and...Morgaine, or Morgana. She always had a feeling the popular legends were wrong....

Her dream-sight flew up away from the three figures on the ridge, and over the field they were looking out upon. Down in the valley was another army, led by another group of three: two men and a woman.

The wing sleeves and split skirt over trousers and boots was where the similarity between the woman's and Cojiñí's clothes ended. Where Cojiñí's gown was modest and blue, the dress this woman wore was wine-burgundy and low-collared. The woman could not have been more different than how Cojiñí appeared in this dream. Pale-gold hair cascading down her shoulders and her ocean-shaded eyes gleaming, this woman had a figure to seduce, and the attitude that she knew it and used it as a weapon.

The man to her right side could only be her brother. Tall, broad-shouldered, impossibly handsome, with the same hair and eyes, there was no mistaking it. The laces on his deep-gold tunic hung open, exposing a good four inches of well-toned, tanned chest, and his hand rested almost lazily on the hilt of the elaborately decorated sword strapped to his hips.

The man to the left of the wine-clad woman was handsome as well, but darker. His pitch-black hair fell in ringlets to his shoulders, mingling with the sable cape flowing from his dark armour, and his grey eyes shone as they caught the light of the noonday sun.

Cojiñí floundered on who these were, then her mind provided the identities as if she had always known. Morgause, her younger brother Mordred, and Cenric, the Black King, sometimes called the Black Knight.

All of a sudden, Cojiñí felt herself being pulled away. What was that annoying beeping noise? It was getting louder...and she awoke.

Cojiñí sat up in bed slowly. That was a strange dream. She rolled out of bed and shivered as her feet hit the bare floor harder than she had intended. She really needed to get a carpet, she mused as she dressed for the day.

* * *

At breakfast, Cojiñí thought about the dream and was silent until Araunya asked, "Co', what's wrong?"

The midnight-eyed girl looked up. "Nothing, just thinking about a very strange dream I had last night."

Scoruş met her eyes. "You had it too?"

"Yeah."

Araunya's eyes narrowed at the implications. Shared dreaming was not a common occurrence, and usually signified something very important.

"Tell me this dream," she commanded the twins.

They seemed to understand the gravity of the situation by the tone of her voice, though they did not know the meaning of shared dreams. They recounted the dream to her, and her eyes glazed in confusion and worry. She had no idea whatsoever what these dreams could mean.

The dream remained on Cojiñí's mind, and undoubtedly Scoruş' and Araunya's as well, on their way to school. Her mind was so preoccupied by trying to puzzle it out, that on the way to her locker she quite literally ran in to Gareth, knocking them both over.

"Are you okay?" She asked as they picked themselves up off the floor. "Sorry, I wasn't paying attention."

"I'm fine." The green-eyed young man said, though he seemed distracted by something behind her head.

Cojiñí turned to look, but there was nothing there, and when she turned back around, he was focussed on searching for something in his locker. She frowned, then shrugged and began to do the same.

* * *

In the mansion on in the mountains, Anwyn watched a pair of captives fight with fists and daggers, one tall and brown-haired, the other stocky and redheaded. It was a brutal fight, for both men knew that to win was to live, and perhaps be set free. Eventually, the brown-haired man came out the victor, dispatching his taller opponent with a quick stab of his long dagger to the gut.

Anwyn clapped politely, and the man looked up. He was handsome, through the sweat-sheen and blood. With a flick of her hand, she summoned servants to take the man away and clean him up. Now to find someone else for him to fight. Eh, she could do that later. Or delegate it to Aneirin to do.

Right now, she needed to continue looking for the Arthur and the Cenric. The Arthur so she could kill him when he wasn't being guarded by Myrddin and Morgaine, and the Cenric, just because. So they would have an ally if Morgaine and Myrddin found Arthur before she did, and so she could have him back. Perhaps this time they could sire an heir to the title of Black Knight—one that could actually be born.

Absently, the golden-haired young woman thought back to how she learned she and her brother were Morgause and Mordred.

They were about ten years old when their parents died in a fire. They were taken in by their great aunt, an old hag-woman their parents had not liked. She was the one who had found the great reserves of magic unlocked by the rage they felt at the death of their parents.

She taught them and trained them in the old ways, the ways she had learned, and one day, she saw in her scrying stone a mark on their auras that signified something old, something odd. She investigated the mark, and on their sixteenth birthday, she told them their heritage. She also told them that there would be a pair of magicals, twins most likely, as Myrddin and Morgaine had been and as they were, that they should destroy—lest they be destroyed themselves.

The next day, the old woman had brought in a young woman and a young man, scantily clad, and by way of these people, taught the two magicals how to seduce and use their beauty as a weapon. These same people were the golden-haired twins' first kill. The old woman was their seventh, and though she could have easily stopped them, she let it happen, as she had foreseen. It was that day, their seventeenth birthday, that they truly became in heart, Morgause and Mordred.

They were just turning twenty now, and though three years seemed like a short time, it was long enough for them to get into their niche and build a mansion in the mountains, fully equipped with servants to wait on them. Last year, they began their sport of capturing strong, handsome young men and women and forcing them to fight to the death. The men and women did not fight against each other—women fought against women; men fought against men. Whichever two came up victorious at the end of the week were the ones that stayed alive, to satisfy the hungers of the gold-haired twins. Usually Anwyn's men didn't mind, but Aneirin preferred his to have a bit of fight still in them. He liked to break them.

Then, after a week, when the new victors emerged from the tournaments, the victors of the previous week were slain, and thrown to the twins' favourite wyrms as a treat. At the moment, it appeared as if this tall, brown-haired man would be this week's victor for Anwyn. She smirked.

Now, to the scrying bowl. Cenric and Arthur must be found.

Chapter 10

GARETH ARCHER LAY ON HIS BED IN HIS ROOM in the house his father owned, staring at the ceiling. A knock sounded on his bedroom door and he replied without looking.

"Yes, Ashton?"

His cousin, who was staying with him for a few days, poked his head into the room, ruddy-gold hair glinting slightly in the sunlight streaming through the open window. His sky-blue eyes were slightly worried.

"Are you all right, Gareth?"

The green-eyed fourteen-year-old sat up and beckoned the few-weeks-younger boy into the room, and closed the door behind him.

Ashton sat cross-legged on the bed next to him.

"I've been selected for Glamdring Secondary, and I accepted."

"So did I!"

Gareth turned to Ashton. "Really?"

"Yep. Me and four to seven others, I don't really know who all."

"Huh. Only about five from Rumen, counting me, accepted."

Ashton frowned. "That's interesting. I wonder why...."

"Because most of us this year are not up to standard for Glamdring."

"Oh."

"Yeah."

"Well, what's the problem?"

Gareth lowered his head, his purple-streaked bangs falling in his face. "I don't really know."

Ashton put an arm around his cousin, and uncharacteristically,

Gareth leaned into the embrace rather than shrugging it off. The sky-blue-eyed boy frowned. Something really was wrong. The problem was—attempting to fix it would be difficult if neither of them knew what the problem was. Perhaps....

"Hey Gareth, do you want to play chess until we can figure this out?"

The slightly older boy looked up. "Sure."

"Your set or mine?"

"Don't care."

"Yours then, as it is closer." He slid off the bed and walked to Gareth's bookcase. From between two science fiction books—ones with knights in space with laser swords and clone armies—he pulled a wooden chess set. It was very nice, if Ashton said so himself. He had given it to Gareth for his eleventh birthday. Just because.

Setting it on the floor, Ashton looked up at the green-eyed boy who slid off the bed. In response to the gold-haired boy's unspoken query, Gareth answered, "Black this time."

Ashton set out the pieces in their proper order, and slid the board a bit closer to his cousin. "White moves first...there." He played his first piece, and the game began.

A few hours later, Gareth was smiling and happy again, at least until Ashton won.

"You do that almost every time!" He complained vehemently.

Ashton shrugged. "Not my fault you're not as good a strategist as me."

"Fair point. But still!"

* * *

The next day was graduation and Gareth tugged slightly on the tight collar of the shirt his father made him wear. He would much rather be wearing his jeans and a nice t-shirt instead of this tight-collared polo shirt and slacks selected by his father and his father's fiancée.

However, he was glad that he had combed his hair with more care than usual when he saw Cojiñí walk through the door to their first shared class—History. Rumen had a large enough eighth grade to split into two sections. Cojiñí and Scoruş were in one, Gareth in the other, and sometimes they shared a class, such as History and English.

Either way, Gareth thought Cojiñí looked more than quite pretty in her button-up blouse that matched her midnight eyes perfectly, her tighter-than-usual black trousers, knee-high leather boots, and silver and blue jewellery—a ring, necklace and dangly earrings—that were shown off especially well because her raven hair was up in a bun on the top of her head. A few strategic strands dangled in front of her ears. The only makeup he saw was a faint touch of silvery eye shadow on her lids, something Gareth noticed only because he had three sisters.

He could even grudgingly admit that Scoruş looked fairly handsome. He was wearing the same outfit—minus the necklace and earrings, except that his shirt and the stone on his ring were a deep forest green. His hair was pulled back tight in a neat queue at the base of his neck with a silver ribbon. He noticed some of the girls giving the midnight-eyed boy appreciative looks.

The odd thing was that, unlike most of the kids who were wearing nicer clothes, the raven-haired twins looked perfectly at ease in their clothing, suggesting that they had chosen the clothes themselves and were accustomed to wearing such getup.

Anyhow, Gareth felt a slight awkwardness being within touching range of Cojiñí. Otherwise, the day went smoothly, at least until lunch, when the day was to end, and the graduating class would have a group photo taken.

* * *

Scoruş watched warily as Edward Carson approached him and Cojiñí as everyone was getting into place for the photo. It seemed the platinum-haired boy had forgotten his part in bullying the twins, and was attempting to charm his way into standing next to Scoruş' twin. Scoruş was beginning to feel that dressing as nicely as they had, was a bad idea. Carson's so-called "charm" was not working at all, and the boy was frustrated at his lack of progress.

Cojiñí looked as if she wanted to hex the persistent brat, and Scoruş was about to step in, but Gareth appeared out of nowhere to stand directly behind the brat, radiating something like an aura of stern confidence that Scoruş would never have expected out of their laughing, fun-loving, stripe-haired friend.

"Carson!" He barked—his voice and eyes sharp as shattered glass.

Carson turned, his ice-blue eyes going wide. "C-Captain Archer!"

Gareth stood so that he was nose-to-nose with the shorter boy. "What are you doing, Carson?"

Carson regained a bit of his former bravado. "I just wanted to stand next to...her." He jabbed his thumb in the direction of Cojiñí, and both she and Scoruş bristled at his tone of disgust and longing. Well, if he wanted Cojiñí, he wasn't going to get her, and all Scoruş would have to do was to restrain her so she would not seriously harm the bully.

Gareth caught the tone as well, judging by the coldness of his eyes. Scoruş felt the temperature to drop a bit, but then got a hold of his anger, as he thought he was the one causing it. He was not needed at the moment. Gareth was doing fine on his own, and Cojiñí could pack much more than a punch if she wanted to.

Gareth spoke again, his voice having grown dangerously calm, an impressive feat for a fourteen-year-old. "It looked to me like that was not all you wanted, and Carson, you should know something. I have heard from the others about your treatment of her and her brother once they became a certain something. And do you know what that certain something is, Carson?"

"What?"

"My. Friends."

Carson's jaw clenched.

Gareth continued. "Be glad that this is the last day, Carson. I did not act until now because I was not completely sure that what I was told was true. I wanted to believe that you were better than that, Carson. Just be aware of this—should you try anything else, you will find yourself in a world of pain, and not only from her and her brother. You are henceforth warned."

Carson left, his metaphorical tail between his legs.

Then the ice that seemed to be creeping through the soles of his feet into the floor disappeared, and Gareth was himself again.

That's when Scoruş realised he had not been the one causing the chill in the air. Gareth had, but he doubted the green-eyed boy knew that.

The floppy-haired boy turned to Cojiñí. "May I have the pleasure of standing next to you, my friend?"

Scoruş redefined his previous observation. Gareth was not quite himself again yet. The Gareth they knew did not speak in that manner. In fact, Scoruş realized he had been ignoring other things lately. Gareth fancied Cojiñí, and did not know how to express it, so he had not tried. The raven-haired boy had a brief surge of brotherly over-protectiveness, and thought that was a very good thing, then neatly placed that portion of his mind away for the time being.

Cojiñí smiled and nodded. "You may, my friend. You have my thanks for chasing away that pretentious brat."

"You are always welcome."

Right then, the photographer called for everyone to look at the camera, and Gareth snapped back to himself just as the man clicked the button. Luckily, he recovered quickly enough to not have a ridiculous expression in the photo. However, as soon as it was taken, the look on his face caused a few kids around him to burst out in giggles.

* * *

All was well then, at least until they were walking out the door. The two boys and girl had been separated by the crush of students, but they were not too worried as Carson had been beaten off and no one else wanted to harass the only friends of the boy who managed to become Captain in all sports he joined. Also, most of the students had heard through the grapevine that the caramel-skinned twins were not to be messed with.

Unfortunately, Carson was more stupid than he had previously appeared. Cojiñí did not glance over when she saw platinum blond hair in her peripheral vision, as there was more than one person with that hair colour, be it natural or dyed, and so it did not seem to be a problem. That lack of action was a mistake.

The platinum-blond person invaded her personal space, grabbed her bum, and whispered in her ear, "My brother says hello, pretty freak."

Cojiñí whirled round, catching Carson in the jaw with her elbow. "Rydych fab gafr!" she shouted at him, her voice a thunderclap in the raining noise of moving people. Heads turned, and a space opened around them.

Carson laughed, proving his stupidity even more. "Spouting gibberish are you now, pretty freak?"

Cojiñí narrowed her eyes and repeated herself a bit more clearly. "You, Edward Carson, are a son of a goat."

"Oh, I'm so scared!"

"You should be." Cojiñí looked behind her, and there, standing at her flanks, were Gareth and her brother. She smirked darkly.

"Thanks, boys, but I can handle this rat on my own if you'll let me."

Scoruş chuckled darkly. "Just don't maim him too much." His voice became alike to a midnight in winter. "Remember, I have a bit of a score to settle with him as well, but I'll let you take care of it since you are perfectly able to."

Gareth did not speak, but the temperature dropped a few degrees, and his eyes became like chips of dark green ice. Call him old-fashioned, but he believed that when a lady was insulted, offended, or treated in any way less than a princess, the perpetrator must pay.

If that payment were dealt by the lady in question, then Gareth would not argue, for he also believed that women were powerful beings in their own right. So he stood and watched, and did not interfere.

Cojiñí grinned, showing too many teeth for that grin to be anywhere near friendly, and felt something rise in her, something old and powerful, and somehow oh-so-familiar. The temperature dropped a few more degrees, and a faint smell of ozone entered the air. A sudden storm began outside, startling those who had chosen to walk in the previously sunny weather.

"Edward Carson," she said, her voice eerily calm and holding a weight and authority of ages past. "You have persecuted my brother and I, and probably others since we came here. And because your brother worked as William Torell's minion, you did not get your comeuppance, no matter what the teachers said to him. Now you have grabbed my rear without permission and in a manner that suggested it was what I deserved for being a 'pretty freak,' as you called me just now. William Torell is trapped in the backwoods of America for good because he tried to do to my aunt what he did to Scoruș and me—taking away something exceedingly important."

She paused, and her eyes to glowed. "Our magic has returned, Edward Carson, and we will not take your mistreatment anymore."

The raven-haired magical turned to the crowd surrounding them, snapping her fingers with a sound like indoor thunder. "Who of you has been persecuted by this goat's son? Who of you would be through with that treatment?"

The crowd rippled and an eighth of the total student population stepped forward. A slender dirty-blonde-haired girl with slightly protuberant luminescent-grey eyes, clad in bright, stereotypical gypsy clothes stepped to their head.

"I, Lea Blake, am tired of Carson's bullying."

She was followed by a pale boy with night-black hair and dark eyes, clad all in black. "I, Ivan Addams, am tired of Carson's bullying."

Another boy, from a younger grade, very slight and pale said, "I, Elliott Blackburn."

Another girl, also from a younger grade, with chocolate-brown hair and leaf-green eyes said, "I, Sarah Austin."

"I, Jaimie Bolton."

"I, Hana Carter."

"I, Jania Dale."

And so on. They all said they were tired of Carson's perceived superiority, and Cojiñí turned back to the boy. "You see, not so 'weak' now that we are all together, are we, Carson?"

Then she noticed that he had assembled his gang around him. Something inside her chuckled at the futileness of that action as all those he had bullied gathered around behind her and her boys.

The midnight-eyed girl's voice went soft so that all had to strain their ears to hear it. "You call me a freak, Edward Carson. Would you like to see what freakish things I can do?"

Her voice rose once more. "Well, then, I shall show you!"

The ring on her ringer made its presence known to all around as it began to glow in time with her eyes. A hand went out, and an unseen force snatched Carson from within the midst of his gang, drawing him up into the air above them, spinning like a top.

Just then, a voice that Cojiñí had never heard before, spoke in her head. Yet it seemed as familiar as her own. *'Cojiñí, sister-me, you must stop. If you do this, you will be no better than him. I know you are justified, but there is a difference between justice and mercy. Let him down. You are better than he is. You know it. Let him go. Give him the mercy he never gave you.'*

'Why should I?'

'Because we are better than those of his mental persuasion, or we can be.'

'But....'

'Let. Him. Go. Give. Him. Mercy. Be. The. Better. Person. Cojiñí.'

With a sigh, Cojiñí gently dropped the brat of a goat's son to the floor, ignoring the sounds of disappointment from the crowd. She walked up to him and knelt down.

"I want you to know something, Edward Carson. I could have let you spin. I could have done worse, but I didn't. Do you know why?"

"W-why?"

"Because if I did, I would be no better than you."

She stood and walked back to her brother, then turned to the crowd, her voice as loud as the thunder that had just ceased. "If I took our revenge, then I would be no better than him. There will be no *show,*" she snapped, the last word full of derision. Then she paused. "There is a difference between justice and mercy, and it is a choice that must be made. Justice, and therefore revenge, would make us no better than him. It would make us bullies as well."

That said, she collected Gareth and her brother, and they walked out of the lunchroom, leaving everyone else standing in shock.

They just barely made it to the back of the library when Cojiñí broke into tears of relief, exhaustion, and assorted similar things.

Scoruş wrapped her in his arms, and silently gave Gareth permission to do the same, as long as he let go when Scoruş did, and kept his hands in appropriate places. The green-eyed boy accepted the conditions, and they all sank to their knees on the floor in the back of the library—the only dry eyes were those the colour of ivy leaves.

Eventually Gareth shifted so that he had his arms around both his friends, and they stayed there until they were found by some of the other kids that had been bullied by Carson: Lea Blake and Ivan Addams to be specific, an hour later. They sat by them quietly until the twins looked up, tear-stained.

"Yes?"

"That was a good thing you did back there. You made us all think." Lea Blake's voice was soft and kind as she laid a gentle hand on Cojiñí's shoulder.

"You are a good person, and you are strong to be able to go that far and still be able to pull yourself back." Ivan Addams sounded proud.

"I almost went too far."

"But you didn't go too far." Mr. Addams' dark eyes shone.

Miss Blake smiled slightly. "You stood up for us all and made Carson pay, but in the process managed to not become a bully yourself. We find that admirable."

Cojiñí and Scoruş untangled themselves from Gareth and each other.

Mr. Addams continued where Miss Blake had left off. "And we would like to be your friends, if you would permit us. Not only for that, though." The last part was said hurriedly, as if he was trying to reassure them that they did not want to be friends only because Cojiñí had managed to keep herself from becoming a bully while at the same time giving Carson his due.

Cojiñí, Scoruş, and Gareth looked at each other. "Are you going to be going to Glamdring this next year? If yes, then certainly. If no, then it might get a bit tricky."

"You were accepted too?" They spoke in tandem, and didn't sound as surprised as the words might suggest.

Cojiñí smiled. "I take that that is a yes, then."

The blonde and brunette nodded, and then smiled. Gareth absently noted that Lea had a nice smile, like a sunny summer day, then he shook his head imperceptibly.

"So, Miss Blake and Mr. Addams...." Scoruş began, but the two cut him off.

"Call us Lea and Ivan, please."

"So, Lea and Ivan, what electives are you planning to take at Glamdring?"

"Well...."

Bonds of friendship were formed there, in the darkness at the back of the Rumen Primary School Library. Many, many kilometres away, on the hidden island of Golauglas, a genderless ghostly figure smiled. Its children were finding their friends and allies.

* * *

Anwyn watched as her two possible toys fought with knives and fists and feet. They were both tall and stocky this time, one fair and blond, the other tanned and dark. She wondered which would win, as they seemed to be evenly matched.

The statuesque woman turned her eyes from the battle and focussed her gaze on her brother's entertainment. Two women, lithe and beautiful, though not even close to her beauty, wrestled on the ground in the ring before her brother's seat. She saw a glint of metal on one of their hands, and realised that the women were not fighting with knives—her brother's usual weapon for them—but rather claws that he had undoubtedly conjured with a flick of the hand. How interesting.

Anwyn observed her brother's possible toys fight for a few moments, bemused by the way he had gone about equipping them to kill, then turned her gaze back to her own entertainment. The fight seemed to have increased in intensity, signalling that it was drawing near to a close. She still could not tell who was going to win, however.

Eventually, the fight ended with the blond tripping over his own foot, and running directly into the dark-haired one's dagger. Anwyn frowned. That was anti-climactic. Oh well, she liked the dark-haired ones better than blonds anyway.

She glanced briefly at Aneirin's toys, noting that their fight was drawing to a close as well. Then she walked down steps of air to her new plaything. She would clean him up herself this time. She waved away her constructed servants. And she would make it...*fun.*

* * *

Khulai Silvertouch glided from one position to the next, his long twin daggers flashing, his scar-covered bare torso gleaming in the moonlight. Just because he was a healer did not mean he did not fight, and it did not mean that he did not fight well. In fact, he was only a short way behind Araunya, and that was only because she had an uncanny talent for it. He just chose not to use it unless it was needed. However, *that* did not mean he would ever let his battle skills get rusty.

The tall man was so occupied with his movements that he did not see that he had an audience of one by the name of Tara Nighthand. Her eyes followed his motions eagerly, from every flick of a blade to every swish of the many braids that kept the entirety of his long raven hair bound and contained. She wondered what his hair would look like unbound—loose locks splayed across his lithe, muscular shoulders.

Khulai's movements picked up speed, and he began to weave in bits of magic with his flashing blades and flying feet, fist, knees, and elbows. Tara watched, fascinated as a safety bubble materialised around him, and everything within it became molested with spells and cantrips and pure energy, all in a rich, bright purple tone of glow.

The brown-haired woman watched what the angularly handsome man was doing as a result of his spells. He was using healing magic to cripple, wound, harm, and destroy. How unconventional.

Her eyes narrowed as she watched his face, then saw the pure pain and desperation etched in the lines of his expression and gleaming through his eyes. He was caught in a memory, she realised, and it was obviously not a good one. What to do? What to do?

Tara was determined. She stood and walked towards the man. This was a risky gamble, but she would do it. With a focussed burst of magic, she shredded a hole in the safety bubble. Ignoring the bursts and small explosions around her, she approached Khulai, carefully levitating the daggers out of his hands and onto the ground. He stopped moving, but even though his eyes were open and nothing covered his ears, he could neither see, nor hear her.

What to do? Well, part of her mind reasoned that she could kiss him, and that most likely would snap him out of it. But the other part of her mind retorted that she didn't want him to know that she liked him like that yet. So what? the first part asked, and when the second part couldn't come up with a reason fast enough, she acted.

As the more rational part of her yelled at her to stop, her hands reached up and grabbed the two braids on the sides of his face and pulled his lips to hers in a kiss that was as chaste as she could make it with the non-rational side of her mind in control. It lasted for only a few moments. Then she pulled back as hurriedly as she could force herself, and took stock of the situation.

Khulai was blinking rapidly—a look of such complete and utter surprise on his face that in any other situation she would have giggled. His mouth worked, but no sound came out. Eventually, however, he managed to form words.

"What was that?"

She bit her lower lip. "You were caught in what appeared to be a nightmarish memory and that was the only thing I could think of to shock you out of it."

He blinked a few more times. "You just kissed me."

Yes, she did, and it was something that she had wanted to do for a long time. "Well, it was the only thing I could think off...."

"You said that already." His wits were returning to him. Well, then, it worked.

Time to go, her rational side said, taking control once more. "Well, you're out of it now, so I'll just...go now. See you tomorrow." She turned around and was ready to bolt away, but he caught her arm.

"Thank you, Tara, for getting me out of that."

"You're welcome." There was an awkward silence, then she broke his grip and teleported home. That was one of the most stupid things she had ever done in her entire life, she thought, as she flopped down on her bed. Then she smacked herself on her forehead. Her tortoiseshell cat, Order, came up to her and started bumping his head against her hand, asking to be petted. She obliged him, and eventually fell asleep, lying on her back, fully clothed, and over the covers, her cat purring loudly on her chest.

* * *

Araunya sipped her tea, then made a face. She had forgotten to let it cool, again. Why on earth did she keep doing that? She had absolutely no idea whatsoever.

"You all right, Aunt Araunya?"

She turned to her nephew. It was a Thursday morning, but school was out for the summer, and it was storming, so she and the twins were inside, curled up on the sofa with tea and hot chocolate and blueberry scones that James had made the day before. They were watching a film.

"Yeah. Tea's too hot."

"Oh."

The film ended, and Scoruş got up to get more drinks and snacks as Cojiñí put the next film in the DVD player. Before the girl pressed play on the remote, Araunya spoke.

"So, remind me what you wanted to do with that cupboard under the stairs?"

Scoruş snorted softly. "It's more than a cupboard, Aunt Araunya. You know that."

"Yeah, but it's so much more a fitting name."

He frowned. "Fair point."

"Names for the space aside, what did you two want to do with it?"

"Make it into a study-reading-writing area," Cojiñí replied, curling up like a cat under the fuzzy blue blanket they had bought the afternoon before. "We figure we can fit two beanbag chairs, a small bookcase, a lamp, and a power strip in there, and we would like to make it so that it will open and lock from both sides."

Araunya was thoughtful. "That should be easy enough to do, especially now that you two don't have school. Although I may be called in to work often enough so that you two will have to do all the setting up yourselves. I was only able to take today off because I worked an extra shift a few weeks ago."

The twins tilted their heads with curiosity. "You never told us what you do. Why?"

She shrugged. "To answer your second question first, I don't know. I suppose it just never came up. To answer you first question, I work at the police station."

"Oh. Okay."

Cojiñí started the film, and she and Scoruș curled around each other like large cats under green and blue fuzzy blankets. What an interesting, yet strangely apt, comparison, Araunya thought as she watched her niece and nephew watch the film, talking to the characters every once in a while, and keeping up an almost constant running commentary.

Then Araunya realised something. Cats. They were like cats. That's what they would end up being—some form of cats. Every magical, whether he or she knows it or not—has an animal form. Usually it is only one animal, but there were exceptions. For example, the Balaur Chief's line had a tendency to have both a mammal form and an avian form. Araunya could turn into a peregrine falcon and a brown wolf. Khulai was a spotted owl and a red fox. Neva was a swan and a chameleon. And Durriken was a red-tailed hawk and a mastiff. Archmages were said to have up to three forms, the third usually being a mythical creature or an amalgamation of the other two forms, sometimes both, depending on the combination of creatures.

So, the twins were most likely cats. That was probably their mammal form, but what was their avian form? Something that would be very much a surprise, Araunya supposed.

* * *

The next day, Cojiñí, Scoruş, and Araunya went to a furniture shop and browsed for beanbag chairs, small bookcases, floor lamps, and doorknobs with locks. Eventually they found exactly what they were looking for, and purchased it all. Araunya discreetly used magic to fit everything in the car.

Once they got back to the flat, they enlisted the help of James and Aidan in carrying the items up the stairs and into number 332C's living room. That done, Araunya pulled a dagger with a twisted point out of the mid-space and used it to drill the old knob and flip-latch off the door, then pulled out a wider dagger and drilled holes in the door for the new knobs to be screwed into. A wave of her hand and a burst of focussed magic, and the door now had a functioning set of knobs that locked from both sides and was impervious to lock picks.

After that, all that was left to do was drag the furniture through the short doorway and into the room that was just tall enough to stand in, and arrange it.

The twins put the bookcase up against the wall directly across from the door. They plugged the power strip into the outlet and pulled the cord so that it was directly in the centre of the bottom shelf of the bookcase, in front of which they placed the lamp. They placed the beanbag chairs on both sides of the lamp. One beanbag chair was green; the other one was blue.

On a whim, they snatched a black throw rug from somewhere and placed that between the beanbag chairs.

"There." The twins spoke in unison, stepping back and admiring their little creation. "Done."

* * *

Gareth moved his knight decisively, but it was taken by one of Ashton's pawns. The green-eyed boy scowled good-naturedly. A few more moves and he would have had his red-blond-haired cousin in checkmate, but no, that never happened. That didn't mean he would stop trying, though. If nothing else, he was persistent. Unfortunately for the purple-stripe-haired boy, he did not notice Ashton's queen nearing check, and soon he had lost yet another game of chess.

They put the board away. "Till next time, cousin?"

The blue-eyed boy nodded. "Till next time." He smirked, "If you feel up to losing again."

"Oh, perhaps you'll be the one losing next time."

"You say that after every game, and I'm starting to think you don't even believe it anymore," Ashton replied.

"Hah. Try me."

"Oh, I will. And I will win once again."

Chapter 11

OVER THE COURSE OF THE SUMMER, Araunya taught the twins how to use the mid-space and, in a mid-space training room, how to fight with a sword, bow, staff, magic, and the body—or at least all that could be taught in a single summer. More training was planned for the following summer. Khulai ended up teaching Cojiñí how to play the pipe organ, and Neva had been instructing Scoruș in the playing of the violin. Both twins had a horrible time trying to read music. In addition, Araunya started tutoring them in the shepherd's flute, her instrument of choice, and in how to speak Welsh, something that would continue over the next school year and on until they were fluent. Khulai taught them healing practices.

Really, the only way the twins were able to absorb all that learning, and retain it, was due to the enhanced magic.

One day, Khulai appeared for their healing lesson with a pair of small white stones in his hand. He gave one stone to each of them saying, "I found these on my nightstand with your names on them. They aren't harmful. I scanned them. However, I have absolutely no idea where they came from."

With curiosity, the twins turned the stones over. On instinct, they enfolded the stones in their hands, closed their eyes, and sent a pulse of magic through them. They felt their surroundings change, and they opened their eyes.

They were in a room made of wood, and very high up, as they could see a panoramic view out the windows—one window in each wall.

Suddenly, a figure appeared—ghostly white and blue, genderless, and clad in a flowing snow-toned robe, carrying a white staff in one hand. It smiled at them and held out Its other hand for them to shake. They did so, surprised they could actually touch It.

Seeming to read their minds, It spoke. Its voice was a double harmonic of a baritone and a soprano. "Most cannot touch me, no. However, you can because you are my children."

They ignored the last sentence, instead opting for "Who are you?"

It smiled again, an expression that seemed both motherly and fatherly, and filled them with a sense of returning home. "I am...well, I suppose you could call me the genus loci of Ynys Golauglas, and by extension, the sentience of the Lodge, as the Lodge was made as a natural formation of the island it was built on, or at least it has grown to be so."

"What do we call you?"

"...Entity. You can call me Entity. Now you must go. All I wished for was to meet you, and you are wanted on the physical plane."

"Physical plane?"

"Yes, did you not know? This is the mental plane, where you may contact me if you are not on Ynys Golauglas. I would appreciate it if you would not speak of this to anyone. Now...depart."

Entity twirled Its staff, and everything went black.

* * *

Cojiñí's eyes fluttered open to see Araunya and Khulai leaning over her and Scoruș, their faces fraught with worry.

"Are you all right?"

"Yeah, we're fine."

"What happened?" Khulai looked curious.

Cojiñí shook her head. "Nothing."

The two adults seemed disbelieving, but they let it slide. For now.

"How long have we been unconscious?" Scoruș sounded calm, just as Cojiñí felt.

"About half an hour or so. Khulai phoned me when you collapsed."

"Huh?"

* * *

School started two-and-a-half weeks later, and so Araunya took them to Glamdring to drop off their paperwork, and to purchase their uniform jackets and trousers. For everything else, they went shopping for white shirts, dark grey ties, and black shoes. They bought a few other school supplies, such as highlighters, pencils, erasers, and pencil sharpeners.

The day school began, that being the first day of September, Araunya dropped them off five minutes early, just to make sure they wouldn't be late. The twins met Gareth, Lea, Ivan, and another boy at the door. The other boy looked familiar—his sky-blue eyes shining, his red-gold hair gleaming in the sunlight. Then they realised. Familiar face, though they had never met him before. Eyes like the clear summer sky, red-golden hair. If they were Morgaine and Myrddin, then this was Arthur to be sure. That supposition was further established when the boy introduced himself.

"Ashton Duncan, Gareth's cousin." It was not his name, but rather his voice that was doubly familiar. As they shook his hand, it came to light in the twins' minds that they'd had this same feeling of familiarity when they had met Gareth, Lea, and Ivan. So if they were Morgaine and Myrddin, and Ashton was Arthur, then who were the others? That was the question. However, they put it out of their minds for now, as they had a school to get to know, and a library and librarian to meet.

The first day of school at Glamdring Secondary had no actual teaching. Rather, it was a day for the students to familiarise themselves with the main building and its connecting additions and wings. For such an exclusive Secondary School, it was awfully big—four floors, and three sections in addition to the main area. It was the second largest building the twins had ever been in. First place went to the Lodge, for though they were able to see only one wing of it, they had been informed by Araunya that each of the four other wings was identical, and the one wing was as large as a small mansion. Just with the wings, the Lodge was huge, and that was discounting the courtyard that linked the wings together.

However, before the students would be led on the tour, and then left to explore on their own, they had to meet the principal. They all gathered in the lunchroom and milled around, wondering when the principal would show up. Eventually, a man stood on a table. The twins blinked. What was Aidan doing here? And dressed in a suit. Hmm.

Aidan Jones pulled a microphone from somewhere and tapped it, getting everyone's attention. "Good morning students. I am your principal, Mr. Jones. How is everyone doing this morning?"

Well, that was just a bit odd.

He continued. "Good? Good. Welcome to Glamdring Secondary. I hope you remember the things you learn here, be it class work or experiences. And I also hope that you memories are not bad. So, that said, time to divide you up for your tours."

From his pocket, he took a sheet of paper and started calling off names. It took a bit, but people soon realised that he was assigning a certain number of students to each of the eleven teachers. Oddly, Cojiñí, Scoruş, Gareth, Lea, Ivan, and Ashton were all in the group led by James, or Professor Allen, as they were now supposed to call him.

"Hello, group. It is nice to see so many of you this year. I'm Professor Allen, your history teacher. Shall we go?"

He led them through the corridors of Glamdring Secondary for at two or three hours before they ended up back at the lunchroom. "Well, that was your guided tour, now, go explore."

As they meandered off, he shouted after them, "No hiding in corners and dark spaces with your SO!" which caused a few of them to giggle. Cojiñí and Scoruş saluted him, smiling. He did not have to worry about them doing anything of that sort, especially as they did not have anyone to hide in corners and dark spaces with, ignoring the fact that even if they did, they were more discreet, and highly aware of what was appropriate.

The twins made a beeline for the library, and their friends followed them, as they did not wish to be separated in such a large building.

Glamdring's library was a lot nicer than the one at Rumen, and undoubtedly had at least a thousand more books, especially because there were more things for the library to have books about.

Cheerfully greeting Mr. Natser, the twins wound their way around the library, making sure to touch and read the title of as many books as they could, to see what seemed interesting. Their friends followed them, curious as to the midnight-eyed duo's purpose. Eventually, they reached the back of the top level of the library where they sat in a corner in a sort-of circle. There they spoke of everything and nothing, as was their wont, until the bell rang for all the students to reassemble in the lunchroom once more.

* * *

The next two months passed well enough, with nothing remarkable happening, and on the morning of Hallowe'en, Aidan, James, Araunya, Khulai, and Ms. Holden set up for a surprise birthday party for the twins, inviting Gareth, Lea, Ivan, and Ashton, who had become a fairly good friend of the twins.

The twins, of course, had no idea that their first actual birthday party was being prepared, and came home from the library completely not expecting what was to happen. However, when they arrived home and the lights were off, they suspected a surprise of some sort. They cast around with their senses, something that Araunya had recently taught them to do, and located nine living beings hiding in various places around the room. They flipped on the light.

The aforementioned nine living beings leapt, or leapt as well as they could in Ms. Holden's case, out of their hiding spots. "Surprise!"

Scoruș and Cojiñí were surprised by the effort their friends and family had put into preparing for their birthday. There were streamers hanging from the ceiling, and their favourite foods, plus a cake on the table. There was even a small pile of presents by the sofa. Others had gotten them presents! That was new.

It wasn't until Lea approached them with party hats that they realised they had just been standing there in shock. Their mouths opened and closed a few times, but no sound came out.

Araunya and Khulai saw the twins' facial expressions and moved forward to wrap them in a four-sided embrace.

"What is wrong, Co', Scor'?"

"It's...so...*new*."

"What is?"

"Having an actual party, with actual friends and family."

The two adults looked at each other. Oh. They hadn't thought of that. Well... "Will you two be okay?"

"Yeah. Just give us a moment."

"Okay."

Araunya and Khulai stepped back and let the twins compose themselves.

Once Cojiñí and Scoruș had gotten themselves under control, they turned to their friends. "Thank you so much for caring about us enough to do this Lea, Gareth, Ivan, Ashton, James, and Aidan." They blinked in succession, which under other circumstances would have been absolutely hilarious.

"You're very welcome, Scoruș and Cojiñí."

A moment of silence ended when Gareth's stomach growled. Everyone laughed, and he flushed.

"Well, then," James said. "Let's eat."

The food was delicious and everyone had difficulty stopping eating it. However, there were limits to how much food a human body, even a magical one, can consume in one sitting, so eventually they had to put the leftovers in the refrigerator. Then they moved to the living room where the small pile of presents awaited.

The twins sat side-by-side, cross-legged on the floor in front of the presents. They each took a box from the middle of the pile, causing it to tumble slightly. They shrugged, checked the tags, switched boxes, and began meticulously unwrapping them.

By the time everything had been unwrapped, Cojiñí had received a few sets of earrings, some embroidery thread and beads, and a silver rose pendant on a chain. Scoruș received a pack of hairpins, some leather cording, and a silver pendant in the shape of a winding tree, hung from a chain by its branches. In addition, they each received a new computer, black leather wristbands etched with Celtic runes, short swords in black sheaths, portable healing packs, and assorted books for their study bookcase, including a few on Norse and Celtic mythology, something that Cojiñí in particular was interested in. Scoruş' interest was more about the myths of Egypt and Ancient Greece.

Later that night, after all the guests were gone, Scoruş and Cojiñí went to their rooms to discover a small box on each of their beds. Contained within the boxes were velvet bags on which were pinned notes reading—*Do not open as of yet. You will know when it is time. I would be much obliged if you told no one....* The words were written in loopy handwriting. The only person that could have managed to get through unnoticed and would say something like that in such a manner was Entity, so the twins did as they were requested, and placed the bags in pockets of mid-space. That done, they went to sleep. They would not be trick or treating that night, or ever. They did not find that activity in any way appealing.

* * *

Christmas came and went. The twins very much enjoyed the music of the extra church service they went to on Christmas Eve. One of the Music, Dance, and Drama teachers, Mr. Erik Chaput, found out about Cojiñí's interest in the pipe organ and took over her instruction in that instrument. Likewise, Scoruş' interest in the violin was attended to by the other music teacher, Miss Cathrine Baudin.

In addition to Mr. Chaput and Miss Baudin taking an interest in the twins' musical abilities, Araunya received a note from Miss Baudin about their excellent performance when dancing ballet together in the school's Christmas production.

Report cards came, and Aidan and James took the twins out for dinner. There was a bit of irony in that act, Araunya thought.

* * *

New Year's, Valentine's Day, and Easter passed without incident, though Gareth acted a bit oddly around Cojiñí on the second day mentioned, as did Araunya and Aidan around each other, and though no one near flat number 332C knew it, Khulai and Tara seemed to be awkwardly avoiding each other in the manner of a pair of magnets turned so that both north poles, or south poles, as the case may be, were nearly touching.

In fact, nothing remarkable happened until halfway through June. Lea, who swam like a naiad—always beating the twins and the boys when they raced—heard from one of the pool volunteers about a teen book club at the public library, held at 7 p.m. on Thursdays. Araunya immediately jumped on that idea and made the twins go.

Her actual words were; "You two need to do more than just spend time with your friends at school. Yes, your dedication is admirable, but you need to do more than homework after school. You are going to this book club, and that is final."

Since Araunya rarely said that something was final, and when she did, she was very serious, the twins went to book club.

The book they checked out the next day was a dystopian science fiction novel, the first in a trilogy. The members of book club were very friendly, and Cojiñí and Scoruş felt welcome there.

Of the members, the four that stuck out to the twins were a brother and sister pair named Kennedy and Rae, and two girls named Mae and Alezandra. They were obviously all friends, and had been so for a long time, but that did not affect their welcoming of the twins, as far as the twins could tell.

Mae was dark-haired, with green- and orange-tinged brown eyes. She was a bit shorter than Cojiñí, with a tendency for dark-toned clothes. Kennedy was a flame-ginger with a crooked nose and chocolate-brown eyes that for some reason Cojiñí thought were blue at first. Like Scoruş, his favourite colour was green. Rae and Alezandra's hair was curly and a pretty blondish-brown, though Alezandra's hair was a bit darker, bushier, had tighter curls, and was slightly shorter. The former was blue-eyed, and the latter's eyes were light green.

* * *

Tara moved through her fight moves slowly and precisely. Ever since she kissed Khulai that night the year before, she had been avoiding him as much as she could. But they worked in the same building and when they did have to talk, she made sure not to make eye contact, still fearing his rage at her actions.

The brown-haired woman spun, and her sword connected with something hard and metal. She opened her eyes to see Khulai, shirtless and in training trousers, one dagger up and crossing the blade of her sword, the other sheathed at his opposite side. She drew back, and he lowered then sheathed his dagger.

"You've been avoiding me ever since the night you kissed me to break me out of my PTSD memory." His voice was not accusing. In fact, it was very, very calm. But she took it the other way.

"Yes, I have. Is there a problem with that?" The words were out of her mouth before she could stop them.

"Why are you doing it?"

That question gave her pause. How to answer? She did not want to lie, and yet she did not want to say the truth either. "Because."

The tall man raised an eyebrow. "That's not an answer."

"Technically it is."

"Very funny, Tara. I'm serious."

"No, you're not, you're Khulai." Oh, great, now she was making bad puns. Yay, fun.

"Ha ha."

Stall for more time? Lie outright? Only tell the partial truth? Tell the whole truth? What was she to do? Her mind was blank for ideas. He knew her well enough that if she lied, he would be able to tell, and if she stalled, it would only take a short time for him to figure that out as well.

What to do? What to do?

She was saved from answering at all when Neva, Khulai's younger sister, came running up.

"Khulai, you are needed at the Lodge. Gorhendad wants to talk to you." The gunmetal-blue-eyed man gave Tara a look as he left with Neva that said though she wouldn't have to answer now, he still wanted an answer. He was not the Head of the entire medical facility for being able to let a problem go at a click of the fingers.

Tara sighed in relief for having more time to mull over her answer. In fact, she was so relieved that she did not even think to be curious about what the Chief wanted to speak with Khulai about.

Continuing with her practice, the brown-eyed woman lost herself in the movements of the sword and feet and hands and magic.

* * *

As Ashton slept, he dreamed of a time gone by.

He was standing on the crest of a ridge, clad in silver chainmaille, a cape the colour of fresh blood emblazoned with a rampant gold dragon streaming from his shoulders. His hair was longer, reaching his shoulders, and he had a beard. He was older, an adult. Upon his head rested a weight; somehow he knew it was a crown of gold. He was a king. At one side of him stood Cojiñí and Scoruș. They were older as well. Their garment ensemble was high collared and slightly wing sleeved. In her case, it was a deep blue split-skirted gown; in his, a dark emerald tunic. Both were girded with swords, and in each of their right hands, they grasped long, smooth, pale-wood staffs carved with runes at both ends. Upon the end directed at the darkening sky was set a dangerously glinting stone of midnight blue shot through with an eerie green and silver, and on the end resting on the ground, an inch of wood was encased in silvery steel.

On Ashton's other side stood four women: an elder Lea clad in shades of ocean-blue and brown, the other women unknown, one raven and the others curly-locked. And three men, one unknown with ginger hair alike to a flame, the other two older versions of Ivan and Gareth. Ivan was not as pale as Ashton knew him to be now, but the black of his leathers under the silvery chainmaille, and his inky hair, though slightly longer, and eyes were recognisable. Gareth's purple hair-stripe

was gone; his hair was longer as well. He was garbed in pale blue battle-robes, clasped a staff alike to a long icicle wrapped in white leather, and a circlet of silver and pale blue resting on his head.

Ashton looked at the field over which they stood. There was an army, led by a woman and man in red clothes alike to those of Cojiñí and Scoruș, and an armoured king all in black and sable. At either side of the king were other figures, blurry, but distinguishable as four women and three men, a dark mirror of those standing beside him.

A hand touched his shoulder, and he turned his head to lay eyes on the most beautiful woman he had ever seen, with shining summer-green eyes and flowing hair alike in colour to the richest milk chocolate, clad in a split-skirted gown the colour of pine needles, and trousers and boots of snowy-white.

Ashton sat up straight in his bed, disoriented. *That was a very odd dream,* he thought. *So vivid...* He shrugged, then lay back down, rolled over, and went back to sleep. He did not dream anymore that night, and little did he know that Gareth, Lea, and Ivan had had the same dream, but without the beautiful woman.

Ivan and Lea, knowing enough about Arthurian mythology, correctly placed Ashton as King Arthur, and Scoruș as Merlin, but of the others they had no clue whatsoever. Thought they had a suspicion about who Cojiñí had been, and though they were correct, they thought it was not enough proof. They were also correct in guessing that Ivan was one of the Knights of the Round Table, as was the unknown man.

* * *

In the lavish mansion in the mountains, Anwyn and Aneirin awoke, slightly unsettled. More players had entered the fray. It was time to start searching for their allies in the other time, including Cenric, Agravaine to combat Lancelot, Meleagant to fight Elaine, Caelia for Branwen, Bruin for Vortigern, Owain for Taliesin, Nyneve to take out Nimue, Morwen to fight Aderyn, and Rhiannon to defeat

Gwenhwyfar, unlike last time this played out, though a good few had not yet been found by the others.

Time was not to be wasted searching for Arthur, as he was already located. Their allies must be found before the other side realised who they were. Hopefully, they would have a few more years to find them, as Morgaine and Myrddin were only adolescents now. As it was, Anwyn and Aneirin were frozen age wise, at least until the time for the battles to begin was reached.

They looked at each other though their metal link, and nodded. They had time. The battles could not begin until their opponents were ready.

With that thought in mind, the pale-golden-haired twins went back to sleep.

* * *

The next day, on instinct, Ashton told Cojiñí and Scoruș about his dream. As exclamations of nearly the same dream came from the rest of their friends, the magical twins frowned in thought, recalling their own shared dream from a year ago. This was very odd. Very odd indeed.

Later that same day, at the suggestion of the twins, the entire group recounted their dreams to Araunya. She muttered something cryptic about the magic of shared dreams, and how this was something she had never encountered before in her life of travels, and that it was something she would have to talk to Khulai about. He knew more about dreams than she did, at least somewhat.

Unfortunately, he knew no more than her in this matter, so they were left in the dark with no answers. So, in the manner of most people, they put the issue to the side and promptly forgot about it.

* * *

The school year drew to a close, report cards came with good results, and Cojiñí and Scoruș invited Gareth, Lea, Ivan, and Ashton to Book Club to read the newest book choice—another dystopian novel.

The summer passed uneventfully, though the twins found out that Kennedy's birthday was during that time, as were Ivan's and Ashton's. Gareth and Lea's birthdays were in the winter, Mae and Alezandra's were during the spring, and Rae's was with the twins' in the autumn.

During the summer, the twins progressed in their magic and fight training, and Araunya began teaching them more complex stuff. She let them spar with blunt metal swords—a step up from wooden ones. She also took them to Ynys Golauglas and had them spend two weeks creating the weapons they would use throughout their lives, and during the ceremony in which they would meet with Chief Barsali and he would choose surnames for them.

* * *

The smithy was hot and dim, lit only by the flames of the forge and a few candles placed here and there. The twins had only two weeks to each create a bastard-sword and Mage-staff. Araunya knew nothing about their plans to make two weapons, but that was what they felt compelled to do.

Scoruș' chest was gleaming with sweat from the heat of the flames and the exertion of pounding the hammer on the steel that was to be his sword. He had taken his shirt off so it would not get soaked or singed. Cojiñí was in a similar state, though she was not completely shirtless, as that would be inappropriate and uncomfortable. Instead, she wore a light tank top. Anyone who had seen them before Araunya had found the twins would remark that they had gained a good deal of muscle, what with the fight training, swimming, and dancing they had been doing since their first summer in flat number 332C.

As the hammers rang upon the steel, the twins wove enchantments into the pattern to keep the blades from growing dull, from rusting, and to fit perfectly into whatever scabbard they were sheathed.

With the assistance of their magics and clever application of the mid-space, the swords were completed only a few hours after the sun set on Ynys Golauglas at the end of the Saturday of the first week. The finished products were truly magnificent. The blades were of

Damascus steel, the hilts of same, yet encased in black leather ridged for a better grip. Within the pommels, each had set a stone, one green, one blue. Along the blades were intricate carvings, disguising powerful enchantments, including the ones previously mentioned. They were written into the steel in a manner so as to never wear thin or smooth. Just below the cross guard was a flat, blank space, intended for a name, their names, to be etched after their names had been chosen.

Next came the staffs. The twins knew not what they would do for certain, only that whatever it was had already been decided.

That night, near midnight, neither of the raven-haired twins could sleep, so they rose from their beds and teleported to the place on Ynys Golauglas where they trained—a wide clearing in the centre of a deep forest, razor-sharp long knives on their belts, even though they were still in their nightclothes.

Cojiñí and Scoruș wandered the moonlit forest for an unaccountable time, until they happened upon a tree. Of course, being that they were in a forest, they were surrounded with trees, but this was a particular one—a strange, old tree, which under the bark had a pale, nearly white wood, strong and durable, perfect for both flexible bows and sturdy war-staffs. It had once been a yew tree, but the magic saturated in the air and water and earth of Ynys Golauglas had changed it.

The tree's name was Barhaol, or Lasting, as no matter what was taken from it, it would stay standing and strong, and it could never be chopped down. Wood from its branches had been used to make the chamber where Entity's ghostlike form resided, and was woven throughout the walls in the Lodge, but it was said that Entity Itself had come from the tree, for due to the over-saturation of magic, it had somehow gained sentience. If that was true, then it was the will of God whom Entity called the White God, as the Druids had done long ago, for something of that sort would not just happen unless that was so. It was also said that this was the tree from which Morgaine and Myrddin had taken small branches and made their Mage-staffs.

Of course, the twins knew nothing of this history, but were simply drawn to the tree and somehow knew they would make *their* Mage-staffs from its wood. And so they carefully levitated themselves up the trunk until they were at a spot where the branches were of just the right thickness to make a stout staff—after narrower tops were trimmed off.

They pulled their knives from their belts, but had to think quickly because all of a sudden, two identical branches broke off and both flew towards them. Catching the branches with both hands, the midnight-eyed twins watched wide-eyed as they saw new branches grow in place of those they held in their hands—just like the legs of a sea star replaced themselves when they were severed.

Scoruș and Cojiñí floated back to the ground, their faces showing surprise. They sensed a presence behind them and turned around, only to see a familiar ghostly figure gliding a few inches off the ground in Its flowing robes. Its translucent feet moved at if It was walking on the air.

"Hello, children."

Its speaking voice was the same as Its telepathic voice—a double harmonic overlay of baritone and soprano, eerie and beautiful.

On a whim, they bowed. "Entity."

The long pale-blue-haired figure looked at the tree behind them, and they turned around once more.

"Do you know what this tree is, children of my magic?"

They shook their heads, and although It was not looking at them, It continued as if It was.

"Its name is Barhaol, the Lasting. When this island was split off from Wales, many, many centuries before my elder children, it was a great yew tree. But then this island was hidden. And because of the endless wards and enchantments woven throughout the entirety of this spot of land, the very earth, air, and water became saturated with magic, and this tree was changed. Why this was the only one to do so, no one on this world, not even I, who came from it, know. But it was changed, became indestructible, and eventually, for some reason known only by the White God, as the Druids and Norsemen once called him, was given sentience."

Entity, or perhaps It could be called Barhaol, paused for a moment, thinking. Cojiñí and Scoruș waited calmly. Eventually It spoke again, suddenly turning to them.

"Those staffs will serve you well. Wield them right, and do not turn from the straight and narrow path or you will be led to your destruction. Do not trust the impossibly alluring beautiful ones, for they will attempt to lead you astray, even though they may not try to kill you. Trust your friends, they have been well for you, and they are valuable allies for what is to come in less than five, but more than three years hence."

That cryptic statement said, the ghostly figure disappeared into nothingness, and the twins stared at nothing for a good long while—until they the sun broke over the horizon. Dawn was coming. Perhaps now would be a good time to return to 332C and go back to bed...

The next day, well, to be precise, the afternoon of the next day, the twins rose from their beds thinking that they had just had a very odd shared dream—until they saw the long, near-white lengths of wood leaning against the corners of their rooms. Judging by the strips of rich brown bark on the floor, they must have stripped them sometime after they returned from their night excursion. Either that, or someone had done it for them as they were sleeping.

Also on the floor were the narrow parts of the branches, smoothly cut, which made the staffs exactly the height they would need to be when the twins were full grown, and yet not too tall for them to use at the height they were now. All that was left to do was carve the runes, set the stones, and encase the end that would touch the ground with steel charmed to never rust. Once the staffs were completed, the twins would need to learn enough to be qualified to use them.

Perhaps they would even become apprentices...but to whom? The only other Balaurs they knew were Araunya, Khulai, and Neva, and only the first two of those they knew well.

Cojiñí and Scoruș descended the stairs to the lower level of flat number 332C. In the kitchen, Araunya was attempting to make three servings of eggy-in-the-basket, and actually succeeding, mostly. Then the pan went flying into the wall, egg going everywhere, and that was the end of that.

The twins burst out laughing. Their aunt glared fondly at them and gave a long-suffering sigh, but she could not hide that she was just as amused with the situation as they were.

Cojiñí and Araunya wrenched the frying pan out of the wall, and mended it as Scoruș pulled out another and began making breakfast, properly. There were never any flying pans when Scoruș cooked. For some reason he had a talent for that, and though Cojiñí could cook a bit, the kitchen was Scoruș' domain. Electronics in the flat, not counting those in the kitchen, were Cojiñí's domain. Araunya did not interfere with either, for although she was the head of their little household, she knew better than to attempt to mess with the twin's specialities. Or things such as flying frying pans and a telly with a frozen screen.

After breakfast, Araunya went to work, and Cojiñí and Scoruș teleported back to Ynys Golauglas to continue work on their Mage-staffs.

It took the entirety of the week to finish the staffs, and more than half a day to find the stones that were to be set in the tops. Eventually, just when they were about to give up looking, Barhaol brought the exact stones they were looking for from somewhere in Its chamber, and they were exceedingly grateful for Its help. Finally, the staffs were done, and they looked exactly like the staffs the twins had been carrying in that strange shared dream from a year before.

The day of the ceremony was scheduled—Wednesday of the next week, to give the twins time to rest.

Chapter 12

THE DAY OF THE CEREMONY ARRIVED in which their surnames would be given or chosen, and when they would be aura-scanned by Chief Barsali to see if they would grow to be Mages. They rose early to bathe and dress in white robes provided by Araunya before going to Ynys Golauglas.

Araunya was waiting for them at the bottom of the stairs, hair loose and flowing down her back, clad in deep-red robes embroidered with silver along the hems, held together with near-invisible hook-and-eye clasps down the centre from high collar to waist, and belted with a woven belt of black leather strips. She held a vaguely familiar black staff tipped with steel and set with a crimson stone.

When she spoke, her voice was formally lilted. "Have you the weapons you wish to present to the Chief and his Witan?"

Presenting the white cloth wrapped long bundles, they spoke in unison, their voices of the same formality as their aunt. "We do."

"Then we shall depart."

That said, they teleported away. The trip through the mid-space seemed both eternal and instantaneous at once, and they reappeared in the clearing where they were greeted by the Witan of Chief Barsali. The Chief was white-haired with age, but his eyes still glinted clear, and his grip and form were still strong.

Barsali spoke, his deep voice resonating through the treeless space in the middle of the forest. "Whom do you bring, Lady Warrior Mage Araunya Ravenheart, to present before us to be named and scanned?"

Araunya bowed deeply, and following her example, the twins did the same. "Chief-Lord Warrior Mage Barsali Oaksword, I bring the children Cojiñí and Scoruș, twin children of Lady Mage Charani Duskflame and Heir-Lord Warrior Mage Durriken Stormeye."

Members of the Witan made sounds of surprise, but a look from the Chief silenced them. "Have they weapons to present?"

"So they have said."

"Present your crafted weapons, children."

Cojiñí and Scoruș stepped forward and unwrapped the bundles, laying the two staffs and two bastard swords on the cloths on the ground in front of Chief Barsali. One white eyebrow rose when he saw that both of them had made two weapons, but it dropped back to its formally stern expression.

He addressed his Witan. "Do these meet with the requirements as they are written and passed down and spoken?"

A nondescript member of the Witan approached the weapons and handled them, scanning them with magic, and giving them a few swings through the air, inspecting them and testing their strength. Finally, he stepped back into his place in the circle. "They do meet the requirements, Chief-Lord Warrior Mage Barsali Oaksword."

The sharp-eyed old man nodded. "That is well." He turned back to Araunya and the twins. "The presented weapons meet the requirements. Have they chosen surnames for themselves, Lady Warrior Mage Araunya Ravenheart?"

She shook her head. "No, they have not."

He nodded once. "Step forwards, children of Clan Balaur. As you have not chosen surnames, they must be given."

Scoruș and Cojiñí did as requested and closed their eyes as orbs of silvery-pale magic light surrounded them, humming and pulsing. They rose a few centimetres off the ground. Though they could not see it, Chief Barsali's eyes had closed as well as he scanned their auras for surnames that would fit.

After a very long moment, the orbs dissipated and Chief Barsali opened his eyes, but he did not yet speak. The twins became even more nervous than they had been.

Although the twins would never admit it, they were a bit surprised when he did speak, as they assumed he had become mute—he'd been silent for such a long time.

"Children of Clan Balaur, son and daughter of Lady Mage Charani Duskflame and Heir-Lord Warrior Mage Durriken Stormeye," he said, then paused. "You were once one in many, easy to be confused with another of your name. Now you are not of that name only; you are...."

He turned to Scoruş. "Scoruş Blackfalcon."

He turned to Cojiñí. "And Cojiñí Seasword."

The white-haired man's gaze rested on both of them. "These are not the only names written in your auras, but I have been requested by a genderless ghost known by Entity Barhaol to not impart you with that information at this time."

Araunya gaped. That was unexpected and unusual. The twins did not seem to think much of it, but their time as scapegoats and whipping boys at the hands of the Tigers had made them adept at hiding their emotions unless they wished otherwise. For some reason, the shared dream that the twins had a year before, and the dream shared between their friends more recently came to mind. But the thought lasted less than a second, and then it was gone, leaving no wake of its passing.

Chief Barsali watched the eyes of the newly surnamed twins, ignoring their carefully blank expressions. He saw the surprise and a flash of a memory of a dream or a dream of a memory cross their gazes for less than a moment. Yes, they had more names, and Barhaol had requested that he not tell them, as they would find out on their own soon enough. They had at least three years, and at most, five years, until the battle against their physical enemies would begin. For now, however, they should have time to enjoy and hate life as perfectly ordinary—he snorted internally at their lack of ordinariness—teenagers, without the added stress of having souls older than their bodies.

He watched calmly as they gathered their weapons. Making two was a wise choice, though they did not know it. They would need both sword and staff when the time came.

Barsali declared the twins to have Archmage potential. One eyebrow quirked slightly at the fact that his eldest great-granddaughter was not surprised at all. However, the reactions of his Witan were humorous. Yes, these two were special. The fact that the Lasting Tree's sentience, which had a form living in the chamber built for it above the Lodge, paid them any attention was telling. The fact that It paid enough attention to *him* to speak to him on their behalf, was monumental.

* * *

Neva Whitefeather moved her pencil on the paper with surety, looked at what she drew, crumpled it, and started over. Once her drawing was done, she examined it for a moment, made sure she had not missed any important details, and then pulled a thick binder full of plastic sleeves from her bookcase. She added the picture to the many others she had drawn.

She exited the room to get a snack, leaving the binder open, displaying the picture she had just drawn. It was a sketch of a rowan tree and a rose bush, both coming from the same root.

* * *

The day school began once again, Cojiñí and Scoruș returned to Glamdring with a new gleam in their eyes, for they had begun their Mage training two days after the ceremony in which they were pronounced eventual Archmages. Araunya explained that the two were essentially the same thing—at least in the amount of training for each—but Archmages had a larger magical core and therefore had more power in which to utilise the training they had received. They did not want to become apprentices and narrow their focuses to one specific thing. Additionally, according to what Barhaol said, they did not have enough time to complete an apprenticeship before whatever battle was coming after at least three years, unless it was a very short one.

Either way, they had a bit more spring in their steps than usual, and though most did not notice, Gareth, Lea, Ashton, and Ivan did, but they did not comment for some reason or another, at least not at first. During lunch, however, Lea, in her usual cheerful bluntness, asked, "So what's different? Have you had a promotion in the magical community or something?"

The twins looked at her, surprised. "How did you...."

"What? Did you think you were the only magicals at Glamdring? Why do you think Carson and his gang targeted me at Rumen?"

The twins' mouths opened and shut with a snap. Oh. Okay.

The dirty-blonde-haired girl continued as if she had not said the last sentence. "Anyhow, I think the magicals here, aside from you two, are me and Gareth...."

Gareth cut her off. "Wait, I'm a magical?"

Lea looked at him as if he were particularly dense. "Yes, haven't you noticed that the temperature drops when you are angry? And when you're really angry, ice comes from your shoes." She paused for a moment. "Also, in that one dream we all had, you had a staff, just as Cojiñí and Scoruș did. It looked like a very big icicle, if you don't remember."

The green-eyed boy rapidly blinked a few times. "Right. Okay, then."

Then Scoruș realised something. "Hey! You can join us in our magic classes after school, and during breaks, and in the summer!"

Gareth shrugged. "I suppose. After all, if I have magic, I need to be trained in how to use it so I don't accidently destroy stuff when I lose my temper."

The group of friends nodded, and they turned their talk to other things.

Later, when Araunya came to pick up the twins, they brought Gareth and broached the subject of him training with them. She agreed, and he called his stepmom to let her know he was going over to a friend's place for the rest of the day, and might end up staying over. She said that was okay, and hung up, though she did say goodbye. His father would have just made some noncommittal noise and hung up without even letting Gareth finish talking.

That taken care of, the three teens piled into Araunya's car and she drove to the flat playing theatre songs the entire way, which the twins did not mind at all. They sang along to some, but Gareth just seemed confused. When asked why, he said it was because he could actually hear words and not just the screaming and machinery sounds, which was what he compared his father's music to. The twins raised two of their four collective eyebrows.

Once they arrived at number 332C, the twins left their backpacks in the car, as did Gareth, to follow their example. Luckily, none had any homework.

Araunya sent the midnight-eyed duo off to their mid-space training room to spar, and followed them with Gareth after she had transfigured his clothes into something easier to move in, as he was not comfortable with going around shirtless when Cojiñí was in the area. However, the glance he took of Cojiñí while she and her brother sparred was very approving, and slightly embarrassed at the same time. She was wearing a tight tank top and yoga trousers.

Once the winter-eyed woman regained the green-eyed boy's attention, his training began. The first thing Araunya had him do was see if he could consciously access his powers. It turned out that he could not, so she worked with him until the alarm rang signalling that it was time to eat. By that time, he could make himself angry, but he still needed practice before using his powers in a controlled manner.

Araunya chuckled to herself as she watched the green-eyed boy carefully NOT stare at Cojiñí as the girl and her brother made snacks for the four of them, but she kept her insight to herself. Gareth knew enough not to try anything with her without asking first—there was a fair possibility that his head and his body would end up separated from each other, or at least in a fair amount of pain.

Gareth did not stay over as it turned out, since he had not brought an extra set of clothes and did not fit Scoruș'. So, at 8 p.m., Araunya drove him home.

The next day, a dark-haired, fair-skinned, dark-eyed man opened his eyes to see a man handsome enough to make this one jealous leaning over his bed. The man had pale golden hair, deep ocean-toned eyes, and a physique to make most women drool.

The awakening dark-haired man was a perfect example of 'tall, dark, and handsome,' but the golden-haired one surpassed him by a league. He looked at the other one strangely, as if searching for something hidden. Eventually the ocean-eyed man moved back, allowing the other to sit and extend a hand. The golden-haired man shook it, answering the dark one's unasked question.

"Aneirin. And you are?"

Even the man's voice made him jealous, but it did not matter. "Haydn. May I ask why you are in my room at this hour of the night?"

"My sister...may wish to meet you, I think." Aneirin spoke as if to himself.

But Haydn replied. "Would I wish to meet your sister?"

The other man smiled, a tinge of malice showing in the display of many snow-white teeth. "If anything is the same as before, yes, you certainly will." The smile disappeared. "But not now. I will come for you later. Await me and my wyrms at the most unexpected time."

Then he was gone as if he had never been there. After a moment, Haydn realised that the other man had been flanked by the most unusual creatures—like dragons, but more akin to serpents.

Little did he know it would be at least a year before he saw the unusual, jealousy-inspiring man again, long enough to nearly forget that midnight meeting on a random day in September.

* * *

Khulai finally cornered Tara after an apprenticeship ceremony, and nearly had to drag her behind the Lodge to get his answers.

"Why do you keep avoiding me, Tara? And why did you run away?" He held a finger in front of her nose. "Don't stall this time, tell me the truth."

Tara's mouth opened and closed a few times, then she swallowed hard. "Why do you want to know so badly?" She was genuinely curious.

"You're stalling."

"Answer me and I'll answer you."

"I asked first."

"So?"

He raised an eyebrow, but the shorter Mage did not back down. "I'm not telling you until you tell me why you want to know."

"I'm curious, and more than a little concerned."

Tara did not believe that was the complete entire reason, but she let it slide.

The brown-haired, brown-eyed, pretty-though-she-did-not-think-so young Mage sighed heavily. *I suppose there's no putting it off any longer,* she thought, and after a long moment she spoke, her voice so quiet that, though she did not notice it because her eyes were focussed on her feet, Khulai had to lean in a good deal closer and a few of his black braids fell over his shoulders.

"I was embarrassed for giving in to my impulses and not being able to think of anything else to do to break you out of that PTSD memory."

There, she said it, sort of. Had she been looking anywhere but the buckles on her boots, Tara would have seen Khulai's look of confusion. But then his eyes widen as the meaning of what she said dawned on him. Oh. Oh! That's what that meant...hummm...what to do? What to do? The gunmetal-blue-eyed man was completely and utterly at loss about what would happen next.

"Um..." The brown-haired woman looked up and was surprised at the proximity of their faces.

She quickly took a step back, and tripped over a stone. Khulai attempted to catch her, but ended up falling too.

They lay there on the ground, staring at the sky for a moment, then at almost the same time, began to laugh, dispelling the cloud that had hung over them for nearly a year.

* * *

The school year passed well, with a majority of good grades, but just before summer break, Book Club began reading a book aloud and dramatically, with interesting results, at least according to Cojiñí Seasword.

The book, well, technically a play, was "Taming of the Shrew," by William Shakespeare, and they were all to read parts aloud, in character if they could manage to do so.

For a reason she could never explain, Cojiñí volunteered to speak as the Shrew, also known as Katerina, Kathrine, or Kate. Kennedy took the role of Petruchio, the man who, if Cojiñí remembered correctly, would end up "taming" the "shrew," and he also offered to play Tranio, if no one else wanted the part. As it turned out, Scoruş took Tranio, and there were enough people so no one had to double up.

During Katerina and Petruchio's meeting scene, Cojiñí was certain that her face, neck, and ears were the exact shade as a ripe tomato, and was very glad that they were only speaking the roles, and not acting them out.

"What's a moveable?"

"A join'd stool."

"Though hast hit it. Come, sit on me."

"Asses are made to bear, and so are you."

"Women are made to bear, and so are you."

"No such jade as you, if me you mean."

A few lines later were even worse, in Cojiñí's opinion, and she lamented Shakespeare's tendency for crude humour.

"Who knows not where a wasp does wear his sting? In his tail."

"In his tongue."

"Who's tongue?"

"Yours, if you talk of tales; and so farewell."

"What, with my tongue in your tail? Nay, come again, Good Kate; I am a gentleman."

"That I'll try."

"I swear I'll cuff you if you strike me again."

On a completely different note, for some reason or another, Scoruş' Tranio had a Scottish accent, which a few, including Cojiñí—when she was not imitating a tomato—found amusing.

They got through two scenes that night, and after the twins returned home, Cojiñí went to bed with an unusual feeling in her head. Something was making itself known.

* * *

That something made itself even more known as the play went on, as Cojiñí had to keep stopping herself from referring to Petruchio as 'Pet,' and blushing every time Kennedy looked at her—while speaking their characters and the rest of the time.

It did not help much that soon after they did Kate and Petruchio's meeting scene, Kennedy showed Cojiñí and Scoruș a video of people acting out that scene on a stage, and therefore made Cojiñí even gladder that they were only speaking the lines. After the video, she said the man playing Petruchio was unattractive to her, but privately, she thought he looked a bit like Kennedy, though a bit more monkey-like and blond. She did not say it, even through her mental link with Scoruș, but she found that a person that looked a little bit like Kennedy was much more appealing than a person that looked nothing like Kennedy. Her interests with fictional characters did not count in this particular census.

* * *

Summer came fully and "Taming of the Shrew" ended. However, Araunya had planned to take the twins to a secluded part of Ynys Golauglas for Mage training for a good deal of the summer, and so they could only watch the first session of the *Taming of the Shrew* movie.

In addition to the training, Araunya rented a few movies for them to watch on weekends. There were two musicals, one the actual movie adaptation of the musical version of *Les Misérables,* and the twenty-fifth anniversary of Andrew Lloyd Webber's *Phantom of the Opera.* The twins were very interested in how those would play out. In the case of *Les Misérables,* they were pretty sure the directors would NOT include the sections on the Battle of Waterloo and 19th century French slang. One of the non-musical movies was based on a comic book about a masked revolutionary in an alternate world where Germany won World War II, and another was a new movie about the Dracula back-story.

* * *

Cojiñí and Scoruș returned from summer vacation stronger, faster, and in more control of their magic. Their heads were full of the new stories, and their vocal cords vibrated with the songs they discovered that they liked exceedingly much.

Those songs showed something few had ever known about the twins—they could sing! Fairly well. Even though they had no training whatsoever. Cojiñí had a difficult time keeping a tune, but she was very good at memorising lyrics. Scoruș was the inverse—good with the tune, not so good at remembering lyrics. As far as ranges went, that was something they had played with in the solitude of a mid-space room in the brief gaps of time in which they could create one.

Scoruș was a tenor, but he could sing bass if he wanted to. Cojiñí was most comfortable as an alto, but it appeared she was able to sing both a high tenor and a low soprano, sometimes even higher if she tried really, really hard and it was a good day.

The fact that they could sing better than okay was discovered by one of their classmates—a kid who'd had musical training before it was a required elective and who could identify students who sang well and those who could not. He heard the twins singing bits from *Phantom's* title song and reported his observation to professors Chaput and Baudin. The professors then contacted Araunya and asked if they could see the twins after school. The twins weren't in trouble, they assured her, they just wanted to do a small evaluation. Araunya consented, and so a meeting was arranged without any knowledge of the twins.

The next day, Music, Dance, and Drama was the last class on the twins' schedule, and Professor Chaput pulled the twins aside when everyone else was leaving.

"May we speak with you two for a moment, *s'il vous plait?*" He was a very tall man and lanky, with an extremely angular face, though not altogether bad looking. He had an odd tendency to pepper his speech with an occasional French phrase, and a voice that could do whatever he wanted it to. He kept his thick black hair pulled straight back, and his nearly amber eyes were piercing. He had an unidentifiable accent, and even with his French last name and interesting speech, no one, not even Aidan, knew where he was from.

The twins nodded as one, curious as to what was about to happen.

At that moment, Professor Baudin walked over. She was a short, spunky, cheerful woman with long, curly blonde hair and shining blue eyes. Her voice—according to the many students who had a crush on her—was that of an angel. Supposedly, she was born in Sweden, but her father was French, hence the French last name.

Suddenly, a realisation hit the twins with all the subtlety and slowness of a lightning bolt. "May we ask you a really random question before whatever that will happen happens?"

The Professors nodded, curious expressions on their faces.

"Have you read and/or watched *The Phantom of the Opera*?"

Both adults seemed surprised, then nodded. Professor Chaput chuckled. "Yes, we have. Or at least I've done both." He turned with a silent question to Professor Baudin, who smiled.

"I've done both as well. I always wanted to be Christine when I was younger, but I wanted to literally smack Raoul over the back of the head instead of metaphorically when they were under Apollo's Lyre on the roof."

Professor Chaput chuckled again. "I always found an appeal to the character of Erik, *Le Fantôme,* though never to the point of actually wanting to be him." He smiled. "I also always found the name similarities to be extremely *amusant.*" Then he frowned. "But we are getting off track, are we not?"

Professor Baudin nodded. "Yes we are." She turned towards the twins, her eyes sparkling. "We have a very important question to ask you two."

"We were wondering...." Professor Chaput began.

"...if you would like us..." The blonde woman was smiling slightly.

"...to tutor you two on how to sing better in addition to the instrument lessons we've been giving you." Professor Chaput's amber eyes gleamed. It was obvious that he liked instructing smaller, more individual groups much better than the large classes he and Professor Baudin were assigned every day.

It also seemed obvious to the twins that the two instructors had too much free time, since they were already teaching the twins to play the pipe organ and violin, and teaching at least two other select students how to sing above and beyond what was taught in the class. And now they wanted to teach them. The question was, why? And how did they find out that the twins could sing? Neither Cojiñí nor Scoruş had sung at all in class.

"Why?" Cojiñí's asked.

"And how do you know we can sing at all?" Scoruş added.

"One of our other students happened to hear you two singing yesterday and told us." Professor Baudin shrugged slightly as she said this, a lock of her curly blonde hair falling over one shoulder. "So, do you accept our offer?"

The twins thought about the implications of the offer. After a moment, they nodded. "We accept your offer, Professors Chaput and Baudin."

The adults' smiles could have lit a city.

* * *

Later that night, Cojiñí remembered something she had realised during the summer, and just forgot to think about. Every single day while she was gone, at some point, no matter what she was doing, she thought about Kennedy. She'd ask herself, *What would he think of this? Would he like that?* It was odd. Then she realised what she had realised. Cojiñí had a crush on Kennedy.

She frowned. Well, that was a complication. They were friends, and she didn't want to ruin that. And yet....

The midnight-eyed girl sighed. Best to attempt to keep it a secret for now, at least from him. She would wait for him to make the first move, and if he liked her as more than a friend, then, well, whatever would happen would happen. If not, then there was no need for her being rejected. Cojiñí nodded. Yes, that was what she would do.

That taken care of, the raven-haired, caramel-skinned, blue-eyed fifteen-year-old Mage-to-be with a crush went to sleep.

The next day was Thursday, Book Club day, and Cojiñí chose to wear a nice green shirt, without really thinking about what she was doing. The same thing happened every Thursday from then on. Eventually, the girl figured out what she was doing, but she continued anyway. It didn't *really* matter that it was Kennedy's favourite colour, she thought. Even though her favourite colour was technically blue, she still liked green a lot.

That day at Book Club, they were to make collages of their summers. Therefore, Book Club discovered about the twins' new movie preferences. They also found out that Cojiñí knew at least one of the numbers from the musicals they had watched. When Kennedy started singing a song from the *Les Misérables* movie, she joined in. No one was surprised that she could sing, for both she and her brother had sung for book club before.

As she was preparing for bed that night, Cojiñí was struck with the urge to do something she'd attempted before but had never succeeded—write a song. She sat down at her nightstand, pulled from its drawer a diary she never used, and a pencil. She began to write. Soon the words flowed, and a melody began to take shape as well, simple but pretty.

Stars fall hard now, break the ties that bind them,
Darkness calls now, hear the songs of night-time;
Light shall fade and return again
Hear the music of time flow by.

Hearts shall still and dreams shall fade,
But I will be always here by your side,
Till night falls no more and the seas no longer roar,
I shall be with you, I shall see you through.

Worlds shall fall and sirens shall call,
But I'll hold true to my promise to you,
I'll keep you safe, I'll do all it takes
To keep you with me for all time.

I'll find a way to live through the days
When you do not believe, I know you will see,
Forever and a day, that will be my way,
Our hearts shall beat as one, till eternity is done.

Stars fall hard now, but we will never fall.

The angularly-pretty girl looked over her wording many times, and once she was satisfied that they fit the melody in her head, she cast a silencing ward over her room and sang her song, being sure to record it on her phone so that she would not forget the tune.

That done, Cojiñí put away her diary and pencil, clambered in bed, and went to sleep.

Chapter 13

THE NEW SCHOOL YEAR BEGAN and on the first day, the twins almost literally ran into someone on their way to class. She was familiar, but not in the way of 'seen her somewhere at school.' More like they had met her before and were friends once upon a time, similar to the way all the twins' other friends had felt when they first met, though the raven-haired duo had not always noticed it at the time.

The girl that Cojiñí and Scoruş ran into was very pretty. Her chocolate hair fell in waves to her waist, and her summer-green eyes shone with innate warmth. She was the same height as Lea, and thought she gave off a "vibe" of being a healer, there was fierceness in those warm green eyes that could not be hidden.

"Hi. I'm Cojiñí." She held out her hand, and the girl shook it.

"And I'm Scoruş, her brother." He mirrored his sisters' action.

"Catrina. It is nice to meet you." Her voice was like a warm breeze that could freeze in an instant, if needed.

"The pleasure is all ours, Catrina. Would you like to be our friend?"

She seemed a bit taken aback by the abrupt offer, but smiled nonetheless. "Sure."

"Great."

As they walked to their next class, a whisper teased at the edges of their consciousness, a whisper in the voice of Barhaol. *They are all found; now for the revealing of who is.*

* * *

Haydn looked up from his book as he realised that there was someone else in the room with him. The dark-eyed man perked up. Oh. Right. The pale-golden man was back.

"It's been a while."

Aneirin shrugged majestically. "I've been busy."

"Is it time for me to meet your sister?"

The ocean-eyed man nodded. "It is."

Haydn stood, and the ever-so-slightly shorter man held out one gloved hand. Hayden took it and they disappeared from the room, leaving only Haydn's open book, *A Collector's Collection of Arthurian Legends,* as proof that there had been anyone in there in the first place.

* * *

The fair-skinned man was awed by the opulence of the hall he found himself in. From out of nowhere, Aneirin produced an enormous dark cloak and handed it to Haydn.

"Put this on. Anwyn doesn't know you are coming, and I intend to surprise her. It is her birthday."

Haydn did as instructed and they set off down the corridor.

After a few minutes, they arrived at huge elaborately carved wooden double doors. Aneirin turned an elegant golden doorknob and entered the room. It was a large office-like chamber, well decorated in black, white, shades of red, and gold. The man entered and Haydn followed, still wrapped tightly in the cloak.

Sitting at the desk was the most beautiful and alluring woman Haydn could imagine. She had a perfect hourglass shape, and yet seemed lithely muscular. Her hair flowed over her shoulders to her hips in a waterfall of pale-gold waves framing a face too beautiful for words, within which was set large, dark-lashed eyes of all the shades of the shining Caribbean ocean. She was clad in a tight, low-collared, wine-burgundy dress trimmed with white fur around the shoulders. When she stood to acknowledge her brother's presence, he saw that the dress reached only mid-thigh. Haydn gulped as his mind registered the almost tangible feeling of power surrounding her. How was he supposed to speak to a woman with that level of beauty and power?

Then she spoke, and her voice was birdsong and bells and angels. "Greetings, brother-mine." Those alluring eyes glanced at Haydn, and he attempted to hold their gaze. "Why, brother, have you brought me a present?"

Haydn could practically feel the angelic man's smirk. "Yes, I have, dear sister, and I think you will like it very greatly."

"May I unwrap it?" The woman's voice held unfathomable degrees of eagerness at that prospect, and Haydn gulped again.

He glanced at the shorter man, and was somehow relieved to see him shake his head, but when he looked back at the woman and saw the disappointment on her face, he was filled with the urge to do whatever he could to banish that negative emotion from her forever.

Aneirin flicked his hand, and the cloak disappeared as suddenly as its appearance earlier. Haydn froze as he felt the woman's gaze travel all over his form, and willed himself to meet her gaze as she looked in his eyes.

She breathed out one word, "Cenric...." and then she was on him, slamming his back against the door, her lips interlocked with his, sparks tingling throughout the air at the touch.

The dark-haired man's eyes rolled back in his head as his mind was filled with images and feelings from a time gone by. His form was assaulted with muscles and calluses and memory of a body reared in the time of swords and bows and magic, and when she pulled back and he could breathe once more, he blinked a few times, then smiled.

"Hello Morgause my dear."

Her eyes were glowing with joy. "My Cenric."

Their lips met again, and they did not notice her brother discreetly slip out to continue his search for the rest of their allies. He was glad his sister had her Black King back once again, and glad they now had Arthur's foil and match in battle.

* * *

A month passed, and the twins' sixteenth birthday drew near. For the celebration, a masquerade had been planned for some reason that the twins did not, and would never disclose. All their friends were invited, and though costumes were not required, they were appreciated. Everyone was allowed to bring a date.

The only dates the twins brought were of the fruit kind, but as the guests arrived, it became clear that Gareth and Lea, and Ashton and Catrina had decided to come as couples, even though the latter had met just one month before.

The twins smiled because all the guests, other than the adults, came in costume. Gareth and Lea were a pair of merfolk. Ashton and Catrina were wood-elves. Kennedy was the Mad Hatter. Mae was Athena. Rae was Artemis. And Alezandra was a sea nymph. Cojiñí and Scoruş had taken a leaf out of Erik Le Fantôme's book and chosen to be The Raven and Red Death, respectively. Ivan was a knight, and for some reason, that was amusing to the twins.

About an hour into the party, an uninvited—but not unwelcome—guest appeared. Barhaol. It had not worn a costume, and perhaps It could not, but either way, It seemed to be on a mission of some sort. Its face was solemn as It looked at the guests. Once the genderless ghostly being was done with whatever it was doing—taking a headcount most likely—It swung Its staff, the end shining brightly pale.

A ring of light spread from the tip of the white staff and collided with the teenagers, knocking them out instantly, and they all crumpled to the floor like marionettes with their strings cut. The adults rushed to the teens, but Barhaol stopped them with a raised hand.

"They have been dealt no harm. Do not worry, and do not interfere. If you do, they will end up harmed, though it will be by no one's fault but yours."

Flashes of blue and silver and black, a woman—black haired and blue eyed—clad in medieval garb. More flashes. Memories of a life lived long ago filled Cojiñí's head, moving through her mind fast enough to blur her thoughts and sight. Somehow, as this happened, she knew a similar experience was happening to all the others.

Her midnight eyes flickered open slowly to see the ceiling. It was a very boring ceiling, she decided, compared to the ones she had seen before Camlann.

She sat up slowly, realising as she did that her clothes had changed. Pity, she had liked the Raven costume. However, her new ensemble was more practical than the black feather-covered, wing-collared, feather-caped gown she'd been wearing. As she stood, she catalogued her clothes. Knee-high black leather boots, practically—yet appropriately snug—black trousers, deep-blue split-skirted high-collared long-sleeved dress, black leather belt. No ring? Then she remembered the small bags that Barhaol had given her and her brother, and summoned hers from the mid-space. Inside was a silver-and-blue Celtic ring, which she slipped onto her wedding finger. It fit perfectly, and she smiled. Then she continued with her mental checklist of herself. Hair braided up and back, good. Keeping it like that kept it out of the way.

The caramel-skinned young woman turned her gaze to her companions. Her brother was arrayed the same as she, though his robe was green instead of blue. The purple stripe in their dark-green-eyed friend's dark-blond hair had changed to icy blue, and he was clad in robes of white and silver and pale blue. Their ginger-haired friend was clad in green, nearly the same shade as Scoruș' robe, but he was wearing a tunic of a bard's cut, with a deep brown leather jerkin. Their black-haired friend's clothing had not changed much—black leather under silver chainmaille under a dark grey surcoat. Their red-gold-haired friend's garb had changed a fair bit. He was arrayed in chain-maille and red, a crown on his head and a scarlet cape emblazoned with a golden dragon streaming from his shoulders.

Their female friends were clad similar to the midnight-eyed young woman in modest split-skirted dresses of varying colours, though none had the particular runic embroidery that was on her hem.

She made eye contact with Barhaol. "Are we still who we were, or are we who we were in times gone by?"

It chuckled slightly, drawing everyone's attention to It. "Yes to both. Your identities are the same as they were most recently, though you have the memories and skills of who you were in times gone by. Those who had been will make their presence known from time to time, however, and in times of great need, may become more prominent so as to nearly completely become you. Do you all understand?"

Cojiñí-Morgaine nodded, followed by Scoruş-Myrddin, Gareth-Vortigern, Ivan-Lancelot, Alezandra-Branwen, Ashton-Arthur, Catrina-Gwenhwyfar, Lea-Nimue, Mae-Aderyn, Rae-Elaine, and Kennedy-Taliesin. She glanced at the ginger-haired young man, but looked away quickly, and closed her eyes momentarily, locking that particular part of Morgaine's memory deep in her mind where she could not access it accidentally or with ease. She did not need to deal with her feelings about Kennedy with Morgaine's similar feelings towards Taliesin complicating things even further. The fact that the two had been married in the time gone by should not, would not affect her in the present, when he had no clue that she liked him as more than a friend, and she was intending for it to stay that way, at least for now. Either way, that did not matter at the moment.

Scoruş rolled his shoulders slightly to get even more comfortable in his robes and tunic. He flicked his hand, and his staff appeared from the mid-space, causing him to blink. He flicked his hand again, and returned it to that timeless, spaceless void.

The midnight-eyed young man turned to Barhaol. "What are we to do now?"

At the question, everyone turned from examining each other's new garments to look at the pale semi-translucent figure.

Ashton stepped forward—Arthur coming to the forefront as far as Scoruş could tell—and he felt Myrddin rising in response to the actions of his friend. At that, the raven-haired young man realised that with Myrddin's memories combined with his, he was closer to the sky-blue-eyed young man than he would have been otherwise. Absently in less than a second, he wondered what would have happened with them had this not happened—but then he turned his attention back to Barhaol, who had begun to speak.

"What you will do now is train and become accustomed to having other, elder people in your minds at every moment of the day and night. The battle is coming and I know that no one wants it to end the way the Battle of Camlann ended, neither in the legends, nor in reality."

Everyone nodded vigorously and It continued.

"Morgause and Mordred are finding their allies and they are all older than you eleven by at least a year, in Taliesin's case, and four years in Elaine's case. Even with the added muscle and mind memory, you will need the two years you have to return to the peak you were at just before Camlann."

Its gaze passed between Cojiñí and Kennedy. "While the memories from the time gone by are fresh now, they should not interfere in the decisions you make now, especially in the matter of relationships. While you have who you were in your minds and sometimes, when needed, bodies, you are still different people now. The choices you make should be your own."

Speech concluded, Barhaol disappeared, leaving the eleven teens and five adults standing in the living room of flat number 332C.

* * *

Cenric sparred with one of Morgause's captured men as she watched. He dispatched the other man in less than fifteen minutes, and she smiled, her ocean-toned eyes sparkling.

Her brother approached and began to speak, but a chiming alarm sounded. The pale-golden-haired twins looked up and grinned, then teleported out of the room.

Cenric sighed, signalled some of Morgause's constructed servants to clean up the body of the man who had been his opponent, and began the walk to where his wife and her brother had the contraption they had built to find the rest of their allies and alert them when it did so.

When he arrived at the room, his Morgause was jotting down in her elegant script the locations indicated by the contraption and the names of the ally or allies that were there as Mordred called them out. A few moments after Cenric stepped through the door, Morgause finished off the location and name with a flourish.

"So, all found then?"

They turned to look at him, and Morgause nodded. "Yes they are, my Black King, and soon Mordred will be off to fetch them."

"Wonderful."

She smiled radiantly and walked forwards, her heels clicking on the stone floor. He backed up, smirking, then turned and took off like a shot towards their room, chuckling at her little growl—her inability to run while in heels. Then there was a pause in the clicking of her shoes and Cenric looked back, only to run harder at the sight of her literally flying towards him, smirking mischievously.

* * *

Aidan stood up from his desk and stretched, then left his office. He was so glad the day was over. Now it was time for tea with James and perhaps Araunya. Their daily tea meetings had petered out after six months or so, and he missed them. They had been fun, at least most of the time. Glancing at his watch, he decided to wait for tea and stop off at the grocery. They were out of milk again, and James would be frustrated with him if he had to do the shopping *again*. Maybe, while he was out, he could find a good Christmas present for Araunya...and presents for James and the twins too, of course. The holiday celebrating Jesus' birth was a week and a half away. Araunya liked birds, right? And he had seen her wearing jewellery at the church they went to.

After the curly-haired man bought the milk, he went into a trinket shop a few blocks from the church. He browsed a few moments then his eyes landed on something in a display case that seemed to have Araunya's name written all over it in bold neon flashing lights. It was a necklace, a pendant on a simple dark-silvery chain, perfectly ordinary. But it was the pendant that caught Aidan's eye. A pair of small ravens with gold eyes—worked in onyx or something else black and shiny—spread-winged and caught in a dive.

He looked more closely at the pendant. Yes, it was exactly what he was looking for. Someone approached and the green-gold-eyed man looked up to see the shopkeeper, a short woman, with peroxide-blonde hair and greyish eyes. Those eyes were fixed on the top of his head. She'd been waiting for him to notice her.

Aidan stood straight and gestured at the necklace. "How much?"

The shopkeeper looked at the necklace, then back at Aidan. "One hundred pounds."

The tall, lanky man shrugged and turned his eyes to the necklace. Not bad for something of that detail, in black onyx and gold. He looked back at the shopkeeper. "I'll take it."

The woman nodded, and called to one of her employees in another part of the shop. "Rose!"

A young woman appeared, no older than twenty-three. Her hair was dyed-blonde, similar to the shopkeeper's, but done more recently since there were no roots showing. Her golden-brown eyes were keen. She had a runner's form, Aidan noticed, and the flecks of gold in her eyes spoke of something otherworldly and ancient. Nah, he tossed that thought away. Seeing that the twins and their friends had beings of legend residing within them was messing with his mind.

The shopkeeper turned to Aidan. "Rose will assist you in completing your purchase." She walked away.

He followed the young woman to the register where she rang up the purchase. After he paid and she was wrapping the pendant in tissue paper, she asked, "Is it a gift for someone?"

Her accent was London, he noticed, with a hint of cockney that seemed to have faded. The voice sounded a bit more cultured.

Aidan nodded. "One of my friends. Araunya Balaur. She works at the police station...." He trailed off, and Rose inclined her head.

"I've seen her a few times, I think. Is she the one with black hair, caramel skin, and eyes like a winter sky?"

"Yeah, that's her."

"Lucky woman to receive a gift like this. Any reason other than Christmas?"

He shook his head. "Nope."

"Hmm." Rose looked thoughtful for a moment, in the manner of someone lost in memories. Then she returned to the present and handed him the small bag containing the purchase. Aidan saw the faint glow in her eyes dim slightly. "Here you go. Have a good day!" she said cheerfully, and with that obvious dismissal, he left.

He had milk to get in the fridge. He would do the rest of the Christmas shopping later.

* * *

Khulai was at a loss, a complete and utter loss. He and Tara had started courting about the middle of November and he had absolutely no clue what to get her for a Christmas gift. Yes, they had been friends for as long as he could remember, but they had never gotten each other Christmas gifts before, usually sticking to cards. And when she was his apprentice, he would often give her a few days off from training to do whatever she wanted, but that did not translate to giving her a Christmas gift as a girlfriend, and by the look of things, probable fiancée.

He wracked his brain and when he disappointedly came up with nothing, he reluctantly settled on Plan B. Ask her parents. He had met her parents multiple times—most recently when she presented him to them as the man courting her—but he had no idea how to ask them what to get her for Christmas. Luckily, her birthday was in February.

Righty-o, then. Plan B settled on, the tall man began his trek to Tara's parents' house. Their home was a simple, single-floor building that and suited Aishe Greenheart and Camlo Ashaxe perfectly.

* * *

Book Club had just ended for the evening and people were starting to go home. Cojiñí, Kennedy, and Scoruș were talking about something or other when Gareth walked up to the ginger-haired young man with a date-stamp in his hand, though no one really noticed it until he had finished speaking.

"Hey Kennedy, you should date Cojiñí."

Cojiñí blushed, the feeling was emphasised when Kennedy said, "No, I don't like inking people."

Later that evening, the black-haired girl felt like hitting something—hard. In her brain, she knew Kennedy most likely viewed her only as a friend, but her heart had decided that it wanted to be *hopeful* about the fact that he didn't say he *didn't* want to date her. And that made her very frustrated—no—angry with herself. That's why she wanted to hit something in a very forceful manner.

Of course she solved that problem by doing just that—going to their mid-space training room and animating five of the training dummies to attack her all at once. Morgaine was not helping at all by reminding her that she and Taliesin had been married in the time gone by.

That was where Araunya found her, in a whirlwind of blade and staff and magic battling of seven training dummies as if her life depended on it. The winter-eyed woman frowned deeply, and with a flick of her finger, severed the tendrils of magic animating the badly beaten-up constructs. She approached the panting girl.

"Cojiñí, is something wrong?"

The midnight-eyed older-than-her-years sixteen-year-old young woman sank to the floor, dropped her sword and staff, and put her head in her hands. Araunya read this correctly as an affirmation of her guess, so knelt and put one arm around the girl.

"What is it, my little Rose?"

Cojiñí looked up, then fixed her eyes on the wall. She told her Aunt Araunya everything, from the thing with the song, and the thing with the other song, the one she wrote, to Morgaine and Taliesin's being married in the time gone by, to the thing that night with the talk about dating and inking, or lack thereof.

Araunya's lips pursed in thought. She had no idea what to say to her niece. No clue about relationships whatsoever.

"Umm...honestly, there is nothing I can say, Cojiñí. I'm sorry."

"That is okay, Aunt. I feel better having told you. But I have a request."

"What is that?"

"Please don't tell anyone else. Alezandra and Mae know, but that's it."

Araunya nodded. "I assume you don't want him to know?"

"That is correct. I don't want to ruin our friendship if this turns out not to be."

"That's very wise of you."

"Thanks." The midnight-eyed young woman said, "I'm hungry."

Araunya chuckled, and they left the mid-space and returned to their kitchen. Cojiñí made herself a sandwich, grabbing a few pretzels from the bag on the counter on the way.

The days passed rapidly and monotonously, except for a particularly nasty storm. Christmas drew nearer. Aidan and James took the twins Christmas shopping on a day when they didn't have school because of sick staff. And when Araunya was working.

Cojiñí used her dexterity and *slight* talent for knots to fashion bracelets for her friends at the Book Club—Alezandra, her best friend, as well as Kennedy, Rae, Mae, Lea, Ivan, Gareth, Ashton, and Catrina. She had something special picked out for her brother and she knew for certain he would like because she liked it and they had similar taste in that sort of thing.

Khulai finally settled on something to get Tara, and more importantly, permission from both of her parents. He was planning to give her an engagement ring, if she would accept it...and him. True, they had been courting for a only a short while, but he felt it was what he should do, even though he knew they were not *quite* ready to be wedded yet. Tara still had to purchase Khulai's gift, but she had the very thing chosen.

Araunya had gotten things for their neighbours that she was pretty sure they would like, though James' gift was also a bit of a test. When she met him, she had been sure she had seen him before somewhere, and being around him nearly every day had only enhanced that feeling. Now, after about two years living in the flat across from the grey-eyed, sandy-haired man had made her almost completely certain where she knew him from. The question now was, was her assumption correct, or was it just a case of a mistaken face, voice, and manner? His reaction to her gift would prove her right or wrong.

Cenric, Morgause, and Mordred had their presents for each other 'purchased,' and Mordred had figured out exactly where their allies could be found. He knew his sister would be glad of that, just as he was.

* * *

Professors Chaput and Baudin had talked to the twins and Aidan, and had entered them as a special act of the school's Christmas Program. They would be showcasing a few of the skills that the two Dance, Music, and Drama Professors had taught during the past year. Because of this, they were exempt from the Christmas play their grade would be performing. They were also handwringingly nervous, and practiced almost every day in the mid-space so that there would be no way for them to mess up.

The day of the performance came, and the twins were so nervous they were hopping from foot to foot backstage. The Professors had scheduled them as the last act of the program, which just made their nervousness increase as each act finished.

Cojiñí absently smoothed her black leotard and mid-thigh-length flowy skirt. She stretched her legs and arms as Scoruș stretched and made sure that his white violin was tuned. Neither of them was going to sing this time, as neither of them felt they were ready. They would each dance and play the instrument they specialised in. Scoruș would start by playing the violin he had borrowed from Professor Baudin, while Cojiñí danced. Then, as smoothly as they could, they would switch to Scoruș dancing to Cojiñí's organ playing.

While not technically a *pipe* organ, the organ sitting just offstage was set up to sound like one, and after trying it out the day before with a tune she had picked up from a pirate movie, the midnight-eyed young woman declared it close enough that no one would notice. Especially if it was disguised just right, a thing done easily enough.

The last act before theirs drew to a close and the twins were surprised to note that they were not as nervous anymore. Instead, now they were filled with a sort of cool confidence. They would perform, and they would do their best. Not only did they want to make the professors proud, and prove that the two adults had not been wasting their time, the raven-haired twins had *personal* reasons to do their best that evening. The entirety of Book Club was in the audience, which meant Kennedy and Alezandra were in the audience.

The student chosen as announcer—a student graduating at the end of the semester—began to speak, and the twins took their places to enter the stage.

Cojiñí closed her eyes and took a deep breath, letting it out slowly. At her side, she could hear her brother doing the same. While not at the skill to dance *en pointe,* ballet was something she was fairly good at, as was Scoruș. They would not fall. And in her opinion, her brother was excellent at playing the violin, which made her a bit jealous. She knew she would never have any talent with that instrument.

Distantly, as if in a dream, she heard the announcer say, "Welcome to Scoruș and Cojiñí Balaur!"

Showtime. She took another deep breath as the announcer came backstage and clapped them both on the shoulder. "Good luck."

They nodded in response, unable to do anything else.

Scoruș walked onstage and Cojiñí took her place just out of sight. The violin rose and landed gently on her brother's shoulder, the bow gently touched the strings, and she stepped onto the stage as the first strains of "O Holy Night" began to play.

Gareth watched as his friend glided on stage and in the back of his mind was glad he had shifted his romantic focus to Lea, due to the looks he had been receiving from Cojiñí. The girl seemed to have her gaze somewhere else—more in the direction of another friend of theirs, one with flame-ginger hair. It was clear, however, that the midnight-eyed young woman most definitely did not wish for said flame-haired friend to know, most likely on the basis that he was a friend, and she did not want to ruin that, something that Gareth could understand very well. Until Lea had smacked him to the back of the head for being so silly. Vortigern and Nimue had been married, and so if Gareth and Lea wanted to date, then there would be no problem whatsoever—that was her logic and he would not argue with her.

Either way, he could still admire Cojiñí's dancing. She flowed from one position to the next, and though ballet was not his forte, he could see that she had put a lot of effort into making sure that this would be as perfect as she could get it, and he expected no less from both her and her brother.

Lea was of the same mind as her boyfriend, though she had never fancied Scoruş. She was the one who had pointed out Cojiñí's fancying of Kennedy. All by himself, however, he had figured out that the raven-haired young woman did not want anyone to know.

There was no real pattern to Cojiñí's dancing that Lea could see, though her knowledge of ballet was limited. However, the grey-eyed young woman could see certain sets of motion reappearing throughout the dancing, particularly in the section of music that was clearly the chorus. No matter what was repeated when, Lea thought that Cojiñí was doing beautifully, and looked the same. The black of her ensemble perfectly complimented her caramel skin, midnight blue eyes, and raven hair. Although she—before "merging" with Nimue, who was technically herself from a time gone by—did not have the best fashion sense in the eyes of others, she knew what looked good on people and could easily tell what was fashionable. That didn't mean she had to dress in that manner—if she chose not to.

Still, she thought that only a fool would think that Cojiñí did not look at least pretty at that moment, dancing to the tune of her brother's violin on that stage.

Suddenly, Scoruş stopped playing, and set down the white violin. Cojiñí spun to sit on the bench of an organ that seemed to have appeared out of nowhere at just that moment. She began to play, "Sing We Now of Christmas."

* * *

The midnight-eyed young man moved just as gracefully as his sister had, as her fingers danced across the two rows of keys. Though he danced in the same style as his sister, and though the manner in which the two danced were indeed very similar, it was clear that they were most definitely not dancing the same way. The faster tempo of the song made that obvious.

Although she would never even think about leaving Gareth, it did not mean that she had any problem admiring the strength and grace Scoruș displayed.

* * *

Eventually the song and the dance drew to a close, and the twins took centre stage and bowed, faces resembling tomatoes due to the sheer volume of the applause. After a few moments, they could not bear it any longer and disappeared through the curtains into backstage.

Chapter 14

A FEW DAYS LATER, DURING CHRISTMAS BREAK, Scoruș walked rapidly through the halls of the city's Swim and Rec Centre on his way to the pool to join Cojiñí, Gareth, and Lea. He literally ran into Alezandra.

"Oh! I'm sorry. I wasn't looking where I was going."

She smiled. "It's fine. I wasn't looking either."

"Ah."

They stood there for a few moments, then manoeuvred around each other and continued on to their respective destinations.

Eventually, the two met up again, this time in the swimming pool. While Alezandra was employed there as a lifeguard, it just so happened that it was her day off, so she joined the members of Book Club having fun in the pool.

It seemed to be swimming day for People Who Have Been Pseudo-Reincarnated, because soon the five of them were joined by Ashton, Catrina, Ivan, Mae, Rae, and Kennedy. For some odd reason, they were the only ones in the pool, but that suited the group of eleven just fine, at least for the moment. Then something happened that was very interesting.

They were all horsing around, and Scoruș leapt at Cojiñí playfully. However, in mid-air he...shifted. Without going through any process of intermediate change, Scoruș was now a large, black, midnight-eyed, winged lion. Suddenly, whatever had affected him hit his twin sister, and she became the same, though still female.

Testing out their new wings, and with the muscle memory that told them that Myrddin and Morgaine had been able to change into the same animals, the twins flew out of the pool and landed clumsily, where they sat like a pair of wingéd sphynxes.

The rest of the group stared, then all of a sudden, they changed too, in the same manner. Where once floated Mae, was now a sleek Bengal tiger, a pair of hawk wings sprouting from its shoulders. And where Kennedy had stood a few paces away, a beautiful falcon-winged panther treaded water—its coat was an unusual shade for the large cat, but it was the same colour as Kennedy's flame-ginger hair. The two of them joined their friends at the side of the pool as they observed the changes the rest of the group was going through.

Gareth and Lea were now a pair of ice-white wolves equipped with magnificent swan wings. Ashton had become a golden gryphon, and Catrina the same in pale grey. Ivan was an inky-black jaguar, a pair of white-tipped wings arching above his back. Rae was an eagle-winged leopard. And like Kennedy, Alezandra became a panther, except of the usual shade, but her wings were those of a raven, like the twins.

On a whim, the two winged lions extended tendrils of magic to attach to their friends, and entered their mid-space training room.

Kennedy-Taliesin, the wingéd panther, was intrigued by his first teleportation in this incarnation. He conveniently, and with some difficulty, ignored the warm, familiar feeling of the midnight-eyed young woman's magic twining around his, towing him along through the mid-space.

The large room in which they arrived was undoubtedly a training centre of some kind. One wall was lined with seamless tall mirrors. A martial arts mat was folded against another wall, and a very large cabinet, most likely full of neatly organised weapons, was next to the mat. On a fairly long rack hung ten wooden fighting dummies.

It was indeed unusual to have six limbs, he decided as he stretched his wings and padded a few steps forward in a not-completely-fruitless effort to become accustomed to the sensation of being on four legs and having those great, feathered extra arms attached to his back. Having a tail was strange as well, the ginger-haired young male wingéd panther thought as he swished his tail back and forth a few times, trying it out.

Out of the corner of his eye, he saw the rest of his friends doing the same things, though a few were starting to fly around the room. On a whim, Kennedy ran a few steps, and then leapt into the air, his powerful wings beating hard. He shot up like a large, furry arrow and, tucking his feet under him, began to soar in a slow spiral.

The ginger panther was soon joined in circling the training room by another wingéd panther of normal colour and a pair of black wingéd lions. And after that, it was only a short time before they were all looping and cavorting in the air above the training room floor, having the time of their lives.

Eventually however, they grew weary, and as they had not built up enough endurance in their wings to fly for very long, the eleven combination-creatures settled on the ground once more, flopping as they landed. Kennedy did not realise that Cojiñí had settled down next to him until she started purring in his ear. He did not physically jump, but the sudden rumbling noise startled him.

Casting a glance around the circle into which they had assembled, the chocolate-eyed panther realised that they had, in a sense, grouped themselves within their group. Ashton and Catrina were beside each other, and slightly closer together than the next group of two—Gareth and Lea. After that, it was harder to determine the mini-groups but Ivan and Mae seemed to have gravitated towards each other, along with Scoruș and Alezandra. Rae was not particularly close to anyone, but she seemed perfectly fine with that. That left him and Cojiñí. The two of them seemed as far apart from each other as were Ivan and Mae, and Scoruș and Alezandra. Hmm. Now, was that her doing, or his? He had no idea.

Kennedy reached within himself to where Taliesin's memories told him his magical core was, and looked for what he should do to turn back into a humanoid form. When that search proved useless, he searched his memories. That expedition produced results. Basically, all he had to do was focus on how it felt to be human, and send out a slight magical pulse, and his magic would do the rest. He did as his memories suggested, and felt himself shift.

The change from wingéd panther to human was sudden because his body did not go through any intermediate process. It just was one, and then in a blink, was the other.

The others were giving him looks, so Kennedy explained what he had done, and where he learned how to do it, then watched as they did the same. When they were all human-shaped again, he asked the question that had been on his mind for the past few minutes.

"So, what happened that made us change like that?"

The question was directed at the two most magically knowledgeable of the eleven magicals—or semi-magicals—in the room, and they looked at each other, then shrugged.

In unison, they replied, "We have no idea, though we could ask Barhaol."

The others looked at them oddly, so the twins elaborated. "The ghostly figure that unlocked us from times gone by."

"Ah."

"How would you contact...Barhaol?"

The twins looked at each other again. "Usually, It contacts us, but we can attempt to get a hold of It telepathically."

As soon as they finished talking, the raven-haired duo closed their eyes and Kennedy-Taliesin could nearly feel their minds reaching out, searching for the mental signature of Barhaol. It took a few long moments of waiting, but eventually their midnight eyes opened.

"It's coming here. It would be easier to explain this in person."

Kennedy nodded, and they waited.

After what felt like a very long while, but was really only a few minutes, the ghostly figure of indeterminate gender appeared, looking exactly the same as It always did. It observed the circle of teens and looked through what had just happened. Ah. So that was why it was summoned.

Sitting down between Its children, Barhaol chuckled. "You became animals because I thought it was time for you to know of another facet of who you are and were."

Raising a hand to stall questions, It continued, "The animals you became are merely...combinations of the others you can become."

It gestured at the twins. "For example, they can become black lions or ravens in addition to what they are now. With practice, they will also be able to turn into black-coated housecats." It paused for a moment. "Also, with practice, all of you will be able to take on physical characteristics of whatever animal you can turn into, when you so choose to, without going through the full transformation."

It saw them nod, and felt their understanding. Good. Now It could go back to attempting to locate Morgause and Mordred. Without a word of farewell, It disappeared back into the mid-space.

* * *

Later that day, Cojiñí and Scoruș sat on the roof of the building in which their flat was located, looking like a pair of gargoyles, since they were in their wingéd lion forms. The reasons they would say they were up there were that they wanted to become accustomed to the forms, and because the stars were pretty that night. However, neither of them really knew the other was there, and they both were up there to be alone and to think. Ironically, what they wanted to think about was essentially the same thing—certain people that they knew.

It was becoming more difficult to tell whether or not it was Morgaine and Myrddin's emotions towards Taliesin and Branwen that were affecting Cojiñí and Scoruș' feelings towards Kennedy and Alezandra. The twins were worried that the feelings from the time gone by were overpowering the ones from now, and they had no way of knowing how to tell.

Cojiñí's thoughts drifted towards Kennedy the person, as opposed to the problem about which emotions she felt, and she unconsciously began to purr softly. Then, all of a sudden, a voice, older than her own and yet very similar, spoke up in her mind.

'I see you need a bit of assistance, my dear.'

Cojiñí was so startled that she stopped purring and shifted back to human form.

'Who are you, and why are you in my mind?'

The voice seemed amused. It had a Welsh accent a fair bit thicker than Cojiñí's own. *'I am Morgaine, my dear.'* The voice paused for a moment. *'Is there any name in particular that you would prefer me to use when referring to you, my dear?'*

The sixteen-year-old thought for a moment. *'You can just call me Cojiñí.'*

She got the feeling that Morgaine was nodding, though the "her" from times gone by was technically just a voice in her head. *'The Rose. A good name, fitting for us. Beautiful, and yet dangerous.'*

Cojiñí frowned. She had never thought of it like that. *'You said you would help me.'*

'Yes, I did. If you would like, since we are technically two people merged and melded into one, I can, if you wish, partition off from your forward mind my feelings and emotions from when I was me and not you.'

Cojiñí did not need any thought to answer. *'If it is not offensive to you, I would very much like that.'*

Morgaine chuckled. *'If it was offensive to me, dear little Rose, I would not have offered.'*

That said, Morgaine went silent, and Cojiñí felt something in her mind alter slightly.

After a few moments, Morgaine spoke again. *'It is done. Does that answer your question from earlier?'*

Cojiñí searched through her feelings. Some of what she had been feeling towards Kennedy was overflow from Morgaine's attachment to Taliesin, but not exactly as much as she had thought. *'Yes, it does. Thank you, Morgaine.'*

Again the internal sensation of the other nodding. *'Very well then, if you do not mind, I will, in that case, be returning to sleep. Fare thee well, my dear Rose.'*

And then the sensation of having someone else within her mind faded away. Cojiñí could still feel it slightly, but it was much less prominent than it had been when Morgaine was talking.

Right, so not all of her feelings towards Kennedy were from Morgaine. She already knew that, but not to the extent it turned out to be. Interesting thing to learn.

She sat for a few more minutes, having transformed back into her wingéd lion form. She stared at the stars, then decided it was time for bed. So she spread her wings and soared carefully through her open bedroom window, transforming back to a humanoid as she landed. She did not know her brother had just gone through a very similar experience on the other side of the roof and was on his way across the roof to his own window.

* * *

Christmas came, bringing with it more snow and icy roads. The group of friends and the adults decided to have their Christmas party in one of the empty schoolrooms, and though it took a bit of time, everyone managed to get there safely.

James made a few varieties of pie, even experimenting with a meat one that of course everyone liked, being that it was James' cooking. The twins were certain he could make the foods they liked least and they would still enjoy them, that's how good his cooking and baking skills were. When they told him that, he dipped his head and shrugged. Even though he had enough talent to be otherwise, he was a modest and humble man.

After everyone had eaten, and Aidan read the Christmas story, the opening of presents began. Lea volunteered to be the one to hand out the presents and they let her.

Aidan was first to open his gift and he grinned broadly at the set of new microscope slides and petri dishes from Scoruş. He liked his experiments.

The green-gold-eyed man was followed by Gareth, who, as soon as he took it out of the box, slipped the leather wristband on that Lea had gotten him, eyes sparkling like deep emeralds. After Gareth came Ivan, who smiled wide enough to show teeth when he saw the carved-ebony pendant from Mae.

Lea was next and she leaped up and hugged Gareth hard enough that Araunya thought she could hear a rib creak. He'd given her a silver swan necklace. The next present Lea handed out went to Alezandra, and was from Scoruş.

Araunya thought she could see the raven-haired young man holding his breath as the green-eyed young woman unwrapped the present and held it up. It was a t-shirt, ocean-blue with a curly-haired mermaid with green eyes on the front. She smiled at him, and Araunya was amused to note that he blushed.

Then came her gift for James, and she watched for his reaction. He slowly removed the wrapping paper, careful not to harm the box, then pulled a folding knife from his pocket to slice the tape holding the box closed. The sandy-haired man's grey eyes narrowed at the sight of the contents. Araunya smirked as he pulled it from the confines of its container. It was a dagger, long and slender, made for both throwing and regular fighting, with a blood-red hilt. It was made in a way that if you pressed one of the small gems on the pommel, it would transform into a pistol, fully loaded every time. When she first saw it used, she was certain that it was somehow connected to a mid-space pocket full of bullets, and that assumption was reinforced now.

James' face conveyed all that Araunya needed to know. He was who she thought he was—Captain Jamison Andrews of the Mercenaries Guard. The Mercenaries Guard were not actual mercenaries, but they were named so because of their willingness to use brutal and up-close methods when needed. They were also used as assassins sometimes, as well as soldiers. Additionally, they were the division of the military that dealt with the things of the magical world.

Araunya had been one of them once upon a time, though she never used her real name or her real appearance. Instead, she chose to be a redhead named Adara Baldwin, although she did not change her voice or accent. She was younger then, and her personal mission was to find and rescue her brother's stolen son and daughter.

She met James on their first assignment. Yes, they had seen each other before—but that assignment was when they first spoke to each other and learned each other's names. His hair was shorter then—a buzz-cut—and his eyes were brighter, but everyone's eyes changed after a war or the missions they were given. He was younger then, too, just twenty-two. She had been twenty at the time.

Their first assignment as part of the Mercenaries Guard was to retrieve the dagger, known for some reason as Tân, or The Fire. That was the dagger he was holding now.

It was supposed to have been an easy mission, as they were just starting, but complications arose. Their com system failure was the first sign that they were getting into deeper water than they had expected. The bubble of restraining magic that surrounded them the next moment only defined that certainty, and the construct guards that encircled them the moment following solidified it.

The constructs relieved them of their weapons and bound their hands before leading them off to one of the many labyrinthine halls in the underground 'lair' where the dagger was supposed to be kept. The only thing that could be viewed as good in that situation was that the constructs led them directly to the chamber that contained the dagger.

The problem was that there were at least fifty constructs and just two of them, not to mention the person sitting on the throne-like chair beside the dagger's case. He was darkly handsome and pale, clad in an obviously expensive tailored suit. His eyes were covered by a pair of costly sunglasses, and when he took them off and smirked at them, Araunya was surprised—and not—to see that the irises were the colour of freshly spilled blood. A vampire, and by the feel of his aura, a powerful one. They were in way over their heads.

The constructs brought them over to the vampire and forced them down onto their knees. Araunya stared at the ground, formulating a plan to escape. If they could not get a hold of the Tân, they would return later with a larger group. And, if they could retrieve it, well then, mission accomplished.

Righty-o then. Constructs could be dispatched just the same as people, however there were too many to combat them all one-by-one. If she used her magic, she could at least take out a few at a time. And because she and Agent Andrews had never worked together before, he probably had a few tricks up his sleeve that would assist the two of them.

Tentatively, because some vampires had an extremely high sensitivity to telepathy, Araunya reached out towards Andrews' mind.

She felt the connection, but all he did was blink and send a query along the temporary link.

'You're telepathic, Agent Baldwin?'

She nodded mentally. 'Yes, well, technically I'm magical.'

'What level?'

'Mage.'

She sensed a mental nod coming from him, then he said, 'I assume, since you contacted me, you have a plan?'

'Not completely. I have one in the making, however.'

Another mental nod, and the link went quiet for a few moments. Araunya waited patiently, and soon enough, the sandy-haired young man spoke up silently once again.

'I assume, because of your rank, you can take out at least five of them at a time?'

'Yes.'

'If you can distract them for long enough, I have been told that I am fairly quick, and I should be able to get a hold of the Tân and return to you swiftly enough for you to teleport us out.'

She was about to reply, but then the vampire on the throne began to speak. He has a very nice voice, the currently-red-haired young woman thought. It took a mental jolt from Agent Andrews to get her back in her own mind. Blast it! The vampire was a Hypnotic!

There were at least three types of vampires, and they all had the same choices as humans in the matters of good or evil. They were said to have souls, but most took the easy path and chose to let Darkness and sin take control of them, eventually leading to their burning in Hell for eternity once they were returned to dust by whomever managed to remove their heads, stake them in the heart, or slay them with magical weapons. Vampires are not repelled by garlic, nor does sunlight destroy them. However, strong sunlight will weaken them and if nothing else, it is painful unless they had a shielding ring or amulet.

Hypnotics, which as their name suggests, hypnotise their prey before doing whatever they want to the mind-controlled person. Telepathically inclined, they hold the middle ground between the other types of vampires she knew of. Then there were the Predators, relying on their highly enhanced strength and speed to capture those they wish to feed off or "play" with. Those are the least telepathically sensitive of all vampires, and a sharp bolt of highly focussed harmful thought can knock one out. Finally, there are the "stereotypical" or "traditional" vampires—a combination of the Hypnotics and the Predators, with strong power for mind-to-mind conversation and viewing through others' eyes. They are known as the Overlords, and are the most telepathically powerful of the three. Dracula was said to be one of the Overlords.

Araunya was glad this vampire was only a Hypnotic, but it could prove very difficult to deal with if she didn't get her most powerful mental shields up immediately—without the red-eyed man noticing, which luckily she managed to do. Still, as he continued to speak, his power slammed against her shields. He was a powerful vampire, and had at least enough magic to animate constructs, which, while not requiring a whole lot of power, took much concentration and finesse.

"I see my constructs have brought me some new ones."

He stood and walked forwards a few steps, taking Araunya's chin in his cold hand and raising her face so that he could look at her properly.

"You're pretty. I think I'll keep you awhile. What is your name, woman?"

Playing the weak card for now, Araunya cast down her eyes and said softly, "Adara Baldwin."

"Hmm." The vampire stepped back and lounged once more in his throne-like chair. "You may call me Master Quirinus."

Quirinus, a Medieval Latin name meaning "spear"—now she knew who he was, and behind her shields, her thoughts grew dark with anger and resentment. This was the vampire that killed Camlo Lightfoot, her grandfather's brother, the last of the IMIH Ward Heads, not to mention he also killed her best friend's favourite uncle. She would be glad if he was one that died that day.

She sent a signal to Agent Andrews before casting out a powerful burst of magic to the front and side of her, sending a good deal of the constructs flying back and tossing a few onto Quirinus himself. When she did that, Agent Andrews shot up from where he had been kneeling and sped towards the Tân faster than she could have thought possible for a non-magical. Perhaps he was not fully without magic after all.

The currently-red-haired young woman cast another burst to knock the rest of the constructs back and pulled her Mage-staff and sword from the mid-space. Quirinus pulled a gleaming rapier from his belt and the deadly dance began.

Araunya lost track of time as they fought, but soon the combination of the more experienced vampire and the forty or so constructs attacking her all at once wore her down.

She heard a shout of surprise from Agent Andrews and she looked over. He had the Tân in his hand, a webbing of blood-red magic twining around him from the hilt of the dagger all the way up his forearm, spreading rapidly. He depressed a gem on the pommel and the dagger shifted into a double-barrelled sharpshooter's pistol. The grey-eyed man grinned viciously as the webbing reached the base of his head, and he pointed the barrel directly at two of the constructs and pulled the trigger. The constructs crumpled. Less than a second later, two more fell to his bullets.

Unfortunately, the few moments it took for Araunya to see what Agent Andrews was doing nearly cost her life as Quirinus stabbed towards her heart from behind. Luckily, she sidestepped at just the right moment to dodge a falling construct, and the rapier did not hit anything vital. She spun around as he yanked the sword from her torso, and then swung her own sword at him as she cast a quick healing and numbing cantrip on herself to keep her going—at least until they could return to base.

Suddenly, the point of a dagger appeared between the vampire's ribs, and he crumpled to dust. Araunya looked up to see Andrews standing there, the web of magic having spread to form a hood before becoming unseen.

They returned to the base, and it was revealed that the Tân had bonded itself to Andrews, who asked Araunya to call him Jamison. So she did.

Over the next few years, Jamison became more and more possessive

of that dagger-gun, and much more vicious in dealing with the targets they were forced to slay. That worried him, and a few weeks after he had been promoted to Captain, he left the Mercenaries Guard, giving the Tân to Araunya with instructions to keep it for him. She left not long after that.

Throughout her time of having the Tân, Araunya discovered that it would bond to only one person, and that there were ways of keeping that person from going mad with bloodlust and the lack of morals that the construction of metal and magic had. She had learned those ways, just in case, and now she was planning to use them.

James looked at Araunya, at the dagger-gun in his hands, and back at Araunya. Finally, he spoke. "Adara Baldwin?"

Araunya smiled and her form shifted to the red haired, fair-skinned, pale-eyed woman he'd had as a partner during his brief stint as part of the Mercenaries Guard, then she shifted back.

"Yes, Jamison. I was Adara Baldwin for a few years, but Araunya Balaur is who I really am."

"Ah." He pointed the hilt of the dagger at her. "We will talk later."

She nodded, and the passing out of presents resumed.

The next present was for Kennedy, from Cojiñí. It was a pair of knotted bracelets made of embroidery thread—one green, blue, and black, strung with red beads; the other green and two shades of blue, strung with blue beads. He smiled and she returned the expression, spots of pink appearing high on her cheekbones.

After that, the presents flowed to their recipients and eventually they had opened everything.

Everyone went home that night happy, full of James' excellent cooking and Tara's apple cider. James, Araunya, and Aidan stayed up late talking about the Tân, and their past, what the winter-eyed woman had learned about the Tân, and how to control the bloodlust and madness that came with being bonded with it. Cojiñí and Scoruş were up on the roof in their wingéd lion forms during that discussion.

* * *

In the mansion in the mountains, Morgause, Mordred, and Cenric were joined by eight others, bringing the list of allies up to the full eleven, and so they, too, were very happy. It was time to make sure everyone was up to speed and ready. Then they would launch the first attack, at a time yet to be decided.

Chapter 15

THE MONTHS PASSED, summer approached, and the day that school let out they were attacked by a pack of wyrms. The friends were gathered in the lunchroom. Aidan had just given diplomas to the graduating students when the serpentine, venomous creatures swarmed in through all entrances and exits.

The twins, Gareth, Lea, Ivan, Ashton, and Catrina, along with the visiting Mae, Rae, Alezandra, and Kennedy, whose schools had let out the day before, emerged from the bundle of students and faculty. Their garments shifted from school uniforms to the clothes they wore in the time gone by. They drew their assorted weapons.

Expressions of wonder and awe, plus a bit of fear, graced the faces of the other students as the eleven Pseudo-Reincarnated teens battled the long-bodied beasts.

There was a multitude of wyrms and only a limited number of people fighting them—seventeen at most. Aside from those who had been Pseudo-Reincarnated, there were Aidan, who had at least learned sword work and could wield a gun fairly well; James, very good at combat, especially with that strange dagger-gun; Librarian Rupert Natser, a fair hand with a quarterstaff; and professors Bishop, Chaput, and Baudin.

Professor Bishop had a pair of pistols, Professor Chaput had a sword and...lasso, and Professor Baudin was equipped with a revolver and long dagger. All the weapons, except for Professor Chaput's lasso, had been provided by the twins when requested by those wielding them. As they were conjured weapons, they wouldn't last more than a few hours, but they all hoped that would be enough time to dispatch all of the wyrms.

Gareth-Vortigern, the Ice Lord, coated sections of the floor with ice, causing some of the wyrms to slip, and impaled those with ice-spikes. The ones that did not slip had their windpipes removed by Lea-Nimue, the Lady of the Lake, in her wingéd wolf form. Nearby, Ashton and Catrina made a good team with the had-been-Arthur wielding his broadsword with deadly accuracy and strength, as the had-been-Gwenhwyfar slipped like a green- and white-clad ghost through the wyrms, her long daggers flashing through their skin, muscle, and bone. Ivan and Mae, back-to-back were effective, too. The once-Lancelot struck home with his sword, and the once-Aderyn, the Hawk Dame, cleaved some wyrms in twain with the sheer power of the strokes of her twin scimitars.

On the other side were the adults, and Alezandra, who had once been Branwen, the Lady of the Ravens. She was standing back-to-back with Scoruș-Myrddin and the pair decimated the wyrms that approached using a combination of magic and silvery blades. Rae, the once-Elaine the Healer, used spells taught to her by Khulai personally. The spells were for draining blood, breaking bones, and using healing magic to kill the wyrms foolish enough to try to take her down. She was not with someone else, but there were times in which Cojiñí-Morgaine could almost see a ghostly figure of a young man fighting beside the light-brown-haired young woman.

Cojiñí-Morgaine felt a presence behind her and chanced a glance. She saw the back of Kennedy-Taliesin—the Bard's head and shoulders. He was armed with a staff similar to hers, though it did not contain a magical stone at the top. He also had a bastard-sword like hers, though slightly longer and broader. Morgaine's eyes closed for less than a second to feel her husband so close to her once again, but Cojiñí stayed alert, and immediately Morgaine was alert too. They felt the strange sensation of merging almost completely fully. It was very strange, the portion of the midnight-eyed young woman's mind that was Cojiñí thought, and the portion that was Morgaine was forced to agree, as she did not like lying at all.

The ginger-haired young man and the raven-haired young woman fell into an easy rhythm, their bodies and weapons moving as one. Time seemed to slow and they lost all sensation of anything except the fight and the closeness of the parts of them from the time gone by. Slowly, the sections of their minds that were Cojiñí and Kennedy were overtaken by memories of Morgaine and Taliesin, of other times when they had battled back-to-back and side-by-side.

Eventually however, time returned to its original state as the battle wound down and the young man and woman came back to themselves and realised that they were completely covered in black wyrm blood. Cojiñí and Kennedy turned around, only to find themselves standing an inch from each other. They froze, and after a moment, Cojiñí stepped back, mentally fighting off Morgaine's urging to kiss him, which turned to slight raging when she did not. Though the caramel-skinned young woman did not know it, Kennedy also had to stay a similar assault by his mental resident from that time gone by, and he stepped back the same time she did.

Now began the process of cleaning up the bodies and blood—and vomit from the squeamish students and a few of the members of the faculty. Once all the dead wyrms had been vanished into the mid-space, with an apology to that Void, and all the black blood washed off the floor—although there were some permanent stains here and there—everyone began to go home, knowing that, in the students' case, their parents *would not believe* what had happened at school today.

No one noticed the solitary wyrm that had not attacked—it merely watched the reactions and looked for weak spots its masters could exploit. Perhaps it could get a head scratch out of delivering the news....

After returning home and showering, the twins curled up on the sofa, completely hidden beneath the green and blue throw blankets they had received as housewarming presents from Ms. Holden when they first arrived at flat 332C. At first, they just sat there, staring at the wall, but when Araunya brought them the blankets, they instantly wrapped up in them and pulled them over their heads.

The winter-eyed woman sighed. They were in battle-shock, which everyone had after their first kill and first battle. It was perfectly normal and they would come out of it, but that did not mean that their aunt—and almost surrogate mother—did not worry about them. Any mother wolf would worry about her pups, even if those pups were a pair of wingéd lions.

After a while, she sat down on the sofa beside the twins and put one arm around them. They snuggled up to her, seeking the silent comfort of her presence. Silent, because she had no words for them right now, and besides, at this moment no words would help, perhaps only hinder. Speaking would come after they emerged from the hide-under-blanket state they were in.

Araunya frowned as she realised that the rest of the Pseudo-Reincarnated teens would be in the same state of battle-shock, and their parents most likely did not know what to do. The caramel-skinned woman sent a telepathic message to James and Aidan to fetch the rest of the eleven, and received a reply that they were just about to do that.

Half an hour later they returned, somehow managing to cart nine teenagers in their two cars, and soon there was a pile of fourteen people curled up in the living room of 332C, the three adults providing quiet support and whatever comfort they could.

* * *

Caelia the Sidhe Queen looked up as she saw the wyrm returning from the mission that Morgause had sent it on. Good. Now perhaps she could learn the weaknesses of whoever Branwen had become. Of course, the others would like to know the weaknesses of their opponents as well, so Caelia brought the wyrm to where the rest of their band had gathered in Morgause's office. This wyrm would be well-received, that was certain, unless the news was not what they wished for, in which case there would be one less wyrm in the world.

A few rooms over, Cenric looked up when Caelia entered the room, a yellow wyrm trailing behind her. Incredulous, he wondered if the battle was over already. Morgaine, Myrddin, and their allies must be reaching their peak quicker than they had reckoned. Or perhaps they were severely wounded by the attack...that was more likely. Perhaps one of their precious little non-magical mortal friends had been killed, or a little kitten or something, and they were beside themselves with grief. Well, whatever happened, this wyrm would tell it.

He stood and gathered with the others, gravitating, as usual, to stand next to his soon-to-be Queen, his Morgause, the soon-bearer of his heir, if they had any say in what would happen next.

Half an hour later, a long, dark-sulphur-toned, serpentine, lizard-like body was cooling rapidly on the white marble floor and they were discussing what would happen next. Eventually it was decided that they would wait a little longer and launch another attack, and that they would do this until the time came for the new Battle of Camlann. Hopefully, it would not end the same as the last one had, and hopefully they would live long enough to raise the next Black King until his coming of age and taking of Cenric's crown. Just in case, however, they would attempt to have him born. If the two of them did not live past the final battle to take care of their heir, one of the others surely would. Or so they hoped.

* * *

In the mid-space, that void between all places and times, the other group of allies was having no such thoughts. With Barhaol as a guest, Morgaine, Myrddin, Taliesin, Branwen, Vortigern, Arthur, Nimue, Gwenhwyfar, Lancelot, Aderyn, and Elaine were holding a council. Nimue was fretting about whether or not the re-born Morgaine and Taliesin, and Myrddin and Branwen would get together, and the rest were letting her pace back and forth on the non-floor, amused.

"Why didn't they do as you two told them? Why?" The dark-blonde Lady of the Lake threw her hands in the air in exasperation. "You said they feel more than just friendly fondness towards each other, so why are they not acting? Tell me that, Morgaine and Taliesin."

The two objects of her ire were lounging on thin non-air, black-trouser and booted legs interwoven comfortably, her head had just been on his shoulder, but the midnight-eyed woman raised it to answer the silver-eyed woman.

"The both of them are waiting for the other to make the first move, and neither wants to ruin their friendship by making that move. Also, remember that Barhaol specifically instructed all of them to not let our feelings interfere in any decisions they make."

Taliesin put in his two copper coins as one lock of his shoulder-length, so-wavy-it-was-curly, ginger hair fell out of its ponytail. "Just because you, Vortigern, Arthur, and Gwenhwyfar's 'new bodies' chose to follow the paths you chose before the Battle, does not mean that the rest of us will." He shrugged. "Who knows? Perhaps Morgaine's Cojiñí will fall into a reality portal and join in with that French police inspector my dear wife told me the girl finds so fascinating." He turned his head to face the midnight-eyed man lounging similarly as he and Morgaine, with Branwen, his own wife. "Perhaps even your Scoruș, Myrddin, will join her and bring back that one 'noble gamin,' as you said he calls her. Only God knows."

Nimue did not seem content with that answer, and sat down beside Vortigern with a huff. "But just because that *may* happen, does not mean it will. They *may* end up the same as you four did. That is still a possibility. They are all still only sixteen years of age, well, in your case, Taliesin, eighteen, but my point still stands. They are young yet."

This time Elaine chose to speak up. "As far as can be told, the only ones actually not following our paths so far, excluding you two—Aderyn and Lancelot—since you took a fair amount of time to do the same as those of us who are wedded..." She paused for a moment to take a sip from a goblet that had just appeared. (Yes, they were dead and did not need nourishment, but it was a hard habit to break.) The curly-haired woman continued, "As far as can be told, the only ones not following the path that you took are Cojiñí, Kennedy, Scoruș, and Alezandra. However, only time will tell whether they take the predestined path or make their own."

"Just whose side are you on, sister-mine?" Taliesin questioned. "Or are you not choosing sides, since that was a decidedly neutral statement."

Elaine replied, "I was not aware there were sides, my dear brother."

He shrugged in acknowledgment of her point, and turned back to Nimue. She opened her mouth, but Barhaol cut in.

"I am aware that you are all enjoying yourselves with all this talk of who will become wedded to whom, but you no longer have indefinite time to chat. The mid-space may be without time, but we do need to get to the point of the matter, and sooner is better than later, no matter how much or how little time is available."

That statement quickly sobered the group of eleven. The reminder that the new Battle of Camlann would take place within two years was not a glad one. That reminder also brought on the thought that if they perished again, there would not be any re-do a third time. As far as they knew, the White God, as Barhaol called Him, would not permit it. There was a slight chance that He may let Barhaol take their consciences and cast them to the winds of time once again, but it was a very slim chance. Time was growing short for their 'new incarnations' and they needed to be ready and have a plan. None of them in attendance would fancy the consequences if Morgause, Mordred, and *their* allies won and took over the earth.

Luckily, last time had been a draw. The way the winds were blowing, however, told them that it would not be so this time around and that made the eleven magicals and semi-magicals worry about the outcome, more so than when they each had been fully them, and not sharing a body with some other person, even if those people had been "holding" them in their minds since before their conceptions.

The topic now rightly steered, conversation turned to how best they could get their new incarnations to train harder and become more prepared for the battle approaching faster and slower than would be expected.

* * *

The clanging of steel-on-steel, the faint whooshing of magic, the crackle of ice, and the roar of wingéd predatory mammals filled the mid-space training room. Dozens of constructs littered the floor, in both normal humanoid form and that of wyrms. Beneath all the noise, a faint rhythm of fast-paced music could be heard. If one looked closely at the eleven forms moving around the room, one could see that within the slashing and casting and pouncing and general fighting, were movements that coincided with dancing.

A powerful kick turned into a pirouette that flowed into a stab, and the dodge of a weapon became a dip in the arms of the person at the other's side. Awkwardness and personal space boundaries were ignored for the sake of this training exercise, as in a real fight, things such as those would be, for the duration of the battle, non-existent. Therefore, when Cojiñí spun into the arms of Kennedy to get out of the path of a simulated blast of fire from one of the constructs, his reaction was the same as hers—that being not die as they dove to the ground in order to be missed by a slicing burst of magic.

The fact that their faces ended up less than an inch from each other when he had been forced to lie on top of her was also conveniently ignored as they rolled out of the way of a slashing sword strike and she used her magic to lift them to a standing position. They broke apart and the deadly dance commenced, though commenced would be the wrong word, as the deadly dance never stopped in the first place.

Three hours later, all the constructs had been disabled in some way or another, and it took only a few minutes of clever and efficient use of magic to have them all mended and put away, which was done by Cojiñí, Alezandra, Rae, Scoruș, and Lea. Then the eleven teens collapsed on the floor in heaps of utter exhaustion. It was the last day of winter break and since it would be much more difficult for all of them to train together once school started—even though they all had eyelet-sized rings that made it possible for them to get into the training room—they had decided to train as hard as they could that day.

Eventually, they all fell asleep because they were so tired. As they slept, they moved around—as is the wont of many when sleeping—and ended up in a dog pile, with everyone holding onto each other in some way or another. Certain ones had limbs tangled.

They woke a few hours later—a few at a time—and those that were awake disentangled themselves from the pile and returned to their homes, to the same time it had been when they left, to sleep in their own actual beds for the rest of the night.

* * *

Khulai was a very happy man as of Christmas morning. The reason for this happiness was that he was now engaged. At that very moment, he and his fiancée were dancing in one of the training yards. Well, dancing was not the *best* word for it—sparring would be a better one, though to the onlooker's eye, it would appear to be dancing, in a way.

Eventually their spar was over, with her winning, which didn't happen that often. For the last couple of days, the dark-haired man had won their little matches, but it seemed as though she was gaining on him in that matter.

So, even though he was on his back on the ground, a sword-point at his throat, Khulai Silvertouch was a happy man because that sword was wielded by his smirking fiancée.

* * *

Aidan Jones was not happy. He was confused. The revelations on Christmas day—that his best friend and roommate had been part of the legendary Mercenaries Guard—and that the woman he happened to fancy just a little bit, were still baffling him. Why his unusually clever and very powerful brain could not wrap itself around the concept that he'd missed these connections, was also a mystery to the curly-haired man.

Three days after school started up again, he was sitting in his office, looking in the Internet for information about the Mercenaries Guard. Previously, all he knew was that it was legendary, which had not been a point of interest to him. However, now that he personally knew two former members, information of that sort might end up being valuable. Also, he was bored again and needed something to do.

The problem was that he could not find much information *about* the Mercenaries Guard. One site seemed promising, but it was blocked by a passcode and he didn't feel like attempting to hack it right now. Therefore, he was left with older news sites and gossip boards...until he saw something else that snagged his attention.

It was one of the those sites run by someone who was just barely on the edge of being a conspiracy theorist, but in his prior investigative researches, those sites had a tendency to be mostly filled with fairly accurate material, depending on the topic of course. However, because the majority of people he knew personally now were at least semi-magical, his interest in the range of topics on sites of this type with accurate material had broadened a fair bit.

As far as Aidan could tell, the site was maintained by a man named Peter Johnson, and it was indeed interesting. However, many of the photos on the site made Aidan grimace, as did the accounts of what the Mercenaries Guard had done and their ruthlessness in dealing with whatever threat was present at the time.

Then Aidan came upon a list of notable members throughout the ages, and that certainly interested him. Near the top of the list was a photo of a very familiar face, though younger and with close-shorn hair, standing beside a fair-skinned, redheaded woman. Glancing at the title of that section, he read that the two dark grey-and-red clad people were Captain Jamison Andrews and Captain Adara Baldwin, and although they were only in the Mercenaries Guard for three years, they were said to be two of the best agents the Guard had.

Clicking on the link at the end of the description lead Aidan to an article that was essentially a biography of the two people in the photograph, with that strange dagger-gun mentioned more than once. He frowned at some things he read, and made up his mind to show the article to James and Araunya to ask how much of it was accurate. That decided, the green-gold-eyed man emailed the link to himself, and set a reminder on his phone so he could show Araunya and James what he had found out about the Mercenaries Guard.

* * *

In a rare show of levity, Morgause and Cenric waltzed in their bedroom as soft classical music played. She laid her head on his shoulder as they moved about the room, enjoying the peace. Last time, it was all "get the army together" busy. Now, they were bound by the contract they had made to be Pseudo-Reincarnated and wait until all of the foes that had crossed the timestreams came of age and launched the attack that would determine if they would live or lose. There was no third chance for them—that had been in the contract as well. Either they won, or they were dead permanently. There were no more re-dos. This was the last time they could vanquish Morgaine, Myrddin, and the allies of those two, or they would perish, and remain perished for eternity.

The other set of magical twins had offered Morgause and Mordred a chance of redemption in the time gone by, as was the wont of those two. But the golden-haired twins had refused. And now, even if they wanted to retreat from their path, there was no turning back and there never would be, not for them, nor for any of their allies. Morgause hoped that she and Cenric would live long enough for their son to be born, as that was something that had not happened the last time. She had been pregnant at the Battle of Camlann, and he had attempted to persuade her not to fight, but she had fought, and would always insist on being at his side. If they lived, they lived together, and if they died, they died together.

The dark- and pale golden-haired duo's dancing slowed to a stop and Morgause stepped back, wondering what was going on. Cenric pulled something from an inner pocket of his vest, and went down on one knee, holding the thing up.

It was a ring with solid gold band and settings holding a large onyx stone flanked by an identical pair of perfect diamonds, princess-cut. Morgause's ocean-toned eyes went wide as her Black King began to speak.

"My Dark Lady Morgause, will you do me the immense honour of granting me something that I did not ask you before. Become my Black Queen?"

The answer did not come in words, but rather by her tackling him to the floor with a joyous and hungry kiss, the ring flying out of his hand to land neatly on the bedspread, guided by her unconscious magic and will to not have the precious thing lost.

A few minutes later, when they came up for air, the ring was picked up from the bedspread and slipped onto Morgause's wedding-finger.

That night, the wedding date was chosen to be exactly a week after they told the rest of their group about the engagement, which would be done the next day. Therefore, they would be wedded a week from the next day, and hopefully their son would be conceived soon after that, so that at least he could be born before the battle took place.

The news was well received, and congratulations abounded. Everyone was glad of the distraction from the upcoming Battle, and wedding preparations began immediately. There was no guest list to make, as they were all already there, and the use of magic made decorations and other setting-up easy. Caelia, as Queen of the Sidhe from the time gone by, would preside over the ceremony, as there were no old-time Old Way-following Druids left to officiate. Therefore, they would not have the ceremony they preferred because they did not have the correct materials to perform a correct Old Way wedding, even with the use of magic.

However, Caelia would do a handfasting, and that was really all they needed, as the rest would be taken care of the night after the ceremony.

Chapter 16

THE WEEK PASSED, Cenric and Morgause were wedded, and almost immediately after the ceremony, they entered their bedroom and locked the door. The rest of their group wisely left them alone for the next few days.

* * *

Aidan spoke to Araunya and James and discovered that all the information he had read on the website was true, and that the man who wrote it had been part of the Mercenaries Guard when they had been part of it. Whether or not he still was involved, or even alive, well, that was a debatable point in the scheme of things.

Cojiñí, Scoruș, Kennedy, Rae, Mae, Alezandra, Ivan, Lea, Gareth, Ashton, and Catrina all trained hard and studied the same. It would not do for the "reincarnations" of some of the greatest legendary figures to fail secondary school and college.

The preacher at Cojiñí, Scoruș, Araunya, James, and Aidan's church finished his very interesting sermon series on the book of Esther, and was now beginning Revelation. The first sermon of that series had the twins hooked, even if neither of them really favoured the first four chapters, instead preferring when it became truly strange, and they were greatly looking forward to the next ones.

A few of those in the mid-space, Nimue particularly, were still a bit peeved that not all of the "new them" were following the relationship paths they had, but they were not to interfere unless it was completely necessary, and it was not as if anyone other than those that lived in the heads of the ones not doing what was wanted could really do anything about it in the first place. Morgaine, Myrddin, Branwen, and Taliesin were all for letting their "hosts" choose their own paths, no matter how much Nimue badgered them about it. Yes, they were married. No, that did not mean that the "new them" had to be married too, and Nimue should really let the situation go. What would happen, would happen. It was not as if being in a relationship would determine the outcome of the Battle.

All was fine, but then Valentine's Day began to draw near. Red and pink, and hearts and cupids were everywhere. The twins wore red, yes, but they also wore black. They did not did really understand Valentine's Day, and so they honoured it in their own way. It was the day the man known as St. Valentine was beheaded, so they wore mostly black, with red scarves. Ivan dressed in similar colours, but he wore mostly black on a regular basis, though he had lightened his wardrobe a bit after Lancelot was "unlocked" in his mind. He also seemed to be after someone—Mae, to be precise. Both Scoruș and Cojiñí had someone they would like to be after, but they did not bother about that at the moment, as they were afraid of the rejection they were sure they would face even though their counterparts from the time gone by had been married to the counterparts of the particular people that they would wish to chase.

Either way, they did not like Valentine's Day very much, ignoring the fact that it was the day a man died, and people somehow interpreted it as a day of romance. If the twins would have uttered those last three words, they would have used all the sarcasm they could muster. It did not help much that there were multiple classmates who kept approaching the twins with the intention of romancing them, though a sharp look usually put whomever it was off and sent them in another direction. However, there were a few who required more of a glare. It seemed as though their little performance the year before had made them desirable targets.

The twin sixteen-year-olds did not appreciate the extra attention.

The fact that professors Chaput and Baudin deemed them ready to sing a duet in the next school program did not help matters much. Cojiñí had developed her higher range and was now able to sing fairly well as a soprano, though she would never be as good as Professor Baudin, and she would always be more comfortable singing as an alto. However, both of them had improved greatly since they started their training two years ago.

Eventually, however, Valentine's Day was over, and the twins went to bed very glad of that fact.

A few weeks after that, the next attack happened. As before, a squad of wyrms swarmed into the area in which the eleven Pseudo-Reincarnated teens were, and as before, all the wyrms were slaughtered, except one who returned to the mansion in the mountains to report, and then that last wyrm was slain.

* * *

Less than a week after the second wyrm attack, Caelia confirmed that Morgause was indeed pregnant with Cenric's heir, and there was a celebration. No one got drunk, especially Morgause, though a few of them thought many toasts would be a good idea. However, Morgause slapped them all on the backs of their heads for even suggesting that doing something to harm her unborn child was a good thing.

Her wardrobe changed after becoming the Black Queen. Although white fabrics made an appearance every so often, black became threaded throughout everything she wore, and blood-crimson joined the shades of wine-burgundy in the closet. She no longer wore anything that was completely or mostly white. The shapes of her clothing changed as well as the colours. Gone were the skin-tight mid-thigh-length dresses, replaced by things just as low-collared but more queenly and elegant. She opted for flowing slit skirts instead of ones that just barely reached her knuckles. All in all, her garb was still provocative, just in a different way. Less seductive witch, more alluring enchantress queen. With the witch, men had a chance, if they were powerful and handsome enough. With the queen, however, any man that attempted to make a move on her would find himself turned inside out or gutted by her husband. However, her beauty was still a weapon she intended to use to its full measure.

And just like last time, she was not against using certain...other things to gain an advantage, or gold, or land, or whatever, though this time she was married, and so would never go as far as she had before her wedding day.

* * *

There was also a celebration in the home of Charani and Durriken Balaur that day, for it was their son, Jardani's, birthday. He was turning six. It was the 13th of March, and the fifteenth anniversary of when Cojiñí and Scoruș were taken by a strange, cloaked figure a few hours before midnight.

They were on the mainland, having decided to go to an opera. Araunya was with them, and they had just returned to the hotel and set down the twins for a few moments. The twins were only a year old and in their cribs, what mischief could they get up to?

They all rushed into the room thirty seconds after they heard the window open, and were greeted with the sight of a dark-cloaked figure holding the children, who were screaming, but silently—obviously under a spell to make them so. The figure looked up, and they saw its gleaming red eyes, then the figure leaped out the open window.

The man and two women followed the figure, transforming into their bird forms as they leapt. They flew as fast as they could, but were unable to catch the cloaked figure. It was in an abandoned field in the middle of nowhere that Charani and Durriken transformed back into humans and collapsed on the ground holding onto each other and weeping at the loss of their children. Araunya did not collapse. Wherever she was and whatever she had been doing for the past three years had made her harder, stronger, more determined.

The winter-eyed sister of Durriken yanked them off the ground and

shouted at them to not give up. They could still feel the twins' auras, correct? At their nods, she grinned savagely.

"Then they can be found, and are alive." That was what she said, and they spent the next six months scouring the entirety of Great Britain and the rest of Europe for the twins, but every time they had a lead as to where the two children may have been, there was no one there.

After that time, Charani and Durriken stopped feeling their children's auras and gave up their search, assuming the twins were dead. A funeral was held, and a gravestone erected in the town graveyard, which caused Araunya to turn hard towards her brother and his wife.

Just because they could not feel the twins' auras did not mean the twins were dead, she said. It was well known that Araunya had the best aura sensitivity—possibly on the entire island of Golauglas, and yet they did not listen, choosing to mourn and move on, though they did not have another child until ten years later. Araunya rarely spoke to them since that day, choosing instead to pursue what they thought was a pointless search.

Either way, that was not on their minds this 13th day of March, fifteen years after the incident previously mentioned. Rather, on their minds was making their youngest son's sixth birthday the best he ever had. Of course, they would not do as they wanted in that, but Jardani would be happy anyway.

Months passed, and as they did, the eleven Pseudo-Reincarnated teens trained and gained experience and skill. Cojiñí and Scoruș' voices and instrument playing improved, though their confidence did not. Araunya and Aidan continued to circle each other, avoiding each other and attempting to become closer, causing James much amusement. He was firmly set, at least for the moment, in his singleness. Cojiñí and Scoruș' noticed, though they were doing essentially the same thing with Kennedy and Alezandra, not that they were aware of this fact.

Then came a very interesting day in June, two days before school let out. Barhaol gathered them all in the mid-space training room and presented before them a young man—brown-haired, dark-eyed, and sharp-featured. The instant the eleven saw his face, something was unblocked in both their minds and the minds of those they hosted.

When he introduced himself, his voice held a slightly foreign accent, tinged with a hint of Italian, yet overlaid with something a bit more Highland Scottish, making for a strange mix.

"Hello, I am Pietro."

They introduced themselves and when he noticed their surprise, he said, "I am very glad to meet you again, my friends. Did you not see me coming?"

* * *

In the mid-space, a man appeared, clad in silver, wavy silver-tipped brown hair just brushing his shoulders.

The eleven stood and bowed in greeting. Elaine looked up first and smiled. "Well met, Geraint."

He bowed in return and took his place beside the curly-haired sister of Taliesin, and then he spoke.

"It is good to be back among you once more."

* * *

In the mansion in the mountains, a wyrm appeared in the middle of a meeting, a tall, pale man at its side. Morgause stood in surprise, knocking her goblet over. The rest of the people at the table rose, too. Meleagant spoke first, her purple eyes inquisitive, and hopeful.

"Peredur?"

He made a showy bow. "That one known as Geraint could not keep me back forever." The pale man frowned. "Though in escaping, I did end up letting him out as well. Unfortunately."

In the time gone by, Geraint and Peredur were cousins, before Morgause's tutor ensnared the pale-haired young man and changed

him from the happy, carefree boy into a grinningly grim man. Geraint made it his mission to get his cousin back, until that same man killed his parents and sister.

From that day onward, the dark-eyed cousin swore revenge on the one he had loved like a brother, and joined the court of Arthur's father, Uther, to take training as a knight, using old, old documents proving he was a descendant of an ancient lord. He became a knight the same day as Arthur and Lancelot, and the three were closer than brothers, spending nearly all their time in each other's company.

He found his first real sense of romantic attraction a few weeks before his knighting, in the eyes of the physician's new apprentice, Elaine, when he met her gaze close-up after nearly knocking her over. He felt even more friendship after meeting her brother, Taliesin, the Captain of the Guard's nephew.

A fortnight before he was knighted, Geraint heard of a few more new arrivals to the court, a caramel-skinned, black-haired woman with strangely pale-blue eyes, and her twin children, who were about the same age he was. They had eyes like the sky on a summer's midnight. The woman introduced herself as Guiomar, and her children as Morgaine and Myrddin, and she said they hailed from the coast at the borders of Uther's kingdom.

Guiomar's tale was one of woe, as she recounted the slaughter of their village, that somehow they were the only survivors they knew of, and that for a reason she would not say, no other village would take them in. Therefore, Camelot was their only option. The twins stood at their mother's side as she spoke—caramel-toned faces set in a carefully blank expression, and midnight eyes glinting with something hidden, something silvery, but that glint lasted a miniscule moment.

Uther, of course let them stay, and granted Guiomar's odd request to assist the Captain of the Guard, since she said that in her village, she held essentially the same purpose. However, he instructed that should a battle actually take place, she was not to participate. That did not make her happy, but she conceded.

Geraint was not surprised when Guiomar showed up at practice the next day. What did surprise him, however, was that both of her twins participated with her, and actually took down and defeated a few of the knights assisting them in their practice.

From then on, Geraint had an undying respect for those twins, and when he expressed that, a friendship followed. Then one day, they returned to the citadel followed by a company of people from a neighbouring kingdom. The raven-haired twins were talking amiably with a few younger ladies-in-waiting riding behind the princess, who had come to visit for some reason or another.

Later in the day, Morgaine and Myrddin introduced the three ladies-in-waiting as Aderyn, Branwen, and Gwenhwyfar. Geraint thought he saw Myrddin looking intently at Branwen the way he admired Elaine when she wasn't looking. Hmm. Interesting.

Over the next few months, their little group of ten grew to twelve people, all around the same age. Taliesin was the eldest, but only by a year in Geraint's case, and three in Elaine's case. Aside from those already mentioned, they were joined by a runaway Northern lord's youngest son named Vortigern, and a young woman from a village near the mountains whose family had left because of a famine. They returned to their home, but she stayed in Camelot as one of the physician's assistants. Her name was Nimue, and she and Vortigern were very...compatible, at least according to Elaine, Aderyn, Gwenhwyfar, and Branwen.

That was how they had all met and become friends, and for many years after that everything was fine and dandy, although finding out some of their number were magically inclined was strange and difficult. A week after Arthur's declaration of engagement to Gwenhwyfar came the appearance of Morgause and her twin brother Mordred, plus their group of twelve, including Geraint's cousin, Peredur.

No one knew it was them at first; everyone believed they were merely foreign dignitaries passing through to another kingdom on the other side of Camelot. The fact that they had a crown prince with them helped in that matter. But as soon as Guiomar and the twins saw the crown prince, they bristled. It was in a secluded corner of a cave under the dungeons that Morgaine and Myrddin explained the reason for their reaction.

"In our village, and the ones around it, Cenric's father was known as the Black King. One would think it was because of the black and sable of his coat of arms, but it is said that one of our Healers looked into his aura and saw that it was black as pitch with malice and cruelty, though unless someone had aura-sight, he could easily seem to be the most perfect man that ever existed."

Morgaine let out a sharp breath of air. "However, anyone aware of what Cenric and his father have done will know that it is all a façade. For example, it was his father who crossed your border and attacked our town, decimating it with the help of an old-woman witch tailed by a pair of twins, one male, one female, beautiful, with pale gold hair."

Morgaine and Myrddin explained about the Black King and his son, and Geraint understood their anger and fear of the man.

It was later that same day that Arthur pointed out to Geraint a young man and woman almost exactly matching the description their raven-haired twin friends had given them, save for being older.

Time passed as it always did, slowly and in the right order, and then came a day in which Uther was murdered by Morgause. Arthur became king, and wedded Gwenhwyfar. Morgaine and Taliesin, and Myrddin and Branwen, became engaged, and Vortigern and Nimue were wedded. Geraint got up his knightly courage and ended up engaged to Elaine, and the same happened with Lancelot and Aderyn.

More time passed and they grew in rank and wisdom. The raven-haired twins were now recognised as Archmages, with Nimue taking on the rank of Mage. Vortigern was given the mantle of the Ice Lord, Branwen became Lady of the Ravens, and Aderyn was knighted and gained the title of the Hawk Dame. Taliesin's semi-magical skill with music made him one of the most famous Bards in Camelot, and many other places as well, and Elaine became a well-renowned Healer even at her young age.

The battles with Morgause and her allies began when she murdered

Uther, but truly gained traction when they discovered a plot to assassinate Arthur. Apparently, Morgause thought Arthur was the leader because he was their king and the people were loyal to him. She figured killing him would set dissention among the people and break them apart. However, she underestimated them, and they grew closer after the attempt on Arthur's life, which luckily had been thwarted by Arthur himself.

The next summer, Morgaine and Taliesin were married, and only a few days after that Myrddin and Branwen did the same. By the end of that summer, the entirety of the group had become wedded, though they were all aware that none of them would be having children anytime soon.

As the fight with Morgause, Mordred, and Cenric escalated, Arthur named the son of one of his cousins as Royal Successor in the event that he and Gwenhwyfar were slain before they were able to produce a proper heir. The rest of them were not royalty, and so did not have that particular problem to worry about, much to their relief.

* * *

Cojiñí wondered why it took so long for one particular member of their group to appear, and why he had not done so when they had been "merged" with the parts of them from the time gone by, so she asked him directly.

Pietro smiled, and when he answered, his voice was eerily calm. "Does Morgaine remember when the tips of Geraint's hair turned silver?"

Cojiñí nodded, confused as to how that was relevant, and she cast into her other self's memories to see if she could tell.

They were hiding in a cave in the woods near Camelot's capital of the same name. Morgause had overrun it and taken control of the kingdom, but they would be back to reclaim Arthur's birthright.

One day, all of a sudden, a white-haired man appeared at the mouth of the cave and asked to speak with Geraint. The magicals of

the group scanned him and found neither malice nor ill intent in this request, and so the brown-haired knight went. Three days later, he returned by himself in the middle of the night, appearing unharmed.

The next morning, it was revealed that the ends of his hair had gained a silvery sheen, and a week later, two centimetres of his hair was completely silver. He would not speak of what had happened, citing that the man had asked him not to, though he did say it would assist them in the battles to come.

After examining the memory, Cojiñí came up blank, and straight out asked the dark-eyed young man. "What does that have to do with how long it took you to appear?"

He smirked at her ire. "Nothing, I just wanted to see how closely bonded you were to who you had been."

She frowned in frustration and he relented, gesturing them to sit on the floor as he began his tale.

"You all remember when I disappeared to battle Peredur and never returned...." As he told his tale, Pietro's mind floated back to Geraint's memory of the events the young man was describing.

He chased his formerly dear cousin through the trees, easily catching up to him, even though the other was on a galloping charger. The extra speed the old man had given him was very useful, especially in a hunt such as this. In a flying leap, he knocked the pale man off his horse, and they tumbled into the underbrush, then rolled into a cave.

As they stood, their fight was distracted by a bright glow. There was a strange urn set on a pedestal. The pedestal itself was plain, rough even, but the urn was elaborately carved with many different runes and inscriptions.

One glance told Geraint exactly what they were looking at, and he quickly formulated a plan and was ready to put it in action. The Urn of Urien was very old, and led to a prison contained in the mid-space that was said to be impenetrable and impossible to escape from without outside help. The thing was, telepathic conversation was restricted to within the "walls" of the Urn, proving outside communication was not possible. Therefore, the Urn was a perfect place to put his so-called "dear" cousin. There was a high chance that he himself could be pulled into the Urn, but since no one could die in the mid-space, he would be in no danger of perishing.

He set his mouth in a grim line and leapt at Peredur, using his speed to open the Urn and throw the other man at it. He turned to leave, but felt himself dragged backward.

Geraint turned to look. Peredur's hand was gripping his armour sleeve. He attempted to wrench the hand away, but his cousin had always been stronger than he was, and the dark-eyed man was dragged into the Urn's prison along with the one he had cast into it.

As Geraint disappeared into the darkness of the mid-space prison, his only regret was that he had not told Elaine of the risk he had been taking, and in that manner, had not said farewell.

Pietro shook himself to bring himself out of the trance he had been in, lost in memories and telling the tale of those events. He looked at the group of eleven surrounding him.

Rae was glaring at him and he winced when she opened her mouth and spoke with Elaine's voice, causing the rest to regard her odd behaviour.

"I am very mad at you, Geraint, and I would like to say that you should NEVER DO ANYTHING LIKE THAT AGAIN!"

He hung his head and spoke as Geraint. "Sorry, Elaine."

The dark-haired young man chanced a glance and saw her nodding. "You are forgiven, but take my words and heed them."

"I will."

Those things said, their respective "other selves" receded back to the past, and the two young adults returned fully to who they were in the present.

Chapter 17

A FEW MONTHS LATER HERALDED the twins' seventeenth birthday, and it was a happy one, just like all the rest since Araunya found them on that fateful day three years before. The presents were not extravagant, but even after three whole years of being loved and having a proper family did not break the twins of the utter wonder of receiving presents. There were times that they still expected to suddenly awake and learn that this was all just a lovely dream, and they were about to be beaten for sleeping in and not doing their chores on time. Not that they would tell anyone, and that included Morgaine and Myrddin, about their fears.

* * *

Late that November, Morgause and Cenric's child was born, with his father's hair and mother's eyes. They named him Pelias seven days after his birth, waiting long enough to be sure he would live. The child proved healthy and strong, and when Meleagant looked at his aura, he was declared to be indeed a powerful man when older. There was a celebration, and though Morgause did not have any wine since she was nursing, she did not begrudge the others of their drink.

* * *

That December, two weeks before Christmas, Aidan asked Araunya out, and she accepted. They shared their first kiss beneath the mistletoe as the sun went down on Christmas Day, causing Khulai and Tara, who had joined their party for a few days, to say it was about time. The latter two had just gotten married and were planning to leave on their honeymoon the next day.

Cojiñí and Scoruș still had not spoken to anyone other than each other and Araunya about *their* feelings towards Kennedy and Alezandra, respectively, and the latter two had not said anything to anyone about their feelings on the matter. However, there was a school talent show coming up in February, and Cojiñí had a plan. She would need help from Professor Chaput, however, but that was not too difficult to acquire.

* * *

He and Professor Baudin will be happy with her, thought the midnight-eyed seventeen-year-old as she pulled her—mostly unused—diary from the drawer of her nightstand and flipped to the page on which she wrote her song entitled "Stars Fall." She would take it to school the next day and ask Professor Chaput to create organ music to accompany it so that she could play it on the same organ she used during the talent show a few Christmases ago.

The next day, she hung back after the rest of the class left, shooing on Scoruș to go ahead and save a spot for her at lunch. He did as she asked, and she was left alone with the two Music, Dance, and Drama professors who showed an eerie resemblance to Erik le'Fantôme and Christine Daae, which she could not shake from her mind.

Realising that there was still a student in the room, the professors turned to look at the caramel-skinned young woman.

"Yes, Mademoiselle Balaur?"

Cojiñí bit her lip and took a deep breath. Steeling herself, she presented the notebook to Professor Chaput, open to the page on which her song was written.

"Could you possibly make music for this song so that I can play it on the organ at the talent show? Please?"

The black-haired professor's nearly-amber orbs scanned the stanzas, and when he looked in her, his eyes gleaming. "You will be singing it as well as playing it, I assume?"

At her hesitant nod, he smiled. "I will make sheet music for you and help you memorise it, but only if you give me the tune you had in mind, and which part goes with which words."

The raven-haired young woman acquiesced, and sang her song in front of the Music, Dance, and Drama professors, humming during the parts where there were no words.

When she was done, both adults smiled at her, and she flushed and ducked her head. Professor Baudin gripped her shoulder.

"Chin up, Cojiñí Balaur. Be proud of your work." Professor Baudin smiled again. "With Erik's help, you will win the talent show...if your brother doesn't make it a draw."

Professor Chaput spoke in a similar vein as his colleague. "I agree with Catherine. Your organ playing is excellent. You have a pretty voice with enough power to sing over the organ without a microphone if you want to. And this," he held up the notebook, "this is unexpectedly good for someone who says she is 'horrible at writing any kind of poetry.'"

His smile told Cojiñí that the wording of the last sentence was not meant to mock and she flushed deeper, then ducked her head again. The professors chuckled and shooed her out to lunch. She went gladly.

As the door shut behind Mademoiselle Balaur, Erik turned to his blonde fellow professor. She was looking at him strangely.

"What are you thinking, Erik?"

He sat down on his desk and she sat beside him, waiting for him to speak. Eventually he did, in French, as she had.

"I'm thinking, Christine, that those twins remind me vaguely of me, in my much younger days."

At the odd look she gave him, he amended his statement. *"Or rather, like they could easily turn into what I was when you met me. However, having their 'aunt,' who treats them more like a mother, taking care of them means that they most likely will never take the path I did."*

Christine smiled at him sadly, and stroked his cheek.

Suddenly he frowned. *"After all this time, it still feels strange to have a proper face—to have a wife to take out on Sundays...."* He trailed off and smiled at her, then continued. *"To not be shunned everywhere I go because of how I look, to not have to hide in a dungeon of my own making...."*

Erik stopped speaking when Christine smacked him on the back of the head. *"Erik le'Fantôme! Stop that right now. What's happened has happened, and we are not supposed to focus on what has already passed, remember?"*

He sighed. *"I remember."*

Three months after he and Christine were wed, three years after the debacle with the grasshopper and the scorpion, not much had changed for him. Yes, he was a better man, Christine's wilfulness, and spirit, and love was the reason for that, but he was still shunned by everyone except for her, and Madame Giry, Daroga Azar Baraz, and Raoul. Yes, he and Raoul were sort-of friends, after Christine knocked some sense into them both. But that was all taken away when they were in the opera house watching, well, an opera, and a fire. Erik and Christine were in Box 5 and the rest were in the box right next to them, Madame Giry having retired a few months before.

With Erik actively watching the opera and providing commentary, and therefore not running around on the catwalks causing mischief, the five in and near Box 5 knew it could not be him that set the raging blaze under the stage, especially since it was near their two boxes. In the chaos that followed, and with the use of secret passages, Erik managed to get Christine to the underground lake and convince her to stay there while he went and fetched the other three. However, when he got back to Box 5, he was just in time to see a chandelier weight swing down and completely crush Box 3, and all of the people in it.

He stood there silently a few moments, until a falling beam alerted him to the danger he was in. The masked man returned down the passageways to the lake in a daze. While he had been no stranger to the sights of killing, and even sometimes participated in some while in Persia, no one dear to him had ever died before his eyes, since he had been a child.

When he got to the lake, Christine was waiting impatiently for him and the rest, but her expression instantly changed to worry when she saw he was alone. Her expression dropped even further at the look in his eyes. No words were needed to tell her that their friends were dead. They embraced as tight as they could, both crying openly, and Erik without his mask, which he had thrown on the floor.

They would have liked to just sit there in Erik's underground lakeside house and mope, but the cave was starting to collapse and that forced them to leave. They bought a small house in the middle of nowhere under the guise of a girl and her widower aunt. They lived there for about a month before something extremely strange happened.

It was noonish, and they were just sitting down to eat whatever luncheon they had prepared. Erik had a habit of leaving his mask off while in the house, though he kept it with him at all times, and Christine didn't particularly mind. However, the mask was back on in a blink when a ghostly, androgynous figure in a white robe, and holding a white staff, appeared in their dining room.

The figure introduced itself as Barhaol in a two-layered voice of soprano and baritone, and offered them a chance for another kind of life, one where Erik was not shunned, where they could live somewhere other than the middle of nowhere, as long as they told no one who they really were, and did not focus on what had happened in the times before the 'shift,' as Barhaol called it.

Before marrying Christine, Erik would have jumped on that offer and grabbed it with both hands and his lasso just for good measure, but now he looked towards his wife. The former Phantom was relieved when she nodded her assent, and he turned back towards the ghostly figure. It smiled at the curly-haired woman's nod, and waved the staff gripped in one hand, the stone suspended in a coil at the top glowing pale purple.

They felt a sensation like falling, and darkness. Then the darkness faded to reveal a room of deep, deep grey, the walls laced with shining purple and bubble-like. Confused, they sat down on a sofa and waited. After a bit, Barhaol appeared and explained that although it would feel like less than half an hour, the new time they would end up in was a few centuries after the one they had just left, and that It had all the necessary paperwork and such prepared for them so that they could just start on their new lives as soon as they arrived. As soon as the ghostly figure finished speaking, Erik felt like a whole new life had been crammed into his head, what with the overload of new memories overlaying the ones he already had. Additionally, it felt as if his face had been set on fire and then he'd been sealed in a block of ice for a few minutes.

When he came to from his brief bout of unconsciousness, Erik was greeted by Christine hovering over him with worry. After he assured her that he was fine now, she "bopped" the tip of his nose. He had a nose! After that revelation, he felt his face just to be sure. He could feel himself grinning! And he was determined that as soon as they arrived at wherever they were going, he would find a mirror.

Erik smiled at the memory of when they first arrived in the "modern times," and when they took the jobs as the Music, Dance, and Drama professors at Glamdring Secondary. It was a pain to have to pretend to not be married, however.

* * *

The day of the talent show arrived, and Cojiñí was nervous. Not only were she and Professors Chaput and Baudin the only ones who knew what she would be doing, all the Pseudo-Reincarnated teens were in the audience, including Kennedy. Morgaine was laughing with delight at the words of the song, and about who Cojiñí had dedicated it to in her mind. Cojiñí was getting ready to mentally slap the midnight-eyed woman.

Luckily, she was not the last act this time. That spot was reserved for a soon-to-be-graduating student, but she did not know his name. Both she and Scoruș were scheduled near the middle of the performances. She was a few acts after her brother, and did not know what he planned to do, but that was perfectly okay in her opinion, and very much fair.

Due to the size of Glamdring Secondary School, there were fifty acts in the talent show, causing it to last an entire evening. Just before the act that preceded Cojiñí's, an intermission took place during which the judges voted on the best performances in the first half. They compiled a list. Following the entire show, the judges would rate the performances in the second half, and *then* choose one, or sometimes two winners. There was no prize, just the satisfaction of knowing that you won something.

Scoruș' act was the last of the first half, and so Cojiñí sat down backstage to wait. She was glad she had brought a book to read, that being *The Phantom of the Opera*. It fit her mood in an oddly good manner. Although she probably knew enough French, thanks to three years of it at Glamdring, coupled with the enhanced learning her magic gave her, she was not exactly ready to read the book in the original version just yet. So she read it in English. She purchased this edition from the library's used book sale, and she liked it very much, partially because it had excellent full-page pictures scattered about.

Eventually, Scoruș was announced and walked onstage carrying the deep-green violin that Khulai and Tara had gotten for him this past Christmas. Cojiñí set down her book and moved to where she could see the stage.

The violin and bow went up to his shoulder, the bow touched the strings, and Scoruș began to play, dancing the entire time. Cojiñí was not sure what song her twin was playing, but it was very fast and quite complicated. What was her simple song, even with the music that Professor Chaput made for it, compared to that?

Even with her doubts about how well *she* would do, she could not deny that her twin brother played beautifully, and she congratulated him extensively once he returned backstage. She told him of her worries, and he wrapped her in an embrace, reassuring her that she would be fine, and if any of the two of them won, it would be her. Cojiñí countered that it would be Scoruș who would win.

The intermission was only fifteen minutes long, so the twins barely had time to eat a snack and use the lavatory before the next act went onstage. Luckily, that act was not Cojiñí, so she had a bit more time to prepare herself mentally, before singing in front of all of those people. At least she could look at the music instead of at the audience, not that she *really* needed to. She had always been good at memorising things, without her magic enhancing it. But she still had trouble keeping in tune, even after over two years of music lessons from the two people who seemed to have walked straight out of the pages of a certain book about an opera house that she liked—even if Professor Erik Chaput was much more..."people-aware"...for lack of a better phrase, than Erik le'Fantôme in the book.

When the student ahead of her came backstage, Cojiñí took a few deep breaths, steeled herself, and walked through the curtains. To distract herself she took stock of what was out there. Good. The pipe organ was at just the right angle. But, oh, dear, there was a camera on the top...probably so that the audience could see her face since her back would be toward the crowd. Having the camera was an interesting development, but she would deal. Cojiñí smiled inwardly when deciding to pretend the camera was not there.

Smoothing a non-existent wrinkle in her deep-blue blouse and black trousers, the caramel-skinned seventeen-year-old woman bowed to the audience and the judges, then slid onto the bench and began to play.

Kennedy leaned forward in his seat, mentally sidestepping a thought message from Taliesin. He did not need to know what the "him" from the time gone by thought of the young woman who happened to be "hosting" within her mind, the wife of the alternate him. *However, she does look pretty today*. Then he shrugged off the thought.

He watched the back of her head as she turned away from the audience and sat on the bench by the school's pipe organ. Then his focus shifted to one of the screens on the sides of the stage when the small camera attached to the organ activated, showing in good detail her face and hands. Her hands began to slowly dance across the keys, and that movement drew Kennedy's eye as he mentally "logged" the notes being played, without consciously noticing of course.

After a few measures of just organ music, she began to sing a song that he had never heard before. It was a simple tune, but pretty, possibly beautiful. Then he heard the words, and his confusion made him thoughtful.

Stars fall hard now, break the ties that bind them,
Darkness calls now, hear the songs of night-time;
Light shall fade and return again
Hear the music of time flow by.

Hearts shall still and dreams shall fade,
But I will be always here by your side,
Till night falls no more and the seas no longer roar,
I shall be with you, I shall see you through.

Worlds shall fall and sirens shall call,
But I'll hold true to my promise to you,
I'll keep you safe, I'll do all it takes
To keep you with me for all time.

I'll find a way to live through the days
When you do not believe, I know you will see,
Forever and a day, that will be my way,
Our hearts shall beat as one, till eternity is done.

Stars fall hard now, but we will never fall.

The song was not just words set to the music, with the organ playing during certain parts. Some sections, such as in between 'till eternity is done,' and the second, 'stars fall hard now,' were pure vocalisations. Overall, however, it was a very nice song, he thought, and apparently Taliesin agreed with him on that front, though the other "him" was a bit more...enthusiastic in his liking of the song.

As soon as her song was finished, Cojiñí stood and bowed to the audience, then disappeared as fast as she could, without being rude, into the wings and then backstage. She liked having talents she could show off, but DID NOT LIKE any sort of publicity at all. If she and Scoruş ever published a book, they would do it under pseudonyms and have either no photo, or only a photo of someone else, or a disguise, on the back flap.

However, neither of the twins could politely dodge the rest of the Pseudo-Reincarnated teens as they exited the building. They were cornered. Cojiñí was wrapped in hugs from the girls, and the boys clapped Scoruş on the shoulder, except for Ashton who gave him a hug. Congratulations, and wishes of winning were said, and they all went to find the adults.

Half an hour later, the judges ascended the steps of the stage to announce the winners of this year's talent show. The twins were both at the edge of their seats, and leaning back in feigned nonchalance. Which was not working very well. Eventually, they settled for sitting cross-legged in their chairs and leaning forwards with their hands in what they called the "Sherlock pose."

After a few moments of shuffling papers, the judges cleared their throats, which caused a few giggles and brought the entire audience's attention to them. The one in the centre, a bald man in a grey suit, tapped the microphone to be sure it was working, then spoke.

"We have debated long, and came to the conclusion that in this case, only a tie will suffice. The winners of this talent show are...." he paused for effect, and a drum roll was played over the sound system. "...Richard Brown and Jane Bishop."

The twins blinked hard. Well! That was an interesting development. Apparently, the judges liked gymnastics and clowning better than violin and organ music. Oh well. They did not enter to win anyway, though that would have been nice.

Standing tall, the caramel-skinned, midnight-eyed, raven-haired twins walked out of the auditorium with the rest of the people. They did not win, but they did not care, not really.

Unfortunately, that serenity was not to last, for though the twins had not yet experienced them, there were bullies at Glamdring—they had just left the twins alone for the time being. However, a few of them cornered Cojiñí one evening as she was taking a walk in the moonlight. Unknowing of their intent, she did not immediately drive them away, curious as to what they would say.

She endured their jibes about her low singing voice for a while, then got fed up. "What are you five over here about, other than to express that you don't like my singing?"

One of them—they were all males—attempted to appear attractive. "You know, boys, this young lady here wants to know why we're here. Why don't we *show* her? How about we *tame* the magic girl?" He wiggled his brows suggestively, and Cojiñí frowned. Was he saying what she thought he was saying?

Then she realised she was surrounded, and ten other young men appeared from out of the shadows. They were led by a familiar platinum-haired Paul Carson. The ice-eyed young man held something glinting in one hand, and before Cojiñí could move, she was restrained and the thing had been clicked around her wrist.

She let out an ear-splitting scream as she felt the pain of the channel to her magic blocked for the second time in her life. The young men, however, didn't seem to mind, and the circle tightened. All of a sudden, there were hands reaching for her, reaching for places where there should never be hands until she was married, and even then those hands should only belong to her husband.

It was when those hands touched her that Cojiñí's training kicked in and she acted, snapping her head around and biting down as hard as she could on the nearest finger. The shout of pain from that attacker gave her a sick sense of satisfaction as she continued her struggle.

The caramel-skinned young woman was glad she and the other Pseudo-Reincarnated teens had practicing fighting without magic as she kicked and punched and bit and head-butted the fifteen young men surrounding her. Finally, she gained enough space to use a trick she had figured out three years before, and pulled on her anger and will to escape in order to overload the circuits of the magic-suppressor.

The shackle-shaped silvery band shattered into a thousand shards in a flash that blinded Cojiñí's attackers, allowing her to summon her staff and sword from the mid-space.

When the fifteen young men regained their vision, they were greeted with the sight of a completely furious seventeen-year-old Archmage with one of the most powerful magic-wielders in British history living in her head and imprinted on her soul.

With a quick cantrip, Cojiñí-Morgaine Seasword had fourteen of the attackers and would-be molesters immobilized. Then she put the point of her sword at Paul Carson's throat. When she spoke, it was both her voice and the voice of the very dangerous woman she held within her mind at the same time.

"I would derive a fair amount of pleasure from removing your head from your sorry shoulders, Paul Carson, if only for causing my brother and I to be relieved of access to one of the only things that kept us alive most of our lives—our magic. Now that you have not only done this again, and attempted to...*tame* me, I am running out of reasons why I should not."

She then revealed a tidbit of information she knew the platinum-haired young man would never expect her to know. "My aunt, who works with the police, spoke with your parents when she discovered who it was that caused those suppressors to be put on my brother and me. She was not overly surprised to learn that you had been disowned many years ago, and that your little brother, Edward, was on the same track if he did not clean up his act."

Cojiñí-Morgaine smiled grimly. "Your family knows nothing of what you have been doing, though they would not be surprised that you will have gotten slain because of it. You have no girlfriend, no children that would be pleased to call you father, and you're wanted by too many towns to count, so tell me, what is stopping me from ridding the world of one more piece of filth?" Her smile evaporated. "Nothing. At. All."

Cojiñí-Morgaine was silent for a moment, then said, "But why should I make myself sink to your level? You'll get the death sentence if I turn you in, removing your head now will only hasten the inevitable."

Another brief pause, then, "It's against God's laws to murder, but this wouldn't be murder, would it? Just justice coming a little earlier than you expected."

The sword point dug a little deeper into Paul Carson's throat, causing him to choke. He had heard from his "contacts" in Glamdring Secondary that the magical twins were the reincarnations of Merlin and Morgana, or rather, Myrddin and Morgaine, and at this moment, he could easily see why so many legends insinuated Morgana was evil. She was dangerous, and had a horrible temper. Desperately, he wondered what he could do to get her to let him go. Unfortunately, he came up completely blank.

Cojiñí-Morgaine watched as the wheels and cogs spun in the platinum-haired young man's mind. He could not escape her, and she knew he knew it when those ice-blue eyes dulled slightly with the realisation that there was no squirming out of this situation. Either she killed him now, or she turned him in to the police, and his eventual death sentence at the hands of the law. The question was—which did she choose?

The caramel-skinned young woman stood there, sword-point to Paul Carson's throat, thinking, for a few more moments before coming to a decision. Her sword moved.

Chapter 18

MOST OF THE LIGHTS WERE OFF, causing a spooky feeling, but Jennifer Grace Hill, called Jen or Grace by her friends, was accustomed to it, so the dark did not bother her. She brushed away a lock of dark brown hair that had fallen out of her up-do from her face and turned the page of her book. It was truly a very interesting story, and she was hooked since the first chapter.

Suddenly her relaxation was interrupted by a heavy knock on the police station door. With a huff, the hazel-eyed woman put down the book. The sight that greeted her was one she would remember for the rest of her life. A dark-haired, caramel-skinned young woman with stunning deep-blue eyes stood there, a vaguely familiar platinum-haired man draped, unconscious, over her shoulder, bound tightly in thick ropes and in a manner that indicated he would not be moving even if he had been aware of his surroundings.

Confused, especially because the young woman seemed no older than twenty years and did not appear *that* strong, Jennifer let them in. Her eyes went wide when ten of the town's worst thugs, ranging in age from sixteen to twenty-six, floated in behind them. They were all bound similarly to the platinum-haired man.

The young woman plopped the platinum-haired man down in a chair by Jennifer's desk, and the fair-skinned woman realised she had seen him before—on a wanted poster in the director's office. This man, bound and unconscious beside her desk, was Paul Carson, wanted for seven counts of homicide and more than that for rape and burglary. He had eluded the police forces of every country he had been in for five years—but now here he was, having been brought in by a young woman whom Jennifer assumed had been intended as a victim.

Taking a closer look at the young woman, Jennifer noticed something odd about her features, not in a bad way, just that she seemed familiar, in a personal way.

"You wouldn't happen to be related to Araunya Balaur, by any chance?" Inspector Balaur was one of the best officers this police station had, and was a fairly close friend of Jennifer's, at least close enough to use a nickname. Jennifer had heard talk that Araunya might be promoted to Chief Inspector in the next few months.

The young woman looked at her and nodded. "She is my aunt. I am Cojiñí." She did not hold out a hand to be shaken, and Jennifer noticed the girl's hands were shaking. And that...Cojiñí's voice was somewhat ...stiff, as if she was tense.

Jennifer gestured to another seat nearby. "Would you like to sit down, Cojiñí?"

The midnight-eyed young woman shook her head with a jerk, so Jennifer perched on the edge of her desk, shifting a few papers and knickknacks aside.

"Are you alright, Cojiñí?"

"Nothing that you could fix, or even really understand. No offence."

Jennifer was not offended. She could tell the young woman was shaken by whatever had just taken place, and understood that the young lady might not wish to speak of such things to a complete stranger, even if that stranger was a police officer.

"Would you like me to call your aunt?"

"No, I'll be fine."

"Are you sure?"

"Yeah."

The young woman began to leave, but stopped when Jennifer called out. "What am I supposed to do with these?" She gestured at the men lying on the floor.

Cojiñí's eyes glinted. "That is up to you. That one," she pointed at Paul Carson, "deserves the death sentence. That is certain."

"You know of what he did?"

"No, I do not know for sure what he did before he came here."

The tone of voice used by Araunya's niece set off an alarm in Jennifer's mind. This young woman had a vendetta against Carson.

"Why do you feel that way?"

The glint in Cojiñí's eyes grew stronger, becoming a faint glow. "I suggest you look up magic-suppressors and their effects, especially on under-aged magicals."

With that, she disappeared into thin air, leaving Jennifer with fifteen unconscious criminals scattered around her floor and no clue what to tell the director.

Cojiñí teleported to "their" clearing on Ynys Golauglas and walked down the riverside to the sea. When she reached the beach, she transfigured her clothes into a swimsuit and waded into the cold, salty water. Lea might be most at home in still waters, and the other girl might swim like a nymph—courtesy of Nimue being the Lady of the Lake, but Cojiñí, and Morgaine felt most comfortable in the waters of the sea. Most of it was because Morgaine had been born near the ocean and in her childhood she became friends with the green, blue, grey, and purple merfolk that frequented the area in that time.

She remembered when they had given her the gift of being able to breathe underwater and swim along with them, a gift she had found negated by chemicals put into modern swimming pools. The raven-haired young woman closed her eyes and let herself sink into water and memory, unconsciously merging fully and utterly with Morgaine as she did so. The woman from the past felt it was needed, and though she knew she would not want to, Morgaine would let Cojiñí be Cojiñí again when she awoke from her tense and exhausted memory-slumber.

Morgaine was not even six summers old when she first met the merfolk that lived beneath the waves near her home. She was playing on the rocks when she slipped and plummeted into the icy-cold greenish-blue water. She had learned to swim, yes, but she was not strong enough to battle the roaring surf, and therefore was sure to perish by drowning.

She had resigned herself to her fate as much as an almost-six-year-old could, when suddenly she felt a pair of long, strong, webbed hands wrap around her waist from beneath and drag her to the surface, temporarily stilling the waves with a harsh, guttural sound. Morgaine had clung to her saviour tightly, eyes squeezed shut against the salt in the spray in the air. It was only when she felt firm ground under her feet that the raven-haired young girl opened her eyes.

The young Morgaine was face-to-face with what was undoubtedly a mermaid. The mermaid's greyish green skin was smooth and slippery; her long, claw-tipped fingers were webbed; fins protruded from her torso and forearms. At the hips, her body smoothly merged with what seemed to be the tail of a silver-scaled fish. And when she smiled gently at Morgaine, her mouth was filled with rows of sharp, pointed teeth, but the five-year-old thought it was one of the most beautiful people she had ever seen.

Morgaine looked the mermaid right in her shimmering silver eyes and held out a hand, saying in her best Welsh, "Hello, thank you very much for saving me. My name's Morgaine, what's yours?"

The mermaid smiled brightly and she shook Morgaine's hand gently, being careful not to scratch her with her claws. She answered in the same language Morgaine had spoken, though with an accent that could only be described as lyrical and fish-like. "I am Mooneye, little fingerling."

Morgaine nodded as formally as a five-year-old could, and said, "It is a pleasure to meet you, Mooneye." She paused, and then said, "Mooneye, do you think you could teach me to swim like you do?"

Mooneye laughed like the falling of rain on a summer day, and nodded. "It would be my pleasure to teach again, little leggéd fingerling."

From that day onward, while Myrddin was learning how to do boy-only things, Morgaine would go down to the beach to call for Mooneye, and the mermaid taught her how to swim.

On her thirteenth birthday, Mooneye brought the Mer-Chief, who just happened to be her mate and husband, and Morgaine was taught to breathe underwater, see underwater, and resist the pressures of the waves. And, with a bit of practice, to swim fast enough to keep up with a hurrying Mooneye.

Her fifteenth birthday brought the newly named Morgaine Seasword more wonders, as Mooneye took her to the merfolk's city, which was absolutely beautiful, and just as magically and technologically advanced as any city on land, though a few areas were a bit different, as would be expected of a city of merfolk under the sea.

When Cojiñí began to awake, Morgaine reluctantly released her hold on the seventeen-year-old's body and returned to her own corner of the young woman's mind, leaving no trace behind that she had been meddling just a little bit, not that anyone would really notice.

Cojiñí opened her eyes to see the rapidly lightening sky above her, and to feel the cold of the ocean water surrounding her. She shivered. Even with Morgaine's resistance to the elements in the sea, Cojiñí was still susceptible to cold. She just could not get hypothermia.

She flipped over and swam with a modified breaststroke to shore, where she used a simple cantrip to dry herself off, and transfigured her swimsuit back into her clothes. While the repercussions of what she had been about to do still had her feeling shaken, she felt better after a sleep in the waves and a memory-dream of a pleasant time of Morgaine's childhood.

The noble-featured young woman teleported away from Ynys Golauglas, glad it was a Saturday and therefore no school. Hopefully, no one noticed that she had not returned home the night before.

As it turned out, no one did notice, though it was close. Scoruș emerged from his room just as Cojiñí was shutting the door to the bathroom to take a shower to wash off the salt water.

At breakfast, and later, Scoruș watched his sister curiously. Something was...off about her. Something was different in her manner and bearing. However, he could not exactly tell *what* was different. That was a problem. The questions were: how could he find out? And how could he help his sister? He could not help her if he did not know what the problem was, and it did not look as if she would be telling anyone anytime soon. He would let it go for now, but if help was needed, he would be there. It was his duty as her brother.

A few days later, Scoruș entered the mid-space training room for a bit of practice, only to see that it was already occupied by someone he wanted to see very much and did not want to see at all—a certain young woman with the name of Alezandra. She was running laps around the room, and he joined her.

After three laps, Alezandra stopped for a drink and Scoruș did the same, not that he was tired, but he was thirsty. When she put down her water bottle, the raven-haired young man asked the question that he had been thinking since he arrived.

"Hey, Alezandra, would you like to practice with me?"

The curly-haired young woman thought for a moment, then nodded. "Spar or defend?"

"Defend."

"Sure."

The group had developed two different ways of practicing fighting. One was just regular sparring, one of them against another. The other they term 'defend,' which was fighting together as a team. They would animate training constructs, then defend themselves as if they were fighting against multiple foes.

Scoruș animated five dummies to attack, and they summoned their weapons—he with his sword and staff, she with her long black knives. And so the fight began.

Personal space doesn't exist in true battle, and so it was in one of these practice melees, as they danced the dance of death around and through their opponents. Time melted around them as they moved. Emerald green and deep ocean-blue magic, and black and silver steel flashed through the bodies of the constructs.

Alezandra spun to avoid a bolt of flame sent by a construct, only to land in Scoruș' arms as he decimated it. That was the last one to destroy. As their battle-adrenaline faded, the two seventeen-year-olds realised exactly how little space was between them.

That final flurry of battle-adrenaline, and most likely the influence of Myrddin, caused Scoruș to do something that would not cross his conscious thoughts at any other time. Technically, it did not cross his mind now—he merely did it. He leaned forward ever so slightly and closed the gap of air between their lips.

It was not a passionate kiss, though Myrddin's experience prevented him from fumbling or being awkward. It was little more than a few-second touch of the lips, and when he drew back, Scoruș was exceedingly glad that she did not slap him.

The caramel-skinned young man's midnight eyes grew wide as, contrary to his expectations, the light-green-eyed young woman merely stared at him.

He managed to stammer out, "I-I-I'm sorry...I-I don't...." before she grabbed the back of his head and closed the gap again.

On instinct, one hand moved to run through her hair, and the other rested on her back—after dropping his sword on the floor with a clatter. Deep in Scoruș' mind, Myrddin grinned.

Cojiñí, who had just arrived, smiled sadly at the sight of her brother and her best friend kissing, arms wrapped around each other. She teleported away to the Ynys Golauglas clearing before the others noticed they were not the only people in the training room.

When they came up for air, they stepped back so as not to get carried away, and after clearing his throat multiple times, Scoruș spoke, his voice a bit shaky.

"Alezandra, who was once Balowen, the Lady of Ravens, would you do me the extreme pleasure of being my girlfriend, and in doing so, allow me to court you?"

She smiled. "Yes, you doofus. Why do you think I didn't smack you hard enough that your brain rattled when you kissed me?"

He flushed. "That's certainly what I expected you to do."

She laughed, and he flushed deeper red, then smiled.

At the next meeting of the Pseudo-Reincarnated teens a few weeks later, Kennedy's chocolate-brown eyes took one glance at Scoruș and

Alezandra, their close proximity to each other, and easily deduced the correct reason for their handholding and sappy looks. It appeared as though they were catching up with the rest in following the relationship paths they had taken in the time gone by.

The ginger-haired nineteen-year-old chanced a glance at Cojiñí, and noticed her distance from not only her brother, but also everyone else in the group. After managing to catch Alezandra's gaze, he directed the sandy-auburn-haired young woman's attention to her boyfriend's sister.

Alezandra whispered something to Scoruş, and the raven-haired young man looked at his sister. Alezandra tugged his arm and pulled him over to sit with Cojiñí. The midnight-eyed young woman seemed glad that someone was willing to sit near her, but also ready to bolt and hide. Was it because her brother and her best friend had gotten together, or something else entirely? A combination of the two? Kennedy did not know, and he was not about to ask. That would be prying into things that were not his business.

After the "meeting," Cojiñí went to her room, grabbed *Frankenstein* and *The Phantom of the Opera,* along with her MP3 player and earphones, and teleported back to "her spot" on the beach on Ynys Golauglas. Putting the earbuds in and turning the music up, with the forest to her back and the sea before her, the caramel-skinned young woman began to read, losing herself in the words of Mary Shelley and Gaston Leroux.

When it started to rain, she packed her stuff to keep the books from getting wet. But once that was taken care of, she remained seated there, on the rocks by the sea in the rain, staring out at the dark green waves.

Closing her eyes, Cojiñí transfigured her clothes into a swimsuit and stored her books in the mid-space, before walking up to a higher point of the rocks. Once she reached her chosen spot, the raven-haired young woman raised her arms above her head, placed her feet, angled her body, and dove into the water.

She was unaware of two people—well, one person and a genderless tree-sentience—watching her from just behind the tree line.

Barhaol watched as Its female child dove into the sea, which was rapidly growing stormy. The young man at Its side was just as silent, though he seemed worried when It glanced at him. His flame-ginger hair looked dark from the rain, and his chocolate brown eyes were dark as well, though not from water. No, it was some unidentifiable emotion that darkened Kennedy's eyes.

He turned to Barhaol, and It silently challenged Kennedy to speak. He pressed his lips together, then turned back to face the sea. Barhaol frowned. It seemed that the young man who had once been Taliesin the Bard was not ready to speak his thoughts about his mental and emotional situation. No matter, It was patient. It had waited over four hundred years. It could wait for a few more months.

All the others had chosen the paths they had chosen before, although if these two chose different paths, it would not affect the endgame, much. However, they must choose something, as this...state of emotional unrest that they were in continued. Though they were all accustomed to the lack of personal space in a melee, that could slip if they found themselves in a...compromising situation. Not as compromising as some...battles may be, however, in the rush of the fight, if they were not in a stable relationship, if something happened as did happen with Scoruș and Alezandra when they practiced together, they would lose precious time and turn the battle in the wrong direction due to their deaths.

Barhaol sighed, and teleported Itself and the ginger-haired young man away.

The water did not seem as cold to Cojiñí's body underneath as it had felt on the surface. And though it was dark, she could see pretty much perfectly. Underneath the roiling waves, the ocean was calm and beautiful, and it was soothing to the raven-haired young woman's mind and heart to be immersed in that serenity.

She continued on the muscle-memory path towards the merfolk city, though she knew that Mooneye might be dead by now. She was intending to check. She did not know the lifespan of merfolk. Perhaps they could survive for longer than the length of time Morgaine was dead and Cojiñí had not yet merged with the Medieval Mage.

The merfolk's city was just as beautiful as Morgaine remembered, and Cojiñí's eyes went wide at the sights. The stone of the buildings seemed as if it had been hewn from the ocean floor. Sections of the sea floor were covered with gardens of underwater flowers of blue, green, silver, and purple, and others were paved with what appeared to be smooth white marble. Flitting throughout the city were vast numbers of multi-coloured fish, as if the city attracted hordes of strange birds.

In the centre of the city square, which was actually a circle, there was a huge statue of a familiar mermaid, a trident in her hand pointing towards the surface. Cojiñí's halted in front of the statue. After a few moments, the merfolk began to notice her and a small crowd gathered, through which many whispers began to circulate. A Leggéd One was in their midst for the first time in a very long while. There was a rumble in the crowd, and a voice called out a name.

"Morgaine?"

Cojiñí turned around, and there was Mooneye swimming towards her. The Mer-Chief's queen's deep-green hair had turned pale silver, and the edges of her scales had turned the same, but other than that there was no sign any time had passed, at least in her physical appearance. Although advanced wisdom shone in the mermaid's silver eyes, and her garments had changed.

When Morgaine first met Mooneye, and when she last saw her, the green-skinned mermaid had been arrayed in kelp and seashells, with a few items denoting her status as Chief's Wife. Now, however, she wore dyed-purple seaweed, pearls, and a silvery metal that would never rust. One item of that metal looked eerily similar to an elaborate breastplate, though it reached only from the end of her ribcage to an inch below the collarbone. Streaming down from that were ribbons of the purple seaweed, forming a sort of short skirt, through which she could see a belt of black pearls encircling Mooneye's hips. In one hand, Mooneye grasped a black-and-silver trident, identical to the one in the statue, and very like the one that had been strapped to the back of the Mer-Chief when Morgaine first met him.

"Morgaine?"

Mooneye swam closer, and grabbed Cojiñí by the chin, forcing her to meet her eyes, which had narrowed with suspicion.

Finally, Cojiñí spoke. *"Hello, Mooneye. It is a pleasure to finally meet you."* As an afterthought, she said, *"Morgaine is asking me to tell you that it is a great pleasure to see you again, and that she is glad you are still alive after all these years."*

Mooneye released Cojiñí's chin. *"By what name are you known now, Leggéd Fingerling?"*

"Cojiñí Seasword, of Clan Balaur."

The silver-eyed mermaid hmmm-ed, and wrapped one arm around her shoulders, then faced the gathered crowd. She raised the trident.

"Our leggéd mermaid has returned to us!"

The crowd cheered, and Mooneye led Cojiñí to her house to explain what had happened in the years since she and Morgaine had seen each other last.

They spoke for at least two hours, there under the Atlantic Ocean, until Cojiñí began to feel that it was time to return home, to flat number 332C. She bid farewell to Chieftess Mooneye, and teleported into her room, using magic to clean herself. She summoned her books back from the mid-space, and returned them back where they belonged, then ambled downstairs to curl up on the sofa.

Araunya and Scoruș were not there, so Cojiñí put one of her favourite movies in the DVD, fixed a snack and a glass of water, and wrapped herself in a fuzzy blanket. She fell asleep just as the credits began to roll. A few minutes later, her aunt and brother walked in the front door. Her brother turned off the television, washed the plate and glass, and carried Cojiñí to her room. Araunya slipped the bed covers over the seventeen-year-old, and Scoruș turned out the light as they left Cojiñí's bedroom to watch something they preferred, but Cojiñí did not particularly enjoy.

Chapter 19

MORGAUSE SMILED AS SHE WATCHED PELIAS sleep in his crib. Her son was beautiful, and she knew he would be the perfect epitome of "tall, dark, and handsome" when he was grown. She just hoped she would be there to see it.

A few weeks ago was the eighteenth birthday of the "hosts" of Morgaine and Myrddin. Morgause, and all her allies, could feel the battle drawing closer, and with great speed. The way things were going, and at the rate the younger Pseudo-Reincarnated ones were becoming closer to how they had been in the time gone by, the Second Battle of Camlann would take place before Pelias turned two years old.

The ocean-eyed woman felt her husband's hands rest on her hips, and her smile changed as she twisted to capture his lips in a soft kiss. The evermore-present danger that they may not live much longer had changed their dynamic as spouses, and made it more urgent, and yet softer. They were attempting to get as much time together, yet savour every moment as if it was an eternity at the same time. The way it looked, Pelias might end up with a sibling, should they survive.

At the thought of her son, Morgause turned her gaze back to the crib as Cenric rested his chin on her shoulder. She stroked his cheek absently, then closed her eyes and drew on a memory that most times she wished she did not still have. Now, however, it gave her comfort.

Though none of them would ever tell anyone, not even those to whom they were married, Morgause, Mordred, Morgaine, and Myrddin came from the same village by the sea. They had been close friends

until one day when the pale-gold-haired twins discovered they had magic, and the raven-haired twins found out the same. They were going to be the unbeatable team of four Archmages, travelling around the countries rescuing people in need.

Morgause smiled then, gently, in a way no one had seen in an eternity of time, then that smile turned to a deep frown as the memory continued and she could not get out of it. Someone was messing with her mind, she thought, before being pulled back into the memory.

Then came the trouble. Morgause and Mordred were playing with their magic as they walked around town. Although they had all made a pact to keep it a secret, at the request of their respective mothers, and in the ocean-eyed twins' case, father. Everything was fine until they were seen making fire-shapes by one of the most superstitious and, unfortunately, influential people in the town. Morgause and Mordred were fated to burn at the stake for witchcraft and no matter what Morgaine and Myrddin tried to do to save them, no one listened, as they were only children at the time, and therefore not worth listening to, according to the town elders.

The torch was about to touch the pyre when the knights of the Black King came riding in like dark saviours. Normally the knights would not care about two pre-teens being burnt at the stake, but the Black King himself was there and dragged them onto his horse before anything could be done about it. The last thing the pale-gold-haired twins saw as they were carried away was Morgaine and Myrddin's despairing midnight-blue eyes staring after them.

The years passed, and Morgause and Mordred were corrupted by the Black King's ways and thoughts, and slowly turned from their dream of rescuing people to the dark ambition of destroying the two people they thought could have prevented them from a horrible death by burning, but did not. Followed by the Black King's wish to take control of Camelot and the surrounding lands. They trained, and became proficient in the ways of dark magic, true witchcraft. Their first kill of a human was on their fifteenth birthday. That was a simple beheading.

Their first execution by torture was on their seventeenth birthday. One day, during Morgause and Mordred's nineteenth year, the Black King approached them with a proposition. How would they like to raid a village? Yes, they would like to raid a village, they said. Which village would they be raiding? When they were told it was the village they had been "rescued" from, identical evil smirks appeared on their faces. That was the day they burned the village that had once been their home, to the ground, unintentionally leaving only Morgaine, Myrddin, and Guiomar—their mother—alive.

Even with that, the raven-haired twins that had once been their best friends continued to offer the pale-gold-haired twins a way back from the path they had chosen, up until the Battle of Camlann, that was, in which case they either never got a chance, or finally got it through their thick skulls that there was no going back for the ocean-eyed twins.

Morgause was finally brought out of those memories by Cenric biting her ear. She smacked him, and he chuckled softly. He was not fighting against people who had once been his friends, as was the case for her, Mordred, Agravaine, Rhiannon, and Nyneve. Or for his family, as in Peredur's case. He was merely carrying on a vendetta set by his father against Arthur's father, and then Arthur himself. Morgause considered him lucky in that, though she knew she and Mordred were the only ones who ever considered the fact that those they were mortally set against had once been the very ones with whom they had shared everything.

The fair-skinned woman turned her gaze once more to her infant son. She had a plan that no one else would know—a plan that would ensure the survival of the babe should she and Cenric perish, and if the rest did the same. It was a dangerous game to be sure, but this darker dream would have an ending, as did everything. Morgause just hoped it would not end in her death, and especially not the death of her child.

* * *

Scoruş and Alezandra waltzed throughout the mid-space ballroom. In fact, the only people *not* dancing were James, Kennedy, and Cojiñí. James was not dancing because he did not have a date, and he had not wanted to dance in the first place, and so did not bring one. Kennedy and Cojiñí neither brought dates of their own, nor did they come as each other's dates, though they could easily dance together. Scoruş had seen enough of their synchronization in fighting practice to know that, yet they made no move towards the dance floor.

The midnight-eyed young man chided himself when he returned his focus to his dancing partner. Alezandra looked absolutely stunning that night, he thought. She wore a sweeping gown the exact same shade as her eyes, and minimal jewellery and makeup, as she preferred. Her curly sandy-auburn hair was up in some complicated style that he could not even begin to describe except to say that it looked beautiful on her. And yet, even as beautiful as she looked now, he still preferred it when she had her hair down.

Why they decided to hold a ball that day, Scoruş did not know, though he was not complaining. Yet even with as much fun as he was having dancing with his girlfriend, he still found his gaze resting on Kennedy and Cojiñí, or more specifically, the distance between them. Even he could see that they fancied each other, at least somewhat, and yet neither of them had an inkling of the other's intentions. It was driving him mad. How they could not see it when everyone else could? It was baffling.

Chiding himself once more, he returned his gaze to his date and put the puzzling question of Kennedy and Cojiñí out of his mind for the moment.

The raven-haired young woman appeared impassive and indifferent, on the outside. Within the privacy of her own mind, however, it was a different story. She did not bother to hide this from Morgaine.

Absently, she smoothed a small wrinkle in her gown, which had caught her eye the moment she saw it in the store. It was the same deep blue as her eyes, threaded with faint glints of silver. It was flowing, and flattering, yet modest, and when she tried it on that day, she felt like a princess, and properly smiled for the first time since she had nearly lost control that day the year before. She fingered her silver-and-blue ring for a moment, then made her way towards the food table. She was hungry, just a bit.

Alezandra was not blind. She could see her boyfriend's worried glances at his sister and she chanced a glance in that direction as well. All seemed fine to her, at least as far as she could tell from looking at the back of Cojiñí's head. Although, she seemed to be eating many more sweets than she usually would.

The green-eyed eighteen-year-old returned her attention to the dance. If something were truly wrong with Cojiñí, the midnight-eyed young woman would tell her. She still considered her to be her best friend after all.

Music filled the room with a smooth, flowing, pulse-pounding rhythm. Ballet-slipper clad feet flew along the smooth wooden floor in time with the beat. A black-leotard-and-tights clothed dancer moved in graceful motions as she spun and leapt around the room.

The dancer's eyes were closed, and yet she dodged cleanly every obstacle in her way. Her long hair was loose, an unusual state for it to be, and it flowed around her like streams of raven silk as she pirouetted.

The music increased in tempo, and the dancer's movements increased in speed. One hand flashed out, a blast of deep-blue light emerging from the palm and impacting a wall before bouncing off and into the dancer's other hand, turning into a glowing ribbon. The ribbon writhed through the air, and the end split into many tendrils. The music's tempo picked up even more, and another multi-tendril ribbon appeared in the dancer's other hand.

The ribbon-tendrils seemed to move in slow motion as the dancer's movements slowed to match the decreasing tempo of the music. Soon she was dancing at the same speed as before, a picture of dangerously controlled grace and power. Eventually, the music faded away and the dancer stopped, letting the glowing ribbon-tendrils dissipate.

She sat on the floor, which, at a thought, morphed into a small, comfy room with glass walls showing deep forest on one side and the ocean on the other. Instead of a proper ceiling, there was a transparent panel showing a starry sky. Where the dancer sat became a long sofa on which she was lying, eyes still closed tight. Different music began to play, soft and slow, and eventually the young woman's form relaxed and she sighed deeply.

After a few moments, Cojiñí stood and walked to one of the glass walls, looking out over the ocean. It was not real, she knew that. None of them was powerful enough yet to make more than enclosed rooms in the mid-space.

Her head snapped up from where she had rested it against the glass. She had an idea she couldn't believe she had not thought of before. The midnight-eyed eighteen-year-old teleported away from the room of her making, the furniture and scenery dissolving into nothing as soon as she left since it was designed to match the wishes of the occupants and now it was empty.

The raven-haired female Mage appeared in a darkened corner of the church sanctuary that she, Scoruș, and Araunya attended on a weekly basis. Her bare feet sunk into the geometrically-patterned carpet as she walked slowly up one of the side aisles to a pew near the front. Sitting down, she bowed her head and began to pray. She never really knew how long she sat there in the dark of the church sanctuary, praying and just sitting in silence, attempting to listen to God. It wasn't something she was that good at, but still she tried.

* * *

Araunya sighed deeply. She was tired. It had been a long day at the station. Though Paul Carson had been apprehended the year before, all the paperwork and such still had not yet been gone through. It didn't help that Jen would not tell anyone about the incident in the middle of the night and the person who dropped off the man trussed like a

Christmas turkey, along with more than thirteen of his accomplices.

The winter-eyed woman ran a hand over her angularly pretty face. Cojiñí had also been acting very strange for the last few months, and Araunya did not think it had anything whatsoever to do with her niece's lack of relationship—other than friendship—with a certain chocolate-eyed and ginger-haired twenty-year-old. Unfortunately, Cojiñí would not speak about it, and was actually doing a good job keeping whatever was bothering her hidden, at least in public. Yet in the times when she thought no one could see her, Araunya observed the caramel-skinned eighteen-year-old's eyes go dark and sad, as if there was a war raging within, or something of that sort.

Another thing Araunya noticed about the change in Cojiñí was that her aura was different, ever so slightly. A path had been taken, and the rest of the paths had been rejected, and whichever path had been chosen had done *something* to her niece.

Well, technically, Cojiñí and Scoruș were the children of Araunya's brother and his wife, however, something deep within the Warrior Mage told her that they should be the children of her and her husband, even though Araunya was not married. Sometimes in dreams, she got glimpses of another life—a woman named Guiomar with twin children and a dead or deserting husband. What was really odd about those dreams was that the children's names were Myrddin and Morgaine.

Araunya ran a hand over her face again and turned back to her work, putting thoughts of odd dreams and odd behaviour out of her mind. Some of the paperwork about Paul Carson had been assigned to her, and there was a new case that had come up—something about a pale man with red eyes hanging around the club district, and a bunch of disappearances that seemed to be connected.

* * *

Cojiñí appeared with a faint whoosh in Barhaol's chamber at the Lodge. The tree-sentience looked up from whatever it was that It had been messing with. When It saw her face, Its eyes gained an understanding and It remained silent as she spoke.

"Why, Barhaol? Why did you do this to us?"

One colourless and translucent eyebrow rose.

"Why did you do this to us? Why take dying and dead minds and force them on unwilling and unknowing random people?" Her voice did not rise, but the few physical items in the room began to shake, and the air took on the distinct smell of sulphur. "Why not just let us live normal lives? Why burden us with this?"

Suddenly, the small chamber was completely full of people as the rest of the twelve Pseudo-Reincarnated young men and woman appeared behind Cojiñí. So...she thought she would need backup perhaps?

Scoruș spoke. "I believe I speak for all of us when I say that I would like to know the answer to that question as well."

Barhaol frowned sympathetically as It looked at those standing there, but Its eyes were firm, though Its voice was kind. "Because you were compatible and because it was not yet time for those whom you bear within your minds to have perished as of yet."

Cojiñí's voice darkened and dripped with sarcasm. "That was *very* helpful."

Barhaol sighed, and all was silent for a few long moments, except for the rattling of the boards on which they stood and which made up the walls and ceiling.

Finally, It spoke. "I will tell you what I told those you host. Only Heaven, Hell, and their respective rulers are eternal, and even the Master of Lies and his domain shall yet fall under the sword of the One that the Druids called the White God."

It looked at them coolly. "You have a duty, and I know that you may have been unknowing when your other selves were unlocked, the process would not have happened if you were truly unwilling. Therefore, do not speak to me as if you were so. And I know you are neither unknowing nor unwilling now, though the natures of who you had been may cause a few...*problems* from time to time."

At the last, Barhaol gave a significant glance to Cojiñí, who looked down as the tumult in the room died down to a near-stifling stillness.

* * *

In the mansion in the mountains, Mordred and Owain were sparring with weapons of steel and wood, as were Agravaine and Peredur, along with Rhiannon and Morwen. Caelia, Bruin, Nyneve, and Meleagant were sparring amongst themselves as well, but not with weapons like the ones that the semi-magicals and Mordred were using. No, these others were sparring using magic, and magic only. Morgause and Cenric were probably playing with their son, or *sparring* by themselves. Or, they could be doing something completely different. Those in the training rings did not know.

The married pair, however, did know because they were there—in Pelias' room. They were not playing with the rapidly growing infant, however, merely watching him sleep, as they often did.

* * *

Cojiñí and Scoruș looked up as the door opened, and greeted their aunt as she came in. She had gone shopping, so the twins assisted her in carrying the bags from the car to the kitchen. Even though both had taken and passed their driver's licence tests, the three of them still had only the one car and Araunya enjoyed driving the twins around, most of the time.

"So how was school?"

"Good. Nothing remarkable happened." Apparently, Morgaine and Myrddin had spoken in tandem in their time, just as Cojiñí and Scoruș did. That was an interesting fact to learn.

It had been two days since the confrontation with Barhaol in the tree-sentience's chamber, and the twins still had not spoken about the *look* the translucent entity had given Cojiñí. Suddenly, the midnight-eyed young woman spoke up.

"Last year I nearly killed a man in cold blood."

Her brother and aunt looked at her in surprise. Araunya nodded for her to continue.

"One night, a few months after the talent show, I think it was in

June...I was taking a walk in the moonlight because I could not sleep. Five of the older kids from Glamdring cornered me in an alleyway and began taunting me about my alto voice. I just stood there for a while, waiting for them to run out of steam at my lack of reaction."

She sighed, and continued, "After five minutes or so, I asked them what they thought they would accomplish by taunting me, and one of them said something about *taming* me. It was then that I realised I was completely surrounded by ten more men, led by Paul Carson. They restrained me. Carson put a magic-suppressor on me. Morgaine helped me break it. I was furious. I immobilised all except Carson. I had my sword at his throat and no reason to let him live. He was going to get the death sentence anyway, so why not have justice come a bit early?"

Cojiñí took a deep breath and attempted to soldier on, but her voice broke, and she could no longer speak. Finally, after a few minutes of silence she said, "It would have been so easy to kill him. So easy. And I had no reason to let him go. No reason whatsoever. Like I said, he was, or is, as the case may be, slated for a death not of natural causes anyway."

Araunya wrapped her niece in her arms to comfort her. "What did you do, Cojiñí? What happened next? Trust me, you will feel better once it's all out."

Cojiñí took another deep breath. "I knocked him out with my pommel and bound him and his fourteen compatriots. I carried him and floated the others to the police station, where I gave them to the officer on duty. Then I left her with the men, and went to Ynys Golauglas. I spent the rest of the night floating in the sea and dreamed about Morgaine's friendship with a Mer-Chief's wife, now the Chieftess herself, named Mooneye."

"Why did you not tell us any of this before?!" Scoruș was concerned and angered, but when Cojiñí answered him, her voice was perfectly level, if a bit cold.

"I was afraid. Afraid you would reject me. Afraid you would hate me. Afraid you would say I was turning dark."

The winter-eyed, forty-year-old woman had the midnight-eyed eighteen-year-old in a tight embrace before she could say any more.

She was soon followed by the eighteen-year-old's twin brother. "We love you, Cojiñí, and I for one will never reject you, nor do I believe there is any way that either of you could turn dark."

After that admission, Cojiñí was back to her normal self, mostly. She ended up telling the Pseudo-Reincarnated group what had happened to cause her to change her behaviour, and was assaulted with a barrage of hugs.

A few weeks later, Aidan proposed to Araunya. She accepted, and James and Jennifer were chosen to be Best Man and Maid of Honour at their wedding, the date of which was set a few months in the future. Although the elder adults were aware that it was not technically their fight, they were planning to do so, and therefore they did not want to waste any time.

At the wedding, which went very well, Cojiñí and Scoruș took on the roles of ring bearer and flower girl. They looked very nice, but on that day, no one could upstage Araunya. She was positively, literally glowing. Her traditional snow-white gown was trimmed with accents of blood red, and among the white flowers in her bouquet, the same red colour shone through.

James was glad to see that his mission-partner had managed to put her *wariness*—from their time in the Mercenaries Guard—behind her and wed his best friend. He, on the other hand, had no intention whatsoever of ever getting married. He was happy being single, thank you very much. However, he did admit that the colleague friend of Araunya's, the brown-haired one, was indeed pretty in her simple, yet elegant, crimson dress that his partner had chosen for all the bridesmaids, of which there were three. Those three, not that it mattered *too* much, were the winter-eyed woman's sister, Neva, her sister-in-law, Tara, and her friend, Jennifer. As the flower girl, Cojiñí did not really count as a bridesmaid.

On a slightly off topic, James did see a certain ginger-haired young man looking appreciatively at a certain midnight-eyed young woman as she walked down the aisle scattering flower petals.

Being a prudent couple, Aidan and Araunya decided to put off their honeymoon in favour of helping the Pseudo-Reincarnated ones prepare for the rapidly approaching Battle.

* * *

In the mansion in the mountains, Mordred and Morgause sat in council with the rest of their allies. The topic of discussion was, of course, the upcoming Battle. Those who could, made arrangements in case they perished and the others not, and Morgause admitted that she had a plan for her and Cenric's son should they all fall. She stubbornly refused to say what it was, however, no matter how much the others prodded. All she had said was that it would work, and it was none of their business. When Cenric said that it was his son, and therefore his business, all he gained was a fierce glare. No one tried after that. If Cenric, her husband, could not pry the information out of her, then no one could—until she was ready to tell. Of course, that was assuming she ever told them at all.

After the meeting, Morgause went by herself to Pelias' nursery and cast the necessary charms and cantrips that she still needed to cast to protect her son. He was probably the only offspring she would ever have, after all.

She placed one hand on the ocean-eyed infant's head and gently stroked his dark hair.

"Pelias, my son, you'll be strong; I know that."

The door opened behind her, and the wine-crimson-clad woman turned. Cenric stood there, smiling, yet he had a tinge of sadness. He walked forwards and wrapped her in his arms. She returned the embrace, laying her head on his shoulder.

"All will be well, my dear. We will live to see our son grown." His voice was comforting, but Morgause was not reassured much.

"We hope."

* * *

"Checkmate!" Ashton leaned back in his chair, grinning.

Gareth huffed. "You always win."

The blue-eyed, eighteen-year-old shrugged. "Not my fault that I'm a better strategist than you."

The other young man frowned, then let it go, just as he had every time his cousin won since they became old enough to not fight about it. He looked around the room.

They were all in the living room of flat number 332C doing assorted things that they felt like doing at the time. Scoruș and Alezandra were attempting to read the same book at the same time. Lea, Ivan, Pietro, Rae, and Kennedy were playing Clue. And Cojiñí and Mae were chatting about...something.

Looking at the pleasant, cheerful scene before him, Gareth suddenly felt a chill run down his spine. It was not the slight chill that came when using his magic, nor was it the feeling he got when someone was watching him. No, it was a realisation that this was the calm before the storm.

Something tapped his shoulder, and the green-eyed Ice Lord jumped. He turned to see Ashton looking at him with concern.

"Hey, you all right?"

Gareth nodded. "Yeah...I'm fine."

Ashton smiled. "Ready to be beat again?"

One dark-blond eyebrow rose. "Maybe I'll get lucky this time and you'll be the one who gets beat."

They turned their attention back to the chessboard.

"Don't count on it, cousin." The blue-eyed young man warned, and the game began.

Chapter 20

THE DAY WAS FRIDAY, THE 24TH OF JUNE, and a storm was mere moments from breaking. All twenty-four of the Pseudo-Reincarnated people could *feel* it. Tensions were high on both sides. In moments of spontaneous irrelevant thought, those of the twenty-four who were still in school were glad it was summer, and therefore they would not miss any classes.

* * *

Morgause and Cenric bid farewell to their son, leaving instructions with the construct servants to care for him until they returned. In private, Morgause also instructed them to let certain people with raven hair, caramel skin, and midnight eyes to take the infant away if they came to do so.

That taken care of, the only formally married couple of their twelve joined the other ten in the antechamber of the mansion. Once all were gathered, an army of wyrms was summoned. Though most of them were certain they would be the ones to survive, taking chances was not an option. They would to anything they could to ensure their victory.

Casting a glance around to make sure everyone was there, they teleported away to Camlann Valley, which, thankfully, was just as bare as it had been all those centuries ago. There they waited for their opponents to make their presence known. This was not a battle to be fought from the shadows, after all.

* * *

Weapons had been sharpened, armour had been strapped on, and all were as ready as they could be for the battle that would begin that day. They were all clad in the garments that those they "hosted" had worn at this same event so long ago. Those who had not been Pseudo-Reincarnated were dressed similarly, if in a bit more modern way because they knew their opponents would have garbed themselves in a similar manner. If nothing else, doing all of the fastenings, and putting on all the layers was at least a distraction from what was about to happen—within the hour.

At ten o'clock, Barhaol appeared. "It is time," was all It said, and then the genderless tree-sentience disappeared.

With grim-set faces and power swirling invisibly around those of them who were magical, the twelve Pseudo-Reincarnated, and five regular people teleported away to where they could feel their opponents were waiting.

* * *

On Ynys Golauglas, Charani Duskflame and Durriken Stormeye looked up from their respective work as a chill ran down their spines. They worried for a moment, and then passed it off as nothing but an open window. However, when they examined the respective rooms they were in and found no open windows, they passed it off as their imaginations and went back to work.

In his bedroom in the Lodge, Jardani, son of Charani and Durriken looked up from his game and frowned deeply. Something was different in the air, he thought, and went to open his own window to let in the summer breeze and wash away the chill that had randomly ...appeared.

Neva Whitefeather set down her pencil and sketchpad, and put on her Mage Robes. She grabbed her staff and preferred other weapon—that being a pair of thin daggers—and teleported to where she felt her sister and brother were. She may not have approved at first, but the twins had grown on her, and she had a feeling that whatever was going on, her help *might* be appreciated somewhat. She wasn't a Warrior Mage, but all Balaurs over the age of ten knew their way around a weapon of some kind.

* * *

The valley known as Camlann was broad and green, and although the sun was in the sky, a cold wind blew and dark clouds gathered in the distance, heralding rain. Luckily, there were no animals around, other than the wyrms milling around behind Morgause, Mordred, Cenric, and their allies.

The twelve and five did not appear on a ridge where they had been standing in those shared dreams. Rather, they materialised directly on the battlefield itself, as the other twelve had.

The two...armies stood across from each other, silent and motionless. The wind whipped all hair not tightly bound into the owner's face, and all clothes with flowing parts became tangled in hip-sheathes and around arms and legs, unless it was kept in place by magic. Then, seemingly, all as one, those who were not wyrms, moved. Swords, daggers, and other bladed things were unsheathed. Axes, maces, and similar weapons were unhooked from belts and magic began to swirl in the air-space.

Unnoticed, Neva appeared and joined the ranks of those fighting with Cojiñí and Scoruș and those who joined them hosting another mind within their own.

Then, almost at the same moment, both sides charged. Wordless battle shouts resounded through the air. Chaos erupted as they met in the near centre of the valley's field. Some blades hit blades and armour with a clang, and others sliced through the forms of leaping or running wyrms, which were dead before they hit the ground.

Cojiñí's blade met Mordred's first, then it glanced off to hit Owain's shoulder-armour. She swung it back, aiming at Mordred's torso, but he blocked and drove her backwards with a burst of magic, causing her to knock into a wyrm, which she beheaded with a clean swipe using magic to strengthen her swing so as to slice through the bone with more ease. Looking once more towards Mordred, Cojiñí saw that he had been engaged by Pietro, who was zooming around the ocean-eyed man and forcing him to do his utmost to block the magically swift young man's strikes.

A pair of wyrms began to attack her, and she dispatched them with without difficulty. Morgaine was leaking through the blocks Cojiñí's "other self" had erected, at the "newer" young woman's request. They had separated themselves mentally, but now they were fully merging in Cojiñí's time of need.

Glancing around, the midnight-blue-eyed young woman saw something that made the world go into slow motion. About thirteen metres away, her brother was in combat with Morgause, and although for a moment, it seemed as if he was winning, Cojiñí soon realised that the elder woman was just playing with him before she made her ending strike.

Cojiñí started towards them when three wyrms descended on her. In the ensuing skirmish, she lost sight of her brother and his foe. The three wyrms that Cojiñí was fighting were particularly persistent, but she was still able to slay them fairly quickly.

Once the wyrms had been dispatched, the raven-haired young woman saw a scene that would haunt her for all of her life, no matter how long it might be. Everything around her seemed in slow motion once more as Morgause knocked Scoruș' sword away and stabbed him in the torso before the caramel-skinned eighteen-year-old could summon up some magical—or other physical—way to defend himself.

The scream of utter agony and rage pierced the air like a banshee's wail as the young Archmage watched her brother fall and lie motionless on the ground. Cojiñí's eyes blazed with a fury even more potent than she had felt when she nearly killed Paul Carson. She advanced towards Morgause, her sword-blade crackling with magic taking the form of azure lightning. Those fighting around her moved out of the way while Cojiñí, no ... Morgaine passed them on her way to kill the woman who killed her brother.

When she reached her, Morgaine struck instantly, her sword sparking. Morgause parried and jabbed towards her right arm. Morgaine sidestepped, and slashed towards Morgause's torso, intending to slice her in half. The other woman sent a sharp blast of magic that forced Morgaine to step back, her swing going wide.

Step, slash, block, jab, fireball, dodge, lightning, slice, kick, block, parry, jab—they lost track of time as they fought. Morgaine's anger cooled somewhat, but her determination to kill her brother's slayer never subsided.

After what seemed to be an eternity and yet no time at all, Morgaine got a lucky strike, and impaled Morgause through the midsection. As the other woman fell, she grabbed onto the front of Morgaine's tunic and looked her in the eye. Suddenly, the midnight-eyed young woman remembered exactly whom it was that she had just mortally wounded. The woman before her had once been her closest friend.

Morgaine sank to her knees, an unconscious shield going up around her and the woman she now held in her arms to keep them from further harm.

"Mor...."

Morgause smiled weakly at the once-familiar nickname they had shared between them. She raised a hand and put it on her former best-friend's shoulder. The ocean-eyed woman coughed up a bit of blood from the internal bleeding the sword-strike had caused.

"Your... brother... isn't... dead..." she coughed. "I... deliberately missed his heart and... as many of... the vital organs... as I could...." Hacking cough. "His magic... has put up... a defence, so... he... should live. You'll... need to get to him... soon, though, or... he'll bleed... out."

Morgaine smiled sadly at her, and Morgause managed to continue, through the hacking up of blood and rapidly weakening muscles. She pushed an amulet into Morgaine's hand. "Take... care... of... my... son... for... me..., Mor." Then her head rolled back and her hand flopped down. Morgause was dead.

Morgaine tucked the amulet away in her tunic and stood rapidly, ignoring her slight dizziness in favour of blasting the wyrms that had decided to attack her into pieces. She had to find her brother. Had the two women stayed in the same place while they fought, he would have been no more than a few metres away. As it was, however, that was not the case. Yet even with that disadvantage, she did locate her twin fairly quickly. They always found each other. Always. No matter what stood in their way. They were Magical Twins after all, so they could not stay separated for long.

The angularly pretty Archmage knelt at her wounded brother's side. Good, he was still breathing. While Morgaine was not as good a healer as Elaine was, she knew her way around a wound, and had much experience healing them. She folded her hands on top of the nearly fatal wound and pushed gentle, yet urgent waves of magic into it, smiling in relief when the bleeding stopped and he was still breathing, although the wound did not close. He had not fully healed, but his own magic could take care of the rest now that he was out of so much danger. She sent him to a small mid-space room so that he would not be harmed any further.

Now that she was certain her brother would live, Morgaine returned her attention to the battle raging around her. She cast her gaze around and it landed on one of the last people she expected to see here. Was that Neva? She teleported closer. Yes, it was Neva, and she was attempting to fight Agravaine. But attempting does not mean succeeding, so Morgaine teleported over to assist her.

After a bit, Agravaine was passed off to Ivan, who was, at that moment, Lancelot. Morgaine nodded at the knight, and one corner of his mouth lifted in reply. Neva spoke.

"Thank you for that, Cojiñí."

Morgaine inclined her head. "You are welcome. But at the present time, I am Morgaine."

The other caramel-skinned woman accepted the correction graciously, and then they were caught up in different bouts with wyrms and moved away from each other.

In other parts of the battle, a few more of the direct foes were slain. Branwen had taken down Caelia with the assistance of her ravens—the birds distracted the Sidhe Queen just long enough for the curly-haired woman to relive her of her head. It was with great personal pleasure that Geraint finally took down Peredur, by way of a double-stab—the pale man had managed to block only the first. Elaine was locked in combat with Meleagant, likewise were Aderyn and Morwen, Gwenhwyfar and Rhiannon, and now Agravaine and Lancelot. Aidan and James had taken on Mordred, and the rest of Morgaine's allies were fighting wyrms. The allies of Mordred, who were not fighting the allies of Morgaine, were taking what respite they could.

Taliesin dispatched a particularly stubborn wyrm with a grunt, then cast his gaze around the battlefield, blowing a loose lock of his flame-ginger hair out of his eyes. Having hair long enough to braid just appear on its own was a bit odd, but it came with the merging, so he dealt. Anyhow, it was more the sudden appearance rather than the length that was the odd part.

The chocolate-eyed man's gaze landed on something he never wanted to see ever again. Morgaine was fighting a fair number of wyrms, and behind her, sword raised to strike, was Owain, but she had no clue. He took off towards them, running as fast as he could, and just barely managed to parry Owain's strike before he hit Morgaine. The slightly older man's grey eyes narrowed at the sight of his direct foe, and his strikes were aimed to kill the ginger-haired man in the most painful way possible, as was his wont when fighting Taliesin.

In the time gone by, Owain had been one of the young men fighting under Arthur, for a time. When Myrddin and Morgaine arrived in Camelot, the grey-eyed young man got it into his head that he was going to wed Morgaine, and nothing would stop him in his pursuit. Of course, Morgaine ended up falling in love with Taliesin, and Owain left Camelot in search of a way to force Morgaine to love him, or at least be willing to wed him. Soon after he left he ran into Morgause, Mordred, and the Black King, and they ended up where they were at the moment.

Taliesin ducked under a strike intended to take off his head and jabbed at Owain's heart with a small dagger that had been in his sleeve. The dagger impacted because of how close they were standing, but it did not hit the other man's heart, although it did puncture a lung. In an uncharacteristic show of pure violence, Taliesin followed up that stab with a punch to the same place where the dagger had gone in, forcing it further into the other man's chest. The angle change from Taliesin's punch not only pushed the dagger further in, it also caused the point to slice through a wall of his heart.

The ginger-haired man had to jump back, bringing the dagger with him as a slender blade suddenly protruded from the air just above Owain's left shoulder, in the body of a now-dead wyrm. The loss of support, and the removal of the dagger that had plugged profuse bleeding, caused Owain to fall limp and sink to the ground. He was dead in moments.

In another part of the battle, a few more direct foes were locked in combat. Vortigern and Bruin nearly ran into Gwenhwyfar and Rhiannon, just as the second half of the latter pair was defeated with a bit of help from Araunya. At the sight of his could-have-been-wife being slain, the brown-haired Fire Lord's attacks gained in ferocity to kill his opponent then destroy the woman who killed her. Unfortunately, while his anger made him more powerful, it also made him reckless, and a well-aimed ice dart from Vortigern slipped past Bruin's flaming defences.

One more direct foe down. Five to go. And, hopefully, none of the others fell while attempting to take down that last five.

Arthur was losing. That was a fact. While the golden-haired son of Uther had been training all his life, the son of the Black King was a few years older and therefore had more training. While Bruin's anger made him reckless because of lack of control, Cenric retained perfect control of his. Therefore, the fact that Morgaine killed Morgause, and Cenric's response made the black-haired man an even more dangerous opponent.

It was already a fairly warm day for Wales, but the exertion and heat of battle caused streams of perspiration to run down Arthur's face and get in his eyes. The temporary blindness almost lost his side their king. Luckily, a certain Balaur artist happened to be less than a metre away and so it was easy for her to join them in time to save Arthur's life with a well-placed kick to the back of Cenric's knee. He stumbled, giving Arthur just enough time to wipe off the sweat from his face and see again. The two men fought for an uncountable—at least by them—amount of time, when finally Cenric was almost run over by a rampaging wyrm and dodged directly into Arthur's sword.

The sky-blue-eyed man pulled out the blade with a squelching noise, and turned his attention to where Gwenhwyfar had been beset by wyrms. He did not just slay his direct foe only to see his wife and queen be slaughtered by those horrid creatures.

The sun was low in the sky, yet the battle still raged and it seemed as if it would continue through the night even though all were exhausted. Elaine had slain Meleagant, but Morwen, Nyneve, Agravaine, and Mordred still lived. Eventually, it was decided there would be an unofficial truce for a few hours so they could all get some sleep.

When morning came, the temporary camp of Arthur's followers gained another person. Scoruș, or Myrddin for now, had returned, and was healed enough to join the fight once more. He was greeted with open arms and tight embraces once Elaine declared him fighting fit, that is. Those that had seen him fall were ever so glad he was not dead, and those who hadn't witnessed the act were glad that he was back from wherever it was that he had disappeared to. Now that they had all twelve of their Pseudo-Reincarnated members, plus the six adults, not to mention that there were only four of their Pseudo-Reincarnated foes left—though they could not forget the still numerous wyrms—it seemed there was a much greater chance they would come out of this battle victorious.

The truce ended once everyone was awake and armoured. Neither army would be heading into the fray unready or unprepared. Branwen smacked Myrddin for going up against Morgause alone, and when he protested that Morgaine had done it, she smacked him again and said, "Well, you are not Morgaine, are you?"

The raven-haired man had shaken his head no, and the matter was not brought up again.

Over in the other camp, Mordred sighed deeply. Counting himself, there was only four of them left. His sister had been the first to fall, soon followed by her husband—the son of the man who made them what they were now. Only he, Nyneve, Morwen, and Agravaine remained. And the wyrms, but they did not count for anything. Wyrms were just animals, incapable of reason or rational thought. However, the impossibly handsome man had to admit, some animals are capable of those attributes—dragons, for instance. Now, that would be a hunt worth having. Before the first Battle of Camlann, hunting had been Mordred's favourite pastime, as it was for most nobles of the time.

Now, however, there were other things on his mind than hunting—mainly trying to figure out a way to survive the day. Even if he was the only one to do so, he knew enough necromancy to attempt to bring back at least Morgause, and then when he succeeded, their combined power could bring back the rest...he hoped. As it was though, there were only four of them left, and of the full magicals, he was the most powerful by a pretty wide margin. Therefore, as it stood, he was the one most likely to survive especially since his direct foe had been taken out of the count.

The ocean-eyed man sighed again. He was tired. Not physically, no, he'd had a very restful night of sleep—without even dreaming—but still he felt tired. No, not tired, more like weary. Weary of the fight, weary of the lack of his Magical Twin, and weary of just about everything in general.

Morwen appeared at the entrance to his tent. He gestured for her to enter. The red-haired woman was followed by Agravaine and Nyneve. Apparently, they wanted to have a council.

The truce was over the moment everyone was out of his or her tent—and that moment had passed five minutes ago. Though there were less wyrms than the day before, the battlefield was still crawling with them. And yet, of the thirty people who had stepped onto the field yesterday, only twenty-two were left, and eighteen of those were on one side. They were heavily unbalanced, but no one was giving up. Too much was at stake. There was no in-between, no matter how much some of the members of the currently larger side wanted a truce. It was clear that that was not to be an option.

Branwen kept an eye on Myrddin as they gathered on the field once more. Hopefully this Battle would end that day and they could go home for some proper rest, and she could take a bath. She knew the other women would like to do the same. Blood, sweat, ashes, and all of the other grimes of battle would take at least a two-hour soak, if not longer.

Soon, chaos ruled as the fighting began again on the second day. As they fought, Branwen thought that future farmers would love this valley when they were done—what with all of the nutrients being soaked into the ground now stained black with wyrm blood. Crops would grow excellently here for the next few years.

However, those thoughts were put out of her mind when she was set upon by three of the creatures whose blood was staining the once-green grass.

Nimue was also set upon by wyrms, but as soon as she dispatched them, she was attacked by something that was definitely *not* a wyrm. Rather, it was Nyneve, her direct foe. Right then, a stream of icy water blinded her, followed by a slice to her torso that was—unfortunately—blocked. Blast, strike, step, duck, kick, doge, slice, jab, for over fifteen minutes before Nyneve tripped over a wyrm corpse, and Nimue took her chance. One dagger flashed and the silver-eyed woman's direct foe was no longer living.

As the day progressed, the number of wyrms diminished, but more diminishing needed to occur before there would be none left on the battlefield. Agravaine knew only three remained now, and the way things were going, there would soon be only two, then one, and then all would have perished at the hands of their direct foes. While not fully magical, Agravaine did have some telepathic ability, which was what had made him such a good scout and spy in the time gone by. As it was now, he was able to pick up on Mordred's plan, should the golden-haired man survive, and the brown-haired man agreed with him. It was a good plan, and from what he remembered of Mordred's necromantic talent, should work.

The green-eyed man's gaze landed on Lancelot, who was advancing towards him. He had fought his direct foe the day before, and obviously, the other man did not win as Agravaine was still among the living. Had this been one of those movies, both men would have drawn their swords, or other weapons, as Lancelot advanced, but since it was not a movie, and both of them already *had* their weapons out, such a thing was not needed. Battle is not glorious, as some would think. No, it is horrible: death and destruction, pain and blood and sorrow and loss. Yes, a victory is good, but even the victors lose something in the winning.

Their swords crossed with a clang, and Agravaine had to take a step back as Lancelot followed that up with an unusually swift strike to his midsection. Swipe to the legs, side-step, duck a beheading shot, missed kick to the knee, Lancelot hissed in pain as Agravaine's sword sliced open his tunic and along his arm. Agravaine smirked. Perhaps he would live after all.

Unfortunately, after another few minutes of fighting, the brown-haired man's luck seemed to have run out against the ink-haired man, and he was hit with a strong kick to the shin, sending him to his knees. He desperately dodged the dark-eyed man's swing as he clambered to his feet, sending a sharp twinge of pain up his leg. That pain, though he tried his best to get through it, made him clumsy, and he was therefore no longer as good a fighter as he had been only a few moments before.

A stray ice-dart from Vortigern, who was fighting wyrms a few metres away, hit Agravaine in the other leg, and he went down again. Though he managed to get up once more, he knew he had little time left. He could feel it was so, and therefore his attacks and defences became more desperate. Even if he did not live—due to bleeding out because the ice-dart hit a large artery—he would still attempt to take Lancelot down with him. Though he did get in a few more good shots, Agravaine was dead and Lancelot was still standing.

And now there were two.

Aderyn and Morwen stood across from each other, weapons ready. The Hawk and the Snake—called such due to the designs and shapes of the armour that they wore. Aderyn had been knighted in the middle of her eighteenth year, and the same happened to Morwen in the winter of the red-haired woman's twentieth. Both were odd-eyed—Aderyn's were green and orange-tinged brown, and Morwen's were a yellow-green. Those eyes were now staring at each other, the lights within shining grim and dark. There was no wind although the sky was cloudy, just as it had been all day.

Unlike the men, they did not immediately rush to attack. Rather, the two women circled each other warily, looking for weak points. Morwen was limping slightly, having been cut while fighting James. A small chunk of Aderyn's shoulder had been stolen by a wyrm. Other than those wounds, however, the two had managed to remain pretty much unharmed.

A few moments after that cataloguing was done, they moved in. Morwen easily parried Aderyn's strike to her upper right arm, and followed that parry with a swing aimed to remove the other woman's sword arm at the elbow. Unfortunately, that was just as easily parried, and without giving Aderyn a chance to attack, Morwen feinted left and drove her sword-point into the dark-haired woman's already wounded shoulder.

Aderyn gritted her teeth against the pain, before Morwen could recover from the attack she had made, the Hawk Dame delivered her own attack, jabbing the talons of her free hand into the side of Morwen. Morwen let out a gasp of pain, and tried to remove Aderyn's head, but the tri-colour-eyed woman merely forced her talons in deeper, and the stroke fell short. Then she removed them with a jerk, and Morwen fell back, clutching the bleeding wound.

With a grim face, the woman known as the Hawk Dame looked down at the woman known as the Snake Dame, and drove her sword into her heart, ending the red-haired woman's misery.

Only one was left now, and he was Myrddin's to take care of. Aderyn needed to find Elaine and get her wounds addressed, or she would bleed out.

She walked across the battlefield towards their camp, miraculously managing to not be caught in combat. Morwen's body was cooling behind her. They would find it later to prepare for burial, and do the same with the rest of their direct foes.

Neva pushed the wyrm's corpse off her and shakily stood. Looking around, she saw her sister and headed that way. But suddenly, she felt a stabbing pain in her midsection. She looked down, cornflower-blue eyes narrowing in confusion, then widening at the sight of a long, silvery blade protruding from just below her breasts. The artistic Balaur of the Chief's Line then looked up to see both Araunya and Khulai running towards her. She spit out the blood filling her mouth. It had a coppery taste. The edges of her sight began to grow grey and her senses started to dim. Then Neva felt the blade being removed, which released the flow of blood. The world went dark and her body went limp. She lost consciousness and then breathed her last breath softly, like a sigh.

James saw Araunya's reaction and heard her cry of rage and sorrow, so he looked to where she was looking. Mordred was standing over the dead body of Araunya's sister. The sandy-haired man growled low in his throat, his mind flashing back to his time in the Mercenaries Guard. Mordred hurt James' partner, so now he was going to pay—no matter that it was Myrddin's job to kill the golden-haired man. James just wanted to...talk to Mordred first, though blades and bullets didn't exactly speak with words.

With the Tân in one hand and a regular pistol in the other, Mercenaries Guard Captain Jamison Andrews snuck up rapidly behind the impossibly handsome monster of a man. He managed to get a bullet from the Tân through the back of Mordred's thigh before the other man realised he was there, then it all went to hell for the grey-eyed Captain-Assassin as Mordred spun around on his good leg and stabbed James in the gut.

James choked, and hoped to high heaven that the blade had missed his vital organs. He most definitely did not want to die that day. The sword was withdrawn. Mordred had become otherwise occupied, probably fighting Myrddin. Distantly, as the world grew grey, the wielder of the Tân heard Araunya run to him and felt her lift his head. Had he fallen over? It appeared to be that way.

He blinked a few times, and his sight cleared somewhat, revealing his partner's worried and angered face above him. He chuckled, or tried to, but it turned into a hacking cough.

"I'm...fine." He managed to say. "I...think it...missed most of...my vital organs."

"But you don't know, James." Worry was the predominant emotion in the winter-blue-eyed woman's face and voice.

He smiled and attempted to touch her cheek, but...he felt so tired all of a sudden. As the sandy-haired man's sharp grey eyes slid closed, he muttered, "I'll...be...just...fine."

Araunya looked up from the unconscious body of her partner at her brother, and he quickly scanned the sandy-haired man.

"He'll live, if I close the wound now."

She nodded sharply. "Do it. I'll watch your back and make sure you're not interrupted."

The caramel-skinned woman passed by the form of her best male friend and her brother and stood, casting a protective ward around the two so that no spells, guts, or anything of that sort would hit Khulai as he worked. After a few moments, she was joined by her husband who took one look at the situation and pulled out his gun to start shooting any wyrms that came within ten meters of the ward-bubble, the ones that she did not take down with her spells, anyway.

Perhaps half of an hour later, Khulai stood, breaking the ward-bubble with a popping sound. The couple turned to him.

"He'll be unconscious for a few more hours, but he will most certainly live if he's not wounded any further, at least until he's healed enough to be fighting fit."

"Good. I'll teleport him to the camp, then, or would you prefer to do it?" Araunya cocked her head and stabbed a wyrm in the eye. It had been trying to sneak up behind her.

Khulai shrugged. "You can take him. I'll take care of Aidan, make sure he doesn't die or get severely wounded."

She smirked, picking up James and slinging him over one shoulder. "You do that." Then she was gone.

While Khulai was healing James, Myrddin and Mordred were locked in fierce combat. Myrddin was angry at Mordred for killing his aunt and nearly killing his other aunt's best friend, in addition to the other reasons for which they were fighting. And Mordred was attempting to fight with a poisoned bullet lodged in his thigh, and with the desperation of knowing he was the only one left on his side, and the only way he would be able to bring the others back was if he survived—something that seemed unlikely, for even if he killed Myrddin in this duel, then Morgaine would kill *him*, if the poisoned bullet did not do so first. So Mordred was in a quandary, and though he knew he would most likely die either way, he would still *attempt* to survive, at least long enough to bring back his sister, who then could easily enough bring him back, and then together they could raise from the dead the rest of their allies.

Sparks flew from the clashing blades, and Mordred felt even more weary than he had been. It was now or never, he realised. Either he killed Myrddin, Myrddin killed him within the next fifteen minutes, or Myrddin's job would be done for him by the poison on the bullet from the Tân. Yes, he knew what it was—very few magicals of his and Morgause's calibre and affinity did not know of the legendary dagger-gun, even though it did not exist yet in the time gone by.

While Mordred was technically more fresh and rested, Myrddin did not have a poisoned bullet stuck in his thigh, leaking liquid death though his bloodstream. So, they were sort-of on even ground in that. Sort-of. Having poison running through your veins is *technically* a whole lot worse than being exhausted from previous fighting.

Myrddin fought with determination and anger. Mordred fought with determination and desperation. Though the ocean-eyed man's strikes were calculated, they were also not as controlled as they would normally be, sometimes going a bit wild. He sent an orb of sickly orange energy, but it was dodged and ended up hitting a few wyrms in the mini-pack about to attack Morgaine and Taliesin. He caught a ball of emerald-green lightning sent by Myrddin, and sent it back at the man, its colour shifting to scarlet in the pale-gold-haired man's hand. Myrddin deflected it with a wave of his hand, sending it off to one side somewhere.

Step strike kick block jab parry slice—Mordred attempted to speed up his movements, and he did succeed, but only a little bit. Suddenly, he felt a sharp burst of additional pain come from the bullet wound in his thigh, and he cried out. He sent a web of energy at Myrddin, then chanced a look down. A small shard of wyrm-talon was impaled in his leg less than a millimetre from where the Tân's bullet had hit him. Reaching down, he yanked the talon from his thigh, and hastily conjured up a clean band of cloth, then bound it around both wounds as tight as he could bear. He would rather his leg be numb than bleeding freely or becoming infected.

As soon as he had bound his leg, he was once again set upon by Myrddin, who was singed from the energy web, but still more fighting-fit than Mordred. The raven-haired man did not attack any harder than he had been, and yet Mordred felt like he was. The pale-gold-haired man was having difficulty blocking, parrying, and dodging the strikes of the other man's sword. He nearly stumbled over the corpse of a wyrm, but managed to leap out of the way just in time, though he landed on his bad leg, causing him to let out another cry of pain.

A few more minutes of fighting, and Mordred realised that there was almost no way for him to live past this day, even if he did live past this battle. He remembered then that the poison on the bullets of the Tân works faster once the wound was bound, unless it was purged first. Mordred certainly had not had time to cleanse his wound before binding it, and now he was feeling the effects. Well, then, better to die in battle from the clean strike of a sword than alone in some desolate place in slow agony from this particular kind of poison.

Mordred stopped defending himself. Yes, he made it a show, but a show was all it was. He was too weary to do more. Then, finally, the end came, and he got his glorious, preferred death as Myrddin relieved his handsome head from his broad and muscular shoulders. The last one was dead. Now, all that was left were the wyrms.

Morgaine saw Mordred fall, his head hitting the ground like a demented bowling ball, and smiled with relief at the death of the last of the direct foes, then she transformed into a midnight-blue-eyed black winged lion. After the turning of human to beast, the wyrms that were about to attack her backed off at the sight of their natural enemy. Morgaine knew that her compatriots who could, were doing a similar transformation from human to creature. As one, they pounced or flew into the fray, slaying many of the wyrms.

When at least half the remaining wyrms were dead, the fully magical creatures carried their allies, the ones who were not magical creatures, back to their camp, then leapt into the sky. They arranged themselves in a circle and transformed back into human form, using their magic to keep themselves afloat. Morgaine chuckled when she saw how utterly confused Araunya, Khulai, and Tara seemed.

Forming a temporary mind-link with the nine people in the circle, the raven-haired woman said, *'On my signal, send a steady blast to the centre of the circle. Myrddin and I will take care of the rest.'*

After receiving assenting replies, Morgaine held out her hands and let out a shrill call. Magic flowed from their hands and met, then streamed downwards, pierced the ground and caused all the rest of the wyrms to perish.

Chapter 21

IT TOOK THREE HOURS AFTER THE WYRMS WERE DEAD to find all the bodies of the Pseudo-Reincarnated's direct foes. Those from the time gone by had not yet let go of the bodies of their hosts, because they decided to wait until at least the end of the day. If nothing else, a slow transition would make it easier on the younger hosts to not go into shock at the deaths they caused, though the merged memories would help with that. Also, they did not want to let go of feeling truly alive—a feeling they they'd not had for many centuries.

Now that the Battle was over, it was time for the funerals. Thirteen had to be planned, and they knew how lucky they were that James and Myrddin did not bring that count up to fifteen. The corpses of the wyrms were piled and burned, but the direct foes, and Neva, deserved proper burials. Araunya and Aidan had anticipated leaving on their honeymoon the day after the end of the Battle, but because Neva, Araunya's sister, was to be buried, they chose to wait the proper two weeks of mourning before going on that trip. Luckily, Araunya had been off duty the past two days, and it was easy enough for her to schedule a week or so vacation time for the trip.

It was eventually decided that they would hold all the burials of the twelve direct foes on the same day, and then have Neva's funeral at least two days after that.

The evening of the day the Battle ended, Morgaine remembered Morgause's last request and pulled the amulet the now-dead woman had given her from her tunic's inside pouch. Examining the palm-sized disk of metal, the caramel-skinned woman discovered a name carved into one side: Pelias.

As she spoke that one word, she felt a pull—a forced teleportation—taking place. She appeared in the most opulent nursery she had ever seen, and yet it was not gaudy. In one corner of the room, near the large windows, was a crib made of well-carved ebony, fitting for the child she assumed was the son of one of the most powerful magicals in the Western Hemisphere and the Black King.

Morgaine walked to the crib and looked down on an infant boy who could not have been more than one year old. His hair was inky-black and held a very faint wave, just as Cenric's had, and when the babe opened his eyes and looked at her, it was with orbs near-identical to those of Morgause. The caramel-skinned woman smiled at the babe and gently picked him up. He did not cry or scream, even though she was a total stranger. Instead, he smiled and cooed at her.

"Hello, little one." Morgaine gently pulled a lock of hair that had fallen from her bun out of the babe's little fist. "Your mum told me to take you. Did you know that, little Pelias?"

The midnight-eyed woman smiled at the ocean-eyed infant again and was about to speak, but heard approaching footsteps. She shifted the child to her hip and made sure she had one hand free, just in case she needed to cast spells at whomever or whatever was coming. She had a banishing cantrip ready to form, when through the nursery doors came a pair of constructs, unarmed, and clad in the manner of female servants in the time gone by.

They looked at her with their painted black eyes, then after a moment of just staring, nodded and began to walk again, but slower. One of them crossed the room and pulled a small chest from a cupboard, possibly full of baby clothes. The other grabbed a satchel from under a table by the crib, and began filling it with things a baby would need. Once those tasks were completed, the constructs made their way to Morgaine. They set the chest down at her feet, and placed the satchel on top of it.

It is not in the nature of a construct to speak aloud—they are not designed for it, although they can see with their painted eyes, and hear with their painted ears. And depending on the strength and type of construct-creating spell used, some can reason—somewhat. In the time gone by, Morgaine heard legends of a magical who created constructs that completely replaced ordinary human life, although the wooden—or sometimes metal—beings could never feel true emotion, and they did not have souls or auras, although their presence could be felt. Nowadays, Morgaine would liken them to robots.

These were obviously Morgause's personal construct servants, for when it spoke in Morgaine's mind, it had a distinct voice rather than the slightly metallic monotone of indeterminable gender a construct usually had.

'The mistress instructed us to assist you in the removing of the young master from here, Archmage, and so we have done.'

Because the constructs could hear, Morgaine did not need to speak mind-to-mind as they did. "Thank you," she said, then, "What are you called?"

The construct seemed to grin—another mark of Morgause's talent for those things. *'The mistress called me Ane.' It...* she gestured at the other construct. *'This is Lara.'*

"How are you able to still work, now that Morgause is...."

'Dead? We do not know. She must have renewed the charm that keeps us functional, in a manner so that we could care for the young master until you came for him.'

Morgause had always been good with constructs, but this was a different level altogether—keeping constructs alive past the death of the one who made and enchanted them, even if it was only two days.

"How long do you have?" Morgaine asked.

'Until you leave with the young master.' She seemed to smile again. *'Do not worry, Archmage. Do not fret, we would rather be with the mistress and no longer functional than functional without her.'*

Morgaine sighed. How Morgause commanded such loving loyalty in spell-animated wood and metal escaped her, but she would comply. It was not as if she could help them "live" any longer, anyway. She didn't have enough talent in that area. She never had.

With a respectful nod at the constructs, the raven-haired woman disappeared into thin air, teleporting back to flat 332C, which is where she had been before activating the amulet. But now she had a baby on her hip and chest and satchel at her feet.

On flat 332C's sofa, James was lying asleep, when Morgaine teleported in. At the faint whoosh that action made, he awoke. He had always been a light sleeper, and his years in the Mercenaries Guard—though long ago—had only strengthened that fact. He sat up gingerly, so as not to jar the still-healing stab wound in his torso, which Khulai estimated would be fully healed by the morning of the next day. At the sight of Morgaine holding a dark-haired babe with light eyes, he asked, "Morgaine...who is that?"

She *giggled* at the look on his face, then quickly sobered. "This is Pelias, Morgause and Cenric's son."

Understanding dawned in his grey sharpshooter's eyes. "She asked you to take care of him, didn't she?" James was concerned. "Why?"

Morgaine sighed, then sat on the floor near James' head, and set the infant down. "In the time gone by, when we were children, she and I, and Mordred and Myrddin, were the closest friends that ever could be, we thought...."

As the medieval Archmage—who was sharing mind with his best friend's niece—explained the story of her childhood friendship, and then their split—the wielder of the Tân realised how painful it had been to battle against her once best friend, and the magnitude of the deceased woman's request, especially because she, Morgaine, was in her early thirties, but Cojiñí was just eighteen years old, nowhere near ready to care for a child, at least not a human one.

"What are you going to do?" he asked, once the tale was over.

Morgaine rubbed her face. "I have no idea whatsoever."

Just then, Araunya walked by, heading for the kitchen. James had an idea. He looked at the child, at his partner, at the child, then back towards Araunya before finally settling his gaze back on Morgaine.

"You could ask Araunya and Aidan to take him," he whispered. "Araunya can't have kids, anyway—the Mercenaries Guard took care of that when we joined—but I know she wants a child of her own. She even treats you two like she's your mother, if you hadn't noticed."

Morgaine nodded with understanding. "That...is something I hadn't thought of. Thank you very much, James."

He smiled. "You are always welcome, Morgaine, just as Cojiñí is."

She returned the smile, picked up the infant and walked to the kitchen. She stood behind her host's aunt. The woman turned around, and took a step back when she saw her niece standing there with a light-eyed, dark-haired infant on her hip. James also laughed at the dumbfounded look on the winter-eyed woman's face.

Araunya tried to speak, and finally got out, "He's not yours, I assume."

Morgaine shook her head. "No, he's not. His name is Pelias, and he *was* Morgause and Cenric's. Now, since those two are no longer living, James and I were thinking that he should be yours and Aidan's."

"Wait. What?"

"Morgause, who had been my closest friend long ago, asked me to care for her son. However, since Cojiñí is only eighteen, she cannot do so. James said you want a child and since you cannot have one of your own, we were thinking that you and Aidan should adopt him." She hoisted the baby directly in front of Araunya's face. "He looks pretty close to your appearance, I think. He could pass for yours when he's older. If you want to do that."

Araunya frowned. "Aidan and I have not been married long enough for us to have a son close to two years old. You know that, Morgaine."

Morgaine settled the child back on her hip. "But you're adopting him, not pretending he's your birth son."

"But you just said...." Araunya began, but Morgaine interrupted her.

"I was saying that when he's older, you won't have to deal with a son that looks nothing like you. He won't be taunted by school bullies about being adopted because it won't be that obvious." Morgaine's face was hard, and not exactly Morgaine anymore. That last sentence was almost purely Cojiñí, and it seemed as if the raven-haired female Archmage from the time gone by was returning the reins of their shared body to the raven-haired female Archmage of the present.

Araunya floundered trying to think of a response. So! That was how Cojiñí and Scoruş found out Brian and Hannah Tiger were not their true parents. There must have been some charm in place to keep them from finding out on their own. It was only when someone else told them outright that they'd been adopted, that the charm had been broken—even with the glamours they had been under. But the midnight-eyed young woman was not done just yet.

"And be sure that once he is old enough, he knows who his birth parents were, but do not bias him against them. And always, always make sure he knows you love him."

Her spiel over, she sighed and hung her head. Sensing her mamá's distress, the golden-eyed pitch-black cat that Cojiñí had found as a tiny kitten on her sixteenth birthday came bounding down the stairs from her room, put her front paws on the eighteen-year-old's hip, and meowed. Cojiñí passed Pelias to Araunya and picked up her own baby, which nuzzled into her neck, purring.

"You know your mamá loves you, don't you, *mon petit fantôme?*"

The cat purred louder, and licked Cojiñí's ear. Rhith was the oddest creature Araunya had ever seen. Sometimes the cat tried to be human. It didn't help much that Cojiñí could turn into a cat herself whenever she wanted, in addition to the wingéd lion and raven forms. As far as Araunya knew, Rhith firmly believed that Cojiñí was her mum, no matter what form she was in, and sometimes the winter-eyed woman caught them speaking telepathically. How that worked, if she was right, Araunya would never know.

Then she looked at Pelias just as the babe grabbed at her earring. She was wearing dangly ones today, as odd as that was. When he noticed her attention on him, he smiled brightly, then tried once more to snag her earring.

Aidan was very surprised when he walked into flat 332C to check on James and he saw Araunya playing with a baby. A dark-haired, light-eyed baby, to be precise. His wife looked up at him from her place on the floor, then used her magic to pull him down next to her.

"Aidan dear, meet Pelias—the closest thing you will have to a newborn son, should you agree with me to adopt him."

"Where did he come from?" As soon as the words left his mouth, Aidan realised exactly what Araunya said in the second half of her sentence. "What do you mean by 'the closest thing'?"

His wife sighed. "Morgaine brought him. Genetically, he is Morgause and Cenric's son. Morgause asked Morgaine to take care of him, but since Cojiñí is only eighteen and unmarried, she has asked us to do so."

"Okay, and what about my last question?"

Another sigh, this one much deeper. "When someone joins the Mercenaries Guard, it is usually for life. It is very rare for someone to leave as James and I did. For the protection of the people, and so they have less things that could compromise them, every person is sterilised shortly after joining."

"Okay...."

"Basically, what I am saying is that I will never be able to give you children. Not genetic ones anyway. I do want at least one more child, though, so I would be extremely happy if we adopted Pelias."

Did he just hear what he thought he heard? "One more?"

Araunya nodded. "Although technically Cojiñí and Scoruș are my niece and nephew, I consider them to be *my* children, as opposed to my brother's and his wife's."

Ah. That made sense. She was much closer to them than their birth parents had ever been. Lost in thought, Aidan did not realise his wife was still talking, and only caught the tail end of what she said.

"...them."

"Pardon?"

She gave him a *look* and repeated what she had just said. "I'm thinking about seeing if we can adopt the twins for their next birthday."

"Their parents are still living Ara...you know that."

"Yes, but they think that the twins are dead, *and* the twins are of age. It shouldn't be too difficult to get the paperwork through, especially if we use Gorhendad's help."

"Gorhendad?"

She smiled. "My great-grandfather, Balaur Chief Barsali Oaksword. He is the only Balaur other than me, Khulai, and Tara that knows the twins are still living."

"Oh."

Her smile broadened. "Yes, oh. The hardest part of this will be keeping this secret until October thirty-first."

"When will we be doing this?" Aidan asked.

"After or during the end of our honeymoon. Your choice."

The day of the twelve burials was June 30, five days after the end of the Battle. It was decided by the Pseudo-Reincarnated ones, now back to their present selves, that their direct foes would be buried in Camlann Valley, side-by-side, all in a row. Neva's funeral would be on July 2, two days later, on Ynys Golauglas. Araunya and Aidan decided that after the funeral, they would be speaking with Barsali about adopting the twins from Durriken and Charani.

* * *

Cojiñí stood over Morgause's open grave, eyes shining with Morgaine's tears for her once-friend. Morgause's hair was unbound and flowed over the coffin-pillow like a pool of pale gold. Her gown was of the deepest wine-crimson—fitting for the Black Queen. And her fairest-above-all face was peaceful, as if in sleep.

"We've passed the point of no return, haven't we old friend?" the black-clad midnight-eyed overlooker asked the still-beautiful corpse with a grim smile. "Perhaps I'll see you on Judgement Day. Until then, farewell...my friend and foe."

The solid black lid materialised over the top of the casket, and a pile of dirt was moved to pack down on the grave. There was to be no headstone for Morgause, or for any of the others.

Placed to the left of Morgause was Cenric, arrayed like the king he was, though the gold and jewels were only illusions crafted to last until the end of the day. Not only did they not have the proper precious stones, they did not want anyone to come to this valley looking for treasure and find the bodies of these twelve.

To the left of Cenric was Mordred, clad similarly, just a bit toned-down. And to his left was Bruin, looking every centimetre like the Fire Lord he was. On and on they went, arrayed in what would have been their finest garments.

As they stood at each grave, the living Pseudo-Reincarnated people—all wearing only the black of mourning—said some small thing to their direct foe lying before them, if they wished to. Aside from Cojiñí, however, only a few said anything, probably because only a few knew their direct foes before they had become foes.

Eventually, all was said that was to be said, and all of the graves were covered with tightly packed soil. The first day of burials was completed. Two days until the next.

The next day, Neva's body was brought to Ynys Golauglas so that it could be prepared for burial. With the twelve, such a thing was simple—just bits of magic to change and clean the appearance and garments. However, a daughter of Clan Balaur could not be buried in illusions in an unmarked grave in the middle of the valley in which she died. No, she must be healed of all her visible wounds, clothed in the best garments of her status, and placed with items she had cherished in life. In this case, those were her sketchpad and art tools, her violin, and her Bible. Also, a headstone must be crafted to suit who she had been, and a place in the graveyard selected in the place where she had lived.

* * *

Jardani watched the proceedings with sharp and solemn sapphire eyes. He was seven years old now, having turned so that past March. Although he was technically eleven years younger than the twins, there was that time between October 31 and March 13 when they were twelve years older than him. He was the type of boy who would be upset by that fact, had he known he had elder siblings.

The young boy ran a hand through his short-cropped black hair. It was kept so because if he let it grow any longer, he would look as if he had just been caught in a windstorm, and because he was not yet old enough to grow it so long, the length would weigh it down. He had not known his Aunt Neva very well, but he *had* known her well enough that her death caused a bit of an impact. He would be attending the funeral—his mum would make him. And he would dress formally in the black of mourning—his mum would make him do that as well. Even though the death of his Aunt Neva was sad, Jardani would rather have gone to play with his friends than stand around staring at a dead person while people talked about boring stuff.

Luckily, there was still the rest of that day before the Day of Boringness. With that in mind, the youngest son of Charani Duskflame and Durriken Stormeye ran off towards the home of one of his many friends. Maybe they had time to play football in the courtyard of the Lodge, or maybe they'd be up to trying to get into that locked West Wing again.

* * *

Jenny Natser was eating lunch with Rupert when Araunya called. Jenny asked if she'd like to come over, but the grim-faced woman answered, "Not now. I have news, Zujenia Natser Balaur. Neva is dead. You and your husband are requested to attend her funeral tomorrow at high noon. You know what to wear."

That said, her second cousin hung up. Jenny slowly put the phone back on the receiver. Neva was dead? How? When?

"Jenny? What's wrong?" Rupert walked over to her and she saw that his blue eyes full of concern.

"Neva is dead." Her voice was flat. "We are requested to attend her funeral tomorrow at high noon. I must locate and dust off my mourning robes, and you need some as well."

"We are going then?"

She nodded. "Of course. Neva was my second cousin and I am still a Balaur. Balaurs do not abandon each other."

Rupert frowned. A lock of his short, dark-brown hair fell forward. "I thought you...."

"I never abandoned them. I left, but I did not abandon. There is a difference. I have always planned to return to Ynys Golauglas. I just did not expect for that time to be something so...like this."

Her husband wrapped her in an embrace, and she returned it. "You are remarkably calm," he noted.

Jenny sighed. "Not really. I...I don't know." Her eyes closed, and she began to weep. Rupert rested his chin on her head, and though he had not known Neva, he cried for his wife's pain.

* * *

The next day dawned clear, grey, and cold for July, even in Britain. Araunya, Aidan, James, the twins, and the rest of the Pseudo-Reincarnated ones left for the Lodge early so that Araunya could grab her mourning robes, and for similar garments to be found for the others, even though the only visible ones would be her, Aidan, and James. Robes to fit them were easily found, and yet they had barely enough time to get down to the cemetery before the funeral started. Luckily, they arrived in time. The Pseudo-Reincarnated ones quickly turned themselves invisible and moved out of the way so that no one would bump into or jostle them. If someone did, it would cause a *bit* of a problem, for why would someone be invisible at a funeral? Not to mention that two of those invisible people were *supposed* to be dead seventeen years before that day.

High noon arrived, and so did many people. Scoruș thought he saw librarian Natser in the small crowd, clad in the unrelieved black of mourning robes. Soon, however, they were out of sight, and he turned his gaze to where Barsali stood beside the grave. The open casket floated above, ready to be lowered once the lid was on.

Next to Barsali stood two other men that Scoruș could tell were directly related to the white-haired man by the similarity of their faces. The one to the Chief's right had greying hair pulled into a short que, a well-trimmed beard with a single small beaded braid in the centre, and dark blue eyes. On Barsali's left was a man who seemed familiar. His shoulder-length raven hair was loose and straight, and his midnight eyes were cold with sorrow. It was the body of his sister lying in that casket after all.

Scoruș frowned at his first sight—since he was a year old—of his and Cojiñí's birth father. He did not *seem* like a man who abandoned his stolen children after a few months' search, but then again, it had been seventeen years ago, and appearances are deceiving. The young man transferred the visual information over his twin-bond with his sister, and received gratefulness in return.

The raven-haired Archmages' attention returned to Barsali as the man began to speak.

"Today we are gathered to mourn the death and celebrate the life of a woman taken from the world of the living so much sooner than anyone who knew her would have preferred—my youngest great-granddaughter, Neva Whitefeather."

He paused a moment, closed his bright eyes, then continued. "I know that many of you wish to know the reason she is no longer with us, but all that I will tell you is this—she was fighting against the thing we all are called to fight against: evil. That she perished in her fight does not mean that it is a lost battle."

Chapter 22

AFTER THE FUNERAL AND SUBSEQUENT FEAST to celebrate all that Neva had done in life, and once everyone else left, Araunya and Aidan approached Barsali with one thing in mind. That, of course, was the adoption of Scoruș and Cojiñí from Durriken and Charani. True, it was not the most perfect time to bring up something like this, yet it was also very much not the worst.

When they presented their proposal, Barsali absently tugged on the braid in his beard. "You do know they are of age now, correct? And therefore you must have their signed permission to go through with this."

Araunya nodded. "Yes, we are aware of that. We are planning to get the paperwork taken care of, and all the things that do not need their signatures—before their birthday. And then present the forms for them to sign on that day." She shrugged. "We just need your help in getting the necessary documents and, of course, as Chief and head of the house, you need to sign some papers as well."

Barsali was amused by the look on his great-granddaughter's face. Outwardly, he smiled and nodded. "I will help you, Araunya, for reasons I will not disclose."

The red-clad woman smiled enormously. "Thank you, Gorhendad!"

This time he actually chuckled. "You are welcome."

Now that they had permission and were offered assistance from Barsali, all that was left was for the couple to acquire the needed forms, and research magical adoptions—for while the twins did not exactly view Aidan as their father, they did see Araunya as the only true mother they had ever had, and the newly-wed couple wanted this adoption to be as final as they could make it. They also had to obtain similar forms for the adoption of Pelias. So, off to the courthouse they went. It took a bit, but after two hours or so, Aidan and Araunya departed with what they needed.

The couple returned home to flats 332B and C. They had decided not to share a room until after the honeymoon. Besides, what would they do about the twins and James, if they had decided to share a room? So they just left sleeping arrangements as they had been for the past four years. At least for the time being.

* * *

In the mid-space, the twelve from the time gone by were lounging on their usual... sofas. Unlike usual however, they were joined by Barhaol, whom Arthur—as the technical leader of the group since he was king—was speaking to in a highly frustrated manner.

"The other twelve have been defeated and laid in their graves. Our task is completed! How much longer would you have us stay in this in-between state? We have all decided to give control to our hosts." Here, he put air quotes around the last word, "so when will you *allow* us to do so? How much longer before *we* can finally rest?" He paused, then muttered under his breath, "Although, the other twelve are not resting, based on where they ended up."

Barhaol sighed and tugged on one ear—a nervous gesture the twelve had seen only when they first asked about why they were there in the first place. The gesture seemed out of place in the immortal tree-sentience. "As far as I know, you have until Christmas, seven years after the...first merging, before you will 'go to rest,' as the saying goes."

The twelve stared at It dumbfounded.

"Five more years...of this? You're serious?" Vortigern's voice was as cold as the ice beginning to seep from the soles of his boots as he gestured around at the lack of individuality in their mid-space room. "At least for the centuries we were in an unconscious stasis."

Barhaol nodded. "I am very serious, and you know very well, Ice Lord, that your Mages and Archmages can easily enough change this room to fit your needs, if that is necessary."

This time, it was Morgaine who spoke, her voice and eyes just as cold as the dark-blond-haired man's had been. "We tried, Barhaol. Nothing worked. The room is *locked*." She waved a hand in exasperation. "It is not as if we can play mind games forever, and 'doing married couple things' would be horribly awkward and inappropriate, and would become boring if that, and mind games, were the only things we could do for five years."

Barhaol frowned. The room was *locked?* It was sure that It had not made it so when It formed the room, but perhaps because Its magic was different than that of humans, being that It was still technically a tree—an icy-pale, humanoid, translucent tree. It reached out with Its magic and carefully altered the "settings," for lack of a better term, of the mid-space room. Once that was done, It opened Its eyes and looked at Morgaine.

"Now try."

The caramel-skinned woman closed her own eyes. Barhaol felt her deep-azure magic thrum through the air and the room changed from the dark, nondescript...thing...it had been, to a comfortable, large sitting room with huge windows looking out over a forest on one side, and an ocean on the other. Because of the lack of proper physics and such in the mid-space, between each window was a door—six in total—leading to separate bedrooms for each of the couples. And yet a person could stick his or her head out a window on either side of a door and see nothing but whatever "natural" scenery existed out there. Additionally, each window showed a completely unique scene, which did not influence the view out the other windows near it. Such was the nature of the mid-space.

Barhaol nodded as Morgaine opened her eyes. "There. Now you have activities to do. I am sure that with your combined powers, you could even make an estate of some kind to wander around in while you are waiting." It knew It sounded condescending, but that was *sort of* Its point. Now that that "problem" had been resolved, the translucent tree-sentience left before any of the twelve could glare at It.

* * *

The two weeks of mourning had passed, and now Araunya and Aidan were leaving on their honeymoon. They had no set destination, only to travel to assorted places around the world in the two weeks they allotted themselves.

Just before they left, Cojiñí and Scoruș handed them each a small square box wrapped in burgundy and silver paper. When the couple looked at them quizzically, the twins smiled mischievously and said nothing. Those smiles lingered as the couple faded into mid-space as Araunya teleported them to their first destination.

* * *

Something was up with the couple and the twins did not know what, but they wouldn't let it bother them...right now. They heard Pelias begin to fuss, and instantly moved to his crib to see what the dark-haired babe wanted. It turned out he was hungry, so Scoruș fetched the bottle and fed him. Once the boy was full, the twins sang for him until he fell asleep again. Pelias slept a lot, and when the twins expressed their concern about this to Araunya, she assured them that it was perfectly normal—he was a magical baby, after all.

The twins did not much like taking care of twenty-month-old boy. Yes, they would do it for Araunya, and they were more than fairly good at it, but that did not mean that they enjoyed it. Both had decided they did not want kids of their own, unless they adopted them at a stage in which the kid or kids could conduct intelligent conversations.

When Pelias did fall asleep, the twins stopped singing and placed an alert charm on him so that they would know when he was about to wake, then they teleported into the mid-space training room. They were surprised to find the rest of the Pseudo-Reincarnated ones were there and appeared to have been there for a fair amount of time, judging by the fact that they were in the middle of a very intense practice session—they were attempting to hit each other with water balloons full of glitter water, for some reason or another.

Eventually the game, practice, whatever, ended and the team led by Ashton won over the team led by Gareth. They began another round, and the twins chose their sides. Cojiñí ended up with Ashton, while Scoruş joined Gareth. The rules were that no magic was allowed, nor was anything that could cause pain. No matter that their ages were seventeen to twenty, they could act like children if they wanted to.

The second round was won by Gareth's team, for even though Ashton was technically the best strategist in their group, the combination of Scoruş and Gareth made a formidable opponent for the gold-haired young man, even if they weren't *quite* as good as he.

* * *

The next two weeks passed quickly, with the only real highlight being that the pastor at the church—attended by the twins, Araunya, Aidan, and James—began a sermon series on Daniel. Judging by the past sermon series given by the bearded man, the twins knew this would prove to be interesting and informative. Araunya and Aidan returned from their honeymoon with all the paperwork ready for the adoption of Pelias, and though the twins did not know it, their own adoption as well, except for the signatures of the midnight-eyed duo themselves.

Now it was time for them to re-work their living arrangements. There were enough bedrooms in the flats for the couple to move in with the other, but it was more space-savvy for Araunya to move in with Aidan and James, and let Scoruş and Cojiñí live in flat 332C by themselves. They were responsible enough for it, the winter-eyed woman felt. It also gave the twins ample opportunity to have personal study spaces. Cojiñí had decided a few years ago that she wanted to write a book detailing Morgause's memories, but because of her lack of personal desk space, she was unable to do so properly. But if they turned Araunya's old bedroom into another study, they could remove the mid-space charms on the cupboard under the stairs and make it a playground for their cats: Cojiñí's yellow-eyed, black-furred Rhith, meaning "phantom," and Scoruș' green-eyed, grey tabby named Jekyll. Araunya had a feeling there would be more cats added at some point, but most definitely not now.

The empty bedroom in flat number 332B could easily be reorganized into a nursery for Pelias, which would become his bedroom when he was older. James opted to stay exactly where he was in 332B, and said that Aidan and Araunya were perfectly capable of putting up a silencing ward around their room whenever they wanted to, and he could be available as another person to care for the rapidly growing toddler, whenever Aidan took Araunya out for dinner, or something.

The day after the living arrangements were decided, the couple whose names both began with the letter 'A,' went to the courthouse to turn in the adoption paperwork for Pelias, or Philip, as he was renamed—the name chosen by Aidan. Araunya would have left his name the way it was, or renamed him Pryderi, that being a Welsh name meaning "care."

Araunya returned to work and was presented with the case of a young man who looked physically similar to Paul Carson. The young man, Edward, was reportedly seen leaving the scene of a crime in a guilty fashion. They were not sure if anything bad had really happened, but due to the obvious relation and extremely similar behaviour patterns, the Department Head wanted to put the recently turned eighteen-year-old under watch, just in case something untoward happened. Araunya was not happy when she saw Edward's photo on the List of Those to Keep Tabs On, with his name underneath.

He seemed familiar, and not in a good way. But from where she knew him, she did not know. Yet. Perhaps she would ask the twins if they knew him.

When she did ask them, they said, yes, they knew him. He had gone to Rumen Primary with them. And that it was a good thing he was on the List of Those to Keep Tabs On because he was Paul Carson's younger brother and proud of it. What they did not say, but Araunya picked up anyway, was that he had bullied them during their time at

Rumen, enough to make them suitably angry to break their magic-suppressors.

Araunya relayed that information to the Department Head, even though she did not *exactly* think it was completely relevant, and the slightly older woman simply nodded and accepted the information, then went back to her paperwork.

Later that day, when Araunya was ready to go home for the evening, the Department Head called her into her office. When she did so, the red-haired woman asked the ink-haired woman to close the door. She did as requested. Then, at a gesture, sat down across the desk from the Department Head.

The slightly older woman held up a few pages of paperwork. "Do you know what this is, Inspector Balaur, or is it Jones now?"

Araunya shook her head. "No, I do not, Madame Stewart. And my name is technically still Balaur, though both names are on the marriage certificate and therefore either will work." Was she in trouble for something? Were those papers her dismissal?

Madame Stewart shook her head. "I may not be a telepath or anything of that sort, Inspector Balaur, but I know what you're thinking, and I am telling you now that what you are thinking is incorrect." She smiled then, an extremely rare sight from the red-haired woman. "These are not your dismissal papers." The smile dropped, and she sighed. "When Paul Carson was brought in by your niece, you had been slated for promotion to Chief Inspector, to take effect a few months later. But someone lost the paperwork. These," she held up the documents in her hand, "are something just a little bit different."

The hazel-eyed Department Head put the documents on the desk and folded her hands on top of them and the golden wedding band on her left ring finger glinted in the light of the office. Araunya waited patiently, wondering what on earth Madame Stewart was going to say next. Absently, she fiddled with her pendant, the gift in the box the twins had given her as she and Aidan left for their honeymoon.

The pendant was a small disk of Damascus steel, carved on both sides with runes of protection, wealth, and long life. Yes, technically, only the protection runes would actually do anything, but the twins liked the look of the others, and Araunya appreciated the thought. Aidan had an identical one.

Madame Stewart looked Araunya directly in the eyes. "What I am saying is, you are overdue for a promotion...."

Yes, it was rude, but Araunya just felt like she had to interject. "Madame Stewart, you really don't need to...."

With a stern look and yet a smile, the hazel-eyed woman continued, cutting off Araunya's attempt to speak, as she handed her a case file with the picture of a red-eyed woman on the front. *Another* one with a vampire? Really? How many troublemakers were in this city? "Go back to your desk, Chief Inspector Balaur. I expect you need to be working on your new case."

* * *

Jennifer smiled at Araunya as the winter-eyed woman passed her desk holding a black case file in her hand. The brown-haired woman frowned. Why did her friend get all those black-file cases? And what was so special about them that they were of a colour different than the usual beige? The woman's frown turned to a smirk as Araunya noticed the new nameplate by her computer declaring her to be: "Chief Inspector A. Balaur" in neat silvery letters.

The fair-skinned woman watched discreetly as her friend opened the case file and looked through it, but all she caught before she had to turn back to her own work was a picture of something that looked eerily similar to a female vampire—beautiful, pale skinned, red-eyed, and dark-haired, with a vicious smile showing two pairs of glittering white fangs. What on earth? She didn't know vampires really existed.

* * *

A few weeks later, the colleges the twins had applied to near the end of the last school year—just in case they survived the Second Battle of Camlann—replied. Nearly all accepted the applications, something the twins had *not* expected as they had a tendency to downplay their achievements. But there was only one school they were truly interested in attending: Albastru University. The name came from the Romanian word for "blue," and was the last name of the man who founded it.

A golden triquetra emblazoned on a field of deep azure was the coat of arms. Students were required to wear a badge of that design at sports events and the like. There were no uniforms, as was typical for most universities in the UK, but different from secondary schools like Glamdring, and that was a welcome change for the twins and their friends. Kennedy started attending Albastru when he left secondary school, and he seemed to like it, so that was another point in the university's favour.

All the adults were happy for them, and though Aidan pretended to be disappointed that he wouldn't be their principal anymore, they knew he was happy, too. They teased him a bit, however, and he was glad they felt comfortable enough around him to tease, so he bore it without complaint.

Although they did not have an upcoming battle, the twins wanted to stay in shape, so almost every day they spent an hour or more in the mid-space training room, sparring with each other or with friends who showed up, and doing obstacle courses, or working as a team attacking training dummies in assorted scenarios. They practiced the skills and knowledge of their "past selves" as well, whenever they could. Yes, their direct foes were dead, but that did not mean they should not improve their fighting skills. What if they were caught in combat with someone more powerful than they were? What would they do then? What about someone faster? A better strategist? More experienced? They would be ready, for life was not perfect, and even the story of a so-called hero is not over after winning against the first villain he or she defeats. That was their rationale, anyway, and when they explained that to the rest of the Pseudo-Reincarnated ones, everyone agreed and began to join the twins for every single practice session.

Araunya would say the younger men and women were pushing themselves too hard, but she knew that their reasoning was sound. She knew what lurked beneath the shiny, clean exterior of their city, especially since she had been assigned the post of Chief Person Who Deals With All Of The Magical And Unnatural Stuff That Goes On at the police station where she worked. It seemed that each department had a person occupying a similar post. Oddly enough, she had not met all of them in the four years she had worked with the police department, though she had run into one or two during a few cases, and had worked with one or two others. She figured there were at least enough that she could form her own team of people that dealt with the strange things, but she did not know how to broach that topic with Madame Stewart, so she kept her mouth shut.

As it turned out, Edward Carson did *try* to follow in his elder brother's footsteps, but because they had him on the List of Those To Keep Tabs On, he was arrested as soon as he attempted to escape after assaulting and mugging a young woman. They had him in a holding cell right now, and were waiting to schedule the trial.

Cojiñí and Scoruş, it turned out, did hold grudges—a fact they did not like about themselves. When they heard the news about Edward Carson, a little twinkle sparked in their eyes. As they said, Edward Carson was not like his brother, not yet, and it was a very good thing he had been arrested before he could become like his brother. They just hoped he would not escape, and maybe actually reap the consequences of his actions. They hoped they would see him change into a better person, but the twins were most definitely not counting on that happening.

* * *

School started up again a few weeks later, and therefore the amount of time the residents of flats 332B and C were able to see each other diminished. Cojiñí was specialising in Architecture and Linguistics, while Scoruş preferred things of a more scientific bent. However, they ended up in many of the same classes, and both prepared to join the school's swim team, although they did not like the competition at all.

The first day they arrived on the campus, they were a bit

intimidated by the sheer size of the place. The first week, the twins did not talk to anyone they did not already know, so basically they did not speak to anyone other than the Pseudo-Reincarnated ones and their teachers—unless it was required for a project. They had intended to stop that behaviour, the lack of interaction, after the first week, but it went on long enough for them to gain a reputation as "the quiet ones." Although they had outgoing natures, the events of their lives, especially before the "first merging," had dimmed that considerably, even though they had trained themselves well in the art of fake expressions...not that they really used that skill lately.

October came, and Araunya heard the twins talking about the "alcoves" they had before the adult Tigers destroyed the rooms, and Cojiñí mentioned something about a book the winter-blue-eyed woman had seen in the Lodge's West Wing library: *Dream Interpretation* by Annaea Sorco. The girl mentioned how ironic it was that the book said she would someday fly, since they now were able to turn into birds and wingéd lions. Scoruș looked at his sister oddly when she said this, but she just shrugged and said that she just remembered it, that's all, even though six years had passed.

Annaea Sorco. What a strange name. Araunya was sure it was a pseudonym, since as far as she knew there had never been anyone with the last name or clan-name of Sorco, though it was possible for a person to have the first name of Annaea. Perhaps she—Araunya was sure the author was a she—was from some other dimension. A very good possibility, as the mid-space connected all dimensions and alternate universes like a complicated and unusual spider's web. Additionally, there had been reports of people travelling to other dimensions, and somehow she had a feeling that she had met one of those people. Although, if the person who Araunya was thinking of was correct, then it was not one dimension-traveller, but two—a certain pair of Glamdring Secondary School Music, Dance, and Drama professors. They seemed a little too much like a certain pair of 18th century French opera singers to be coincidental, and the way they had deflected her subtle probe when she pointed that out was just a bit suspicious to the highly-trained aura-sensing female Warrior Mage.

The twins' birthday was drawing near, and Araunya and Aidan were nervous about the twins' acceptance of their birthday present. Philip, the child once known as Pelias, could walk and talk now, but as he was just about to turn three, it was not expected that he do either well—even though he was a magical child. And even with that "handicap," he made it very clear that he wanted to get birthday presents for "Co-gee-nee" and "Sca-whoosh." His adopted parents, whom he had taken to calling Mum and Dad, indulged him, and took him on a trip to the mall.

He made them not look as he chose what he wanted to buy, and hid whatever it was under his jacket until it was time to purchase the things, then he asked them to cover their eyes again, and asked the cashier to put them in the bag without the adults seeing, even though the presents were for Co-gee-nee and Sca-whoosh, not them. His reasoning for that was—if they saw the presents, they might "ax-ee-den-tally" tell the twins what the presents were. Araunya and Aidan assured their son that they would not tell, but he stubbornly refused, saying in the most adorable way that he was just "tay-keen prah-cauh-sheens."

Chapter 23

THE DAY OF THE TWINS' NINETEENTH BIRTHDAY dawned clear and chilly, a seemingly perfect October morning. The twins had not planned anything extra special, as it was not one of those extra-important birthdays, like their last one, having been their coming-of-age. And yet, they suspected something was going to be different from the last eighteen birthdays. But what that was, they could not guess, and even if they did, whatever their guess might be would likely be incorrect. Although, the only basis that they had for that—other than a vague feeling—was that Araunya and Aidan were acting odd, almost nervous about something. And Peli...Philip seemed very excited, almost as if it was his own birthday. But he knew his birthday was in November.

The rest of the Pseudo-Reincarnated ones had all been invited, of course, being that they were Cojiñí and Scoruș' friends, but not all of them could come. That was okay, the twins told themselves. It was not as if there was anything overly special about this particular birthday, and if something interesting did happen, they could always tell the others later.

As it was a Monday, the small party was scheduled for after school and after swim. Luckily, it was not a meet day, since the swim season had not started yet. However, the twins decided they would practice with the times, so there would not be an abrupt change when swim season did start. Also, they enjoyed being in the water—Cojiñí more so than Scoruș.

The midnight-eyed duo returned from the city pool laughing about some movie reference, and after they showered, dressed in t-shirts and jeans, they went downstairs to the kitchen to grab a quick snack before everybody arrived at 6:30. Yes, there would be food at the party, courtesy of James, but Scoruş and Cojiñí preferred to eat something a *bit* healthier and more savoury, before the rich, sugary deliciousness of James' baking.

At 6:15, a knock sounded at the door. A bit confused, Scoruş went to open it. An equally confused Cojiñí trailed behind him. There stood James, arms crossed and a mock-stern expression on his face.

"You do know that the party is supposed to be over in our flat, right?"

They shook their heads. "No."

He sighed. "Well, get over here then! Before everyone else arrives and we have to start the party without you." His grey eyes took in the sight of their bare feet, and when they noticed what he was looking at, they reached for their shoes. "You don't have to put on shoes just to cross the hall, you know, especially since I know that you'll just take them off as soon as you get through the door."

The shoes fell to the entry floor with a thump, and the caramel-skinned twins followed the sandy-haired, tan-skinned man to his flat for their nineteenth birthday party.

When the trio entered flat number 332B, the twins were glad that the lights were still on and no one was hiding behind the furniture. On the table was a chocolate fudge cake, made by James of course, as no one could bake as good as he could—in the opinions of the residents of flat number 332C, though Araunya made excellent soups and stews, and her baking was...close enough to that of the grey-eyed man for a fair comparison. While not as good as James, Araunya's skill with cookies greatly surpassed anything else that the twins had tasted. Aside from the cake, there were blueberry scones, a particular favourite of the birthday duo, apple pie, another favourite, and ham and cheese croissants, also particularly favoured.

Near the sofa was a small pile of presents, one that would be added to as each guest arrived, even though both of the twins had insisted that no one needed to get them anything, that their mere *presence* was enough. And still their guests brought gifts. The workings of human minds escaped them sometimes, even though the twins were human themselves.

Everyone that was going to come was there by 6:30, and the small party began. First would be the singing and cake, then presents, then they would watch a movie agreed upon by all the guests. The cake was, as usual, absolutely delectable and delicious, and also extremely rich. The twins thought that James had made too much again, as they finished their first and only slice, but then they realised he had done it on purpose, so that people could take some home and the party could continue a few days longer.

Finally, it was time for the presents to be opened. First came the gifts from Rae and Kennedy, having been delivered by Alezandra, as neither was able to attend. Scoruș received a black leather scientific journal and a set of ink pens in various shades of green, and Cojiñí received a pack of drafting tools and a silver-and-blue necklace that she put on the instant she unwrapped it. Following those were gifts from Alezandra—a wing-patterned t-shirt and a snakeskin cuff bracelet. Next were those from Mae, then Ashton, Catrina, Gareth, and the rest of their friends. James gave them tickets to a musical they liked, although they would have to pay for their own food afterward, he joked.

Finally, all that was left on the floor by the sofa was a box wrapped in silver and burgundy paper, the size of a piece of letter paper. Though there was no tag, the twins could tell by the paper that it was from Araunya and Aidan. The box was not heavy, and when Scoruș shook it, it sounded like it was full of paper. The twins looked at each other. What could it be? Off came the silky silver ribbon. The burgundy paper was carefully removed—which is how the twins unwrapped every present they received, unless they were short on time.

Once the paper was off, the raven-haired, magical duo held a plain white cardboard box, neatly taped shut on all sides. With a carefully aimed slicing cantrip, the tape was cut. Now all that was left was to lift the lid, which was done.

The twins' eyes went wide, and they looked at Araunya and Aidan, disbelieving and yet hopeful. Even though they were newly nineteen, and had been through a battle in which they had to kill people who had once been their friends, they looked so young at that moment.

"Adoption papers? Are you serious? Please say this is not a cruel jest." They spoke in tandem, in a manner that showed their desperation for this legal sealing of a bond they considered already made.

The only married couple in the room nodded and smiled. "All that is left is for you two to sign the papers. Then we will submit them to the courthouse and to Gorhendad."

Araunya and Aidan found their arms full of exceedingly grateful nineteen-year-olds, and returned the four-way embrace. They glanced at the other occupants of the room, and saw them all smiling as well. On a whim, the couple invited the rest of the birthday guests to join them in the joyful embrace. They did so, and the hug became a dog pile of people, all of whom were over eighteen. Anyone who looked in on the scene would have been confused—not that anyone would do so, and not that anyone in the pile of people would care.

Eventually the pile of arms and legs and torsos and heads broke apart into separate people, and they all took their previous seats on the floor, sofa, or armchairs. The twins smoothed the adoption forms that had been crumpled, and conjured elegant steel-tipped quill pens with a wave of their hands. Having a medieval being living in one's head and providing one with his or her memories and skills made it more than easy to write with such a tool. And because they could use their magic to erase mistakes, keep inkblots from forming, and prevent the ink in the pen from running out, the twins preferred to use the tool whenever they could, and especially for formal documents.

On a whim, Araunya turned on her aura-sight, and as the twins signed each of the papers with a flourish, the winter-eyed woman saw another set of hands overlaying those that belonged to her soon-to-be son and daughter. The hands belonged to Morgaine and Myrddin—she was sure it was them. And she was honoured that the people her twins had been in the time gone by approved of this adoption. What she didn't know, of course, was that she—face, manner, and bearing—was extremely similar to the mother of those twins from another time.

Cojiñí and Scoruș smiled to themselves when they felt Morgaine and Myrddin's acceptance of their choice, and the utter agreement that came with that acceptance. They had become very close with the people who were their "other selves," and felt as if they would be devastated if they had to leave. Though sometimes extremely frustrating, it was comforting to have someone else in their heads to help them through their bouts of depression and provide council and a sounding board for ideas.

They let the pens dissipate. There—the last paper signed. Now all that was left was for the documents to be delivered to the proper places, and then they would have a mum and dad. A proper mum and dad, too, not ones who were abusive, or ones they had seen only once since they were a year old. But a real, proper, actual, official, caring, loving mum and dad. The fact that the twins were nineteen, and therefore did not need legal guardians or anything of that sort, was conveniently ignored.

Adoptions of someone older than thirteen, much less twins from one magical family to another magical family were uncommon, and so no one realised the significance of—or noticed the oh-so-faint tingle of magic that ran through the room as the pen-tips left the last paper's signature line.

That Friday, as soon as school let out, Araunya, Aidan, and the twins—who had not yet told their friends who weren't at the birthday party about the adoption—teleported to the library of the West Wing of the Lodge where Barsali was waiting for them in the duelling circle. Araunya gave the white-haired man the papers, and as he looked over them, she looked over him.

He did not look very well, was her conclusion. He seemed to be as strong as always, but she knew the end of his life was drawing near. Even magicals are not immortal, though they healed quicker and have a longer natural lifespan than ordinary humans have. Barsali was 147 years old. The very highest reach of a Balaur lifespan was 155, and only a few had ever reached that age. And even fewer had stayed strong for all those long years. Although Barsali was strong and still vibrant, Araunya read in his aura that he did not have much time left—five years at the most; one at the least. She could tell, however, that he would not die before his next birthday. He would be at least one hundred forty-eight before passing into the next existence.

The clan of Welsh-Romani magicals known as Clan Balaur never called what happened after death to be "the next life." Although death is not eternal, what happens afterward is nothing like life on Earth, or life in any dimension. Either it would be the perfect paradise in Heaven, without pain or trouble or worry, or it would be the worst compilation of the most horrible tortures imaginable, without comfort or peace or rest.

But whatever the Balaurs called or did not call the time after death, their Chief and the great-grandfather of one of their best Warrior Mages was nearing that time, and not in the slowest manner.

Barsali Oaksword, Chief of Clan Balaur, watched his eldest great-granddaughter watching him. If he could, he would have transferred heirship from his eldest great-grandson to her, but that choice was not his to make, resting rather with the father of both—who preferred the son to the daughter, perhaps because the son did not go "gallivanting around the world getting herself into trouble," as Danior termed what his winter-eyed daughter did. He had always had this outdated, restricting view of women, and thought they should not *be* Warrior Mages in the first place. He preferred that she remain sitting in the home making pretty things, or doing healings, or making and caring for children, or playing soft gentle music. Barsali often wondered where Danior got that idea, as his father—Kennick, Barsali's eldest son—most definitely did not think that way, and his mother was not like that, being very fiery, even if the warrior's path was not the one she chose. His eldest great-granddaughter was much like her namesake—Kennick's wife—now that Barsali thought about it, and yet somehow Danior did not see it that way, choosing instead to see only her stubborn, spirited, and wilful actions rather than her heroic ones. Araunya Flameheart, grandmother of Araunya Ravenheart, both had winter-blue eyes and a warrior spirit.

Durriken Stormeye, the heir of Danior, and by descent, the heir of Barsali, was a Warrior Mage, but nowhere near Araunya's level in the arts of battle and fighting. Neither was he as good a negotiator, having had much less practice. Araunya had no equal in her generation in the ways of war, but she had always preferred peace instead of bloodshed. That quality had been in her since she was a child settling disputes between Durriken and his friends, and some of his not-friends.

Durriken however, enjoyed fighting just for the sake of the fight, and as a child would often incite the quarrels that Araunya attempted to diffuse, simply because he knew he had a good chance of winning. While the winter-eyed woman did enjoy the rush of adrenaline and thrill of combat, it was only during the fight. She did not go out of her way to cause quarrels in the hopes they would turn into brawls just so she could have the glory of winning. Yes, she had incited her own share of arguments, she was a sibling after all, but it was almost never for the mere purpose of having an argument.

All in all, Barsali felt Araunya Ravenheart would make a better Chief than Durriken Stormeye, but Durriken was the firstborn, and unless there could be proof provided against his taking the title and responsibilities and privileges, or if he was slain, he would gain that title.

However, that was not the most important thing at that moment, and Barsali Oaksword returned his attention to the adoption documents in his hand. Everything seemed to be in order. Now he just needed to run it past his Witan to make sure they agreed with that assessment. Then all would be finalized and finished, and his eldest great-granddaughter would have two nineteen-year-old children in addition to the three-year-old she adopted earlier in the year.

The white-haired man took a chance and activated his aura-sight on a whim. While he may not have as much talent for it as Araunya—no Balaur in generations did—he had a fair skill in feeling, smelling, seeing, and deciphering nimbuses of coloured light. His own aura was an earthy amber tone, and carried within it the scent of an approaching storm. The white-haired man's eyes widened in wonder when he saw—overlaid with the signatures of the twins—another of signatures done by similar, but ancient hands. *Must be the signatures of Morgaine and Myrddin,* he thought, and then let his aura-sight fade. The overlaid second signatures faded with the nimbuses of coloured light surrounding the four people before him.

Barsali looked up from the papers and smiled. "Everything is in order. I will submit it through my Witan, and then the legal requirements will be completed. As it stands," his voice rose and thundered with authority, "I, Chief-Lord Warrior Mage Barsali Oaksword, do declare Lady Warrior Mage Araunya Ravenheart and Lord Aidan Jones to be the rightful parents of Lady Archmage Cojiñí Morgaine Seasword and Lord Archmage Scoruș Myrddin Blackfalcon, in magic and in bond."

At those words, a thrum of magic passed through the clearing where they stood like a strong summer wind, indoors.

The next day dawned rainy and cold, but that did not bother the twins. What did bother them, however, was that they felt different. Not bad, just *very* different, aside from the warm feeling of having proper parents, that is. Their eyes felt odd, but not physically—more of a mental *there-was-some-other-way-they-could-be-looking-at-things* sort of way. In addition, they were tripping over their own feet, as if they had grown taller overnight. When they looked at their faces in the mirror, their eye-shape had narrowed and their noses had become more aquiline. Was this supposed to happen with adoption? There was no way for them to tell, as they knew nothing about that sort of thing, and Morgaine and Myrddin were no help whatsoever, as they had never had to deal with anything like that either.

It was with some slight difficulty that the midnight-eye twins dressed for the day. They were extremely glad that they knew how to alter their clothes magically, for not only had they gotten taller, their body shapes had shifted slightly, making them just a bit more wiry, like Araunya and Aidan. Cojiñí was glad of the diminishing of certain aspects of her form that gotten in the way of crossing her arms properly, and driving her elbows down from over her head to the forearms of someone theoretically wrapping his or her arms around her waist from behind. Once they were suitably dressed for the day, the two caramel-skinned Archmages trooped down the stairs and out the door to cross the hall to flat number 332B so that they could talk to their new parents, but being very careful not to trip over or bump into anything with their new height.

Araunya looked up from her book as she heard the door open. She sat up on the sofa. Her eyes narrowed at the sight of two people who appeared *very* similar to Cojiñí and Scoruș. It took her a few moments, but then she realised that they *were* Cojiñí and Scoruș. Once that realisation clicked, the winter-eyed woman began to catalogue the changes and from where those different features originated. The twins were taller, but by three inches at most—that was from Aidan since Charani was not the tallest of people. They had slightly more aquiline noses—also from Aidan, or someone along his line of relatives. Faintly narrower eyes—those were from her, that was certain.

Then she noticed the looks they were giving her.

"What? Come in and close the door, you two. No need to let all the warm air out into the hall."

They smiled at the sort-of joke, and the door clicked shut on its own when they came and sat down next to her. She put the book down and sent an *insistent* mental message for Aidan to come downstairs *right now*, as he was needed by their children. Also because his assistance was needed to provide an explanation.

The curly-haired man immediately came down to the living room, thankfully fully dressed. Not even being married had cured him, *yet*, of his odd habit of sometimes going around the house wearing only a bed sheet. It was kind of cute the first two times, but then it just got annoying, especially when they made plans to go somewhere and he had to take the time to get dressed, being that he was not a full magical and therefore could not do it simply with a thought.

He sat down in the armchair to the left of the sofa, facing the trio *on* the sofa, and said, "Yes, Araunya?"

She narrowed her eyes at the tone of his voice. He pouted. "Have you noticed, Aidan, anything different about our eldest children?"

His green-gold gaze focussed on the twins as he went into deductive mode. "I suppose that the adoption changed their genetics as well as their legalities?"

"That is how it seems to be."

"Is this usual?"

"I do not know. Perhaps. There is most likely information about these kinds of things in the Lodge's West Wing Library."

"Well then, what are we waiting for? If something has gone wrong with the adoption of our twins, I want to know what, and how to fix it." It seemed that Aidan was taking his job as the twins' father very seriously.

"You do know we are nineteen, correct?" Scoruș asked.

"So?"

Their search in the library proved fruitless until Scoruș stumbled on a narrow, leather-bound, ancient volume stuffed into the back of one of the shelves in a remote corner on the other side of the duelling ring. It had no title, no author, and was written in what seemed to be Old Norse. But once the resident Linguistics student, that being Cojiñí, deciphered it, it was revealed to hold the exact answer to their question. As it turned out, changes in physical appearance after a magical adoption are perfectly usual, but it is rare that adoptions are done after the age of thirteen. Not only do physical changes occur, magical ones do too. In a magical adoption, the person being adopted is transferred completely from one family to the other, thus altering the adoptee's genetic magical skills to more closely match those he or she would have had if he or she had been born to the family he or she was being adopted into.

It was at that point the twins mentioned the odd feeling in their eyes that had been present since they awoke that morning—the feeling that there was a different way they could be viewing the world, rather than using their "regular" eyes. Araunya thought about this and asked them to "poke" at the part of their mind that was telling them this.

Their eyes fluttered closed. When they opened them again, they said, "Wow."

Everything was different, bright, glowing, beautiful. The walls were latticed with threads of shining silver, as was the ceiling. Out the window, the sky was a tapestry of eerie blue, although the day was grey and cloudy. The raven-haired twins turned their gaze to the other people in the library, and their eyes widened. Araunya was surrounded by a nimbus of scarlet light, reaching at *least* fifteen centimetres away from her in every direction. Aidan had one too, though its glow was much smaller, eight centimetres at the most, and its colour was a greenish-gold shade. The twins guessed that those glows showed magical strength, or were auras, or something. For some reason, they could smell the odd combination of apple-wood smoke and chemicals coming from the latter glow, and leather and fresh-cut pine from the former.

They turned their gaze to each other and blinked in surprise. They knew they were supposedly more powerful than most, but they did not expect what they saw. They were each surrounded by a glow reaching at *least* thirty centimetres from their skin to the edge, and so very bright. The one Scoruș saw enveloping Cojiñí was deep, electric azure, threaded in places with an eerie emerald green, and it gave off a scent of roses, leather, and old books. The glow Cojiñí perceived embracing Scoruș was an inverse of her own—dark, eerie, emerald green threaded with azure and emitting an aroma of a deep forest, leather the same as his sister, and smoky incense.

They turned to Araunya. She was smiling, and her eyes were glowing, but it was different than the nimbus that surrounded her whole body. She summoned a book over to her, but it looked no different to the twins than it would have without this odd "other sight."

"What is this, Mum?" Scoruș asked, and to his own and his sister's ears, his voice sounded double-toned—an older voice, Myrddin's voice, overlaying it.

"This is what is known as aura-sight, a magical talent that has been rare the last few centuries. Those most powerful in this talent are able to see magic when it is activated, as I can. That is why I levitated the book. Did either of you see anything when I did that?"

They shook their heads, and she sighed before continuing. "Another facet of aura-sight is that some can read a person's life, past and possible futures as well. Those take the form of different-coloured threads woven through the cloth that is each person's aura. Dare I ask if you two can see that?"

Cojiñí and Scoruș shook their heads again, then "poked" at the place in their minds where they had found the button activating their aura-sight, and the world faded to normal as Araunya did the same.

The following day, the twins had a very interesting idea. Just before the communion meditation at church, they activated their aura-sight. The result nearly blinded them. It seemed as though that particular talent not only showed magic, a thing of earth, it was a talent of its own given by God for a reason that only He knew, a reason that only He would ever know. Everything was glowing, and it was all glowing a clear, pure white-gold-silver, a colour that Araunya said would never be anyone's aura, and that no magic was on any world in any dimension. But was not just a combination of white, gold, and silver—no, the white was the kind that came from combining all the colours that have ever existed and will ever exist. It was breathtakingly, blindingly, painfully beautiful, and though it hurt like nothing the twins had ever experienced, they wanted *so bad* to keep looking, especially when they looked straight at the crucifix behind the communion table and the glow where it was a thousand, a million times more intense.

Luckily, their sanity was saved when their aura-sight...turned off by itself. Blinking the spots out of their eyes, the twins turned their attention to the member of the congregation who had been asked to give the communion meditation. He had just stepped up to the podium.

Chapter 24

THE YEAR PASSED, and during the summer of the twins' twentieth year, a trip was scheduled to Ynys Golauglas. An official trip. It was time for the Balaurs to know about their stolen and found children of the Chief's line. Charani and Durriken were going to be furious, and Durriken may even call for a duel, but Araunya knew that even without using any of her tricks, she could defeat him fair and square. The twins could probably do so as well, what with the added skill and experience that came from Morgaine and Myrddin.

They knew for certain that the trip would happen, the question was, How? Did they want to be dramatic and have the twins appear in deep-hooded cloaks and throw the hoods off? What did they want to accomplish? Eventually they decided it would be easiest for them to just walk around as if it was perfectly normal for people who were supposed to be dead for nineteen years to wander around. After a bit, Barsali would call them up to the dais in the city square and *introduce* them. Anything that happened after that was up to fate, as it is said.

The day on which the twins were to reveal themselves to the residents of Ynys Golauglas dawned warm and grey. They dressed in long-sleeved t-shirts in their favourite colours, the calf-length black leather jackets they received for their twentieth birthday, sturdy black jeans, and knee-high boots, and even though the latter were out of style, they liked them and so they wore them. All in all, they chose clothes good for fighting, if that was needed. They knew Araunya and Aidan were dressing themselves likewise, though Aidan still was not particularly the best at fighting with his newly discovered magic yet.

Just after breakfast, they teleported to the area outside the city designated for out-of-island travellers and were greeted by Khulai and Tara, clad in a similar manner to the four new arrivals. They were also visibly armed, whereas the others had their weapons hidden just out of sight in a mid-space pocket. Together they trooped into the city, though it was tricky for the elder adults to not appear as if they were guarding the younger ones, which is what they wanted to do. Araunya and Aidan were very protective of their children, no matter that those children were two years more than the coming of age.

High noon arrived with the sky just as grey as it had been earlier, though it did not seem like there was a chance of rain. Barsali climbed upon the dais. The cameras that had been set up in strategic places around the area were switched on with a simple thought on his part and they began to record as he began to speak.

"My ever-dear people of Clan Balaur, I know this is a surprise, as there was nothing signifying that I would be addressing you today. However, I have an important announcement to make. Something that has not been said for far too long."

The white-haired chieftain gestured for the twins to come up on the dais with him, and they went, albeit a bit reluctantly. He guided them so one was standing on either side of him. He put his arms around their shoulders.

"May I present our long-lost, presumed to be dead, former children of Heir-Lord Warrior Mage Durriken Stormeye, now adopted as her own by my great-granddaughter, Lady Warrior Mage Araunya Ravenheart, and her husband, Aidan Jones...." He paused for effect, then continued once the whisperings of 'who did he say?' and 'has he said yet?' had died down.

"Lady Archmage Cojiñí Seasword and Lord Archmage Scoruș Blackfalcon, found, by their now-mother after having been stolen thirteen years before then, and nineteen years before now!"

The whisperings were back, full force. Araunya and Aidan moved to join the twins on the dais, but they were intercepted by a furious couple by the names of Durriken Stormeye and Charani Duskflame.

Charani was first to speak. Her sapphire eyes were ablaze, though her voice was low. At least she knew enough to not cause a scene. Araunya just hoped that Durriken had mellowed some since the last time she spoke to him.

"What gave you the *right* to do such a thing?"

Araunya's eyes narrowed. They give up on their firstborn children after only six months of searching and now she dares to ask what gave her the right to keep searching? To find the twins? To keep that finding from them out of respect for their now three-year-old-son? To formally adopt a pair of young people she already considered her children?

Her voice was just as low, and she could feel Aidan's eyes narrowing to match hers and her near-dangerous tone. "The right to do *what* exactly? Adopt them? They were of age and I already considered them to be my children, having lived with them for over four years...."

Durriken cut her off. His voice was not so low, which caused a few people around them to stare. "What gave you the right to hide from us that you knew where they were, to keep our own children from us?"

All right, that was it. Normally she would have reacted calmly, but one—this was her brother talking and he and she had never gotten along. And two—who was he to say such a thing? Yes, losing children is a great pain to bear, and grief makes people do unspeakable things, but to abandon your search for stolen infants, your firstborns, just because you cannot sense their auras because you do not have the talent for feeling them, and then to ask the very person who had actually searched for them what right she had to keep them safe and to train them for battle so that they would not perish, was the last straw. Araunya snapped, and her aura nearly became visible to all as her eyes began to glow and an invisible wind commenced to blow the loose strands of hair that had fallen out of her bun.

"What *right* did I have? What *right?*" Her voice truly was dangerously calm now, but if either her brother or his wife pushed any more, she would shout.

Unfortunately for Durriken, he nodded, seeming to miss his sister's rage. "Yes, what right did you have as my younger sister to keep vital information to the heirship of the Chief's Line from me, the third Heir?"

So he was playing the Heir card, was he? Well then, he would meet her wrath and that should deflate his ego a bit. She was not at the shouting point yet, but the wind grew stronger around them, and her jaw was set, then it became deceptively relaxed. More people turned to look, guessing correctly from whence the sudden wind had come. The midnight-eyed man smiled, obviously thinking she had relented. He really had not spent much time around her, had he?

"I *was* going to tell you, *elder brother, dear,* when I first found them, but do you know what? Neva asked me not to, so that you could raise Jardani. Out of respect, I acquiesced to her request. I grew to love them as my own children, so on the day they turned nineteen I presented them with the adoption paperwork, drawn up on Aidan's and my honeymoon. They signed it that very evening."

She paused, and Durriken opened his mouth to speak, but the winter-eyed woman cut him off. "Do you know how they were living when I found them, Durriken? In the basement of a house belonging to their so-called foster family, on hard cots, showing signs of frequent beatings, being treated as slaves by the people who were supposed to be taking care of them. They had been trapped with magic-suppressors as well. Do you know how they had been living before that? The same, but without the magic-suppressors, although they had figured out how to create alcoves to hide in within the mid-space. They are experts at hiding their emotions because that was one of the things that kept them alive for the first thirteen years after they were stolen from us."

Durriken interrupted her. "How can we believe any of what you say is true, Araunya? You were always good at telling tales, and your time in the Mercenaries Guard only made you better at deception and sneaking around. How can we know this is not some elaborate hoax you and Gorhendad are playing? If so, it is in very poor taste." He seemed to think of something then. "Or...have you somehow tricked Gorhendad? It is no secret he is aging quickly, and it is common for the elderly to be..." he tilted his head, "easily deceived."

Araunya was quick to speak before Charani could chime in. "You seriously think that little of Gorhendad, that I could possibly trick him into something like this? As a joke? You think little enough to seriously believe that I would sink so low as to attempt something like that?" Her voice was hard and cold.

Durriken looked at her as if he couldn't imagine why she would dare to question him, and something deep inside Araunya split in two. The wind that had faded slightly whipped into a gale as the winter-eyed woman began to glow scarlet, the exact same shade as her magic and aura. And her voice became amplified with rage.

"YOU MAY BE THE ELDEST CHILD, DURRIKEN STORMEYE, BUT KNOW THIS: I HAVE ALWAYS BEEN THE MORE POWERFUL, AND NOW YOU WILL LISTEN TO ME, AS YOU HAVE NEVER DONE DURING THE ENTIRETY OF OUR LIVES!" She felt the presences of her twins and her husband beside her, and the scent of sulphur betrayed the fact that she was not the only one filled with wrath against Cojiñí and Scoruș' former parents. The people that had assembled now formed a wide ring around them.

"I SWEAR TO YOU, *BROTHER*, ON EVERYTHING THAT YOU HOLD DEAR, THIS YOUNG MAN AND WOMAN ARE INDEED YOUR LOST, DEAD, ELDEST CHILDREN. WHEN I FOUND THEM AT A CHURCH SERVICE WHEN THEY WERE FOURTEEN YEARS OLD, THEY HAD BEEN TRAPPED INTO MAGIC-SUPPRESSORS, AND WERE LIVING IN A BASEMENT WITHIN AN ABUSIVE HOUSE THAT DOES NOT EVEN HAVE ENOUGH WORTH TO BE CALLED A HOME. EVERYTHING I HAVE TOLD YOU IS TRUE, AND THERE IS NO WAY I WOULD ATTEMPT TO DECEIVE GORHENDAD INTO A TRICK THAT WOULD RESEMBLE THIS TRUTH, NO MATTER HOW LOW A REGARD YOU HOLD OUR *CHIEF* TO EVEN SUGGEST SUCH A THING!"

She took a deep breath and continued, this time not bothering to shout, as her magic was amplifying her voice anyway, and though she was absolutely furious, that was no reason to blow out everyone's ears.

"I rescued them from a life that would have driven them to suicide and you have the gall to ask me what right I had and to accuse me of deceiving Gorhendad—as if he could be deceived by me. I would have returned them to you once they healed after breaking the magic-suppressors they had been bound with, but Neva had enough respect for you and for your young to request that I wait until he was at least in school, and I accepted. Then...."

Cojiñí and Scoruș cut her off. They were glowing as she was, and speaking in perfect tandem, their voices cold and dark. "Then we learned that we were to fight in a pre-destined battle once we were of age, and so Mum trained us, as well as our first real friends, to fight and survive. You abandoned us after six months of searching when you could not sense us anymore, even though you knew perfectly well that you are two of the least aura-sensitive people in the Chief's Line, and nowhere near Mum's level. Grief may make someone do unspeakable things, but to abandon young children because *you* could no longer sense them is beyond unreasonable."

They adopted mock thoughtful expressions. "One would think a grieving parent would do anything he or she could to *find* their firstborn children, not give up after less than a year of searching." The thoughtful expressions evaporated. "If there was one thing that Mum taught us, if nothing else mattered, it is that Balaurs do not abandon each other, for we are all family in spirit and in Christ, if not in body."

They were about to say more, but then Barsali appeared directly behind Durriken and Charani. "Well said, young ones."

The accusing couple spun around and saw the disappointed and angry eyes of Chief-Lord Warrior Mage Barsali Oaksword.

"You may be the Third Heir, Durriken Stormeye, but I am still Chief, and until I—your great-grandfather—and your father are dead, you will not become Chief-Lord! And even though it is your father's choice whom he makes his heir, I can still change the line of succession while I live, so tread carefully."

"But they are *our* children! We had a RIGHT to have them back when they were found!"

Barsali pursed his lips. "Charani Duskflame, you are a mother. A mother should not give up on her children. Yes, I know, you think your children are dead, so why listen to the mocking sister-in-law, who has never married or given birth, who says that she can still sense them?"

The sapphire-eyed woman opened her mouth, but the white-haired man continued. "But one would think, as your former children said, that a mother would do anything she could, use all the resources she could, to find the lost children. And yet you stopped searching after only six months. The question is, why?" He nodded at Durriken. "Same to you, *Third Heir*. Why give up?"

Dead silence followed the question. Not even the gales created by the wrath of Araunya and the twins made noise, for they had calmed down considerably as the Chief spoke, or at least got themselves under control. Up started the mutterings again, as the Chief, the Third Heir and his wife, one of their most powerful Warrior Mages and her husband, and two twenty-year-olds that were supposed to be dead nineteen years, all just stood there staring at each other.

Eventually, Araunya sighed at the lack of response from her brother and his wife. "I'd hate to be disrespectful to Gorhendad by imitating him, but *why*, Durriken and Charani? Why do such a thing?" she said tiredly. Then her ire showed again. "Why not do all you could to find them? Why not be like others in that situation and firmly disbelieve that they were dead and stop looking only where there was no proof of their living in any dimension? Even with all your faults, you are not completely uncaring of life, Durriken. And Charani, you were always so kind and loving of the twins before then, so why abandon them?"

Charani put her face in her hands. Araunya, and everyone else, waited. After a moment, she looked up again. "We did not stop searching because we could no longer feel their auras. Yes, it was true that we could not, but if it was only that, I at least would have accepted your help in looking, Araunya, even if Durriken is too proud to do so."

Durriken looked as if his wife as if accusing her of betrayal, but the sapphire-eyed woman ignored him. "We...received a note, from a ridiculously anonymous sender, that said that there was no use looking anymore, we would never see our children again, no matter if we searched through all the universes and dimensions with a fine-toothed comb. While Durriken was busy destroying furniture in reaction, I took the note to Hennain Dorenia, who verified that it was written in truthfulness."

She sighed, but soldiered on. "I brought that information to Durriken and he believed me. We knew no one else would believe us, so we kept it a secret and we asked Dorenia to do so as well. We couldn't think of anything else to do."

Araunya accepted that explanation, as she could sense no lie in Charani's aura, but that answered only one of her questions. She voiced her other. "What makes you think it was my duty to turn the twins over to you when I found them?"

"Just because we wouldn't find them, doesn't mean that you wouldn't."

The winter-eyed woman spoke again. "The note said you would never *see* your children again, not that you wouldn't *find* them, Charani. Or did you tell me wrong?"

Suddenly, Cojiñí spoke up. "And she still hasn't seen them."

Araunya turned. "How do you mean?"

The midnight-eyed young woman tilted her head. "We are not her *children* anymore, even ignoring the fact that we have now been of age for two years. We are your son and daughter, Araunya, *Mum*, so says the adoption paperwork and our changed appearances and aura-sight."

Scoruș agreed. He'd had the same thought as his sister, at the same time. Araunya considered the concept, then rose when she realised what the twins meant, and that they were exactly correct. She turned back to her sister-in-law, who looked startled. Obviously, she hadn't thought of something like that.

"But...but...."

Scoruș interrupted his former mother. "My sister is correct, Charani. We are not your children anymore. We have not been since we stopped wishing someone would come and rescue us from our abusive life before Mum found us. Therefore, the note was correct. You will never see your twin children again. They did die, as was thought...."

Cojiñí completed his thought. "...but later than was thought. Your children died, not when they were a year old, but around their seventh birthday."

Araunya sent her brother a challenging stare as he opened his mouth to speak, but Durriken ignored her and continued anyway.

"But genetically, you are still our children, and so no matter mental and emotional considering, you are still ours."

Aidan spoke for the first time in the conversation. "Have you not been listening, Durriken? Changed appearances and aura-sight—they are not genetically your children anymore, as of their nineteenth birthday. Adoptions are not just legal, you know. A magical adoption alters the genetics and abilities of the adoptee to be a closer match to those of the adopters."

The very muscular man's mouth formed an O at this revelation, then he scowled. He seemed ready to say something, most likely something tactless, in anger, but Charani interrupted him.

"I suppose that both of you have been taken out of the Heir's Line with the adoption?"

Araunya nodded, but Charani was not looking at her. Instead, the fair-skinned woman's focus was on the twins, who appeared confused.

"Heir's Line?" they said.

Araunya commandeered the conversation. "Durriken is the Third Heir, meaning that unless something changes, he will become Chief after his father and grandfather, being the eldest-born. You two would have been the Fourth Heirs, being the firstborns, had your adoption to become my children not taken place, as I am the second-born and have not been specifically chosen by my father to be his heir."

The twins looked at each other, their faces deep in thought. Araunya wondered if they were dismayed that she honestly, completely forgot about that until Charani mentioned it now. She bit her lip, a nervous habit since her childhood. The sharp-featured woman hoped neither of her twins decided they wanted a position of power that very moment because if they did, the adoption could easily be reversed due to their age.

Araunya was in luck, or so it seemed, because there was no wish for a leadership role in the twin's nature, even though they would make excellent Chiefs *should* it end up that way, although they did take smaller such roles when others required it of them. Even though the midnight-eyed duo were not *opposed* to being people of great power, power was not something they hungered for.

"Why would we care?" The twins' snippy reply was directed at Charani.

Araunya breathed an audible sigh of relief. She was a fool to think the two twenty-year-olds, whom she had known for six years, would turn their backs on her for a thing like that.

Charani's reply proved even further that the sapphire-eyed woman knew nothing of the caramel-skinned, angularly handsome male and female twins that Araunya was proud to call her own.

"Do not all young people dream of power and prestige?"

Cojiñí and Scoruş scoffed. "You are over generalising, Charani, if you think *all* of any kind of people are anything other than loved by God. We are all different. Yes, the natures of some can be very similar, but there is no one exactly the same as anyone else. Not *all* young people are power-hungry."

The woman who had previously been their mother conceded. "Point taken."

Durriken spoke in a manner that revealed how little he had been listening, and nearly dissolved the tentative peace beginning to form between the two small groups. "No matter that you are of age and magically adopted, you are still under my lineage, as the required paperwork did not go through the Ynys Golauglas court."

Charani muttered something in the man's ear, but he ignored her, and the twins were silent as their mother refuted his claim.

"It went through the Witan, Durriken, or are you accusing our esteemed Chief of professing falsehoods? Additionally, you are neither on the Witan, nor the court, so why would you know in the first place?"

Durriken removed a band from under his sleeve and threw it on the ground at the feet of Araunya and the twins.

Had he been wearing gloves or gauntlets, those would have taken the place of that wide band of embossed white leather. He was elder, and more experienced. He could easily take down any of the three who answered his challenge. The fact that Araunya had always been better than he in the arts of battle was conveniently ignored.

"I challenge you for the rights of parent-ship over Cojiñí and Scoruş Balaur."

Durriken's words were directed at his sister, but she did not move. Did not even blink. Instead, two hands—similar to those of his sister, with elements of the hands of Aidan Jones, his brother-in-law—reached out and lifted the challenge-band. The hands were both left hands—Araunya's dominant hand—and apparently the dominant hands of the twins. He looked in their faces, and grim midnight-blue eyes met his. Those eyes could have previously been traced to him, but now could never be, for the lights within were different.

Twin voices, one a rich tenor, the other a strong alto, both as grim as their owners' eyes, spoke in perfect harmony. "We, Lady Archmage Cojiñí Seasword and Lord Archmage Scoruş Blackfalcon, accept your challenge, Heir-Lord Warrior Mage Durriken Stormeye, and will fight for our own parent-ship, as we are of age since two years past."

This was definitely unexpected, but ceremony must be followed.

"Terms?"

Durriken was brought out of his thoughts by the voices belonging to his former children. "First blood, if I win, you are ours and the adoption is annulled. If you win, Charani and I will no longer speak of it again, and will leave the matter alone."

A moment of silence, and then the twins nodded. "We accept your terms. Collect your weapons."

So they would not wait and do it later in a proper fighting ring? Very well, he could improvise well enough.

Durriken drew his sword from its sheath at his hip, slid into a fighting stance, and waited. Then he realised that neither of the twins were wearing weapons. Were they going to fight with magic only? That issue was resolved, however, when a pair of well-crafted bastard swords appeared out of thin air and popped into the twins' hands. They slipped into fighting stances with an ease Durriken had not expected, and yet he should have. They were trained by his sister, after all, and twenty years old.

The duel was over quickly, ending with Durriken on his back on the ground, bleeding from small slices on both cheekbones, two sword-points at his chest. For all his supposed experience and skill, he was no match for his two opponents—they were younger and faster, and they had been through a Battle. Durriken hadn't. Not to mention the added experience and skill from having certain medieval persons living within their heads, which Durriken had no clue about whatsoever.

After they met assorted cousins, Cojiñí and Scoruş returned home to flat number 332C, where they immediately removed their shoes and jackets, and dropped onto the sofa to watch a movie.

* * *

The years passed, three years to be exact. Cojiñí finally learned how to play the violin, and while Scoruş could have done the same with the pipe organ, he chose the guitar as a secondary instrument—as opposed to the shepherd's flute, which was Araunya's chosen instrument. Catrina and Ashton, Lea and Gareth, and Mae and Ivan became engaged in the summer of the second year after the duel with Durriken. Rae and Pietro became engaged soon after. Scoruş was planning to ask Alezandra on the New Year's Eve, after his twenty-third birthday.

The Christmas before that New Year's Eve was absolutely beautiful, as if the weather was attempting to compensate for something. That night, as the party wound down, the thing the weather seemed to be compensating for happened.

They were lounging in flat 332C's living room, expanded with a clever use of a portal into a mid-space room. All of a sudden, the Pseudo-Reincarnated ones felt an odd pull, as if they were being stretched, and then they were assaulted by a flood of memories from their "other selves," from their birth to the end of the First Battle of Camlann. Their eyes opened after the onslaught of images and feelings, and they saw their other selves standing before them, translucent and glowing. When Cojiñí realised what was happening, she attempted to grab Morgaine's hand—to keep her from leaving. But her own hand passed through Morgaine's, as if through smoke.

Morgaine's smile was a sad one. "There is no stopping this, my dear Rose-thorn."

The twenty-three-year-old woman's tears pricked against her eyelashes, and knew through her twin-bond that her brother felt the same. The Pseudo-Reincarnated ones had become very close to those they "hosted" during the past seven years, and the fact that they were leaving was a sad one.

"Must you go?" They spoke, unconsciously in sync, all twelve of them.

The other twelve nodded, then Nimue spoke. "We wish for this, dear ones. Our time here is done. We welcome greatly the restful state of death, and the Paradise to come, where we will meet again."

As the elder twelve began to fade into nothing, they called out as one, "Remember this, dear ones: only Heaven, Hell, and their respective rulers are eternal. And even the Master of Lies and his domain shall yet fall under the sword of God."

About the Author

FROM THE EARLY DAYS OF HOLDING A PENCIL, to her current teenage years of typing novels, Sharon Rose has been interested in sharing creative and engaging stories. As an avid reader, she is heavily influenced by modern and classical fantasy and science-fiction writers. *Flower and Tree* is her first finished novel, but by no counts is it the first started one.

Sharon was born in Eugene, Oregon, three months early. Now she lives in Toledo, with two black cats, the younger of which she considers to be her own child, her sister, and her mother.